APSARA

By

PEARL WHITFIELD

This is a work of fiction. King Jayavarman VII, Queen Indradevi, and Indravarman are historical characters. I have taken some liberties with their lives (the little we know from the historical record), as explained at the end of the book. The issues of water and empire are mostly accurate. Other than that, all characters and events are products of the author's imagination, including specific Cham invasions in the story.

Apsara. © Text copyright 2021 by Pearl Whitfield.
Cover images and maps of Kampuchea © Pearl Whitfield

First Edition published by PonderosaSage
Printed in the United States of America

ISBN: 979-8784990266

To contact the author, please email PonderosaSage@gmail.com

DEDICATION

To the people of Cambodia,
now and throughout history.

CONTENTS

AUTHOR'S NOTE

This is a work of historical fiction that grew from an experience I had in 2013, in Cambodia at the museum in Siem Reap. I had spent several weeks at the complex usually called Angkor Wat.

Angkor Wat itself left me cold, despite its intricate and spectacular bas reliefs. But Bayon, built some time later in the 12th century by Jayavarman VII, drew me day after day. This is the story of that experience. It starts when Bopha is about 7 years old. Many of the chapters have dates to anchor them in time.

To help readers, I have included a map of the Kingdom of Kampuchea and one of modern Southeast Asia, a chapter list, a character list, and a glossary of Khmer words. In the back, after the end of the story, those who want to know more about Cambodia and what liberties I took with history, can read the Afterword, Historical Notes and References.

Pearl Whitfield

Eastern Oregon, November 2021

MAP OF KAMPUCHEA UNDER JAYAVARMAN VII

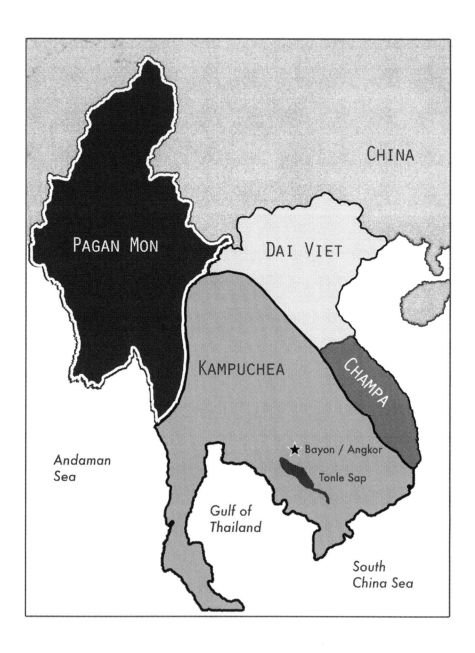

MAP OF MODERN SOUTH EAST ASIA

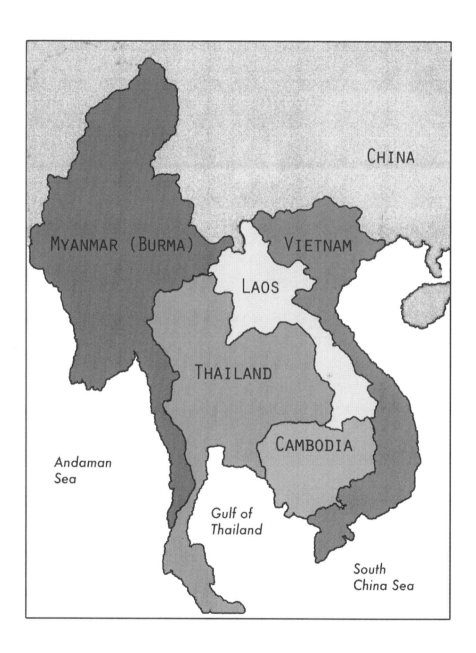

CHARACTER LIST

Preah Chan Bopha   "Bopha," the Apsara. Name means "Moon Flower"

Reasmey   Bopha's little sister. Name means "sunshine"

Rithy   Bopha's brother, "strength and courage." Becomes monk Nimith Vireak, meaning "transformation","absence of desire"

Boran   Guard for King Jayavarman VII and Apsaras. Name means "ancient"

The King's Man   Kiri, "mountain." Would be considered Prime Minister today

Apsaras:

   Sophea   "clever, wisdom"

   Nary   "small beautiful bird"

   Thida   Bopha's mentor in the Apsara courtyard, "girl born of royalty"

   Tevy   Sophea's mentee, "angel"

   Kalienne   Bopha's dear friend, "sweet darling"

   Theary   "helper"

   Nuon: Shared sleeping mat with Bopha, "soft and tender"

   Kesor   Woman in charge of older Apsaras, "heavenly lady"

   Dara Davuth   Boy dancer, "star money"

King
Jayavarman VII   "Jaya". Most famous of Cambodian Kings, came to power at age 50 in 1178 (or age 60 in 1181, depending on your source). He reconquered Angkor Wat from the Cham; built Bayon Temple; expanded Kampuchea into Thailand, Laos and Cambodia; and made Buddhism the State religion *(influenced by his first wife, who died before this book begins)*.

Garuda   Bird-god of Hindu legend, half man and half bird. Sanskrit for "eagle"

Khosal	King's Minister, just under Kiri. Finance Minister. Name means "clever, magical"
Muni	King's Minister for Public Works, "wisdom"

Palace Women

Chariya	Bopha's maid in the palace
Khun Thea	King's favorite sister, Kiri's wife
Indradevi	Jayavarman's 1st (current) wife, stern sister to his deceased wife
Mach Botum	Jayavarman's 2nd wife, plump and jolly. "Melodious princess"
Sao Nang	Jayavarman's 3rd wife, married as an alliance to the Shan in Burma
Mony	Khosal's wife, "precious gem"

Children of the King still living at Bayon:

Malis	Youngest daughter of Mach Botum, "jasmine"
Nimith Sokhem	Sao Nang's first child (a son), "transformation and hope"
Arun Veha	Kalienne's son, "morning-sun sky"
Samang:	Bopha's guard, grandson of Boran, "lucky"
Sikha:	Village healer, "peaceful, content
Thom	First Twin, full name Apphoutheto Thom, "miracle big/oldest one"
Vanna	Second Twin, full name Phnheaphaael Vanna, "surprise, golden"
Chou	Twin's nanny, "refreshingly beautiful"
Kravann Chivy	Daughter of Bopha, "small golden-brown flower," "life"
Visothirith	Son of Khosal, 'heavenly, pure"
Poeu Meaker	Youngest son of Boran, "youngest," "greatest"
Xiuying	Chinese language teacher, "brave and beautiful"

GLOSSARY

Amok
fish amok is famous Khmer steamed fish curry, with a delicate blend of flavors

Apsara
a female spirit of the clouds and water in Hindu and Buddhist culture, who is a superb dancer. Apsaras dance to bring heaven to earth, blessing the land with prosperity

Arkoun
thank you

Aupouk
Father

Avelokiteshvara
in Buddhist belief, an earthly manifestation of the cosmic being, the embodiment of the compassion of all Buddhas

Baray
reservoir; part of the intricate ancient waterworks system

Bong
"older brother." Term is used as honorific among peers; for women, "Bong Srey"

Cham, Champa
Cham are the people, Champa the land. Now southern Vietnam.

Chitea
Grandfather

Chop
Stop

Dai Viet
what is now northern Vietnam

Dengue
mosquito-borne illness also known as "break-bone fever." There is no treatment to this day, and still no vaccine, as well as no immunity. A person who gets infected a second time often gets fatal bleeding into their brain

Durian
a fruit, much prized by Cambodians and Chinese. Strong smell stinky to others

Eightfold Path
an early summary of the path of Buddhist practices leading to liberation from the painful cycle of rebirth, in the form of nirvana (enlightenment)

Four Noble Truths *Taught by the Buddha:*

1. *The Truth of Suffering.*
2. *The Truth of the Cause of Suffering.*
3. *The Truth of the End of Suffering*
4. *The Truth of the Path leading to the End of Suffering.*

Garuda *eagle in Sanskrit; bird-man from Hindu mythology, the mount for the god Vishnu.*

Jeeb *dance position for hands, feet, arms, legs. There are more than 4,000 jeebs in traditional Cambodian dance. Much of the tradition was lost when outlawed by the Khmer Rouge.*

Kampuchea *early name for Cambodia, now in disfavor because used by Khmer Rouge, who terrorized country in 1970s, killing millions*

Karma *concept in Hinduism and Buddhism, which both believe in reincarnation, that your actions have consequences, not just in this life but in your lives to come*

Khim *ancient Cambodian stringed musical instrument similar to hammered dulcimer*

Khmer *both the language and the people of Cambodia, pronounced "Khmai"*

Kromah *ubiquitous checkered scarf, used as wrap, turban, bag*

Lok *honorific for man*

Lok Srey *honorific for woman*

Mdeay *Mother*

Mon *part of what is now southern Myanmar (Burma)*

Naga *snake in Sanskrit*

Pagan *ancient Burmese kingdom, now part of Myanmar*

Rishi	*Sanskrit for sage or teacher, great yogi who is enlightened*
Sampeah	*traditional greeting with palms together*
Sampot	*traditional garment, long cloth worn around lower body. Can be draped in different ways including as loin cloth*
Sangat	*administrative division. From the Sanskrit for fellowship, especially referring to followers of a teacher/sect*
Sok	*Khmer for afterbirth*
Soursdey	*hello (familiar term, as opposed to formal)*
Srijivayan	*an empire in part of what is now India*
Taa	*grandfather. Also "Chitea"*
Tohkeay	*lizard, large gecko whose name is the sound it makes*
Wat	*Temple*
Yeay	*Grandmother*

PROLOGUE

She stood on the parapet before the sun rose, a lithe figure with hair pulled tight in two buns, one on each side of her head. Her left hand rested on the cool stone balustrade. She could hear, distantly, the sounds of many people already hard at work. They were preparing for her husband's funeral, soon to take place on the Terrace of the Elephants. Unable to sleep, she took refuge here, high above the waiting world. She turned her head left, then slowly circled until her back leaned against the supporting stone. Everywhere she looked, his face beamed back at her with that beloved, enigmatic smile. Some said the faces were Avelokiteshvara. To her, they were both.

The eastern sky was red as Preah Chan Bopha turned toward it. She put her hands together palm to palm, raising her arms. Lifting her right knee up and to the side, she started to dance

CHAPTER 1

1184, Chosen

For a long as she could remember, Preah Chan Bopha had loved to dance. When the troupes came through her village, she would go with her brothers and sister to watch. At home, she would try to remember exactly each gesture and movement. She would dance to the river, a wooden bucket in each hand. On the way back, the buckets heavy and sloshing wet over her legs, she walked slowly. But her mind was still dancing.

Her family called her "Bopha," which meant flower. Her full name was Preah Chan Bopha, moon flower. "The moon was full on the night you were born," Mdeay said, "and you were as beautiful as a flower. I had waited so long for a girl. Your father had his boys, and I love them. But I wanted you to be a girl."

It was a long and fancy name for a village girl, but no one teased her. No one dared. Her five older brothers protected her and her little sister, Reasmey, who was just starting to walk. Reasmey had been born in the middle of the day during hot season. Bopha danced in the shadows between the stilts and listened to her mother groan in the house above. Early that morning, shortly after her father and brothers had gone to the fields, Mdeay told her to go get their neighbor, Pich. "Tell her 'It's time' and ask her to come."

Pich brought her baby and climbed the ladder to the house. Bopha started to climb also, but Pich told her to wait below until she was called. After a long time, there was a very loud groan from upstairs, so loud it stopped Bopha in mid-step. Then a thin wailing, and laughter. Pich said, "You have another girl!" Mdeay mumbled. Pich called to Bopha, "You can come up now."

Pich had wrapped the baby in layers of blankets and was putting a hat on her when Bopha entered. The baby looked more like a tiny monkey than a sister. "Her name is Reasmey," Mdeay said, "because she brings sunshine and it's the middle of the day." Pich put lots of blankets on Mdeay and went down the ladder to start a fire. Mdeay and Reasmey needed to be kept warm, she explained.

Bopha was already hot from dancing, but she wanted to be with Mdeay, so she stayed upstairs. Her sampot stuck to her sweaty body. Reasmey sucked on Mdeay's breast then slept. Mdeay closed her eyes. Bopha watched a while, then climbed back downstairs. The sun had climbed over the roof and was beating down the earth around the house. Bopha sat in the shadows as far as she could get from the fire pit. She didn't feel like dancing.

Reasmey wasn't much fun to play with for a long time, until she started to crawl. Bopha would watch her while Mdeay worked around the house. Then, when her sister started to pull herself up on things, Bopha had to watch carefully. One day, Reasmey pulled on a bucket and fell over, the bucket on top of her. There was blood on her mouth where the bucket hit. "Reasmey, you have to be careful. Here, hold my hands. That bucket isn't heavy enough to keep you up."

They would walk all over the yard, and even over to Pich's house, Reasmey holding on to Bopha's hands. It meant Bopha couldn't dance as much, only when Reasmey was sleeping in her hammock. Finally, Reasmey was able to walk on her own. Bopha showed her how to do the steps and make the hand gestures. She and Mdeay would laugh when Reasmey tried to dance.

One day, Mdeay told her excitedly, "Guess what, Bopha!". She took one full bucket from her daughter, grunting as she hefted it to pour into the big earthenware jar they used for a cistern. The top of the jar was taller than Bopha. "Pich told me that the King's Man is coming! He's looking for beautiful girls that can dance."

Bopha was disappointed. She couldn't understand Mdeay's excitement. "Is he going to dance? Are the beautiful girls going to dance here?"

"No, little cucumber. He wants to take girls from here and teach them to dance for the King. Would you like that? You were born to dance, I can see that. But there's no way for you to learn more here."

Bopha wasn't sure. "Can you come too? And Reasmey?"

Mdeay put the bucket down and rubbed her back. Her belly was huge above her sampot. "No, we have to stay here and take care of Aupouk. Who will make his food if we leave?"

2

Bopha thought it over. "How about Pich? She's a good cook. Aupouk liked her fish amok so much when she brought it over after Reasmey was born."

Mdeay laughed, "Yes, he did. And you are right, Pich is a very good cook. But she has her own family to feed. When I heard about the King's Man, I talked with Aupouk. He agrees that we should take you to the Sangat when he comes."

"Okay." Bopha brightened. "Can he teach me the Wishing Dance?" One of the dancers had told her about this dance the last time they came, and showed her some of the moves.

"Yes, I'm sure of it," Mdeay said, hugging Bopha to her, sideways since the new baby took up too much room for a regular hug.

* * *

The King's Man arrived one evening soon after this. Aupouk had gone to the Sangat with all the other men to greet him and have a feast. "I told him about you," Aupouk told Bopha the next morning, "and we are to meet him this afternoon. So you'd better bathe." Bopha had tripped going up the muddy bank of the river, dumping the buckets. She refilled them and put them ahead of her, one at a time, as she climbed back again. But she hadn't washed. Besides, everyone knew that a coating of mud was good for keeping off mosquitos.

The whole village was gathered in the yard outside the Sangat. Bopha had washed herself at the river, careful not to get muddy again. Mdeay pulled her hair into many braids, then wrapped her own silk kromah around Bopha's head to make a turban, with the braids hanging below. Bopha was wearing her best sampot, the one with a beautiful pattern of yellow rumdol flowers against pale green leaves.

Last New Year's, Yeay Mony had given it to her. She said Bopha was old enough to to have something beautiful of her own. Yeay Mony was her mother's mother. She lived with them as long as Bopha could remember. But before the hot season had given way to rains, Bopha climbed the ladder to their house, holding a sprig of rumdol to give her grandmother. The fragrance filled the hot room. Yeay Mony had been sick that morning, and Bopha knew how much she liked rumdol.

3

"Yeay Mony, I brought you a present," she called, walking fast to the pallet where her grandmother lay. But Yeay Mony had not awakened. Bopha leaned near. In the dimness, she could see her grandmother's eyes were open. "Yeay Mony!" Nothing.

Bopha touched the wrinkled shoulder, but there was no response. She backed away, crying for her mother. The rumdol flower fell onto Yeay Mony's motionless chest.

Bopha wished her grandmother could be with them now, to see how beautiful her sampot was and to celebrate as Bopha danced. Mdeay stood next to her, holding Reasmey so she didn't wander away in the crowd. Aupouk had also bathed, and stood across the Sangat courtyard with her brothers and the other men. To one side, Bopha could see men with instruments. She recognized Pich's husband with his fiddle. The musicians played a few chords, testing, then testing again to get the sounds properly tuned together.

People had come from all the surrounding villages and were shouting greetings and catching up on news. Bopha was pushed aside by a fat woman, who usurped her vantage point so she could no longer see her father.

Suddenly, the crowd hushed. Bopha squeezed hard against the fat woman until she had a view of the plaza. A tall man was stepping into the sunlight. Her father and the other men bowed in sampeah, palms together at heart level. The fat woman bowed, her breasts pushing against Bopha's head.

The little girl could see everyone was bowing, but she couldn't take her eyes off this man. His sampot was bright red. He wore a belt of small golden balls that hung to his knees. His hair was braided like hers, but on his head, which he held high and straight, was a pointed helmet that flashed in the sun. Bopha had never seen anything like this.

Her mother's hand reached past the fat woman and pushed Bopha's head into an unwilling bow. The man started to speak. Everyone in the crowd lifted their heads, placing their hands together at their hearts briefly, then relaxed and strained to hear. His voice was high and clear.

"Kampucheans! I am honored to come here today in the service of our King, Jayavarman VII. As you have heard, his Royal Majesty has sent me to find the best dancers in all the land, the

4

most beautiful girls, the most talented boys. In his mercy, he wants to bring these children to Angkor, to learn to dance for him and the Court." The crowd murmured appreciatively. "Your Sangat leader will now proceed with the auditions. He assures me that you have several very talented contestants."

The man stepped back into the shadows, where Bopha could see he sat on a high chair draped with fluttering silk. She pushed back to where her mother stood. "Mdeay, what is auditions? And what is contestants?" Before her mother could answer, the Sangat leader, a short squat man with very powerful shoulders, stepped into the sun.

He bellowed, "Who has brought a child to dance for the King's Man?" The crowd shuffled. Bopha couldn't see anything, so she squirmed past the fat woman again. A man she didn't recognize walked forward and bowed to the King's man and the Sangat leader. He mumbled, not standing up straight, and gestured to someone in the crowd on the other side of the courtyard.

People opened a path for a very small but very beautiful girl. Her father, as Bopha guessed the man to be, mumbled again. The girl walked to her father, then bowed to the Sangat leader. Both she and her father turned to bow to the King's Man. The girl stood straight, her father was still somewhat bent.

"Sophea has traveled three days to come perform for us," announced the Sangat leader. "Please, you may all sit now." The crowd jostled and sat. Once they were quiet, the Sangat leader gestured to the musicians. Flutes, drums and strings began a tune that Bopha recognized.

Sophea was smaller than Bopha, with delicate features. Her hair was dressed similarly to Bopha's and her sampot was bright orange. She stepped into the center of the plaza, put her hands together at her heart, bowed to the King's Man again, and started to dance. Each movement was precise, and perfectly coordinated with the music. Her tiny figure turned and bent and stretched, the bright orange sampot twirling. Bopha was transfixed, as was the crowd. At the end of the dance, Sophea again faced the King's Man and bowed. Bopha could just see him lift his hands back to her in sampeah.

The day was getting hotter and Bopha was hungry. She scooched back until she was next to her mother. "I'm hungry," she

5

whispered. Mdeay reached into her kromah and passed Bopha a piece of dried fish and a small lump of rice. Bopha ate both quickly, then wished she hadn't. The rice stuck in her dry throat. "Can I go home and get a drink?" She managed to ask. Mdeay shook her head, but handed her a small pebble from the kromah.

"Suck on this and your thirst will ease," she advised her daughter. As Bopha sucked on the stone, she watched the next dancers, two girls she knew from her village. Neither was anywhere near as good as Sophea. Then a little boy shyly approached the Sangat leader with his father. Bopha didn't expect much, since he couldn't even lift his head.

But when the music started, the boy became another person. He raised his head as he raised his hands to his heart. With his first step, he captured the crowd. When he leapt high in the air near the end of the dance, the whole crowd gasped. A collective "Ahhh" of appreciation filled the plaza when the last tones died away. The boy couldn't help but smile a little as he faced the King's Man.

Suddenly, it was Bopha's turn. Her father stood and gestured to her. She stepped over knees that blocked her way, and entered the circle. The sun pounded down and sweat trickled down her back. Thanks to the little stone, she was no longer thirsty, but she needed to get rid of it. When she lifted her hands to the Sangat leader, she bowed over them and was able to spit the pebble between her palms. As she and her father turned to the King's Man, Bopha tucked the small rock into her sampot, then performed a deep sampeah. Her father walked back to sit with the men. The Sangat leader gestured to the musicians. Bopha listened, letting the music fill her.

Before she knew it, the instruments became quiet, a last trill of the fiddle string hanging in the hot and silent air. Bopha bowed to the King's Man and heard a long "Ahhhh" from the people. The King's Man was smiling as he lifted his hands to her. She bowed again then walked back to sit beside her mother.

Mdeay touched her shoulder, nodding. There were tears in her eyes. "That was beautiful, my little durian," Mdeay said softly. "I've never seen you dance any better."

Bopha was surprised. She could barely remember moving. Her body felt like it was in a dream, and there were spurts of sharpness pinging up and down her back. She was shivering and sweating at the same time, but she didn't feel sick. Mdeay' smile faded as she looked at her daughter. "Are you okay, little one?" Bopha nodded, unable to speak, the jolts of energy too much for words.

There were only a few other dancers. Bopha sat watching, without seeing. Her back finally relaxed and she was exhausted. She leaned against Mdeay's arm. Mdeay patted her knee. "You are better?" Bopha nodded. Reasmey had fallen asleep in Mdeay's lap.

"Just tired," she whispered. "The stone worked, but now I'm thirsty again." She dug in her sampot, but the pebble was gone.

The Sangat leader walked into the circle and announced that there would be a break. When the drums sounded, people should return to the courtyard. Everyone stood up and stretched. The fat woman told Bopha she had been the best dancer of all, then waddled off to relieve herself in the bushes behind the Sangat.

Mdeay led her children back through the village to their house, and drew water for them. As they drank from the coconut bowl, Aupouk returned. "Preah Chan Bopha!" He was smiling broadly. "That was the most amazing dance. I didn't know you could do that."

Bopha ducked her head. "I didn't know either." She wasn't sure exactly what she had done. And she didn't say anything about the sparks in her back or the dream in her body.

They heard the drumbeats, slow and deep, and followed their summons. The crowd was more subdued now. The sun had passed behind the big trees that surrounded the courtyard. People settled into the shadows quickly. The King's Man walked solemnly into the center of the circle.

"Kampucheans," he announced. "You can be justly proud of your children. Their performances this afternoon were a tribute to His Majesty." He stopped, looking around at the crowd. "I am pleased to say that tomorrow three of your dancers will come with me to Angkor." The crowed chattered excitedly. He waited for the chatter to subside, then continued.

"As I call your name, please enter the circle." He paused. "Sophea Srey!" The crowd ahhhed. The tiny girl walked to the

7

center, bowed to the King's Man, then stood next to him in the place he indicated, her head high. "Dara Davuth!" The boy walked slowly into the circle, bowed, then joined Sophea but didn't lift his head. Bopha heard his father hiss at him. Dara sighed, raising his chin. Bopha was surprised he could be such a wonderful dancer yet so shy without music. Peiple ahhhed, but not as loudly.

"Preah Chan Bopha!" She heard Mdeay's gasp, saw Aupouk smile and lift his hands in sampeah. The crowd moved aside for her and she entered the open plaza. The King's Man smiled at her as she bowed. His face was lean and his eyes were very dark, but kind. Bopha looked at him for a second, then turned to stand next to the two other children. Dara was her size, Sophea half a head smaller. They faced the crowd, which ahhhed and patted the ground.

"Thank you for giving our King this wonderful gift," the King's Man said. He brought his hands together and bowed slightly. The children and all the people bowed deeply in return. "You may all leave now. Tomorrow morning at sunrise, bring the children to me here." He turned and walked into the shadows. After a moment of silence, the crowd got to its shuffling feet.

Bopha, Dara and Sophea looked at each other. "See you tomorrow," Bopha said quietly. Her father was coming for her across the yard. Dara whispered the same, as his father arrived. Sophea just looked at her, then at Dara, and nodded, head high. Her father was last to come. Bopha watched her walk away, her back so much straighter than her father's.

* * *

Bopha woke in the dark. She could hear her father's slight snore, her brothers' quiet sleeping breaths. Reasmey was curled into her on the small pallet they shared. Even though she couldn't see, Bopha knew from the sound that Reasmey had two fingers in her mouth. She listened but couldn't hear her mother.

Gently and silently, Bopha uncurled from Reasmey and stood. The birds were still sleeping but night insects hummed and creaked. A tohkeay suddenly squawked loudly — "tohkeay!" — under her feet and Bopha caught her breath involuntarily, even though she knew the sound well. A big one lived in the beams

8

under the floor, a sign that their home was blessed. Was that what had woken her?

She could see a little in the dimness now, and made her way around her sleeping family. Mdeay wasn't in her spot next to Aupouk. Bopha lifted the cloth that covered the door. Slipping outside, she stopped. There was a dark shadow in the courtyard. When a cloud lifted from the half-moon sky, Bopha could see the shadow was Mdeay, kneeling at the family altar under their big neem tree. She smelled incense. She climbed quietly down the ladder and joined her mother, who glanced at her then closed her eyes again, hands in sampeah at her forehead.

The ground was cool and gritty under Bopha's knees. Mdeay had put a stick of precious incense into the clay pot filled with sand, which sat on the painted wooden platform of their family altar. She could make out, in front of the incense, a small banana, and a white lump on a banana leaf which was likely rice. Her mother was making a special offering. But why in the middle of the night? She knew better than to interrupt her mother's silent prayer.

After what seemed like ages, when the incense was nearly burned down to the sand, Mdeay took a deep breath and lowered her hands. "Why are you up in the middle of the night?" She looked at her daughter. In the moonlight, Bopha saw tears gleaming in her eyes.

"I just woke up, I don't know why. Why are you making an offering in the middle of the night?" Bopha asked.

"When everyone gets up, I will be too busy," Mdeay said, pulling Bopha so close she could feel the new baby jumping in Mdeay's tummy.

She laughed quietly, "The baby is jumping! Is he happy to be outside with you in the night?"

Mdeay smiled and released her daughter. "This is a very busy baby, he or she. I will miss your help." Bopha could see the smile fade as she said it.

"But what are you praying for?" Bopha asked.

"I'm asking Buddha, and all the gods, and all the spirits of the forest, to protect you on your journey and in your new life," Mdeay said.

Bopha had forgotten. Even when Mdeay said she would miss her help, Bopha hadn't remembered. But now she did and felt like she had when the water buffalo calf ran into her. Her chest was tight. "I don't want to leave you," she whispered.

"I know," Mdeay said, hugging her again. "It's a big honor to be chosen to dance for the King. But it's a big change to leave here."

"Can't I stay?" Bopha was begging, tears pouring down her face. She could feel Mdeay shake her head.

"It will be better for you if you go. At first, it will be hard and you will miss us. But you will be so happy to be a dancer. And you will meet new friends. Imagine, seeing the temples of Angkor!"

Bopha had of course heard about Angkor. Her oldest brother said it was only half a day's walk to the big road that led there. He told her about the five tall towers, and all the monks who lived there. Their village had only a very small Wat, with three monks. One was so old and shriveled that Bopha didn't know how he could even walk. Their house was close to the Wat, and the old monk would stagger into their yard every morning and hold out his bowl in trembling hands. Mdeay always saved a special treat for him, maybe pouring sugar syrup onto rice, or giving him two of the sweet little bananas Bopha loved so much.

"Can I come back to visit?" she asked.

"Maybe," said Mdeay, getting to her feet. "That would be nice. I'd love to hear all your adventures."

As long as they were already outside, they went to the bushes before climbing the ladder. By now, Bopha could see the sky had gotten much lighter, with pink streaks in the gray.

"Let's start cooking now," she said to her mother. "I don't think I can go back to sleep."

"Me either," said Mdeay, smiling a little. "Good idea."

They worked quietly, the tasks known so well they didn't need more light. Bopha got some twigs from the firewood pile. Mdeay squatted by the pot that kept the embers overnight, in a bed of ash. She scooped out layers of ash, then carefully lifted a few chunks and put them in the fire pit. She blew gently and the chunks went pink, then orange. Bopha carefully laid the twigs in a cross-cross

10

pattern over the chunks, while Mdeay continued to blow until there were a few tiny flickers of flame on the twigs. Bopha brought bigger sticks.

While Bopha blew on the fire, and fed it more wood, Mdeay dipped water from the cistern. She got rice from the big covered storage basket. It was now less than a quarter full. She hoped the gods would bless them with a good harvest by the time the new baby was eating. With Bopha gone to the King, there would be one less mouth to feed until then.

The family clattered to life upstairs, the boys pushing each other on the ladder until Aupouk said, "Chop!" Bopha wasn't hungry suddenly, but she squatted with her banana leaf plate and ate a few bites of rice and a banana. Her stomach was fluttery.

After the meal, Aupouk gathered them at the altar and lit incense. As he prayed, Bopha caught glimpses of her brothers looking at her solemnly, almost in awe. She was going to dance for the King. They would stay in the village, walking behind a water buffalo and squatting in a rice paddy, planting, weeding and harvesting. Bopha had wrapped her rumdol sampot and a wooden comb in a new blue and white kromah Mdeay gave her.

She wore her everyday sampot, with its stains and a few worn spots. The only other thing she owned was a thin gold arm bangle. Mdeay pushed the bangle up onto her arm as high as it would go, and handed her the knotted kromah. Bopha held onto her mother tightly, the unborn baby kicking her away. Mdeay gently put her hands on the little girl's shoulders and held her away. "Go in peace, my child," she said softly.

Aupouk looked at the sky, now almost fully light. "It's time," he said, and started to walk toward the Sangat, his family straggling behind. Bopha turned back to look at the house and the neem tree. One of the farm cats came out of the shadows, stubby tail held high. It looked at her briefly, then sat down and started to groom.

Many of the villagers had come to the Sangat to see the three dancers leave, and get another glimpse of the King's Man. This morning he was wearing a deep green sampot, with yellow vines. A teenage boy held the reins of a big brown horse off to one side of the courtyard. The horse's mane was braided tightly and evenly, and on his back was a thick brown blanket. Several men and a few women stood nearby, dressed more formally than the villagers.

The Sangat leader, quite a lot shorter than the King's man, stood stiffly next to him.

As the first rays of the sun hit the peak of the Sangat roof, the leader stepped forward.

"Bring the dancers here." Aupouk touched Bopha's shoulder and she followed him into the center. Dara and Sophea came out of the crowd, following their fathers. The three men and three children stopped in front of the leader and bowed. The leader gestured to the men, "Leave now." Aupouk didn't touch Bopha's shoulder this time, but he nodded and smiled into her eyes. He bowed again to the Sangat leader and, more deeply, to the King's Man, then returned to Mdeay's side.

The King's Man spoke, "Thank you for the gift of these dancers. May the King's blessing be upon us all." He turned and walked to the horse. The teenage boy cupped his hands and the King's Man stepped into them, then up onto the horse in one fluid motion. The teenager handed him the reins. Without a backward glance, the King's Man urged the horse forward, and the nearby men fell in line behind him.

The children in the middle of the courtyard weren't sure what to do. "Go," bellowed the Sangat leader. Two of the women, standing where the horse had been, waved to them with "come here" gestures. Sophea immediately went, Bopha following, still a little uncertain. Dara Davuth, head hanging, was the last to move.

As the caravan trailed along the high embankment between brilliant green rice paddies, the villagers seemed to wake up and started to follow. They could have easily kept up with the procession, but there was no room on the path for more than two abreast. Besides, the excitement was over and there was work to do.

Even Bopha's brothers soon gave up, and stood watching as their sister got smaller and smaller against the dull brown path. Aupouk called them, and they turned and followed him. Mdeay was hugging Reasmey to her chest, resting the little girl on the shelf of her pregnant belly. Two of the women in the procession were behind Bopha, and soon Mdeay couldn't see her daughter.

12

With wet eyes, Mdeay returned to her home. Today she would have to take Reasmey to the river to get water for the family.

CHAPTER 2

On the Road

The women behind the children were carrying baskets on their heads, and they chattered among themselves, excited to be heading home and bickering about who would do which chores as they traveled. Bopha, Sophea and Dara walked in silence. The path between rice paddies went straight for most of an hour. Villagers squatting to weed would stand and stare at the procession, giving sampeah to the horseman in the lead. By the time the sun came up, they had gone further than Bopha had ever gone, which was the next village. She could see trees in the distance. The air became hot and heavy. She was thirsty and hungry, her stomach having settled, but the group kept moving.

When they finally got to the trees, the King's Man halted. The men put down their bundles and the women their baskets, scattering into the bushes. One of the women hissed, "Go now, if you need to. We won't stop again for a while." The children did so.

The trees were deep and the brush thick. Bopha squatted, then heard a gibbon screech, and another screech in reply. The tree branches rustled. Looking up, she could make out their furry bodies scampering high above. She liked monkeys, though her mother said they were a nuisance. It was true that they would swing down and try to get the lids off any food jars. Mdeay forbid the children to feed them.

Bopha stood up, tears in her eyes as she thought of home. She looked around and didn't see anyone. The tears fell down her cheeks. Then two women stood up nearby and Bopha pushed through the bushes toward them. "Here you are," scolded the older one. "Don't get lost. And don't dawdle." Her skin was smooth except for frown lines between her eyes. Her full breasts swung as she moved.

The younger woman was pretty, with small firm breasts. She gave Bopha a gentle nod. "Are you thirsty?" She handed her a water bag made from a pig bladder. Bopha took it in both hands and looked it over. The small end was folded inside a knotted cord. The woman showed her how to take off the cord, hold it up and squirt liquid into her mouth, without touching the bag to her lips. Bopha tried to do it that way, but got a lot of the water on her chin and chest. The woman chuckled.

"You'll learn," said the young woman reassuringly. "I'm Achariya, What's your name?"

Bopha whispered, "Preah Chan Bopha, but I'm called Bopha."

"Okay, Bopha." She turned. Bopha saw that Sophea had appeared near them. "And who are you?"

"Sophea Srey," Sophea answered in a normal tone.

"How pretty," said Achariya, offering her the water. Sophea drank without spilling a drop."

"Hurry up," the scolding voice intruded.

"Coming, Heng," said Achariya, walking ahead of the girls. She picked up her basket and settled it on her head. "Let's go."

As the troupe set out again, Dara walked closer to the men, in front of the women. There were five men, in addition to the King's Man and the teenager, four women, and the three children. By now the air was hot and heavy. They walked another hour on a small track through the forest, unable to see beyond the next trees. When the path opened into rice paddies, the sun blazed into their eyes. Bopha squinted into its glare and could see a long way ahead, where two separate villages huddled in the green.

Many people were working the paddies. They stared at the travelers. The sky started to fill with clouds, and the hot little girl gave thanks. It wasn't much cooler but at least her eyes didn't burn in the glare. By the time they got to the second village, the charcoal sky threatened storm. The headman of the village met them with a deep bow.

"Please, come in until the rain is past," he offered, gesturing to a large house. This village was much bigger and most of the dwellings were fancier than where Bopha lived. Thunder rumbled as they gathered under shelter. Bursts of wind lifted dust from the courtyard and spat it into Bopha's eyes. She turned her back to it, wiping her eyes.

15

But the tears didn't stop. She looked around, recognizing no one but the other two children, Heng and Achariya, and the King's Man. Dara was squatting with his head down, making patterns in the dirt with a small stick. Sophea stood straight, near one of the pillars. Bopha closed her eyes and remembered Mdeay at the altar, the smell of incense. It seemed so long ago, she couldn't believe it was still the same day. She wiped her eyes again. This time her vision cleared.

A lot of villagers clustered with the newcomers, talking over each other, asking questions. Heng and Achariya joined a group of women and began to prepare food. Bopha made her cautious way to them through the crowd. "Can I help?" she asked Achariya, who was on her haunches by the fire pit.

"Do you know how to keep the fire going?"

"Yes."

"Okay then, here's the wood. Don't let it get too hot."

Bopha shook her head. "I won't." It was good to have something to do. Whenever she lifted her head, she saw Dara and Sophea in the same places. Sophea was sitting now. A few little boys squatted near Dara, looking at what he was drawing.

The rain poured down, thunder sometimes so loud people stopped talking. The men squatted near the front, some of them smoking. The women were clustered near the fires. It was such a large house that there were two fire areas. LIttle children toddled and ran among the grown-ups. Several girls, younger and older than Bopha, watched her and Sophea closely.

One crouched next to Bopha. "Is it true that you are going to dance for the king?" Bopha nodded. "How exciting. I wish I could dance," the girl continued. Bopha said nothing. She wasn't excited, just tired and hungry and homesick. Luckily, Heng came by and looked into the rice pot.

"Time to eat," she pronounced. The other girl got up and went to join her family.

By the time the meal was done, the rain had rumbled off and the sky was light. When the King's Man stood up, everyone else did too, bowing. Bopha found her kromah bundle where she had left it, and followed Achariya to where the horse stood, its coat much darker after the rain.

They walked for hours, through more woods and past more villages, stopping only once to relieve themselves deep in the jungle. The lowering sun was in Bopha's eyes. Her legs were tired, and her heart heavy. She stumbled and fell into Heng, who said sharply, "Watch where you are going." Sophea was still standing straight and walking easily.

Not long afterwards, the procession came to a big village. At a fine house in the middle of the village they stopped at last. The setting sun shone golden in the treetops. A tall man, as tall as the King's Man but more broad through the shoulders, was waiting there. He bowed after the King's Man had dismounted. Bopha could hear him making what she now recognized as the usual welcome speech. All she wanted was to sit down and eat.

Heng pushed her and Sophea forward. Dara was standing in front of the King's Man, facing the head man. His head was up for a change, Bopha noted. The three children gave sampeah to the Sangat leader, who bowed back. "Welcome, young dancers. Tonight you can rest. Then tomorrow you will dance for us!" He turned to the King's Man. "We also have some talented children, as you will see at the celebration." The King's Man nodded and the two men walked into the shadows under the house, followed by a crowd of other men and youths. Dara went with them, leaving Bopha and Sophea standing where they were.

Achariya pushed through the women and girls who had gathered. "Come," she said, and led them through the courtyard to a house at the back, big but not as big as the headman's house. The village females surrounded them. Bopha felt like she was being crushed and could hardly breathe.

"Are you all right?" Achariya looked at her with concern. Bopha nodded, looking down. She couldn't talk past the lump in her throat. "Sit here. We'll eat soon." Bopha sat, and watched the woman's bare feet walk away through the dirt. The feet soon came back, and Achariya squatted next to her with a small pot of water. "Drink. You'll feel better."

Bopha managed a small sampeah, and drank all the water. It tasted funny and hit her stomach hard. She was afraid the water might not stay down, and willed herself to breathe, staring at the ground, still holding the cup. Mouth open, small breaths. After a moment, she took a deeper breath and looked up, handing the cup to Achariya. The young woman reached out a hand and patted Bopha's shoulder. "It gets easier," she said. "I do know how you feel."

Heng's sharp voice interrupted them. Achariya got up and went to Heng, murmuring something. Heng shook her head impatiently. Achariya murmured. Heng's head shook less vehemently, then finally nodded slightly. Bopha looked back at the ground, rested her arms on her knees and closed her eyes. All she wanted to do was curl up next to Reasmey and go to sleep.

The evening was a blur of unfamiliar faces. There were a couple of torches under the house, and more in the courtyard where men and boys were milling around. Bopha could make out the tall lean figure of the King's Man, and once saw Dara with a group of boys. When dinner came, the fish amok was good, though not as good as Pich's. Bopha ate her portion fast, not realizing how hungry she was. Achariya offered her more, and Bopha ate another small amount. "Looks like you feel better," the pretty young woman suggested.

"Yes, thank you," said Bopha. "And thank you for your kindness." Achariya smiled and closed one eye fast. Bopha was startled. What was that? Achariya chuckled and did it again.

"It's called a wink," she said. Bopha tried it and her face scrunched all up on one side.

"Try the other eye," suggested Achariya. Bopha did, and it was easier. "Now do it fast, so it almost looks like you didn't do it. So people wonder, 'Did I see really see that?'"

Shortly after the meal, Achariya took Bopha and Sophea upstairs, where the girls shared a sleeping mat. The one big room was full of women and girls, who were just dim murmuring shapes in the gloom. In the courtyard, instruments started, then singing. Bopha fell asleep despite the noise. She woke twice, the first time unsure where she was, her ears filled with shouts, singing, laughter. She felt a back against her, but it was too big to be Reasmey. Torchlight from the yard seeped between the beads that hung in long strings from the tops of the windows, and she remembered. Sophea was curled away from her. The second time Bopha woke, the village was quiet and dark.

In the morning, Bopha went with the King's women and Sophea to bathe in the river.

Here the water was deeper and faster than at home. At a bend, there was a calm pool. Bopha washed her old sampot and laid it over a bush. Sophea was lying on her back with her feet up, in the water. "What are you doing?" Bopha asked.

"Floating."

Bopha carefully leaned back into the water. But when she tried lifting her legs, her head went under and she spluttered and splashed.

"Don't splash." Sophea's voice was annoyed.

"I can't help it. How do you do that?"

"You work too hard. You have to be relaxed. Start out over by the bank, then push yourself slowly away with your hands."

Bopha watched Sophea, who looked at her impassively then closed her eyes. She went to the bank and lay down, then followed Sophea's instructions. It worked. Bopha felt herself lifted by the water. "It's working!" she shouted to Sophea. But the effort of shouting unbalanced her and she went underwater again. This time she tried not to splash, but she was coughing. When she caught her breath, she looked out at Sophea, still floating with her eyes closed. She was smiling.

Bopha checked on her sampot, which was dry enough. She climbed out of the water and dried off with her new kromah, then wrapped the sampot around her narrow hips. After breakfast they would be dancing, and she would wear her new rumdol flower sampot. Yesterday Bopha hadn't even thought about dancing, but in this morning's sun she was excited, and did a few bends and steps. Her gold arm bangle flashed as she twisted her arms in a few intricate patterns of the Wishing Dance. She didn't know the whole dance and was eager to learn.

* * *

19

There was a much bigger crowd today than there had been at Bopha's village. She, Sophea and Dara stood to the side with the King's company. They would dance last. Bopha realized that she would not see any of the other dancers, the adults completely blocking her view. She whispered to Achariya, "Can we go somewhere we can see?" Achariya shook her head.

Bopha could barely see the tip of his golden helmet when King's Man spoke, but his clear voice carried. He made the same speech, and the Sangat leader made a speech very much like the one in her own village. She heard him say there would be twelve contestants. It would be a long day. But when the crowd sat down, she and the King's company had a clear view after all. Bopha watched intently as eight girls and four boys performed, with a break after the first six dancers. These children were good, she thought, with the exception of two girls and two boys. People cheered lustily, louder for the best dancers but still honoring the four that weren't so good. "Wah! Wah! Wah!"

How many dancers does the King want? Bopha found herself wondering. What happens if there are too many good dancers?

It was mid-afternoon when Bopha's group danced. Sophea went first, her small body moving precisely and beautifully through the moves. The "Wah!"s and ground patting went on and on after she was done. She stood in sampeah in the center of the courtyard, smiling. When it was finally her turn to dance, Bopha didn't feel the same energy that she had at home. She didn't make any actual mistakes, but she hadn't done as well. The "wahs" reflected her own assessment. Dara came after her and was, if possible, even better than before. His was a finale to remember, and the crowd knew it.

When they went to bed that night, three more girls squeezed next to Bopha and Sophea. Two boys had been chosen to join the company as well. Heng was too busy scolding the newcomers to bother with Bopha. One of the girls was a taller than Bopha and her nipples were just starting to grow. Her name was Kalienne, and she had a gentle smile. Another was smaller than Sophea. Her name was Nuon, and she seemed as soft and tender as her name. She cuddled into Bopha, and Bopha could feel her little shoulders quiver in the darkness. But she never made a sound as she cried.

The next morning was hot before dawn and Bopha woke before the sun. She untangled from Nuon and made her way down the ladder and out to the woven mat that served as modesty shield. The moon was low in the sky and a little bigger than it had been when she left her village. She remembered the smell of incense under the neem tree with her mother, and her mother's eyes gleaming with tears in the moon's light. The family altar here was elaborate, with several shelves. Bopha knelt in sampeah but had no incense.

Could the gods hear her prayer if it wasn't carried on that smoke? She hoped so. "Take care of Mdeay and Reasmey, and let me see them again. And help me to be the best dancer I can be."

After breakfast, the large crowd watched as the King's Company set out, the five girls toward the end of the line with Heng and Achariya behind them. Bopha could see the horse turn into the sun at the corner. When she got there, she saw that the narrow street was crossed by a very wide one, and that the King's Man was heading straight into the sun. Villagers caught up to their procession, and surrounded them. The crowd followed beyond the end of the village, and little boys ran next to them for another half-mile before stopping.

This must be the road her older brother, Rithy, had told her about. It was wide enough for two horses to walk next to each other. He said the King had made big roads to connect the whole kingdom, which was very big. He said, "It takes a month to walk to the ocean."

"How do you know that?" Bopha asked. "And what's ocean?"

"The second oldest monk told me. He grew up in a village on the road to the ocean. Ocean is a river so big you can't see across to the other side.   And if you go out on it, you can't see land anywhere."

"How do you go out on water?" Bopha asked.

21

"In a boat," her brother said, proud of his knowledge. "It's like a pot, but big enough for people to sit in it. Some people even live on boats in Tonle Sap."

"Is Tonle Sap ocean?"

"No, it's a lake. Lakes are also big, but ocean is very big. And ocean water tastes like salt." Her brother wanted to become a monk and learn to read and write, but Aupouk said no. He needed Rithy to help in the fields, at least until his brothers were older.

Bopha shook herself. The caravan had stopped just before a village. Heng shouted, "Go now, children."

She looked around but there were almost no bushes. Heng was squatting behind a woven mat hung between two poles. Dara was with boys, their backs turned away from the road. She envied men and boys. They could pee so easily. She waited till Heng was done, then went behind the mat herself. Sophea went after Bopha.

"Sophea," Bopha tried, when the other girl came back to the road. "Did you walk on this road with your father?" Sophea looked surprised.

"Why do you ask?"

"The Sangat leader said you had walked for three days to get to our village."

"Yes. But we came from the north." Sophea pointed. "Angkor is to the south." She turned toward the sun, now halfway up the sky.

Bopha nodded. "You danced so well, even after such a long walk. I don't know if I could do that. I'm tired already and we only walked for one day. I didn't dance very well yesterday."

The smaller girl looked Bopha up and down. "You get used to it." Then she added, almost grudgingly, "And we stayed with one of my mother's relatives for a few days before the contest."

"So you got to rest a little?'

"Yes." Sophea turned away and walked toward the women, who were gathered at a large cistern, filling the water bags. Bopha followed her straight little figure. Would she get used to it? To any of it?

CHAPTER 3

Arrival

They walked on for many days, Bopha at the end of the line, just ahead of Heng and Achariya, and a man who was now bringing up the rear. He started when the caravan came to the big road. Achariya said it was traditional for any group sent out by the King to have guards in front and in back. The area where Bopha lived was very remote, and there wasn't much chance of any trouble there, so the rear guard had been in front with the other men. He carried a long stick with a pointed metal end. Just below this point were thin silk banners, blue and gold, that waved in the breeze as he walked. Bopha couldn't see any guard in front. Maybe it was the King's Man himself, or maybe another of the men went on ahead. What kind of trouble? She wondered but was too tired to ask and Achariya was busy.

Many of the villages along the road were very big. Every day or two they stopped for a dance contest. Bopha could just about recite from memory the speech of the King's Man and whoever was the Sangat leader. Always the same. It was interesting at first to see so many people and the fancy houses. But the moon became full and started to wane again, and Bopha trudged along, glad for Nuon's company. She was a sweet child, and chattered about the monkeys and the dust and the shapes of the clouds. They walked by twos and threes, except for Sophea, who kept to herself, her little back still as straight as when Bopha first saw her.

Rainy season was almost over, but they still got soaked a couple of times by sudden storms. Mostly they walked into the sun, and wrapped their kromahs around their faces. Once in a while their group would have to get off the road for a band of mounted horsemen, galloping past them, heading north. Then dust would fill the air. Bopha had danced twice more, still not feeling good about it. The energy that filled her that day in her village she had never felt before or since, but she missed it. She hoped that when they got to Angkor, and were settled into a routine and being taught more about dancing, that the sparking up her back would return.

More children were added to the column, and the dancing was rotated among them all. Except Dara. He danced every time. Bopha thought he was getting even better. He looked different too. Instead of hanging his head and dragging his feet, he seemed to be the leader of the boys. The men would laugh at him and clap him on the back, and he would grin.

Before the moon was dark, there were ten girls and five boys. One night, Achariya told the girls that tomorrow evening they would sleep at Angkor. It was a restless night, as ten excited girls tossed and turned in a room too small for them. Several times an irritated Heng shushed them. "It you wake me again, you'll be sorry," she finally said. Whether that did the trick or whether they were all just exhausted, Bopha didn't wake again until the sky was getting light.

"Will we see the King?" "Where will we stay?" "Do we dance all day every day?" Voices and questions buzzed around the back of the procession as they started out for the last walk of their journey.

Even calm Achariya said, "Enough. No, you won't see the King. He is away on a campaign. And you will find out everything else when you get there."

As the sun lengthened their shadows sideways, the King's Man finally halted the column in a place where the road spread out to the west. On the other side, a long baray reflected light off its placid water. He gestured for the children to come near, and they gathered around him. He did not get off the horse, who stood and blew loudly out his nostrils. Bopha had trouble focusing on the King's Man because the space was filled with people. Vendors squatted next to small braziers, cooking strips of chicken and fish. Others called out "Crickets!" and "Snails!" There were displays of vegetables and the potent smell of durian permeated the thick air. She had never see so much to eat. Her stomach rumbled. Heng swatted her shoulder and Bopha pulled her gaze from the food to the tall man.

"We are late, so each of you can get something to eat here. Be quick. We will eat as we go the rest of the way. It will be dark when we get to Angkor." Achariya, Heng, and another woman who had started working with them, shepherded the girls to get food. Two other women were in charge of the boys. Bopha got two pieces of hot chicken in a banana leaf, with a ladle of rice. She couldn't see the durian, so she got a banana. The mangos looked perfect, but she couldn't eat one and walk. She was so hungry she bit into the chicken before it was cool enough, and had to put her kromah over her mouth while she panted.

A sudden loud whistle quieted the crowd. It was the signal to start moving again. Bopha saw Boran, the rear guard, waving his spear and pushed through the crowd to him.

He was about her father's age. His face was marked by many small scars and one long one across his forehead. She had learned from Achariya that his name was Boran, which means ancient. But Bopha thought he was just old, not that old. He volunteered to go with the King's Man to find dancers because he liked children. He had many, she said, and one of his girls would teach them to dance at Angkor. Once Bopha heard him chuckle when Nuon said in her piping voice, "That cloud looks like an apsara!"

Now he said, "So, little Bopha, you are soon to meet my daughter. It's been a long journey. We will all be glad to get home." Bopha's face fell at the word. Boran noticed and said, "Ah, that's right. This is not your home." Then he added, reassuringly, "Not yet. But it will be. I think you will like it very much."

Nuon was at Bopha's elbow. She was quite shy, but Boran had won her over and she ventured, "Will your daughter be our dance teacher?"

"Yes. She teaches the youngest children. She loves to dance and is beautiful to watch."

Heng shooed the last of the girls into line and they started moving. Sunset turned the baray bright pink. Then the road turned away from the water as the tropical night fell suddenly. They could smell fires and see glints of light through the trees on each side of the road as they walked. Murmured conversations and occasional shouts of laughter proved that the trees were full of people settling in for the night. It was fully dark but the road was smooth. Bopha just followed the sampot of Kalienne ahead of her, one step and then another. She was too tired to be excited. Besides, in the dark, how could they see Angkor?

Bopha was nearly asleep on her feet and bumped into Kalienne when they finally stopped. Torches were lit around an

26

enormous courtyard. A large wooden building was dimly visible. Suddenly they were surrounded by voices, laughing and talking, welcoming them. Nuon reached for Bopha's hand, and Bopha was glad for the touch. Kalienne held her other hand. The three tired girls stood in a little line. They could hear Achariya's voice in the crowd, then she was there. "Here you are," her voice was smiling and excited. "Let's get you to bed."

She was in charge of Bopha, Kalienne, Nuon and Sophea. Bopha felt sorry for the older girls who had Heng. After they each had a drink of tepid dilute tea, which left a bitter aftertaste but was better than being thirsty, Achariya showed them where the privy mat was, for them to step behind. Finally she led them to the big building. There were stairs at each end, not simple ladders. A covered balcony ran from one end to the other. It was Bopha's first time on stairs, and she decided those steps were definitely easier than rungs. "You'll be in this room," Achariya told them. Six other girls were already there and had laid out sleeping mats for them. Bopha couldn't remember any of their names, and sank onto the mat she shared with Nuon, falling asleep immediately.

* * *

B opha was wakened by the sound of doves in the rafters, and the subdued chatter of little girls all around her. Nuon still slept in a little ball but she could see Kalienne and Sophea were rolling their mat. She stretched and stood. Her sampot was dingier than ever after days of dusty travel. She asked Sophea, who always seemed to know everything, "Do you know where we can wash?"

"Achariya will take us to the baray in a few minutes," Sophea informed her. "Then we'll have breakfast."

"We have to go all the way to the baray?" Bopha asked in dismay.

"No, not that baray. Not the one we passed yesterday. The King has been making barays all over, and there are two near us."

The sound of hammers pounding stone started in the distance outside, at first just a few, then hundreds. The noise was not quite deafening. Sophea raised her voice a little, "They are building Bayon. It's the King's newest temple."

27

"How come you always know everything?" Bopha asked in amazement. Sophea shrugged, her lips curved up a little. "Have you seen Angkor? Can you see it from the porch?"

Sophea shook her head. "No. It's an hour's walk from here. We'll go in three days."

Bopha was disappointed. After all she'd heard, she wanted to see the towers for herself. But she didn't have much time to think, since Achariya came to take them to bathe. Then it was non-stop busy, meeting all the dancers, learning her way around the complex, which even had a kitchen building with special people to cook. There were nearly fifty girls. Bopha couldn't count but she knew it was a lot. Nuon was the youngest and Kalienne one of the oldest. But since Kalienne was new, she would stay with Bopha and the younger girls for now.

The children who had been at Angkor for some time were instantly recognizable. Their posture was erect, like Sophea's, and they moved like water. They placed their feet carefully without looking like they were. They would sit instead of squat, so they could practice twisting their hands and feet into dance positions when they were't doing anything else. Bopha found herself standing taller, and she watched Sophea more closely, trying to imitate the way the younger child carried her head.

After a breakfast of rice and fruit, the girls gathered in the center of the courtyard. Huge trees surrounded it, so the early morning sun just lit their tops and left the yard in shadow. Gibbons ran up and down, jumping between the branches and chattering. Heng and Achariya sorted the girls into four lines, with the smallest in front, then joined the other women in a semi-circle around the girls.

There was a commotion on the road. The King's Man rode into the courtyard, followed by Boran and several young women who walked like dancers. He stopped his horse in front of the line of girls. His clear voice rang out, "By the mercy of our King Jayavarman VII, you are here to learn to dance. Follow your teachers' directions, and practice continuously. Being chosen is a great honor. You must live up to it. In three days, you will go to Angkor for the ceremony of reception into the community of Apsaras. In a few months, when the King returns, he will want to see you all, so prepare yourselves to dance for him."

The King's Man wheeled his horse and rode off fast, dust puffing up from each step. Boran, carrying his spear, led the young women to face the line of children. There was no wind, so his silk flags lay against the haft, the yellow gleaming in the shadowy light. In his gruff voice, he introduced the teachers. Bopha thought he sounded proud when he said, "And this is Ponnleu, who will teach the youngest dancers."

The teachers gathered their charges and each group went to a different corner of the yard. Bopha followed Ponnleu, along with Sophea, Nuon, Kalienne and five others.

Ponnleu, whose friendly smile lit up her beautiful face, wore a light green sampot. "Today, we will get to know each other, and start to learn some jeeb positions. This afternoon, musicians will come, and each of the new girls will dance. After that, the teachers will decide the best class for each of you." She started by having each girl say her name, and would remind the shy ones to keep their chins up and their eyes focused straight ahead, with a little smile on their lips.

Bopha knew there were many many jeeb positions for the legs, and even more for the hands. Now she started to learn their names and meanings. She was so absorbed she was surprised when the lunch gong sounded. This was a large metal circle hanging from the porch. One of the cooks hit it with a padded mallet. The notes hung in the hot air. The sun was directly overhead and shone into the center of the courtyard. The edges were still in shadow, but Bopha's sampot was damp with sweat.

* * *

Three days passed in a blur of active learning. On the morning that they would go to Angkor, everyone rose early. After bathing in the baray and washing her hair, Bopha put on her rumdol sampot. She admired the lovely swirl of colors as Kalienne braided her hair for her. Then they all ate a bit of rice and dried fish. Just as they finished, the King's Man and four guards arrived. Bopha saw Boran was wearing a bright red sampot and his lance caught the sunlight. They started to Angkor, a long line of girls walking four abreast, with the short line of boys ahead of them and two guards ahead of the King's Man on his horse. Boran and another man followed behind. All the young dancers were going to the ceremony.

In the early light, Bopha could see many shelters nestled among the trees, more and more as they got closer to Angkor. Wooden houses, all larger and fancier than almost any they had seen on their journey, lined either side of the road. Between the houses, under huge trees, people were selling things she had never imagined and couldn't identify, as well as all kinds of food. The road here was so wide that horses and wagons could pass the procession easily. The closer they got to Angkor, the busier the road. Men and boys herded pigs and water buffalo. Women carried live chickens and ducks in wicker baskets yoked over their shoulders. Little girls carried pots of flowers as big as they were. Everyone was selling something. Sing-song vendor cries filled the air.

Despite this throng, the line of dancers was never jostled. The crowd parted for them, and Bopha could hear whispers, "The Apsaras!" She stood a little straighter and could feel Nuon next to her, lifting her head up higher as well. Bopha stopped looking around and focused on placing her feet just so with every step. Excitement coursed through her. Apsara! She was going to be an Apsara!

Suddenly the line halted. The road here was so wide it was almost a pavilion. In the distance, Bopha caught sight of the famous towers. Everything else faded away. Angkor. The voice of the King's Man carried on the light breeze. "Children of Our Beloved Jayavarman. From now until the end of the ceremony, you are not to speak a word. When it is time for you to dance, you will be told. You have ten minutes to refresh yourselves. Next time we stop, it will be inside the temple."

Achariya and Ponnleu led their charges to the mat, and when they had relieved themselves gave them each some fruit and a piece of pork belly, followed by a drink of the weak, bitter tea. Bopha wasn't hungry but didn't know when they'd eat again, so she swallowed her food. Despite the fluttering in her stomach, the meal settled okay when the King's Man whistled them back into line.

The towers got bigger and bigger. Bopha had never seen anything so big. Each one was bigger than all the houses in her village stacked on top of each other. Finally, they reached the end of the road and the vendors disappeared. In front of them was a huge stone causeway, arching over a baray so big it might even be a river. Stone lions roared and likenesses of Sesanaga, the thousand-headed serpent, greeted them on each side of the bridge. From the temple floated chanting, deep and constant.

Bopha's body wasn't big enough to contain her excitement as she placed one foot then the other onto the stones, barely warm so early in the day. She was on the causeway. Stepping. Stepping. Standing tall. So aware of her feet and her hands and her arms and her head. Morning sun glinting on the still waters. Before she knew it she was in the shadows of a deep corridor that stretched away on both sides. Carved into its stone walls were three levels of figures, a story in pictures. The carvings were brightly colored and some shone with gold. Ponnleu nudged her gently, and Bopha tore her eyes from the bas-reliefs and turned left into a small courtyard.

Several hundred saffron-robed monks sat in the shadows of the corridor, droning prayers. As the girls entered in silence, their teachers pointed where they should stand. They formed two half-circles, facing the tallest structure of stone. Rising in the very center of the complex, this temple building was completely covered in gold leaf. When the girls stopped moving, so did the chanting. A bronze gong sounded. The note echoed against the towers.

Burning on the bottom tier of the structure was a large bronze brazier. A group of priests, holding incense in sampeah, climbed the first few steps and lit the joss. Sandalwood smoke filled the still air. The sun suddenly seemed very hot. The chanting started again. One monk in brilliant yellow robes started up the steps. Two by two, the rest of the priests climbed the narrow stairs, carrying their incense in sampeah, until there were two monks on each step all the way to the very top, where the first man stood alone. He held his incense up to the heavens. The other monks did the same.

Bopha's neck was getting tired of looking so far up, when the chanting stopped again. After the gong, the highest monk started to climb down. The courtyard was completely silent, except for the distant call of birds and chattering shrieks of gibbons. And the constant hammering from Bayon. The priests gathered in a half-circle facing the dancers. Everyone held their hands in sampeah.

For three days the girls had been practicing for this moment. Bopha had been placed in the second class. Kalienne, although oldest, was with the youngest along with Nuon. Sophea was in the third group, the most advnced. They would now dance inside the temple, once around the tower for each class. The boys made up the fourth group of dancers.

The first group were herded by Ponnleu and Achariya into a line with their backs to the tower, facing the corridor full of monks. The monks who had climbed the tower melted into the shadows and sat to watch. The rest of the dancers also sat. By now the sun was beating down into the courtyard, heat bouncing off the stones onto the girls. Bopha's nice new sampot was sticking to her legs as she crossed them. The gong sounded. When the notes had faded completely, unseen musicians began to play. Nuon, the smallest, started the dancing. When she returned to where she started, the music stopped and the gong was struck.

Nuon's group was sitting together but Bopha caught her eye as she passed, and nodded her head slightly, smiling. Nuon smiled back. Bopha's group rose and took their places around the tower, waiting for the gong. She was in the middle of the group and watched closely as their leader, a somewhat plump girl named Leap began the dance. Bopha was hot and her initial excitement had wilted somewhat, but the music revived her. As she circled into the shaded side of the tower, her spine began to tingle. She could feel the jeebs moving her arms and hands. She smiled. The rows of seated monks followed her movements with their eyes.

The King's Man had been seated to the side, in the shade of the corridor. As she danced past, her smile met his. He nodded slightly. Her spine tingled and warmth spread up to her heart. Bopha gave herself to the music and was surprised to hear the gong and feel the sun hot on her face. Her back hurt as the tingling tightened into spasms when she walked to her place. She sat and tried to breathe. Achariya had told them that breathing would help relieve tension and calm their nerves. Bopha watched the other two groups dance, but saw nothing except when Sophea and then Dara passed in front of her eyes. By the last prayers and gong, Bopha's back had eased, but she was exhausted.

Instead of sitting, the boys stood in their group, and the girls stood up in their lines. The monks materialized from the shadows and reformed their half-circle. The King's Man strode into the center of the circle and faced the monks, giving them sampeah. Then he walked to a spot at one side, where the priests' line met the girls'.

"We give thanks to our Beloved Jayavarman, who has brought us here, and to Suryavarman II, who built the wonders of Angkor. You have been blessed today, and welcomed into the society of Apsaras, sacred to the Gods and Beloved of our King. May you earn this honor by training your bodies to His service."

After a moment, the seated monks chanted one more prayer, blessedly short in Bopha's opinion. After the gong, the King's man strode out, followed by the high priests. Then the monks stood and filed out. Last, the girls were released. They walked in silence through the corridor and out into the brilliant day, across the causeway and the sparkling waters, into their new lives.

CHAPTER 4

1185, Reunion and Loss

Bopha worked hard to learn the dances and at night her muscles and joints cried. Achariya was one of the teachers for the second group. She gave the girls a liniment that burned, and smelled rotten. But if you rubbed it at bedtime into whatever body part hurt, by morning you could move without pain. Every day, dancing. Dancing in the morning and dancing in the long afternoons. Music and movement filled her life, and she fell onto her mat after supper.

Weeks turned into months, and one day she realized that she hadn't thought about Mdeay or Reasmey or Aupouk or Rithy or her other brothers for ... how long? She didn't know. Mdeay's soothing voice said in her ear, "It's okay, little one. It's okay for you to enter your new life. Do not worry. We are one in love, forever." Tears sprang to Bopha's eyes. She was lying on her mat in the midnight dark. Quiet breathing of a dozen girls whispered in the silence. Nuon was lying on her back, her side against Bopha's back. Bopha let the tears fall, but did not make a sound. Next thing she knew, light was pouring in the open door.

"Get up, sleepyhead," said Nuon, standing over her. "How can you sleep? Don't you remember? The King, Jayavarman the Beloved, is returning today!"

Bopha was up in a flash, rolling the mat. How could she have forgotten? Half her head was still in the village, hugging Mdeay's huge stomach, the baby inside kicking her chest. She felt herself divided into two parts, one here at Angkor, one at home with her family.

She wasn't really at Angkor. The dancer's compound, she had learned, was nearer to Bayon, where the King was building a new city, with a new palace and a new temple. The dancers would go this afternoon to greet him. The place was called Terrace of the Elephants because there were larger-than-life elephant statues holding up the stone foundation. The King and all his courtiers would sit on the pavilion and look out over the parade ground. Sometimes, she had heard, his soldiers would march in front of him for hours, so many you could never count them, more than the stars in the sky. That was what they would do before they went to war. Today, it would be the dancers on the parade ground.

The dancers' compound comprised more than her building and the kitchen building. Next to the younger students' area was another, larger courtyard, with several buildings where the older Apsaras lived. Sometimes, Bopha could see them through the trees, practicing. But it was far enough away that their music was just a hint of tones in the air. Today, she would see all the dancers perform.

The morning seemed to last forever, and Bopha wasn't alone in having trouble concentrating during dance practice. Suddenly a group of people ran past the entrance, shouting, "The King is coming! The King is coming!" All the children ran to watch, as did the teachers and the cooks and all the helpers. Down the road there was a big cloud of dust from which came a steady, deep drumbeat. Boom-Boom-Boom. Bopha heard horns sounding, Ta-Ta-Ta-Ta. Pause. Then closer, Ta-Ta-Ta-Ta. The dust got closer and the sounds louder. She couldn't see much until the procession was upon them. First many soldiers wearing pointed metal helmets paced in unison to the drum. Their lances pointed straight up into the cloud of dust. Then the drummers, almost staggering as they carried the big instruments. Boom-Boom-Boom. Bopha's heart jumped in time to the beat.

Then the horns, very long and pointed, with big open mouths. The men who blew them were big and their faces very red as they puckered and blew. Ta-Ta-Ta-Ta. Next pranced horses of every color, with fancy head-dresses. Their manes were cut short and braided to stand up on their necks. The riders carried shields and also held long lances, but these they held at the ready, as if they were going to run someone through. Bopha shivered to think what would happen if a lance hit you.

The biggest horse was blacker than a night with no moon. He was in the center, and slightly ahead of the others. As he approached, people fell to the ground. Before she did the same, Bopha looked up into the rider's face. He happened to turn his head just at that moment. His face was stern, eyes as black as his horse, and his face dark from days of riding in the sun. His lips were full, and as he caught her peeking, they turned up slightly.

That's all she saw. She replayed the moment, as she stared down at the road next to her face. There were small pebbles mixed with the light brown dust. The King had smiled at her.

* * *

There was no more dance practice after the King's company had passed. The girls bathed in the baray as the sun was at its highest, then dressed in their best sampots. Bopha's gold arm band was getting tighter and didn't go as high up her arm as it had. She could tell she was growing, since she also had to tie her garment at a different place around her hips. What could she do if the bangle got too tight? Bopha decided to ask Achariya later.

Kalienne still braided her hair for her, and she was now in the dance class with Bopha. As she wove tight strands, she whispered to Bopha that she had gotten her moon bleeding, so she would not dance today. Several of the older girls would just watch the dancing without participating for the same reason. Kalienne's nipples were darker now, and her breasts fuller. Her beauty shone. Bopha's heart squeezed a little as she looked at her friend. There wasn't another girl as beautiful among all the dancers.

"Does it hurt?" Bopha whispered back.

"A little. Like if your bowels are loose." Kalienne grimaced a little, and Bopha wrinkled her nose. She wasn't eager to grow up that much.

"Well, I don't want it."

Kalienne chuckled, a warm, deep, soft sound. "I don't think you have much choice in the matter, little cabbage. It's your fate as a girl child." She tugged on Bopha's head as she finished the last braid. "There you go." She looked at Bopha, up and down. "You look beautiful," she pronounced. "May you dance as well." Bopha flushed and ducked her head.

"Thank you," she murmured. "Thank you for braiding my hair — and being my friend."

Kalienne touched her shoulder gently. "I'm glad you are my friend. It makes being here easier, knowing you are with me."

36

Sudden tears filled both their eyes as they gazed at each other.

The other girls had been leaving while Kalienne worked on Bopha's hair, and they were alone in the big shadowy room. They heard many steps on the stairs, and voices in the courtyard. "We'd better go," Kalienne said. She reached for the smaller girl's hand and the two friends stepped into the brightness of the afternoon.

Shortly after, the King's Man arrived. The procession formed and traveled in the same fashion as when they went to Angkor, with guards keeping the crowds at a distance. It was a much shorter walk, only half an hour, and they took a different road. This one went straight through the jungle, just as wide and busy as the road to Angkor. Bopha stared up at a huge stone arch as they approached it. On top was a pedestal, carved with a stone face. It had the same features as the King, but this face was gentle and peaceful, not stern. She could see the same face on each side of the pedestal as they passed under the arch. She shivered, feeling the King was watching her from all directions.

The noise of construction grew louder and louder as they walked. Suddenly, it stopped. The jungle rang with silence. It was a few minutes till birds and monkeys started their chatter. The road opened up into a broad, flat area of packed dirt. To the left, Bopha could see there was a higher place overlooking the flat arena. Pennants waved in the light breeze. As they got closer, she could see the elephants, carved of stone, holding up the pavilion. On top, high wooden benches ran the length of the terrace, several rows of them, the rear benches higher than the lower. In the center, in front, the bench was raised a few feet, with a canopy over it, and flags flying.

"Is that where the King will sit?" Bopha whispered to Kalienne, then remembered they were supposed to remain silent. Kalienne nodded. Achariya shot her a glance, her sweet face more stern that she had ever seen. Bopha nodded, chagrined.

All the dancers had come, the young students and the adepts. The children would dance first. They formed into two half-circles, the children facing the older dancers, leaving a large space in the center as a stage. They stood in the sun, as musicians filed out from an opening on the right side of the elephants. Under a large canopy at ground level, a long bench was set between two of the

37

elephants. The men carried their instruments to the bench, tested the sounds, then waited. Even the gibbons stopped squabbling. Everything waited.

When the drum started, it filled Bopha's body. The King was coming. She was going to dance in front of the King. She could barely catch her breath.

A double line of priests walked sedately into view on the pavilion, hands in sampeah. They split at the King's canopy and took their places to each side, in front of the first row of benches. Behind them came lines of brightly clad men with turbans. Some took their places in the first row, some in the second. Then came women with fancy headgear, jewelry sparkling in the sun. They sat behind the men. All the time, the drum kept up its steady beat.

When the horns sounded, there was a gasp, as the entire company collected its breath to receive the King. The people on the terrace made sampeah, turning toward where he would appear. The dancers in the arena lifted their hands as well, but higher, over their heads. He was coming. Bopha could barely see his head at first, just the glint of gold from his crown. As he walked between the rows of people, they bowed their heads but did not prostrate themselves. Then, Bopha saw him, standing in a purple sampot, with gold chains around his waist and golden necklaces covering his chest. Now his face was not stern, but more like the face on the arch. He looked at each dancer in turn, and each bowed their head at his gaze.

Bopha felt his eyes taking in the whole of her as she bent her head, standing straight, hands still high in sampeah. She wanted to look into those dark eyes again, but she did not dare.

King Jayavarman VII nodded in satisfaction, then sat on the cushions on the high bench under the royal canopy, folding his legs gracefully into lotus position. The priests chanted a short prayer and rang a deep gong. The King's Man had been in the center of the dancers, between the children and the young women. Now he stepped forward and made a short speech, offering to the King these new dancers, gathered from the far reaches of the Khmer Empire, declaring that the King's Apsaras were the best in all the world. Bopha wondered how it was that his voice could sound so clear in the hot afternoon air. He bowed to the King, then walked to the musicians' canopy and sat to watch the dancing.

38

This time, Bopha did not feel jolts in her spine as she danced, but she felt the music carry her into the moves and steps that she had practiced. She faced the King many times as she twirled, and she sought his eyes. Was it her imagination that he was looking back at her? She never even noticed all the rest of the crowd, the courtiers and priests. She was dancing only for the King. When the music ended, the crowd patted the wood of the benches, and cheered, "WAH! WAH!" The king smiled and made sampeah to the children, who bowed low.

While dancing, Bopha hadn't noticed the sun or the heat, but as she sat watching the rest of the children perform, she could feel sweat trickling down her back. She wished she had a little pebble to ease her thirst, and she moved her tongue around as if she had. That helped a little. But she forgot her discomforts when the final performance started. These were the adepts, the real apsaras. Never had she seen such dancing. As the final notes faded into the late afternoon sky, there was total silence in the arena. The dancers held their final positions.

Then the King stood, hands high in sampeah, a big smile creasing his face. He shone in the angled light. Truly he is like a god, thought Bopha. She barely heard the crowd start to cheer. Kalienne nudged her. It was time for all the dancers to rise and bow.

Bopha did so, but almost like in a dream. She felt the King's eyes had entered her very being, and chased out all other thoughts. When she lifted her head from the final bow, he was looking directly at her. She nearly fell over, but felt Kalienne's warm arm touch hers lightly. It helped. She could feel her feet on the ground again.

The King turned away at last, and Bopha took a deep breath. She watched him walk back toward the huge distant trees. The pavilion crowd recessed behind him. The dancers gathered into lines behind the King's Man and started walking home. Now there was murmuring among them, a festive, relaxed air.

"Don't you think he's handsome?" Leap was stating a fact in the form of a question. Bopha nodded absently. Leap continued, I can't wait to dance for him again. When he looked in my eyes, I could hardly breathe."

Bopha looked at Leap, suddenly all attention. Leap felt that the King had looked in her eyes? Did all the dancers feel that? She listened to other conversations. Yes, they all thought he'd looked at them. Maybe she wasn't as special as she'd felt. Her heart sank, and with it her body. The rest of the walk home she was silent and didn't even care to stand up straight, till Achariya reminded her.

After supper, she found Kalienne sitting under one of the big trees, stretching her feet.

Bopha joined her and asked, "What did you think of the dancing?"

"It was amazing. I wonder if I'll ever be able to dance like the real Apsaras. Even though I couldn't dance today, I felt like I belonged there when the King looked at me."

"He seemed to look at each of us."

"Yes. I've heard his eyes are magic."

Bopha considered this. "Do you think so?"

"I've never felt so ... accepted." Kalienne was quiet a moment. "What about you?"

"I don't know. At first I felt like he was looking into me, like I was somehow special. But everyone seems to feel that way. So maybe he is magic," Bopha was thinking out loud. "He is the King, but maybe he's more."

* * *

As the months went on, Bopha began to forget she had had another life. One day as she was drinking the bitter tea, she remembered going to the river in her village for water. Here, as an Apsara, her needs were provided for and all she had to do was dance. She tried to picture Mdeay and Reasmey but couldn't. She gasped, and inhaled the tea. Coughing and crying, she tried to focus on Mdeay's face, but it was covered by mist.

"Are you okay?" Kalienne asked.

"Yes ... No ..." Bopha stammered. "I can't remember my Mdeay's face."

Kalienne's beautiful face clouded. "I know what you mean. Me neither," she admitted.

"It seems like we've been here forever." She paused. "I love the dancing, but I wonder how my family is. I heard the cooks talking. The King is going to war, somewhere near Banteay Chhmar. The Chams have invaded."

"My village is not far from Banteay Chhmar," Bopha worried. "I never went there but my brother Rithy told me about it. He hasn't been there either. It's more than two day's walk."

Kalienne nodded, "Mine too."

Neither said, I hope my family is okay. But both girls knew the murderous reputation of the Cham.

The next day, the King galloped past on his black horse. So many soldiers marched four abreast after him that it took almost two hours before the last one passed the dancers' courtyard. The dust took a long time to settle, but Bopha's heart did not. She had a sinking feeling when she thought about her family.

* * *

D ancing took her mind off everything else, and she was grateful even for the pain she felt after practice. It distracted her mind. There had been no news of the war in the weeks since the King left.

Late one afternoon Bopha sat with Sophea, Nuon, Kalienne and Leap, doing hand exercises in a shady corner. A very ragged boy came to the gate posts. He looked all around. His sampot was so torn it barely covered his private parts. His hair was long and tangled and his face filthy. He was almost black from the sun and skin hung on his bones. Boran was leaning against a tree next to the gate. "No beggars, please," he told the boy in a deep but gentle voice.

"I'm looking for Bopha. Preah Chan Bopha? She was taken to be a dancer many months ago," the ragamuffin said.

Bopha heard her name ring through the heat. She jumped up and ran to the gate.

41

"Rithy?" She stared at the stranger. The boy nodded, tears trailing through the dust on his face. "Rithy, what happened? How come you are here?" She threw herself into his filthy arms and he held her tight, his tears turning to sobs.

Boran touched Rithy's shoulder gently. "Son, are you Bopha's brother? The one who wants to be a monk?" Rithy nodded, still choking with tears. "Let me get you some food and something to drink. Follow me."

Bopha released Rithy but stayed next to him as Boran led them to the cooking house.

"Bong Srey," he addressed the middle aged woman stirring a pot. "May we please have a bit of food for this young man? He had just arrived from a long journey."

The woman made a sour face as she looked at Rithy, but her respect for Boran won out and she ladled soup into a small pot and handed it to him. Boran took it with thanks, but stood waiting. The woman sighed and reached for a piece of dried fish from a bag hanging from the rafter.

"May you live long and may your children have as many babies as there are stars in the sky," Boran told her, making as much of a sampeah as possible with both hands full.

"Arkoun, but I have too many babies already," the cook retorted.

Boran turned to Rithy and winked. "Here you go. Let's sit in the shade and you can tell us why you are here."

Kalienne had told Achariya about the stranger's arrival, and they both joined Boran, Rithy and Bopha under a big banyan. "Eat first, my son," Boran said. Rithy needed no further encouragement. The food was gone in moments.

"Thank you for your kindness. I've been on the road for two weeks but had no money for food," he told Boran.

"But why are you here?" Bopha burst out, unable to wait any longer.

Rithy's face contorted in anguish. "Oh Bopha, I'm so sorry. But the Cham came through our village. I had eaten something

42

that didn't agree with me and was in the bushes at the edge of the field. There were so many soldiers, they covered the field.

Aupouk begged them to let the boys go, but their faces were hard and angry. They beat Aupouk to the ground, then kept beating him. Other men caught our brothers, who were running for the jungle." Rithy couldn't continue. Bopha stared at him in shock.

"Aupouk is dead?" Rithy nodded. "And our brothers?" Rithy bent his head. "What about Mdeay and Reasmey?"

Rithy didn't say anything. Boran patted him on the shoulder awkwardly. "These things are too hard to talk about all at once. Let's let your brother rest for now," he told Bopha.

The group sat in silence. Rithy bent over his folded legs, head between his knees. Bopha scooched next to him, so their legs and shoulders touched. "I'm glad you are here, my dearest brother. I'm so glad you are safe," she said, weeping. Rithy leaned his body a little into hers, briefly.

News of the arrival of Bopha's brother and his terrible news raced through the compound. Knots of girls and boys gathered under the trees, murmuring and looking at their group. The sour cook appeared, with a sad and apologetic look. She handed Rithy another pot, this with rice and slices of mango. "Thank you," he managed. His voice sounded strange and strangled. She left, and Rithy put the pot down on the ground. "I'm sorry, I can't eat any more."

Achariya put her arm around Bopha, who was sitting in a stunned stupor next to her silent brother. The boy's master, Samphy, approached, Dara behind him carrying a clean sampot. "We heard your sad news," Samphy said, squatting in front of Rithy.

"For now, you can stay with us in the boy's dormitory. Dara will take you to the baray."

Rithy nodded, in a daze. Samphy stood. "Come now."

Rithy gathered his bones to stand, grunting a little with the effort. He followed Dara out of the courtyard and down the road. By now there were clots of people at the gate, and they followed the boys. Boran yelled at them, "Leave the poor boy alone!" They scattered.

43

When Rithy and Dara returned, Rithy looked more like Bopha remembered. He was taller, but so skinny that you could see his bones move under the loose skin. He seemed years older. "Thank you," he said to Dara. "It feels so good to be clean."

"You can share my sleeping mat," Dara told him, smiling. Rithy nodded, but didn't smile.

Bopha had kept watch over her brother's rice and mango, carefully covering it with her hands to keep out eager bugs. "Here's the rest of your lunch," she told him. "Can you eat now?"

"Yes, thank you," Rithy said. "It's been so long since I ate that my stomach can only hold a very small amount at a time." They both looked at his stomach, a concavity under protuberant ribs.

"You're very skinny," Bopha told him. She wasn't sure what to say. She wanted to ask more, but was afraid of the answers, and Rithy seemed skittish, like a wild cat. "I'm glad you got here. How did you find me?"

"Most people wouldn't talk to me. They just shooed me off like I was a fly. But I kept asking, where's the road to Angkor. A couple of times I got lost and had to back-track. I don't know if the people who gave me those directions were being mean or just didn't know. Most people only know their own village and a few others. When I got nearer, I asked where the Apsaras lived."

Bopha nodded. Rithy ate the rice slowly, then put a slice of mango in his mouth. He rolled it around on his tongue, and sucked it gently before chewing. "This is so good," he said.

Boran had sent a runner with the news to Bayon, for the King's Man. Now he rode into the courtyard. Boran caught the reins as the King's Man jumped down gracefully. "Here he is. His name is Rithy. He's the brother of our dancer Bopha." Boran pointed to the two children, who had stood up side by side, hands in sampeah.

Under the shade of the porch was a bench, and the King's Man went to it, gesturing to Boran to bring the boy. Bopha followed closely, even though she hadn't been invited. The King's Man sent her a sharp look, but she lifted her chin a little and stayed next to her brother. "This will be a story that is hard to hear," the King's Man said, not without compassion. "Are you sure you want

44

to stay?" Bopha nodded. She didn't want to hear but she needed to know.

Because Rithy had been squatting in the jungle at the edge of the rice field, the Cham had not seen him. When he saw what happened to his brothers and his fathers, he stayed there until the soldiers had run into the village. He could hear screams of women and children, pigs and chickens. The cries went on and on, then finally it was silent except for the crack of wood being shattered. Then there was the smell of smoke. He could see it climbing into the sky. Rithy circled around the fields, keeping to the jungle, until the village was in sight. Or what was left of the village. He watched as the soldiers lifted the bodies of pigs onto their shoulders and marched down the path to the next village. They left bodies of people in the dirt.

Rithy crept closer. Houses were burning all around and the smoke made it hard to see. He got to where their house was. Mdeay was lying on her back, her intestines spread out around her and covered with flies already. Reasmey was barely recognizable. She lay under the banyan tree. Her head had been smashed into it and the altar was in fragments on the ground. There was no sign of the baby. Then Rithy saw a tiny foot sticking out from under Mdeay. He hated to touch his mother's body, but he had to know. It was hard to pull Mdeay onto her side. He wished he hadn't. The baby had also been disemboweled. Rithy vomited.

The house was fully engulfed in flames now, and the crown of the banyan was on fire. It was too hot to stay. Rithy crawled a safe distance to the edge of the field, between bouts of vomiting and diarrhea. He lost track of time. Next thing he knew, it was full night. There was an orange glow from the remains of the village. He lost consciousness again.

When Rithy roused again, it was early morning. At first, he didn't remember why he was lying in the field. Then he did. There wasn't anything left in his stomach when he gagged. Except for birds and monkeys, the whole world was silent. Rithy walked in a crouch to where Mdeay and his sisters had been killed. The house had collapsed on top of them and was still smoldering. He didn't know whether to wait and see if he could move enough of the wreckage to bury them, or just leave. When he heard the shouts of soldiers, he knew. Rithy ran into the jungle. He would go to Angkor. He would find Bopha. She was all he had left.

CHAPTER 5

The King Returns

Gentle shaking woke Bopha. She was gasping and crying, still running from the Cham soldiers. Achariya was rocking her shoulder. In the dimness, Bopha could make out Nuon. "Hush, shh, shh," Achariya said softly. "You must have had a bad dream."

"You were screaming and screaming," Nuon said. "The whole compound is awake."

Achariya gathered Bopha into her arms, and the little girl wept into her warmth. Achariya rocked. Nuon squatted next to them. "The soldiers," was all Bopha could say.

"They are not here. You are safe here," Achariya reassured her. "And the King has gone to kill the Cham and make his whole Empire safe again."

Bopha didn't know what empire meant, but she remembered the King's eyes looking into hers and felt better. "I'm sorry to wake everyone," she sniffed.

"It's okay. Everyone understands the shock you have had." Achariya handed her a cup of tea. "Here, have a drink then lie down again. It's the middle of the night." Bopha sipped but her stomach was upset and she ran to the porch railing and vomited into the darkness. Achariya followed her and rubbed her back, pulling the girl's hair away from her face. Bopha was spent and sagged into the kind woman. "Come now. Try to get some sleep."

Bopha could hear rustling from all the mats, but after being outside, the room was too dark for her to make out any shapes. Her mat was in the middle of the room, and when Achariya had guided her to it, she sank down into a fetal position. Nuon reached for her arm and patted it, then for a change she curled around Bopha, instead of the other way around. Her warmth soothed Bopha, who was shivering. Nuon pulled a cover over them.

When Bopha woke, the room was empty, morning light pouring in the open door. Kalienne squatted next to her. "Good morning," she said softly. "The teachers said to let you sleep." Bopha sat up, groggy and muddled, then remembered her dream and Rithy's arrival. Her face crumpled. Kalienne moved closer and hugged her. "Rithy is waiting for you," she said.

"Rithy!" Bopha said, scrambling to her feet. Kalienne followed her down the steps.

Sure enough, Rithy was sitting next to the bottom step, a pot of rice and dried fish with crickets in front of him.

"Bopha," he said. "I saved you some breakfast," then added softly. "I heard you last night." Bopha nodded and squatted next to him. She did not reach for the food. "Boran is going to Angkor Wat today, to talk with the head priest. He says maybe I will be accepted there, to become a monk." His thin face almost smiled, then fell into sorrow. "It's what I always wanted. But not like this." Tears welled in Bopha's eyes. "But Samphy says I can stay here. Near you. At least for now." Bopha nodded, unable to speak. "Here, try to eat."

She dipped her fingers into the bowl and made a small ball of rice, which she gagged down. Her stomach curdled. She pushed the bowl to Rithy. "I can't. Not now. Not yet." After a moment her stomach settled.

Kalienne was squatting on her other side. The dance groups were gathered in their corners and the musicians were tuning instruments. "It's time for me to go," Kalienne said. "Can you come?" Bopha wasn't sure. Dancing was the last thing she wanted.

"Try it," Rithy urged. "Sometimes it helps to do something. Movement can keep your mind off your troubles."

Bopha stood slowly, then trailed after Kalienne. She recognized the music as her favorite, the Wishing Dance. She felt Mdeay hug her and say, "Yes, I'm sure of it." So long ago, Bopha had asked her if the King's Man would teach her this dance. Suddenly Bopha realized that if she hadn't been chosen to become an Apsara, she would be dead. Her shock registered on the faces of the other girls, who gathered in a circle around her then lifted their arms into the first jeeb position. None of them were smiling but she could feel their support easing her heart. She raised her arm, and the circle began to dance.

48

Rithy had been right. He was so smart, her brother. Bopha hoped that he would become a monk. He would be able to help people. She wondered what had happened to the monks in their village. Had the Cham burned the temple as well? How about the old monk? Surely they would spare him.

Her thoughts stopped her body, and the next girl in the circle bumped into her. "I'm sorry," Bopha murmured, returning to the dance. By now she knew the music and the steps by heart, and picked up where the music had gone. They were dancing more slowly than usual. Was it for her, to help her? Bopha was glad for it, anyway. She tried to focus.

She had never heard of the Cham before coming to Bayon. Her village was so small, so far away. Now Bopha had learned all kinds of things, not just about dancing. The girls talked about the King, his exploits at war, how he had extended the Empire over the northern mountains as well as far to the east and west. She learned that the Cham, who lived beyond the northern mountains, had come to Angkor itself not so many years ago, killing and burning. They hadn't been able to burn the stone temple, but had broken off some of the bas reliefs and stolen all the gold and jewels.

Boran had been at the King's side when he reclaimed Angkor. Sometimes in the late afternoon heat, as she sat stretching in the shadows near the gate, the soldier would give in to imprecations and weave amazing stories. Bopha never got tired of hearing how the defeated Cambodians gathered when Jayavarman became King, how he led them to victory. Boran's sonorous voice brought to life the screams of the elephants and cries of horses and men, the crash of swords and shields. The boys would inch their circle closer, and listen without moving till Samphy cleared his throat, reminding them to exercise as they listened. Samphy was listening too.

Bopha hoped the King would kill all the Cham. In her village, Buddhism was new, so people prayed to the Buddha, but also to Hindu gods and goddesses, as well as to the spirits that lived in trees and streams. Buddhism was the path of peace. King Jayavarman VII was a Buddhist, but also a King. Defending his Empire and his people was his job, even if it meant going to war. She didn't understand it all, but she pondered these new ideas.

49

When her dancing was over, Rithy came up, smiling broadly. "Boran says the priest will let me live at Angkor!" It was nice to see him smile. Bopha had forgotten how it lit up the world around him. She did a little twirl, hands high in sampeah.

"That's wonderful," she said. "When do you leave?"

"There's a ceremony in five days. The dancers will be going, and I'll go with you."

It was the first Bopha had heard of the ceremony. There had not been any new dancers since she arrived. Sophea said the teachers had enough children to teach, and the King's Man was staying at Bayon. He was in charge during the King's absence. Bopha, of course, followed the cycle of the moon, but days and weeks flowed into each other. She had no real idea of years.

What was the purpose of this ceremony?

"It's to honor Garuda," Sophea told her. Garuda, the bird-man god on whose back Vishnu rode. Bopha was fascinated by the statues of him, taller than she was. In the market not far from the dancers' compound, there was a street of carving studios where men chiseled stone. Some early mornings, the girls were allowed to go out to shop. Groups of four or more would hold hands and wander through the crowds of farmers setting up their stalls.

Brightly colored monks went from stall to stall in pairs, holding yellow umbrellas over their heads. They would stop and hold out their begging bowls. Most vendors would put a little something into the bowl, and the monks would drone a prayer of blessing while the vendor bowed in sampeah. In general, Kampuchean men and women wore only a long sampot wrapped around their hips. But monks had flowing red or yellow or orange robes, and covered their shoulders and upper bodies as well.

Bopha always wanted to go watch the carvers, especially the ones who were shaping Garuda's feathers. They would take small hammers and chisels, chipping away shards to reveal one feather, then another. In some sculptures, he looked more like a bird, with feathered legs and claw feet. In others, he was a man with both wings and arms, and a large hooked beak instead of a nose. She liked all the sculptures, but was most intrigued when he had more bird features.

The girls had been learning a dance about Garuda killing the Naga people. This dance was done with the boys. Dara had been chosen to dance the part of Garuda, and when he leapt you could almost see his huge wings unfurl and thrash the air, then his talons would tear the snakes into pieces.

On the day of the ceremony, Rithy walked in front of the Apsara procession, next to Dara. He was taller than all but one of the dancers, almost as tall as Boran. He walked with shoulders straight and head up but his feet met the earth flat, like a monk not a dancer. Bopha, toward the end of the line, watched her brother. She was glad he would be a monk, glad he would be near enough that they might see each other from time to time.

When the towers of Angkor came into view, Bopha's heart thrilled. What a sight. She watched Rithy stop and gape, staring at the huge stone towers silhouetted against the clear blue sky. It was a very hot day. Bopha realized that it was nearly rainy season again. She had been with the dancers so long that Bayon did feel like home. Boran had been right. Besides, now it was her only home. Her heart broke again.

She and Rithy had lit incense with Boran, Samphy, and Achariya one day. The King's Man arranged for a dozen monks to come perform a ceremony for their family and village. As the chanting droned on, incense filling the air, Bopha felt her heart ease. The gong entered her body and shook out sorrow, letting it float away with the sweet smoke. She found herself next to the King's Man after the lavish meal, after the monks and the men had all eaten.

Bopha put her hands in sampeah and whispered to the tall man, "Thank you, Your Honor, for giving my family this ceremony."

The King's Man looked down at her and smiled, both gentleness and sadness on his face. He returned sampeah and said, "I am sorry for what happened. And so is our beloved King." He looked into Bopha's eyes until she dropped her gaze to her prayerful hands. Then he turned to Rithy, who had come up next to his sister. "May you work hard on your studies, and bring honor to the King."

Rithy nodded, saying nothing. The King's Man turned and walked to his horse. Bopha and Rithy watched him mount and ride

51

off toward Bayon. "He seems very kind," said Rithy. Bopha thought about his eyes. He seemed to look into her, not as deeply as the King, but there was some mystery in them.

The line of dancers moved again and Bopha stepped carefully, standing tall. Achariya had told her that she would be joining the third class soon. For today's ceremony, the children would go first, all groups dancing together. Then they would watch the adepts. As their line crossed the causeway, a single cloud floated over, its shape reflected in the still baray and its shadow covering the dancers. It was a relief from the stifling heat, but Bopha wondered if it was a good omen or a bad one.

During the ceremony, as Bopha moved her arms carefully from jeeb to jeeb, lifting her legs precisely into each position, she had a sensation of wings fluttering behind her, where Dara and the boys were. The hot still air lifted in a gentle breeze. As she danced around the stupa and into the shadows where the King's Man sat, she felt his gaze on her but stared straight ahead, curving her lips into the requisite smile. Feathers fluttered in her mind, chips of stone dropping on packed dirt.

Bopha was entranced, but her body followed the steps learned in rigorous training. Muscle memory merged with the music. She was surprised, when the music stopped, to find herself in the sun. It didn't feel warm until she moved to sit with the other children. Then the flagstone floor burned her calloused feet as she squatted to watch the older dancers perform.

Rithy had been allowed to watch the ceremony and the dancing, sitting with Boran. After the monks and the King's Man had filed out, the dancers left the sun for the shadowed corridor. Rithy stepped next to Bopha, and kept pace with her. He whispered, "I have to stay here. One day soon, we'll see each other again." Bopha nodded, without turning her head. Her hands were in sampeah already. She felt Rithy step away. On the far side of the bridge, when their line was released to mill about, Bopha looked back to Angkor. She thought she could see Rithy in a flock of monks, walking to the dormitory building.

"Blessings be with you, beloved brother," she thought. "Tell me all about what you are learning when we meet next."

* * *

The moon waxed and waned and waxed again. Bopha was dancing with the third group now and spent more time with Sophea. She stilled shared her mat with Nuon, and the two would usually sit with Kalienne for meals. Sophea often joined them. Under her carefully practiced exterior calm, Bopha sensed some turmoil. One day she asked, "Are you okay?"

"Of course," Sophea answered.

"Well, you seem different," Bopha struggled to put words on her feelings. "Like there's something going on inside. I mean, you look the same on the outside, but ...". She trailed off. Sophea looked at her. "I just hope you're okay." The two of them were sitting alone under one of the big banyans. Kalienne and Nuon had gone behind the mat. Clouds were massing and the heat was almost overpowering.

Suddenly Sophea crumpled. "I know what happened to your village," Sophea wept. "My village is even further north than yours. I haven't heard anything, but I'm afraid ..."

Bopha put her arm around Sophea's trembling shoulders. The smaller girl stiffened reflexively, then leaned into Bopha's embrace. "My mother is a tyrant. She pushes my father like he was a water buffalo. I couldn't wait to leave. Once I told her I wished she were dead. She was so harsh that she would become a cockroach in her next life. But I didn't really mean it. I don't want them to be dead."

Bopha's shoulder was wet from Sophea's tears. After a moment she reached for her kromah and offered it for Sophea to dry her face. "Thank you," Sophea said, then added in a tiny voice, "I just wish I knew."

"Whatever happens, it's not your fault," Bopha told her. "It's just karma, and we don't know how it all works. But it's not your fault." Sophea snuffled into the kromah, nodding. Unconvinced. "I mean, our thoughts are powerful," Bopha continued,

"But it's still not your fault." She paused, then smiled softly. "You are one powerful little girl, yes. But not all-powerful."

Sophea managed a crooked smile. "My mother always told me I was difficult. Stubborn. That I'd come to no good end." Sophea paused. "I liked to dance and one day when I was quite small the King's Man came through our village, gathering little apsaras. I swore that I'd be chosen the next time he came."

"And you were," Bopha finished softly. Sophea nodded.

"But I don't love to dance. Not the way you do. For me it's more like ..." she looked for words. "Like rules to follow." She looked at Bopha for the first time. "But for you, it's love. When you dance, everyone can see the love moving through you. I don't know how to let myself go into the music that way."

Bopha didn't say anything. More and more often she had felt herself giving over to the sound and movement, letting it dance her. Was that something you could learn? She had never tried to learn it, it just happened.

The dinner gong sounded, Nuon and Kalienne appeared. They looked concerned when they saw Sophea's tear-streaked face. "What happened?' Bopha shook her head in warning, but didn't say anything. It was up to Sophea what she wanted to share. They looked at Sophea, who started crying again.

She finally whispered, "I'm afraid for my family, my village, up north." The girls helped Sophea to her feet and wrapped their arms around her. Sophea actually kept her hand in Bopha's as they walked to the kitchen.

* * *

Not long after this revelation, the King returned. It was a cloudy afternoon, promising rains at last after a scorching hot season. Leaves burned as crops stood in parched fields.

The helmets of many soldiers had big dents in them, and many arms were bandaged. But they marched proudly in front of the King. This time Bopha knew where to look, and stared at the mounted figure as it came near. She knelt, in sampeah, but looked into his face again. His eyes seared hers, and she fell to the ground. His horse's hooves made soft popping sounds in dirt as he passed. Only when the sound faded did Bopha lift her head.

The King sat straight in the saddle. His broad back had an ugly red gash, running all the way down from his armpit to disappear under his sampot. Bopha sent prayers for his healing,

54

as she rose. She stared after her King until Kalienne touched her arm.

"Bopha, are you in love?" she teased.

"Did you see his back? He was wounded!" Bopha said. "I'm going to light incense for his healing."

Kalienne linked arms with Bopha, who was almost as tall as her now. "I'll light some too." Thunder rolled, then crashed right over their heads. They ran for the shelter of the porch as the clouds opened, pouring down hard rain. Bopha thought about King Jayavarman riding through the storm. Would the pounding rain hurt his back? Would he stop and shelter? She thought he would ride on until he reached Bayon, a beacon of hope to all who saw him.

CHAPTER 6

1186, Apsara

Bopha and Rithy met sooner than either expected. Achariya came to Bopha and Sophea during lunch and told them to go wash. The King's Man was coming. In the dormitory, Bopha knotted her rumdol sampot around her hips. Achariya herself braided Bopha's hair, and Bopha asked her what she could do when her bangle no longer went over her elbow. Already it was closer to her elbow than her shoulder.

"When you graduate from the third class, you will get three bangles, and two new sampots, so you can be most beautiful for the King."

Bopha considered this. "Does the King give them to us?"

"Yes. He is most gracious to his Apsaras. He gives us everything." Achariya held Bopha's braid and gestured around the room. "A place to live, food, clothing, teachers."

"Were you an Apsara?"

"Yes. I danced for many years. But one day a wild pig came into the market. He tore through, upending tables and smashing vegetables. People were running everywhere and screaming. The boar ran right into me. My ankle twisted as I fell. I could feel the crunch as my weight landed on my ankle. For many months I could hardly walk. Even now, there are positions that I cannot perform."

Bopha nodded. She had noticed that one of her teacher's ankles was bigger than the other and sometimes seemed stiff.

"When it was clear that I could no longer dance well enough for the King, the King's Man let me stay here as a teacher." Achariya paused, a little smile playing her lips. "He is a very kind man."

Bopha looked at her, feeling something underneath the words but unsure what. Achariya returned to braiding with a vengeance, pulling Bopha's head so she forgot to think about what the mystery might be.

"There. You look beautiful. Beautiful enough to please our King."

Bopha thought Achariya was just using the expression, but when the King's Man arrived, Rithy was walking with a group of monks behind him. At first Bopha didn't see him. He stood tall, in the red robes of the novice. All the other monks wore gold robes.

When she did see him, he nodded to her, smiling. Then he winked. Bopha had forgotten about winking. Where did Rithy learn about it?

All the children and teachers had gathered to see the King's Man. Bopha and Sophea stood next to each other. "Are you ready?" He looked directly at Bopha, who looked around herself to see who he was talking to. Achariya nudged them forward, out of the group of dancers.

"They are," Achariya looked up into the face of King's Man, whose gaze softened as he regarded her.

"Let's go. We must not keep the King waiting." What did he mean? Why were monks with the King's Man? Bopha looked back at Achariya, who made a shooing motion. Boran came up and gestured for the girls to walk behind the monks. He brought up the rear of their small procession. A few soldiers walked in front, parting the crowds that watched from the gate. Whenever the King's Man went anywhere, it was the stuff of rumor and conjecture.

Bopha heard "Apsara," and lifted her head. She walked like a dancer, but her mind was whirling. What was going on? They took the road to Bayon. "We must not keep the King waiting." "Beautiful enough to please our King." Was she going to see the King?

She and Sophea were the only Apsaras in the line. And why was a novice like Rithy coming?

There were no answers during the half-hour march. Bopha felt more and more excited, especially when they passed under the arch of faces. She began to believe that, yes, she was going to see the King.

This time, when they got near Bayon, they took a broad road that turned away from the Terrace of the Elephants and into the huge trees behind it. Bopha caught sight of curving roofs. Coming closer, she saw many large buildings scattered among the trees. Water caught the sunlight and flashed it back from several barays. Women were swimming in the waters of one, and Bopha heard their laughter.

Flags flew from the largest building, which had many windows. The porch was wide. Its deep eaves would cover six people from wall to railing. Soldiers in crisp sampots and gleaming helmets stood at attention on each side of the steps, their lances flying the King's colors. They stared straight ahead as the King's Man stopped. Dismounting, he gestured for the monks and the girls to follow him. They climbed the broad stairs, passing the motionless guards. Bopha's heart was pounding with excitement. This was clearly the King's palace.

Two more soldiers guarded the entrance, whose double teak doors were thrown back. A wide strip of red cloth ran from the door into the room. The King's Man entered, his hands in high sampeah, then he prostrated himself. The monks knelt in deep sampeah. Then it was the little girls' turn. Boran gestured that they should do as had the King's Man, and he did the same. The red cloth was heavy and scratchy and thick. It didn't move when they stood. Keeping his hands in sampeah, the King's Man led them forward.

Open windows on all sides, and the open doors, let in lots of light. Bopha saw a platform at the end of the room, with a high chair. On it sat King Jayavarman VII. More guards stood to each side of the chair. There was a low bench on one side of the room, where men and women in fancy sampots and jewelry sat watching the arrivals.

"Welcome to Bayon." The King's deep voice thrilled Bopha. "So, my dear friend, you have brought the children from Kohl's Chek, and the girl from Serei Ksan."

The King's Man bowed deeper, then motioned for Rithy, Bopha and Sophea to come nearer.

"Yes, Beloved Lord. This is Rithy, who brought the sad news, and his sister, Preah Chan Bopha. She was chosen to train as an Apsara last year. And this is Sophea from Serei Ksan, who is also an Apsara."

"Very good." The King's voice smiled. "Come closer, my children." Bopha was trembling all over but kept her hands in sampeah, her head up, and her eyes focused slightly downward. She could see the King's flat stomach covered with long gold necklaces. Rithy's red robes accompanied her the few long steps to the platform, Sophea's brilliant blue sampot on the other side. The King's feet were large, his toes long, peeking out from under his sampot as he sat.

Bopha lifted her eyes into King Jayvarman's. "Ah," he laughed. "The little girl who peeks at her King!" Bopha dropped her eyes, blood rushing to her head. "I remember you from the gate of the Apsara courtyard." Stunned silence throbbed through the room. Bopha's blood drained out of her head just as suddenly as it had come and she felt dizzy. "It's okay, Preah Chan Bopha. You may look at me now." After a moment, Bopha could feel her feet touching the scratchy cloth on the floor. She looked up. The King was smiling at her. His gaze entered her, as it had on the day the Apsaras danced for him at the Terrace of the Elephants. She caught her breath, but didn't look away until the King nodded.

He turned his attention to Rithy. "And you are the brave boy who always wanted to become a monk. Are you studying hard?" Bopha could feel Rithy bobbing his head.

To Sophea, the King said, "I look forward to seeing you dance one day soon." Sophea glanced up at him, then back at her hands. Tears filled her eyes but did not fall. It was only a few days since the news about her village had finally arrived. There were no survivors. By some quirk of fate, Dara's village, just south of Bopha's, had been spared.

King Jayavarman lifted his voice to include the waiting monks, and placed his hands in sampeah at his heart. "We are in sorrow at the devastation in our land, the wanton destruction suffered. Especially for these children, our heart is heavy." He turned to them. "This is to honor your villages, and the other villages that were hurt by the Cham." He waved his hand to the monks. "You may start the ceremony."

The King's Man joined the courtiers on the bench, motioning for Boran to bring Bopha and Sophea. Rithy went with the monks to the golden altars which gleamed on the opposite side of the room. After the deepest gong Bopha had ever heard, the chanting began. Sweet incense filled the room, carrying Bopha into a dream-like state. Preah Chan Bopha. The King had called her by her full name.

The King himself lit incense at the end of the ceremony, then invited the whole company for a feast. Neither Bopha nor Sophea had any appetite, as they sat with the court ladies in front of platters piled with rice and duck, pork and vegetables, pots of fish amok, mounds of fruit. They ate a few bites, but the excitement was too much. And the sorrow. Both together, Bopha thought, looking around the big room. How was it possible to have both feelings at the same time?

One of the court ladies had more bangles and larger necklaces than the others, and a circlet of gold held her braids back from her face. She sat on an embroidered green cushion. She looked at Bopha. "Are you not hungry?"

Bopha's stomach twisted. She didn't want to insult the King's hospitality. "It's delicious," she whispered. "But I'm too ... "

The woman sniffed. "Not every little girl gets to meet the King," she said to the ladies surrounding her, who shook their heads, expressions flat. It was the closest to disapproval that was still within the bounds of politeness.

Bopha wished she could sink through the floor. The woman had singled her out, not including Sophea. She was grateful when the monks finished their meal and chanted a final prayer. The children were herded in front of the King again. "Go in peace," he said. "May we all go in peace." He looked again at Bopha. And winked. She stared. Had she really seen that? She dropped her eyes to her hands. They all backed out of the great hall — monks, Boran, the children, the King's Man, hands in sampeah to the King.

The hot, still air of afternoon promised rain as they emerged on the porch. Sure enough, thunder rumbled as they neared the Terrace of the Elephants. A few raindrops fell when they went under the arch of faces, followed by a downpour on the bridge of Garudas. They were so wet that they just walked on, not trying to shelter. At the crossroads, the monks peeled off toward Angkor.

Rithy turned to nod at his sister before his line trudged away in the other directions. Bopha nodded back, unsure whether she was

60

crying or her eyes were just filled with rain. Sophea was still straight and her steps sure. Bopha lifted her chin and followed suit. At least the rain kept the crowds under shelter, though hundreds of pairs of eyes watched them pass.

* * *

Moons passed, many moons. Bopha did not see Rithy. Life as an Apsara went on, with practice then ceremonies. Dancing every day. Bopha had been moved up to the third class long ago. One day, Heng gathered all the children. "Tomorrow, we will choose which of you are graduating and will move to the adept courtyard as full Apsaras." She shushed the excited murmuring. "Some of you will continue to study here. Some of you will be leaving. Not every child can become an Apsara. This is the moment when we must decide."

An uneasy silence followed these words. Heng gestured the children to leave. Groups clustered in the shade, faces taut.

"What will I do if I cannot dance?" Kalienne worried aloud to Sophea, Leap, Nuon and Bopha. "I love it, but I know I'm not the best." No one answered. None of them knew for sure, but they had heard stories.

Some dancers became servants in the palace. One they knew had sunk to selling fruit in the market. It was even said that some sold their bodies to pleasure men. At the edges of the market, the girls had seen women in thin sampots, their eyes outlined with kohl, standing in unusual postures. Once Bopha had seen a man follow such a woman down narrow alley. They disappeared into a doorway. She had heard about what men and women did, mounting the way she had seen dogs and pigs and cows do. She shuddered. How awful.

Bopha had not yet gotten her moon blood, but her breasts were very tender these days, and getting bigger. She was taller than any of the other girls except Kalienne, taller than most women and even some men. Because she was a dancer, she held herself erect, not trying to be shorter. She felt the eyes of men in the market follow her. It made her uncomfortable. She was glad to walk hand in hand with other girls at those times.

61

Nuon was still in the second class, and Leap had just started the third, so they would likely continue dancing. Bopha reached for Kalienne's hand. "You are so beautiful. Surely if you don't become an Apsara, you will move to the Palace. The King's Man watches you whenever he comes." Kalienne blushed. Everyone had seen it.

Just then Achariya walked past. Her face had a hint of sadness. Bopha wondered if Achariya had heard her words. She remembered what her teacher had said about the King's Man, how he looked at her with such gentleness.

The darkness rustled all night as the girls tossed and turned, wondering what their fates would be when day came. Bopha felt sluggish when she opened her eyes, her body torpid as she helped Nuon put away their mat. All the music had drained out of her. She felt like one of the puppets they saw in the market, whose movements were jerky when the vendor pulled hidden strings. The room was quiet, the children absorbed inside themselves. No one ate much breakfast, and the meal lacked its usual chatter and laughs. The boys were as subdued as the girls, not smacking each other on the shoulder or poking their neighbor in the ribs just as he tried to swallow something.

The young dancers drifted into the middle of the courtyard before Heng appeared, flanked by the other teachers. Heng wasn't one of the teachers, but she seemed to be in charge of everything, and would turn up anywhere. The children had learned to be careful with their tongues, to look around for her before gossiping. When her short, sturdy body stopped in front of the quiet crowd, everyone looked at her.

A line of dancers approached, down the shadowed path from the adepts' courtyard. All eyes turned to watch them. They gathered in silence behind the teachers. Just then, the King's Man rode into the yard. Heng bowed in sampeah after he had dismounted. His tall figure dwarfed her when he took his place in the center of the teachers.

"Today is very important," he declaimed. "Not just for you children, but for our Empire, and for the pleasure of our King. He has sent me to welcome his newest Apsaras." He nodded to Heng.

62

"These are not decisions we take lightly," Heng said, her voice sharp and clear, "for your futures are at stake. We," she gestured to the teachers on either side of her, who all looked sober, "have watched you for two full cycles of moons, and we have talked much among ourselves. Our goal is always to please our King. You have all worked very hard, but hard work is not always enough. Which of you children are the best dancers in the whole Empire, dancers fit to entertain His Majesty? That has been our question." She paused. An anxious stir shivered through the quiet children.

"We will start with the dancers who have been chosen to continue. When your name is called, please come forward. If your name is not chosen, your teacher will meet with you afterwards to talk about your future." Heng stepped back one step, so the King's Man was slightly in front of her. Over the past two years he had spent enough time watching the young dancers that he knew each of them, though they were not aware of that. Now he called out the lucky names.

When he pronounced Sophea's name, she rose gracefully and walked toward him, head high and hands in sampeah at her heart. He murmured to her. Sophea nodded.

Achariya stepped forward and handed the little girl a bundle wrapped in a bright blue and white kromah. Sophea bowed to her, took the package, and turned to face the crowd, standing next to the King's Man. His height made her look even smaller than usual. A few more names were called until there was a short line next to Sophea.

"Preah Chan Bopha!" The name hit her chest like a stone. Bopha slowly stood. The trees overhead swayed a little. Then she got her balance and stepped forward. The King's Man watched her come nearer. She lifted her gaze from her hands to his eyes and felt him steadying her, then almost pulling her to him. "Congratulations, Preah Chan Bopha. I knew the first time I saw you, dancing in your dusty village, that you were born to be an Apsara." His full lips curved into a warm smile.

Bopha was too overcome to smile back, at least to smile for real. She nodded, looking at her hands again. Over the months of training, her lips had learned to curl up, even at rest. But in her heart she was too stunned to smile. The weight of the moment, of her future, pressed down on the young girl. She took the bundle Achariya offered, green and white, and held it to her chest.

The King's Man gestured to her to stand on his other side. Her head reached his shoulder. Out of the corner of her eye she could see a few dark chest hairs surrounding the heavy gold of his necklace, which lay flat and wide across his collarbone. Tiers of gold connected in a V shape all the way to his navel, where a thick gold chain draped down across his sampot. She smelled a slight muskiness from his body. Bopha focused on the green kromah in her arms.

Dara joined her, then another boy. Red, black, green, blue, orange, yellow, brown. The kromah bundles made a rainbow in the children's arms.

"Thank you all for your hard work, these many months. Both teachers and students have done well. Congratulations, Apsaras." The words of the King's Man rang through the trees. Early morning light caught in the gold of his necklace. The children stood holding their gifts as he turned to give sampeah to the teachers, who held their hands at their foreheads.

Then he strode to his horse and swung up gracefully. The crowd at the gate made way for him. He sat straight and looked neither right nor left. Bopha followed him with her eyes until the black tail of his horse, with yellow ribbons braided into it, disappeared behind a tree.

Suddenly children and teachers and adepts were swirling together. A fine-boned young woman, with large sweet eyes in a rounded face, full breasts, and many bangles on both arms, came to Bopha. "I am Thida. I will be your mentor." Bopha managed an awkward sampeah with the kromah package in her hands. "Go get your things, and meet me under the dormitory porch." The younger girl nodded and pushed her way through the crowd toward the steps.

She was getting her old sampot and her comb when she heard soft weeping from the dimness in one corner. Kalienne had not been chosen to dance. "What are you going to do?" Bopha asked with concern. Kalienne wiped her eyes and sniffed.

"Achariya is taking me to the Palace," she said. "It's an honor to work there, I know. But I will miss you so much. And Nuon.

64

And even Sophea. And all the teachers. I will be a maid to one of the court ladies. I hope she's nice."

Bopha didn't know what to say. She hugged her friend. Their breasts pressed against each other for a long moment. Bopha's were very tender, but the pressure felt good. Her cheek was against Kalienne's, and she turned her head to look at her friend. Her eyes had adjusted to the light and she could see tears caught in Kalienne's long lashes. She lifted her lips to kiss them away, but Kalienne met her mouth, pulling her even closer. This was Bopha's first such touch. She was flooded with sensation, from lips to breast to ...

Footsteps came up the stairs and the girls pulled apart, staring at each other. Bopha's heart was pounding like she had just run all the way to Bayon. She could see Kalienne's chest raising and falling the same way. Their nipples were hard. A small shadow filled the door. "There you are," Nuon's high voice reached into their corner. "Thida is waiting. She asked me to get you. She wants to take you next door and settle you in your new dorm before lunch."

"I'm coming. I was just saying goodbye to Kalienne." Bopha squeezed her friend's hand, then hugged her again. "I know we'll see each other. I mean, I'll just be next door." She stopped, stricken. Kalienne would not be next door, but somewhere in the Bayon Palace maze.

Kalienne nodded, trying to pull her sweet, beautiful face out of despair. "Yes, we'll see each other. For sure."

"Thida seems very nice," said Nuon. "But I don't think she likes waiting."

Bopha quickly gathered her few belongings and wrapped them in the kromah that Mdeay had given her, which was now somewhat bedraggled. She picked up her bundle from this morning, realizing for the first time that they must be the gifts from the King that Achariya had told her about. Arms full, she made sampeah to Kalienne, whispering, "May the Buddha bring you to a mistress as sweet as you are."

Thida was indeed waiting at the bottom of the steps. "I'm sorry I'm late," said Bopha. "My friend ..."

But Thida had started walking. All the young dancers were lined up to say goodbye, with the teachers in a line opposite. Sophea stood with a beautiful young woman almost as delicate and short as she. A slim young man with very well defined arms stood next to Dara. Bopha caught up with Thida. After lots of bowing and smiling on all sides, the line of new Apsaras and their mentors reached the path that twisted between huge old trees, and left the children's compound behind.

Chapter 7
1188, Dancing at the Palace

Thida was as sweet as she looked. Bopha knew how lucky she was. Sometimes she heard other Apsaras chiding the girls in their charge. Sophea's beautiful mentor was not sweet. She scolded Sophea almost every day, and didn't wait for a private moment to do so. Sophea and Bopha shared a mat, and sometimes in the night Bopha felt Sophea's shoulders shake with silent tears.

Come morning, Sophea was as straight and precise as ever. Bopha tried to be extra nice to her friend. Sophea was indeed becoming a friend, though Sophea found it hard to share much of her inner life, wrapped as she was in protective layers of exactness. Her dancing was beautiful, but somehow distant, like the little girl herself.

Bopha found herself protective of Sophea, vaguely sensing a fragility deep inside.

Every month or so, the adept Apsaras would go to Bayon for ceremonies, the newest ones dancing in the back row. Usually they would perform two different dances, including some of the younger dancers in each. There were thirty-four women and ten young men.

Some of the Apsaras would dance for the King and his court at other times. It was exciting to see them prepare for these more intimate times, preening, only four or five dancers chosen. Bopha learned to listen to the cooks as they gossiped about who was visiting the King from far-off places. He always wanted to show off his dancers. She recognized that three of the same young women would be chosen almost every time. Sophea's mentor was usually in the group. Why them? Who decided?

One day Bopha asked Thida, as they sat in the shade after morning practice, pressing their hands back as far as they could go, stretching their thumbs.

"Oh, the King's Man decides. He comes here every few days and watches us practice."

Bopha nodded. She had seen this. "He is very close to the King, and knows what he likes in a dancer." She paused, a flush coming into her cheek. "And what he likes in a woman."

Bopha wasn't sure what she meant. It must have shown on her face. Thida seemed flustered. "Anyway, usually he knows and the King agrees. Sometimes, though, the King will ask for another dancer."

"How does the King know about the dancers?"

"His man tells him all about us. And the King watches carefully during ceremonies. You've seen that?" Bopha nodded. She could feel his eyes entering hers again. She felt at such times that he actually knew her, maybe knew her more than she knew herself. "So that's how. The King's Man, and the King himself, decide."

Bopha thought about this, and paid close attention in the coming months to which dancers were chosen when. One afternoon, Sophea's mentor stayed in the courtyard as five other young women followed the King's Man. She harangued Sophea when the younger girl failed to turn on the correct beat during the next practice. Bopha felt sorry for Sophea, who seemed to have traded her mother for a tyrant Apsara.

The next time dancers went to Bayon, Sophea's mentor was in the group, but she no longer went every time. Had she somehow fallen out of favor? There was no doubt that she was the most beautiful. But perhaps the King's Man had heard about her sour disposition, and how badly she treated Sophea. Apsaras were supposed to be the embodiment of the celestial dancers. Beautiful inside and out, their sacred rituals brought prosperity to the land, bringing heaven to earth.

Sophea would always be petite and fine-boned, but she was growing. By the time Bopha began her moon-bleeding, Sophea's breasts were starting to fill. Most of the dancers would bleed around the same time, so ceremonies were scheduled accordingly, if at all possible, since they did not dance while they were bleeding. After six moon cycles, Bopha still lagged a week behind the rest. Everyone knew exactly who could dance when, including the

68

King's Man, so he looked more somber than usual when he rode into the courtyard one morning shortly after breakfast.

It was already very hot and his horse was dark with sweat after the short ride. The King's Man swung down and motioned to the older woman, Kesor, who was in charge of all the Apsaras in the courtyard. They walked to the shade under one of the dormitories. It happened to be Bopha's. She was inside, changing to her practice sampot.

"I know the timing is terrible," she heard the King's Man say. "But His Majesty wants five Apsaras for tonight. Emissaries from China arrived late yesterday, and there is a feast of welcome."

"It sure is terrible. Only six Apsaras are not bleeding. And two of those are new." Kesor's voice was worried. "Though both show great promise."

"Which ones?"

"Sophea and Bopha."

"Ah, that's perfect," the man's voice was pleased. "The King has been asking about them."

"Can I choose which dances? They are not yet competent in some of the more complex patterns."

"I guess we do what we have to do," the man's voice was calm. "Have them ready before the sun is halfway down."

Bopha's heart was leaping and her whole body trembled. The King had been asking about her? How could she be ready to dance for the King in such a small group? She heard her name being called from the courtyard and stood up shakily. By the time she got to the door, her head was high and her step sure. Kesor and the King's Man were facing the other dormitory as she slipped down the stairs. She was glad because she thought her face would betray that she had eavesdropped. Even though she hadn't intended to do so, she felt guilty.

"There you are." Kesor saw her. "Where's Sophea?"

"I haven't seen her since breakfast."

"Sophea!" The woman called loudly. Sophea materialized behind Bopha. The King's Man was watching them.

Kesor continued, "Here you are. You two are excused from practice this morning and must go to the baray to wash. You will be going to Bayon this afternoon."

Sophea's face was blank, then shocked. Then she smiled broadly. Bopha watched her friend process how this news could be possible. She tried to do the same, but from the expression on the face of the King's Man, she might have failed. He looked surprised that she wasn't more shocked.

"I'll be back later," he told the Kesor, striding toward his horse.

"We'll be ready," she assured him. Kesor called for the other three Apsaras and explained about the Chinese visitors. "So the King wants to show them what real dancing is." By now all the dancers had heard the news, and gathered around the chosen girls. The excitement was contagious. Thida was going with them, along with one of the dancers that usually went, and another dancer that Bopha didn't know well.

The sun baked the baray to body temperature, so washing was not refreshing. Then some of the other dancers braided their hair. It was an intricate process, many braids that had to be just so. Bopha was not yet proficient, though it wasn't something you could do for yourself. She missed Kalienne's sure yet gentle touch. The young woman helping her now pulled hard on each hank. She hadn't seen Kalienne since coming to the adept courtyard but Sophea said she had indeed gone to Bayon. Maybe she'd see her tonight?

The day became more and more hot. The Apsaras gathered under the porch to wait for the King's Man. When he arrived, they followed him out the gate. Boran was one of the rear guards. He gave Bopha a huge grin, then recomposed his face for the walk. The girls had umbrellas to protect them from the worst of the sun. The whole country panted for the rains to come, but it would likely be another moon till that relief.

Bopha was glad that she had been to the King's palace before. It was hard enough to know she would see him, and he would watch her so very closely, without the added uncertainty about her surroundings. The Apsaras that usually danced in a small group had talked with her and Sophea about where they would perform, and what to expect. Now their line was silent, as befitted their

70

station in public. The crowds parted and Bopha could hear "China," and "Apsara," and "So young!"

Instead of going to the Great Hall, the Apsaras were led into the courtyard for women, behind the main palace. Here they waited in the shade of the biggest trees Bopha had ever seen. The late afternoon heat throbbed in the air and the only noise was frantic cicadas. After a light supper, the dancers changed into their best sampots. Kesor had come with them, since the group had so many new dancers. Now she gave each a gold necklace to wear for the evening. Bopha had never worn such a beautiful thing. It was just like the one the King's Man wore, except more delicate.

Bopha was looking at her chest, where her breasts rose below the gold that shimmered in the torchlight. The tropical night had fallen suddenly and little boys had gone all around the courtyard, lighting torches. It was still very hot. The dancers squatted in a little group near the trees, waiting to be called into the Great Hall.

"Bopha!" The whisper came from behind one of the trees. "Hssst. Bopha!"

Bopha left the group, which was talking about the heat and the walk home so late in the night. She looked behind the tree. Kalienne! The girls fell into each other's arms. "I can't stay. I just heard the dancers were different tonight, and came to see if maybe ... Oh, Bopha, it's so wonderful to see you." Kalienne's eyes filled with tears. One drop fell on Bopha's finger as she reached to stroke her friend's face.

"Are you okay here? Is your mistress nice?"

"Yes, it's okay. She's okay. But I have to go." Kalienne kissed Bopha's full lips, and disappeared into the night. Bopha leaned against the tree. The visit almost seemed like a spirit had held her, not her real friend. But her lips tingled and her arms still felt the pressure of Kalienne's body against them. She shook her head to clear it, and detoured to the mat to collect herself before returning to the other dancers.

A gong rang, vibrating through the courtyard from the Palace. That was the signal.

The Apsaras stood as one, and followed a little boy who carried a torch much larger than he. The King's Man stood at the foot of the huge stairs up to the Great Hall. The dancers gave him sampeah, passed the immobile guards, and paused at the door.

Light poured out, along with heat from all the torches inside. Large woven fans hung from the ceiling, pushed by boys in white sampots that gleamed against their tanned skin.

A crowd of people in fancy clothes milled about the room. Bopha could see the King sitting on his chair, with men on each side dressed in strange robes that covered their whole bodies. They must be hot, she thought. The King's chest glistened in the light. Was it sweat? Or oil? His necklace shone so brightly she could hardly look at it. Silence drifted over the crowd as the King raised his hand. All turned to watch the Apsaras file in behind the King's Man, then bow in front of the King. Rustling of clothes was the only sound as people took their places on the rows of benches. The Apsaras would dance between the benches and the altar. The musicians were set up next to the altar, behind the dancers.

"Welcome, Beloved Apsaras!" The King's deep voice filled the room. "You are here to perform for my esteemed visitors from far-off China. They will see, through your dancing, more of the glory of Kampuchea."

The King's Man sat where he had before, while Kesor joined the women on the benches behind. She needed to watch so she could help the dancers correct in future any missteps. The musicians tuned up for a moment, then complete stillness filled the hall, except for the high shrill of cicadas. A gibbon shrieked. The gong sounded again. The dancers raised their hands and legs into the first jeeb as the khim began the song.

Bopha forgot everything as the music filled her body. The last drum beat echoed through the hall, then the deep buffalo horn, bringing her back. Her eyes had been open, but she had not seen the King, nor the King's Man, nor the admiring gazes of the Chinese visitors. Her heart pounded, but she controlled her breath. Focusing on that, she bowed with the other dancers. Standing straight again, she looked directly into the King's black eyes. He had a broad smile, and his hands were in sampeah. After a long moment, he looked away, to the next Apsara. But Bopha felt him still inside her.

The Chinese were bowing up and down, and the courtiers, both men and ladies, offered sampeah.

"Now you have seen my Apsaras," the King said, pride and pleasure in his voice. "Once more tonight they will dance for us."

This time, when the khim strings vibrated, Bopha stayed in the room with her body. Her low back was vibrating to the music, almost painfully, with little shocks of energy pulsing up her spine. Once, when she twirled through a movement, she ended up facing the King's Man. He was watching her intently, and caught her eye. He nodded almost imperceptibly. She twirled away again, completely focused. She and Sophea were on either end of the line of dancers, Thida next to Bopha. As they held the last jeeb, Bopha could see Thida's breasts rising and falling as hard as hers were. The excitement started to drain out of the dancers as they bowed.

The King stood up, and everyone else quickly followed suit. He stepped off the dais and walked to the line of young women. Bopha could hear murmuring from the courtiers, but only when they got back to the courtyard of women did she learn how unusual this action was. He bowed to each dancer in turn. When he reached Bopha, he was so close that she could smell sandalwood from his skin. So it had been oil, that glistening. He didn't touch her, of course, but she felt that he was. The sensation was like when Kalienne kissed her. She kept her slight smile, as he looked into her, but could feel her nipples stiffen.

At last, he turned, and standing next to Bopha, he gestured with his right hand. "These are the Apsaras of Kampuchea! We are indeed blessed." His hand was in front of Bopha's chest. Each finger had a heavy ring with a gemstone embedded its gold. She looked at the tiny black hairs across the back of his hand. He dropped his hand. She felt Thida start to bow and did the same, hands in sampeah.

King Jayavarman VII strode to his throne and sat. The Apsaras walked backward out of the hall, joined by Kesor. The King's Man stayed behind to participate in the feasting that would follow. The darkness on the porch nearly blinded Bopha after the brilliance inside the hall. Sophea led their line down the steps, then waited for Kesor to lead them to the women's courtyard. They were quiet as they followed the wavering torch.

73

Kesor had a woven bag from which she drew a dark wooden box. Its lid was clipped on all four sides by curved metal hooks that fit over protruding metal posts. She unclipped the hooks and removed the lid. Soft red cloth lined the inside. Kesor collected their gold necklaces, nesting them in the box. She closed the lid. Serving women brought the dancers fruit and bitter tea. Bopha wondered if that was one of the things that Kalienne did, bring refreshment to her mistress. She wished they had more time to talk. Her body and mind were getting more tired by the moment, as the thrills of the day faded.

Finally, the Apsaras started for home. This time, the King's Man did not lead them, but four guards were in front and three joined Boran behind them. It seemed like a long half hour until they reached the dancers' courtyard. The other girls in their dorm were sleeping. Someone had set up their mat for them. Bopha and Sophea undressed in silence and darkness, and fell asleep immediately. The soft sound of drum, khim and flute echoed in Bopha's mind as she slept.

CHAPTER 8
1190, Kalienne

L ife in the dancer's courtyard had its own rhythms, the moon cycled through its stages over and over. Bopha was often chosen to dance for the King in a small group, often with Thida, sometimes with Sophea. But she felt her friend slipping away, more distant as the moons passed. She was bleeding now, but her cycle was not connected to that of any other dancer.

One morning Sophea's mentor did not come to breakfast. The dancers in her dormitory were unusually subdued. "What's going on?" Bopha whispered to Sophea, who seemed more relaxed and happy than she had in a very long time.

"The gods have heard my prayers," she whispered back. "I will have a new mentor, starting today — Nary."

"That's wonderful," said Bopha. Nary meant small beautiful bird, a perfect name for the gentle Apsara who often danced in their small group. "But why?"

"Kesor and the King's Man got fed up with how mean that horrible woman was to me. She was sent away last night."

"To where?"

"I don't know and I don't care," hissed Sophea. "But not to the Palace. She is banned from dancing, except at fairs in small villages. Serves her right."

"She was really mean to you," Bopha agreed.

"I couldn't take any more," Sophea confided. "I didn't want to go on living."

Bopha was shocked, then realized that on some level she had known that. "I would miss you," she said, touching Sophea's shoulder gently. Sophea tensed slightly, then took a deep breath and nodded.

"Thank you. You are my only friend," Sophea said softly. "But you seem to have lots of friends."

Nuon had graduated to the Apsara courtyard some moons ago. But Leap and most of the other dancers did not. From the many village girls who arrived, few were chosen to continue dancing. "Mostly Nuon," said Bopha. "And you." And Thida, she thought, and Nary. She did have a lot of friends.

Over the next weeks, Sophea's dancing changed in a subtle way. Watching her one day, Bopha realized that her friend seemed to be enjoying the movement, not going through automatic steps but engaged with the dance. Bopha was glad. Then she shivered. How close she had come to losing this strange, gifted friend, wrapped like a caterpillar in her lonely cocoon.

Bopha had rarely seen Kalienne on her trips to Bayon. The older girl was always in a hurry, scared to be caught leaving her tasks to look for the dancers. It had been many moons since the last time. Then one day as she, Nuon and Sophea held hands through the market, Bopha glimpsed her, turning into an alley.

"Kalienne!" Bopha ran.

The figure turned toward her, then continued walking away, faster. Bopha had seen her shape. Her belly was big above her sampot, and the sampot had seen better days. "Kalienne!" Bopha raced past vendors who stared after her.

She caught up, and blurted out, "Oh my dear friend," Bopha said. "I'm so glad to see you. But ... "

The two young women faced each other in the narrow street. Kalilenne looked at Bopha, then down at herself. Bopha gently lifted her chin, then drew her close, as close as she could. "Oh, Kalienne." They stood hugging until Sophea and Nuon, who had followed Bopha more slowly, caught up and stood staring in silence. Bopha released Kalienne, but kept an arm around her waist. "Tell us. What happened? Are you still at the Palace?"

Kalienne shook her head. "No. I live here, just down this alley." She gestured to where the house walls got so close together that pedestrians would have to walk single file. "I have a room." Her voice broke.

"Who?" Bopha's voice was sharp. "Who did this to you? Are they going to take care of you?" She had come a long way from the day that Thida told her how the dancers were chosen. She now knew what Thida had meant, "What the King likes in a woman." The Apsaras were in a special category, and they had more choice than most women, Bopha knew. But someone without that protection, someone at the Palace for instance, was not so lucky."

"Yes. He is paying for the room. And he gives me money for food," Kalienne's voice was tiny. She didn't say who.

Bopha's whole body was hot with anger. "So you won't say who?" Kalienne shook her head. "I hate that you have been treated this way." Anger melted into sadness. Bopha pulled Kalienne into another embrace. She was almost as tall as her friend, but Kalienne had developed a stoop, so their heads were at the same height. She whispered, "Will you tell me if you need anything?" Kalienne nodded. "Promise?" Kalienne nodded. "Who will help you with the birth? Can I come?"

"He has talked to a woman. She lives in the next alley. She will come." Kalienne paused. "Oh Bopha, I would so much love to have you with me. But you must not do anything to get yourself in trouble. Life for an Apsara is enchanted. You can't risk it."

Bopha shook her head impatiently, pulling away to look into her friend's face. "I will come. No matter what. Promise to tell me when it happens?" It was Kalienne's turn to shake her head. Bopha grabbed her upper arms, harder than she meant to. "Kalienne!

Tell me!" Kalienne looked at Bopha's hands, and Bopha let go. "Please!" Bopha's eyes filled with tears. So did Kalienne's. "Please let me decide what is most important in my life."

Kalienne stared at her, then touched Bopha's mouth with a finger. "Thank you," was all she said. "I have to go."

The three dancers watched Kalienne pick her way through the dung and trash, her step still sure but her posture slumped.

"I wonder who the man is." Nuon broke their silence. Bopha shrugged, heart breaking when the alley twisted, swallowing Kalienne.

"Well, she's protecting him," observed Sophea. "Though I don't know why. He's not protecting her." She harrumphed, and added, "Men."

"Maybe she's in love with him," said Nuon.

Bopha said nothing. She wished she could follow Kalienne now, lie with her, hold her in her arms, stroke her long smooth hair. Snuggle as close as she could. Protect her from all harm. And hear the whole story of Kalienne's life since she left the dancers' courtyard. She sighed, all the way to her toes.

The girls walked quietly back to the market, all interest in shopping sapped. Sophea's head was up and her back straight, as usual, which helped Bopha do the same. "Do you think she'll be okay?" No one answered Nuon's question. They turned toward home in silence.

Bopha went to the market every day, with anyone who was going, but saw no sign of Kalienne. One day she told her companions she had to do her business, and slipped away, agreeing to meet at the Garuda workshops. After she made the turn in the alley, where Kalienne had disappeared, Bopha saw a wrinkled old woman, skin sagging off every bone. She squatted in the street, wrapped only in a small kromah, wringing water from an ancient sampot.

"Yeay, have you seen the young woman who is with child?" Bopha politely called the woman grandmother, and gestured a big circle in front of her own flat stomach. The woman's eyes were cloudy and she had a few wisps of white hair on a knobby skull. She looked closely at Bopha however. Bopha waited, then gestured again.

The woman seemed to come to some decision and stood up, slowly and with some difficulty. She thwacked the sampot in the air, releasing wrinkles and droplets of water, then tied it around her meatless hip bones, pulling the kromah out from underneath once the sampot was settled. She looked again at Bopha. Then she creaked away from her own doorway, into the deeper shadows further down the alley.

Bopha followed. The alley was a toilet and a trash dump, and smelled like it. Bopha knew that people had to go to the baray on the other side of the market to get water. Poor Kalienne. Who would get her water? She raged again at the man who had gotten her friend into this mess. The woman stopped in front of a narrow door, then stepped back so Bopha could enter.

It was nearly pitch dark inside, the fetid alley air seeping in around Bopha's body as she pushed aside the curtain and entered a tiny room. The street was so narrow that little light made its way between the houses, and much less into the room. Bopha's eyes adjusted and she made out a bench with a bowl on it. There was a form on the sleeping mat, facing away from her.

"Kalienne?" she asked, very softly. The form moved slightly. Soft sleeping breaths were the only sound. No bird song here. The room was so far from the market that the bustle there was less than a whisper. Bopha took two steps into the murk, placing her feet carefully, not sure what might be there. Two steps was all it took. She knelt beside the woman on the mat, still not sure it was her friend. "Kalienne?"

The woman woke with a start and rolled onto her back, her eyes catching the little light as she stared at Bopha. "Kalienne, it's you!" Bopha lay down, stretching her length against Kalienne's body. She could feel her friend's hip bones, where the baby had taken all the nourishment it could get. Reaching one arm under Kalienne's shoulders and covering her chest with her other arm, Bopha pulled her close.

"How did you find me?" Kalienne's voice came out as a croak.

"An old yeay showed me. Do you need a drink?" Bopha could feel Kalienne shake her head. "I can bring water," Bopha offered. But she did not let go of Kalienne, except to stroke her hair, over and over. Kalienne turned into her embrace, and wept gently.

"Kalienne?" A man's voice broke over them. Bopha knew that voice, and scrambled silently into the corner. "Kalienne, are you here?" The King's Man! Bopha could dimly see him stooping to get under the door frame. He took the two steps, then stopped.

Bopha stood up, facing him.

"You!" The single word hissed in the dark. "You did this to my friend."

"Who is here?" His vision had not adjusted yet.

"Preah Chan Bopha." She pronounced her full name, each syllable crisp in the darkness.

"Ahh. Preah Chan Bopha." His voice was full of sorrow. "Of course."

"Kalienne, I'll come back as soon as I can."

"Bopha, please don't say anything," Kalienne pleaded. Bopha's eyes bored into those of the King's Man, but he couldn't see that in the dark. "Please."

After a long moment, Bopha said softly, "Okay." She slipped past the man and out into the dank, dim alley, walking fast till she got to the market. Her mind was racing. What would the King's Man do, now that he knew she knew? Now that he had found her in the forbidden alleys of the market, alone?

"Where were you? Are you constipated? It took you forever," the dancers teased her when she got to the sculpture atelier. Bopha's eyes had trouble focusing in the bright sun of the market and she stepped under the awning. There were four artisans, working in close quarters. After glancing up at the beautiful young women and smiling, they returned to their chisels. Tap. Tap-tap. Tap. They knew not to gawk rudely at Apsaras. One of the Garudas was larger than life. Well, larger than a human. Who knew how large a Garuda was, really? Bopha felt her anger and fear and sadness ease as she looked into the huge stone eye above her.

"All will be well," she heard a deep, creaky voice say, inside her head. "Do not fear."

Bopha's heart pounded and her knees weakened. "It is as it is." The voice grated but was not actually unpleasant. "Go in peace."

She opened her eyes, having not known she closed them. The huge stone eye stared at her, unblinking. Well, of course, stone wouldn't blink, she told herself. But she was shaken.

"Have you done all your shopping?" Nuon's voice broke into her dream. It was time to return for morning practice.

"I'm done. How about you?" Her friends didn't seem to notice Bopha's state, and she took a deep, careful breath.

"I'm ready," was all she said, and remembered the voice. 'All is well. Go in peace.'

80

T he King's Man did not come to the Apsara courtyard that day, nor the next. Bopha alternated between worry and peace. Luckily there was a huge celebration coming soon. The dancers were practicing the most complex performance, so she was distracted physically and mentally most of the time.

Then he arrived, as the afternoon heat gathered clouds. It would rain today, and soon. Bopha watched him dismount, each movement graceful. He could have been a dancer. Maybe he had been one, she suddenly thought.

Thunder cracked, interrupting both her thoughts and the preparations for afternoon dancing. Everyone ran for shelter as a hard rain started very suddenly. Being far from the buildings, Bopha went under the biggest banyan. Then she realized the King's Man was standing there. She had never been alone with him. Her face was stony, despite the little practiced smile.

"Preah Chan Bopha," he began. She didn't want him to besmirch her full name, pronouncing it with the same lips that had touched her beloved Kalienne. "I'm sorry you found out."

"Well, I'm not," Bopha shot back. "I'm just sorry you did that to my friend." She couldn't stop speaking. "And why can't you keep her at the palace, like any other courtesan? The most beautiful and gentle of all the dancers — and you put her in a stinking hole in a stinking alley!" Bopha was shaking with rage. Instead of glancing at the King's Man then dropping her eyes, Bopha was staring directly at him, hands curled into a jeeb of distress.

He held her blazing eyes, then dropped his. "It's complicated," he said softly.

"Complicated," she spat. "What a sorry excuse." She knew that she was losing her temper, and his calm put her at a disadvantage. It was all well and good for a man to go into battle and cut off the heads of his foe with a sharp sword, or slice a jugular with sharp palm fronds. But to show anger outside of war? No. And never acceptable for a woman.

Bopha struggled to regain her composure. The rain beat down, some finding its way through the branches onto her bare head. He was wearing his usual gold helmet.

81

They stood in silence, listening to the storm, studying the ground between them.

"Bopha, I know you are Kalienne's friend. I can't explain it all to you. Not now." She looked up at him. "Maybe sometime. But I won't punish you for supporting her."

Bopha nodded slowly. "I have never felt about anyone the way I feel about her. But at this time, I can do nothing to draw attention to the situation." Bopha stiffened. He noticed. "I will make it possible for you to be with her when she is laboring. But that's the most I can do for now."

Tears welled up in Bopha's eyes and dripped down her cheek, along with the raindrops. She looked at the King's Man. His eyes were shiny but no tears fell. She knew he told the truth. Did he feel for Kalienne the way she did? Her heart froze to think of it. But that was better than if he didn't care. Bopha's mind whirled as the thunder rumbled off, taking the rain with it. She put her hands in sampeah, and bent her head to the tall man. She could see his hands rise together in response.

Then he was gone. Bopha watched him meet Kesor as she came out from under the biggest dorm. They talked a few minutes. He did not stay to watch the afternoon dancing, but leapt onto his horse and cantered onto the road, gawkers scattering in front of him.

She saw him again at the ceremony at Angkor Wat. The King's Man sat in the shade next to the King. From the corner of her eye, Bopha saw that they occasionally leaned their heads together. She felt both men following her movements closely.

As the Apsaras recessed across the bridge, a tall boy in orange robes followed. Rithy!

Bopha threw her arms around her brother, who hugged back then put her at arm's distance. "I'm sorry, brother. I forgot. You are now a monk."

Rithy laughed. He still had the radiant smile she remembered. "It's okay, little one. But just this once. And you are no longer the little one." He looked at her closely. The top of her head reached his nose. "My little sister is all grown up." Bopha ducked her head.

"When did that happen?"

"When did you get your orange robes?" Bopha countered. "Even though we are so near, I don't get news from Angkor Wat."

"I know," agreed Rithy. "I've seen you at every ceremony, but usually can't find you afterwards. Your dancing is amazing," Rithy continued. "When you move, the story comes to life. Everyone who watches can see it. All the monks agree."

"The monks talk about the Apsaras?"

"We may be monks, but we are humans at the same time," Rithy chuckled, then sobered. "Bopha, I may be moving to Bayon."

Someday the temple at Bayon would be complete, and the King would have the biggest celebration in living memory. That's what Boran said. "You are moving before it is completed?" Bopha asked.

"Yes. Next week. We are starting to focus more prayers there. And I have been learning to write. I love it. They need more scribes at the Palace. So I'll do both."

"Pray and write?" Bopha smiled. Her brother had wanted this so much. "I'm happy for you. And I hope we see each other more when you are closer. Sometimes I dance for the King with a small group of Apsaras, so maybe ..." She trailed off. Maybe.

She wished ... what? She wished for more freedom, she suddenly realized. Though she was well cared-for in the dancers' courtyard and was doing something she loved to do, she couldn't just decide to go visit Kalienne, for example. Other people told her what to do, and she had to do it. Or what?

"Bopha?" Rithy was looking at her with some concern. "Are you okay?"

"Yes," she said slowly. "I guess so."

"You looked like you were in another world in thought."

"Yes. I was." She burst out with it, "I just realized that I can only do what other people tell me to do. Even the dance moves are prescribed. I can't just come and see you, or even make arrangements on my own for it to happen."

Now Rithy really looked concerned. "Bopha," his voice held a note of warning, "Apsaras agree to do the King's bidding when they come to Angkor. As I agree to do the bidding of my superior monks. We are none of us free to choose ... "

He broke off, seeing Kesor approach. He bowed to her and Bopha turned around. She put her hands in sampeah, then said, "Good afternoon, Kesor. This is my brother, Rithy." She added, unnecessarily, "He's learning to be a monk here."

Kesor looked at them sharply. "We are leaving now," was all she said. The siblings bowed to her. She walked off, calling the Apsaras into formation.

"Goodbye, dear Rithy."

"Go in peace, Bopha. Till we meet again."

Bopha watched her brother turn back across the causeway, his robes brilliant against the pale gray stone. The towers of Angkor Wat stood stark against the late blue sky of afternoon, sun gleaming long on the baray and shining from every speck of gold that adorned the huge temple. "Goodbye, dear Rithy," she murmured   again,   "Go   in   peace."

CHAPTER 9

1191-1192, Morning-Sun Sky

Bopha didn't dare try to visit Kalienne again. The weeks dragged past. One night she was awakened by Kesor. The full moon poured through cracks between the wooden shutters. "Come," the woman whispered. They walked silently down the steps to the courtyard, and into the shadow of the big banyan. The tall figure of the King's Man separated itself from the tree. He gave Kesor sampeah and motioned to Bopha to follow him. No one spoke. His horse snorted as they walked away, leaving it tethered under the tree.

Walking in silence from tree to tree along the side of the road, from shadow to shadow, the two figures passed through the sleeping market and down the alley. A dog barked twice, shrilly. The full moon light didn't reach the street here but lingered on the upper walls. Once Bopha slipped in a pile of something slick. The King's Man turned quickly to steady her, his hand very strong on her arm. As soon as he was sure she wouldn't fall, he let go.

At the door to Kalienne's room, a pale light flickered through the curtain. The King's Man pulled back the cloth and motioned Bopha inside. There was a motherly figure squatting next to the mat. The small torch lit up beads of sweat on Kalienne's face as she looked up at the man and girl. "You came," she said softly, then groaned. Bopha fell to her knees beside her friend. The King's Man stood in the doorway. "Thank you," Kalienne said, when the contraction had passed, looking past Bopha into his face. Bopha followed her gaze.

In the dim light, and seen from below, his face was deeply lined. His eyes were soft and worried as he looked at Kalienne. He nodded. "I'll return when ... " Kalienne groaned again, a guttural sound that pierced Bopha's heart. The midwife stood up and shooed him out unceremoniously. The curtain dropped behind him.

Hours later, Kalienne screamed, "I can't do this! Stop! Stop!" Bopha was squatting behind her, supporting her back as Kalienne also squatted. The room was close and hot, all the women drenched with sweat. With one hand, Bopha dipped a cloth in a pot of water on the bench, squeezed it, and drew it gently across Kalienne's forehead. "Stop! Stop! Leave me alone!" The cries reverberated around the tiny room.

"Shhh, shhh, shhh. Yes, you can. You are doing so well," the midwife murmured consolingly. "You are nearly there."

"I can't!" Then another scream, louder and longer.

"Kalienne! Listen to me." The midwife spoke with loud authority. "Look at me." Kalienne and Bopha both looked. "You need to stop screaming. I can feel the baby's head. You are almost there, but you have to take this pain and turn it into pushing. When you scream, you lose that power. Now, take a deep breath and slowly let it go."

Both girls breathed.

"When the next contraction starts, take a deep breath and hold it, pushing like you were moving your bowels," the midwife instructed. "Do you understand?" Two heads nodded.

Kalienne groaned. The midwife repeated, "Take a deep breath. That's good. Perfect. Now push. Keep holding your breath and push, push, push." The girls did. Bopha felt like she was going to faint.

The midwife was squatting in front of Kalienne. "I'm going to reach in now and feel the baby." Kalienne winced but didn't scream. "Okay, good. Kalienne, you are doing a very good job. Next time you feel the pain, do the same thing. But if I tell you to stop, you have to stop pushing immediately. If I say pant, start to pant like a dog." She panted to demonstrate. Bopha and Kalienne panted.

"But don't pant unless I say so." The girls nodded. Bopha had her arms around Kalienne and was gently pressing her thighs apart, as the midwife had showed her.

Kalienne took a deep breath. The midwife leaned in, her hands in the birth canal. The torch flickered slightly, making three huge shadows on the walls, like mythical monsters. None of the women noticed. "Push, push, push." Bopha and Kalienne did.

"Now stop. Stop! Pant!" The girls panted and the midwife moved her hands, feeling for the umbilical cord. "Keep panting. I've got the cord. It's wrapped around the baby's neck, so I'm going to unwind it." The contraction was over and Kalienne sank against Bopha's chest.

"There. Got it." The woman's voice pulsed with relief. "Next push, you'll have your baby."

The torch flickered, the shadows towered, the women waited. Then Kalienne gasped.

"Deep breath. Hold it, hold it. Now push!" The midwife was firm. She reached between Kalienne's open legs. After the longest moment of Bopha's life, her friend screamed once more, an almost animal sound. "Good girl," said the woman. "Here's the head. That's the hardest part. Next push, we'll see whether you have a boy or a girl."

Bopha couldn't see over Kalienne. The head! Almost done now. She hugged Kalienne, then breathed deeply with her as the next contraction came suddenly.

"Arrrggghhh."

The midwife moved her hands rapidly, catching the slick body as it jetted into the world.

A thin short wail filled the room. Bopha and Kalienne gasped. The midwife nodded. "You have a boy!" His second cry was lusty and long. "And he's a big one. Good thing you are tall and have broad hips."

The woman lay the baby on a kromah on the mat, reached for the two thick pieces of string lying ready on the bench. She put one around the umbilical cord and pulled it tight. Bopha could see the cord pulsing and blue in the light. When the string was tight, the pulsing stopped. The midwife knotted it, then tied the second cord near the baby's body. Then she turned the baby on its side, slid a small stone under the cord, and hefted a knife. With one hand steadying the baby, she sliced through the air. Thwack! The two halves of the cord separated neatly. The woman watched carefully. No blood seeped from either half.

She wrapped the baby in the kromah, then in another piece of fabric. He continued to wail as she handed him to Kalienne. "Here

87

you go, daughter." The dim light glistened on her nearly toothless gums. "You can nurse him while we wait for the sok to deliver."

Kalienne shifted from a squat to stretch her legs out, and leaned back against Bopha. She reached for the squalling bundle and held him to her chest. Bopha could see his eyes were open. He stopped crying and seemed to look into his mother's eyes. "Hello, little cucumber. Are you going to stop crying now? It's not so bad, being in this world," Kalienne crooned.

Bopha supported her friend as she offered the baby her breast. He nosed around, mouth open, then took the nipple, hard. "Oh!" The midwife looked up, grinning. "He knows how to suck, eh? Such a smart baby!"

"Does it hurt?" Bopha asked, in awe.

"No … Yes … But in a nice sort of way," Kalienne tried to explain. "Oh, here comes another contraction." She leaned back further, Bopha taking her weight.

"Just let it come," said the midwife, "this is the last contraction. Once the sok is out, you can rest."

* * *

The room was quiet. The midwife had gone to get more water. Dim light from the morning sun outlined the pattern of the door cloth. Kalienne lay on her side on the mat, cuddling the baby, who was asleep, making little squeaks and funny breath sounds. Bopha was lying behind Kalienne, her face in Kalienne's hair, one arm around her friend and touching the baby's foot. Once in a while, the baby's foot jerked against her hand.

"What are you going to name him?" Bopha asked softly.

Kalienne stirred, and turned her head toward Bopha. "Kiri will decide. If he were a girl, I would. But this is the first boy Kiri has."

"Kiri? That's the name of the King's Man?" Kalienne nodded shyly. Bopha had never thought of him as having a name. Bopha felt anger stirring in her stomach as the man's presence entered this intimate moment.

"He's so beautiful, don't you think?" Kalienne had turned her head to watch the sleeping infant. It was Bopha's turn to nod. She didn't trust her voice.

The two young women were dozing when the curtain opened and a tall shadow filled the room. Bopha immediately awoke. The King's Man! She separated from Kalienne and rose, cramped between the wall and her friend's sleeping body. He stood in silence, looking at the new mother.

"I met the midwife at the baray. She told me," his voice was low and gentle, but it woke Kalienne.

"Kiri, you are here! You have a son!" Kalienne's pride and pleasure filled the room. Bopha stepped around her. She no longer felt welcome. Kalienne reached for her hand. "Bopha, thank you. I could not have done it without you."

Bopha squeezed her hand and whispered, "You were amazing. I am honored to have been with you. But I have to go back now."

The King's Man stepped back to let her pass. "Thank you, Bopha. Kesor will take care of things, don't worry." Bopha met his eyes and nodded. She started down the dim and dingy street after he entered the room she had had to abandon. She could hear his voice, a deep murmur, and Kalienne's a higher one in response, then their mingled soft laughter. Bopha quickened her steps.

* * *

Kiri was true to his word, Bopha had to credit him that. Over the next few weeks, Kesor found ways to let the young woman go to Kalienne's every few days. She also let Bopha know she was not pleased with the request. "The King's Man has told me that you are needed. But it cannot continue. The other Apsaras are starting to talk."

Arun Veha, "morning-sun sky," was already much bigger than he had been at birth. Bopha and Kalienne sat under a tree near the baray as Kalienne nursed. Kalienne finally told her the story of how she and Kiri came to be together.

"My lady was the wife of the King's Man. She is very nice, but has deep sorrow inside. They had been married for many years, but she only had daughters. Five of them. Then, many years before I came to work for her, my lady nearly died giving birth to her sixth child. It was a son. But he did not survive. After that my lady, her name is Khun Thea, could not stand to," Kalienne stopped, flushing. She dropped her voice. "She said something had happened to her insides during that birth. It hurt so much when her husband lay with her that she could no longer be his wife. The King's Man was kind to her and did not put her aside, as many men would."

Bopha was braiding grass into a long rope as she listened. She said nothing. Kalienne lifted Arun Veha and patted him till he burped. A big blob of milk drooled onto the kromah over her shoulder. Bopha wiped the baby's face with a corner of the kromah. Kalienne met her eyes. Bopha shrugged. "Shall I continue?" Bopha nodded, quiet.

"I worked for Khun Thea for a long time. She was always kind to me. The King's Man would come and talk with her when he came back from trips, sitting on a bench while Khun Thea was getting ready for the feast that always followed his return. Sometimes I would come into the room when he was there, and I felt his eyes follow me. But if I looked up, he always looked away. Sometimes he would leave suddenly if I came in. One night there was a full moon festival. The Palace was full of people. I was helping my lady —gathering her silks, braiding her hair, fixing the clasp on her necklace. I left the room to get something, and walked right into the King's Man. I mean, right into him.

"My breasts rubbed against his chest jewelry, and I could feel him suddenly stiffen." Kalienne stopped. "I mean, he stiffened as would anyone who gets run into, but also his ... manhood stiffened. I looked up at him in that moment, into his eyes. He stared at me, then backed away, and didn't look at me again. I ran down the corridor, hardly able to breathe. When I came back, he was gone."

"Then what happened?" Bopha couldn't help asking. She didn't want to hear, but she had to know.

"Later that night, after I helped my lady prepare for sleep, I was walking to my room. The King's Man and his lady live in one wing of the Palace. He is such a close friend to the King. They have known each other since childhood. Khun Thea is the King's baby sister, his favorite. That is part of the problem. Kiri doesn't want to hurt Khun Thea and he doesn't want the King to know about Arun Veha.

"Anyway, the servants live in various buildings behind the Palace. Maids like me live just behind the Palace, the cooks live above the kitchens, grooms by the stables. Like that. There is less light behind the Palace than in the front courtyards. As I passed a tree in the darkest part of the path, someone stepped in front of me. I was surprised, but not scared. If I screamed, many people would come quickly.

"'Kalienne,' the person said. I recognized Khun Thea's husband. His shape and voice were so familiar to me. I stopped. He beckoned me to come nearer. 'Will you come with me?' He sounded so sad, so pleading. I knew how kind he was — to Khun Thea, to everyone. And I had a funny feeling all over, all the way inside."

Bopha had been looking at her, but now looked away. "Oh, Bopha. You know that feeling. You and I have had it."

Bopha nodded, eyes welling. Kalienne reached for her hand. "You are my dearest friend. But we can't be together like that. You know it." Bopha looked at her and nodded again, her tears leaking onto their clasped hands. "I hope you can find that feeling with a man sometime."

The baby farted, loud and long and wet, but kept on sleeping. Bopha and Kalienne grinned at each other, lopsidedly. Kalienne took a deep breath. "It's okay," Bopha reassured her. "You can finish the story. I want to hear it, even if I don't like it."

Kalienne looked at her gratefully, and continued, "Kiri lifted his hand toward me, palm up, inviting me. When I touched him, I felt something pour into me through our hands. He led me to an empty room where he had set a soft mat and cushions, with small torches in holders on the wall. His touch was so gentle. I felt myself melting, then his arms were around me."

She stopped talking, a soft smile playing on her full lips. "We met as often as we could. I could hardly get enough of him, and he said the same. But he didn't want to hurt Khun Thea. He loves her and she is a good woman."

91

"Does he love you?" Bopha's voice was shaky.

"Yes. I think so. I'm sure. He tells me so. And he has taken many risks to keep me safe, to have you come visit. When we are together, he is so tender that I almost weep to remember."

"But you had to leave the Palace?"

"Yes, when I knew my condition, I told Kiri. I left before Khun Thea guessed. Neither one of us want to hurt her." She paused. "Or to have the King know."

"What about now? What about Arun Veha?"

Kalienne looked down at the baby, and shrugged. "I don't know. Kiri comes almost every day. You should see him with Arun Veha. He is not the King's Man then, but a father smitten by a little baby. He lifts him up high in his hands, like he is offering him to heaven, then drops his hands suddenly. Arun gurgles and laughs. I think he likes it, that sudden movement." Kalienne's face dropped. "Kiri is going on another trip next week. He'll be gone for more than one moon. But he has given me money, so we'll be okay." She looked at Bopha, "and he says you can come."

"Can't you move to a nicer place?" Bopha asked.

"Not yet," said Kalienne.

The baby woke, and they bathed him in the baray, then walked back to the room, Bopha carrying two big water buckets. Arun Veha started to cry when Kalienne put him on the mat, but she hugged Bopha tightly before sitting down to nurse. "See you soon," said Bopha, warmth from the embrace filling her.

* * *

But it wasn't soon. Almost a moon passed before Kesor told her she could go. When Bopha got to the little room, there was no sign of Kalienne and Arun Veha. She panicked and ran to the baray. When she saw them sitting under the tree in the early morning sun, Bopha's heart slowed from its mad pounding. "I'm sorry, I couldn't get away," she said breathlessly.

"Kesor sent word," said Kalienne, "that you would be delayed."

Bopha was surprised to hear that, but glad. There seemed to be many layers of intrigue around this situation. How many people knew? How long before Khun Thea would find out? And the King? She was becoming aware, as she lived near the Palace, how many eyes watched and reported, how much gossip surrounded all of the notables.

All she said was, "How are things going?" She couldn't believe how much bigger Arun Veha was after just those few weeks. When he finished nursing, Kalienne passed him to Bopha. "Hey there, did you have a nice lunch?" Arun looked into Bopha's eyes and gave her a big smile. "A smile! You learned how to smile!"

"Smiling for Auntie Bopha," said Kalienne, leaning into her shoulder.

"I can't stay. Tonight a few of us are going to the Palace. Can I get you anything at the market?

Kalienne shook her head. "We're good. I'll stop on the way home."

"How about water?"

"That would be great," Kalienne smiled. "You always know."

"I carried a lot of water before I became an Apsara." Bopha felt a sudden pang for her family, her village, the baby she never met that was so cruelly murdered.

* * *

Boran led the guards, in the absence of the King's Man. Tonight there were only three Apsaras going to dance. Bopha wondered at that but did not ask. She and Thida and Nary walked together as the sky darkened. A sliver of moon was high in the sky. Rainy season was nearly over, and the air was what passed for cool so close to the equator.

Bopha had goose bumps on her arms and wished she had brought her kromah. Boran led them not into the Great Hall, but to a different part of the Palace. They climbed a set of stairs, beautifully crafted, though narrower than the usual grand entrance. There were the usual two stiff guards at the bottom and the top.

The windows were shuttered and the door closed when the Apsaras stopped half-way down the porch. Boran knocked, then the tall door was opened by another guard. Teak walls gleamed black, reflecting torches in brackets on the walls. Boran bowed deeply in sampeah, but did not prostrate himself. Following him inside, Bopha saw that only the King and one other man were in the room, besides three musicians. It was warmer inside than the evening chill outside, and Bopha's goose bumps relaxed.

A table covered with a thick, embroidered cloth was against one wall. On it she could see plates of fruit, a stack of bowls and one of cups, and a pitcher. The King reclined on a wide bench covered with silk fabric and thick cushions. The other man sat relaxed on another bench. Bopha thought she recognized him from other events. His gold necklace was a very different design than the King's and the King's Man. Kiri, she thought. The King's Man is Kiri.

"Welcome, Apsaras." The King's voice reeled her back into the room. "As you can see," he gestured around the room, "tonight is not the usual fancy occasion. There is no ceremony, no celebration. We just want a few short dances. And after," he gestured toward the table, "we hope you will honor us by sharing a small repast." He looked right at Bopha. The room suddenly seemed much warmer. The King leaned back against cushions. The musicians started a simple melody that the dancers immediately recognized. It was a village wedding song. They all knew the steps. Thida led them, weaving and turning through the happy movements.

When the song ended, the dancers were formed in a triangle. Bopha facing the King, Thida the other man, and Nary the musicians. The King inclined his head to her, his full lips curved into a smile. She felt the smile warming her, and she returned it. Her King was happy. The Apsaras bowed and reformed their line. This time, the musicians played a very fast tune and Bopha had to concentrate hard. The King was laughing out loud when they ended. "Beautiful!" He chuckled again, then said, "Lest we wear you out, let the next dance be more gentle.

The flute lifted Bopha slowly and gracefully, then the khim droned deep in her center. This dance opened the hips, the drum beat rotating and rocking the dancer's pelvis. Suddenly Bopha was soaring, arms outstretched, then back into her body, curling into herself while energy pulsed from between her legs up to the top of her head, around and around. Despite the slow pace, she was panting when the last chord died away. Her back continued to zing and tingle and she couldn't control her breath. Her eyes were locked into the King's when she fully returned to her body.

Thida glanced surreptitiously at her, her beautiful eyes asking "are you okay?" Bopha gave her a tiny nod. The dancers bowed in sampeah until the King said, his voice husky, "Thank you." He cleared his throat, but his next words were still deeper than his usual deep. "May we offer you some refreshment?"

A servant had entered the room, poured a cup and sipped it. The King watched. The man nodded. Then the King stood, and led the young women to the table. He himself poured each of them a cup from the pitcher. The other man and Boran had come near. The King handed Nary a cup, then Thida, and lastly Bopha. When she reached for it, his fingers burned into hers. She caught her breath and looked up at him. He was Kiri's height, so her head was somewhat higher than his chin. The height of his lips, her mind told her. His eyes were smiling. She dropped hers and took a step back.

Jayavarman VII invited each to take a bowl of fruit and bring it, with their cups, to the benches. The Apsaras sat in a line, the King sat next to Bopha, and the other man and Boran sat at the other end, next to Thida. The King lifted his cup, "To my Apsaras, whose celestial dancing brings prosperity to the land." He sipped. Everyone else lifted their cups and took a sip.

The liquid was cold and hot at the same time, cool on the tongue, hot in the throat. Bopha felt the burn all the way to her stomach. She coughed, a little cough, much to Jayavarman's amusement.

"So, Preah Chan Bopha, you have never had such nectar?"

She shook her head, trying not to cough again. She saw Boran look at her with concern. After swallowing a few more times, Bopha managed to say, "No, my Lord. Nothing like this. It is cold, but it burns." All the men laughed. From the King and Boran, the laugh felt gentle, soothing. But the other man's had a hard edge that made her uncomfortable.

"That it is," said the King. "And, how do you like being an Apsara?" He was still talking to her. In a tiny voice, Bopha managed, "I love to dance, my Lord. Thank you."

The King turned his attention to Thida and Nary, asking them similar questions. He lifted his cup again, and everyone took another sip. This time Bopha knew not to take too big a one. It tasted better, somehow, and she began to feel better. The butterflies in her stomach flew away. When the King looked at her, she smiled at him again. He said, "Have some fruit. Please. The bounty of our orchards, for the most beautiful women in the land."

Bopha had chosen one of the sweet little bananas, easy to eat. She saw that the other dancers had done the same, but Boran had taken slices of mango and the other man durian. They each ate, the men with gusto, slurping a little, the women nibbling daintily. Bopha peeled more of her banana and was about to take another bite when the King turned to her.

"We have invited your brother, the monk Rithy, to come to Bayon and be with us. He is a very smart young man. It is not easy to learn reading and writing, but he does it like he has done it before. Who knows? Maybe he was a famous scholar in a previous life."

Bopha nearly dropped her banana. She looked at the King. "Yes, my Lord. He is very happy about that." Then she added, "and very grateful to your Majesty for this chance." Something impelled her to add, "Ever since he was a little boy, he wanted to become a monk, to travel and to learn. When we were still in our village, he told me about the wide roads you had built that go all over the Kingdom, and about boats, and about the ocean."

The room was very quiet. Everyone looked at her. Her head felt a little funny. What was she doing, talking like this to the King, as if he were one of her friends? She gave an apologetic shrug.

The deep voice reassured her, "It is nice to hear someone talking as if the King were a friend. Not everyone dares to do that." He smiled gently at her. He had read her mind. Out of the corner of her eye, Bopha thought she saw the other man stiffen. Boran was nodding very slightly. "You will have to come again and tell me more."

Soon after, the King dismissed the dancers. "Now there is some business that cannot wait," he said. "My Minister Kosal has much to discuss with me."

Bopha felt a little unsteady when she stood, and her head felt even more funny. Boran waited until the dancers had passed, then walked behind Bopha. She felt his presence supporting her. At the bottom of the steps, she whispered to him, "Thank you. I think that cold-hot liquid is not good for me."

"Probably not," he agreed. "But the King may disagree." They walked in silence the rest of the way home, Bopha replaying the evening, and Boran's words.

CHAPTER 10

1192 - 1193, Telling Truth to Power

Before the moon cycled again, Bopha was summoned to the Palace. This time, Kesor went with her, but no other dancers. They were escorted to yet a different room. This one had high stools, set in front of tall benches that faced long windows. It was late afternoon and golden light poured in, filtered through huge trees. Monks were sitting on the stools. Bopha had seen scribes in the market, and recognized what they were doing. Writing! The figures the scribes drew looked so funny, some of them dancing, some floating on their backs.

But why was a dancer in a room full of monks writing? Bopha and Kesor stood in the doorway. The monks, well-trained, never looked up from their tasks. Boran looked around, then walked to a bench in the far corner. At his approach, the monk there looked up and Bopha recognized her brother. Boran offered sampeah, returned by Rithy, then motioned him to follow.

Bopha remembered not to hug her brother, but her smile enveloped him, as his did in turn. Boran was also smiling warmly. Kesor's smile was stiff, like a dancer in pain.

"Come," said Boran. "The King is waiting."

King Jayavarman VII was in the room where Bopha last saw him. He was alone, except for the guards outside the door. There was no sign of the cushions or the table. The windows were open. The same golden light that filled the writing room welcomed them. The King gestured them to come close.

Where the light touched the King's face, Bopha could see that he looked tired. He was not a young man, but not yet old. She thought he was probably older than Aupouk. She lost her smile, thinking of what Aupouk looked like the day she left her village. She wondered about the gash she had seen when the King came back from fighting the Cham. Had it healed?

"No smile for your King, Preah Chan Bopha?"

"I'm sorry, Your Majesty." Bopha was flustered, and floundered on, "I was thinking about your face, and then about my father. And about the wound you got from the Cham. The one on your back."

"My back?" It was the King's turn to be surprised. Bopha could see Rithy, Kesor and Boran all looked stunned.

"Yes, Your Majesty." Bopha looked at him, concern on her beautiful face, "I saw it when you came past the gate of the young dancers' courtyard. It looked so red and sore. And so big." Stop, Bopha's mind told her. Be quiet.

But the King leaned back, gazing at the young woman in front of him. "That was years ago." Bopha nodded. "And you remember that I was hurt." She nodded again. He nodded. "I am touched by your concern. Rest assured that, by the will of the gods, my back is a strong as ever." He looked at Rithy. "And you, young monk Rithy, what about you?"

Rithy, hands in sampeah, looked confused. "Your Majesty?"

"What do you have to say to your King?" Before Rithy could muster words, the King looked at Boran and Kesor. "You two may wait outside. We won't be long." The two adults bowed and backed out the door. Jayavarman VII turned back to Rithy, "Well?"

"I don't know what to say, Your Majesty," Rithy fumbled, looking at his prayerful hands.

"Well, I don't want to hear whatever you think I might *want* to hear. Your sister has twice told me just what was on her mind. It is not common for a monarch to hear such truth. Since you are her brother, I thought you might also risk honesty."

Rithy stood up a little straighter and lifted his eyes. "In all truth, your Majesty, I am honored. And I am afraid. I am afraid not to tell you what I think, but that I have to tell you my mind is blank." He almost chuckled. "That is what we monks seek, but right now it is not what I would want."

King Jayavarman VII stared, then chuckled, then laughed out loud. Rithy snuck a glance at Bopha then both of them just stood looking at the King. His laugh was infectious, joyous, and they had trouble not to join with him. "I got what I asked for," said the King, and started laughing again.

This time Bopha started to giggle. Once started, the more she tried to stop, the more she laughed. Within a few moments, Rithy was having the same trouble. The three chuckled and giggled until they were almost gasping.

Finally the ruler of all Kampuchea, builder of Bayon, conqueror of the Cham, wiped his eyes and squeaked, "I haven't laughed like this since ... I don't know when. Maybe when I was a young boy and got the giggles during a very solemn ceremony. Kiri and I actually had to leave the King's audience hall. It was very bad." He paused, grinning, "But so funny!" He chuckled, then added, "We were beaten with thick straps afterwards. But it was the only time we were."

He took a deep, shaky breath, still smiling widely and looked at Bopha and Rithy. "Thank you. You cannot know what a gift it is for a King to hear the truth, and to laugh without restraint. We will meet again." He winked at Rithy, which caused Bopha to chuckle. "Next time, bring your King a few more thoughts."

He winked at Bopha, and she, without thinking, immediately winked back. They smiled at each other. "Preah Chan Bopha, you are a most beautiful woman, a most gifted dancer, and a treasure of truth for your King." He gave sampeah, looking in her eyes. She lifted her hands the same.

Then Rithy and Bopha bowed and backed out of the room. On the porch, Boran and Kesor were smiling but looked confused. Even the guards had slight curls at the edges of their lips. Rithy returned to his work in the writing room, which was just down the porch a few doors.

No one spoke until they were off the Palace grounds. Finally Kesor asked, "What was that all about?" Bopha tried to explain, but it was impossible, partly because just thinking about it stirred her to fits of giggles. "Well, it seemed like the King was happy, whatever it was," Kesor said.

Bopha nodded, then said thoughtfully, "It isn't easy to be King. You have wealth and power, but maybe not truth."

Boran was studying the young Apsara. "I think you are right," he said slowly. "There is so much ceremony and protocol in a King's life, vying factions, intrigue. During battle, there is not so much of that, especially not for a King like Jayavarman VII, who fights right alongside his soldiers." They reached the big road and stopped talking. But Bopha considered his words, the corners of her mouth still happy from the unexpected laughter.

* * *

Arun Veha was holding Bopha's hand tightly, walking with a sailor's tipsy gait. "He's so strong," Bopha told Kalienne. They were strolling along the baray in late afternoon heat. Clouds had bunched up, covering the sky.

"I know. It won't be long before he'll be running," said Kalienne. Bopha swung the toddler up in her arms and met her friend's eyes.

"When will you move? I know it's better than being in that tiny room in a filthy alley, but I'm going to miss you." She gently swayed the baby side to side, his legs dangling. He laughed so hard he got the hiccups. "And you're going to miss Auntie Bopha, aren't' you?" She moved him to her hip, and grabbed Kalienne's hand as they headed back to the room. A few raindrops splattered on the dirt of the road.

Kiri had rented a small house half a day's walk from Bayon. It was only an hour or so by horseback. They had chosen the village for the sake of discretion. "I wish I could ride a horse," Bopha said suddenly. "Then I could come easily."

Kalienne grinned, "That would be a sight! A woman on a horse!" Sobering, she continued, "I wish you could come easily as well. I'm not sure when we go — but before the next full moon." The raindrops became heavier. The young women picked up their pace, then ran down the alley. By the time they made the turn, it was pouring. Bopha put Arun Veha down and got a kromah to dry his dripping hair. He pulled away, wanting to go back outside.

"You'll get wet," Bopha cautioned the little boy as he stepped past the curtain. The alley had become a small stream, and the rain poured off the roof in sheets. When the water hit his head, he started to cry.

Kalienne laughed. "That's what you get for not listening to Auntie Bopha," she told him. "Come here, little silly." She squatted, reaching out her arms. Arun Veha, sniffling, snuggled his soaked body into her. "Oh, you are so wet!"

Bopha crouched next to them, "This is called rain," she told him. "Sometimes it's just a little bit, a few drops. But now it's rainy season, and the water comes down as if the gods had turned over a bucket in the sky." She mimed lifting a bucket up high and pouring it out. Arun Veha looked at her closely. He lifted his arms. "That's right," she told him. Then she stood and showed him a few dance positions. He tried to stand on one leg but started to fall. Kalienne steadied him.

"Do you think he'll be a dancer?" Bopha suddenly asked. "When I see the King's Man getting on and off his horse, I wonder if he was a dancer." She couldn't bring herself to call him Kiri, even in private.

"I wonder. Kiri loves dancing," Kalienne said. "If he weren't of noble birth, he would have done that. But the King told him, way back when they were children, that he needed Kiri to be his friend and counselor when he became King." The two young women looked at the sturdy little boy, who was now squatting in the doorway. He put his hand out into the stream of water coming from the roof, then pulled it back when the stream hit, then put it out again. "He's so inquisitive. I hope he can play with other children in the village."

"How will you explain yourself there?" Bopha asked.

"Some of the truth. I went to Bayon to be a dancer but wasn't chosen. My village was destroyed by the Cham so I stayed in this area, since I had no family left. I got married but my husband died. One of his cousins is watching out for me. When Kiri comes, he will ride an old horse and dress plainly." Kalienne stopped, then added, 'I thought I could offer to teach children dancing."

Bopha nodded. She knew it was too risky for Kalienne and Arun Veha to stay near Bayon. Every few months, the King would call for her and Rithy to come "tell him the truth." She hoped he never had reason to ask about this situation. A chill ran up her spine and the hair on her arms raised. She reached for the kromah and dried her hair and body. "I'd better be going." Kalienne stood up with her and the two friends hugged. Bopha loved the feeling of her friend's breasts against hers, and held tight. But just for a moment. She kissed Kalienne's cheek and Kalienne touched her lips.

"Kiri will make sure you can come before we leave."

"He's been good about that," Bopha admitted grudgingly. "But Kesor will be glad when it is over. I don't know what story she concocted about my absences. People understand that Apsaras sometimes are summoned to go alone ... somewhere."

As she walked back to the dancers' courtyard, Bopha wondered again what Kesor had said. Lately, when she and Rithy went to Bayon, the King had been looking at her more deeply. He never touched her, but sometimes she felt like his eyes were stroking her.

Her nipples stiffened as she remembered the last time. Maybe Kalienne's hope was coming true, that she could feel for a man the way she felt when she was in Kalienne's arms.

* * *

"I am going to have dancing here next week," Jayavarman told Bopha, his eyes searching hers. She and Rithy were sitting on either side of the King. The young people faced the king, whose bench was higher than theirs. "But you will be the only dancer."

Bopha's eyes widened and she saw Rithy's do the same. "Rithy will come as well. After two dances, I want you both to stay, sitting on benches to one side. My minister, Khosal, and I will confer. You are to watch him carefully. He will not be pleased by your presence." The King looked troubled. Bopha wished she could make him feel better."

"I will do whatever you desire, my Lord," she said. He reached his hand out, but didn't touch her. She felt warm energy on her arm where he didn't. She looked at her arm, then at him. He nodded.

"Thank you, Preah Chan Bopha. Thank you for being honest with me. You and this monk Rithy," he turned his gaze to the young man, who met it calmly, "will leave before the two of us are done talking. But I will send for you in a few days to hear your thoughts about Minister Khosal." He looked like he was going to say more, but stopped. "You may go now."

103

Bopha's heart was pounding. For some reason she felt uncertain, almost scared, as she and Rithy backed out of the hall, hands in sampeah. The heavy door had been closed after them when they arrived. Now Rithy opened it. Outside, the guards stood stolid. Kesor no longer accompanied her to the palace, but Boran did. He was squatting in the shade on the porch. The sun was setting on the other side of the building. Boran stood and looked at her, but didn't say anything.

Rithy and Bopha felt a weight between them as their eyes met. He lifted his hands and nodded, then they bowed slightly. Rithy went down the porch to the scribe's room and Bopha followed Boran down the stairs. She had seen Minister Khosal many times when she came in small groups to dance. He always seemed tense. When she felt his eyes on her, Bopha felt somehow dirtied. Not like when the King's Man or the King looked at her.

Too soon the day came. Thida braided Bopha's hair. Kesor gave her the box with her necklace in it. She showed Bopha how to do the clasp at the back of her neck, and watched till the young woman had done it correctly several times. Kesor's face was almost grim when she made sampeah to Boran as he and the dancer left. Two guards Bopha vaguely recognized walked in front of them. The sun set as they approached Bayon. The walk seemed to take no time at all.

Rithy was waiting for her at the top of the stairs. He was wearing yellow robes. Bopha wished they could talk. She wondered what wisdom her brother could give her to calm her muddled mind. The door was open, and they entered. Then the guard closed the door.

King Jayavarman VII sat on cushions in his accustomed place, Minister Khosal to his left. The musicians were waiting, next to the altar. The table was again set against the back wall. The scent of fish amok cooking in the kitchens wafted in the west windows on a light breeze. Bopha was glad for the air. As if reading her mind, the King picked up a small bronze bell and rang it. A door she had never noticed opened at the back of the room. Two little boys came in and started to work the huge fans. The creak of the ropes was the only sound.

"Welcome, monk Nimith Vireak and Apsara Preah Chan Bopha." The King's deep voice filled Bopha with pleasure. But why did he call her brother Nimith Vireak? There was no way for her to find out now. Rithy bowed and sat on a far bench. "Now, let the dance begin."

The first notes tingled in Bopha's back. Once, as she turned, she met Minister Khosal's eyes. It was like looking at a stone, but not like the stone eyes of Garuda. These glittered with malevolence and Bopha felt suddenly cold. Then the music carried her to the King. He looked concerned, and she smiled more fully. Her King was a good man, and he would protect her. Knowing that, she relaxed into the sound and movement, feeling herself carried on huge soft wings, as she twirled and swayed.

After two dances, that seemed short to the Apsara whose back was on fire with energy, the King again rang the bell. Several servants brought plates and bowls filled with food. Bopha hadn't realized how hungry she was until the smell hit her stomach, which growled loudly. The King and Minister Khosal had preceded her to the table. The King turned when he heard the grumble. "So, Preah Chan Bopha, the King's feast appeals to you?" His voice was laughing.

She smiled into his warm, dark eyes, "Yes, my Lord. Apparently that is the truth." He chuckled. She felt Minister Khosal stiffen with disapproval but she did not look at him.

One of the servants put rice and fish amok on a plate, tasted it, and nodded to the King, then poured a cup of liquid and did the same. "Well, I guess I won't die of poison tonight," said the King. Bopha was startled. Another thing that was hard about being a ruler! The servant brought the plate and cup to the King's seat. When everyone was served, the servants left but the fan boys remained. Bopha was glad, since the evening was hot with the promise of more rain.

Conversation was stilted as the four of them ate. Bopha was aware of Minister Khosal watching her closely. She sat straight and said little. Rithy too said little, but Bopha could tell he was tracking every nuance. After the meal, King Jayavarman rang the bell. Servants cleared the plates, closed the windows to the front porch, and left with the fan boys. Thunder rumbled and more wind came in the west windows. Bopha and Rithy had moved to a bench slightly behind the King while the servants were working.

"So, my friend, Minister Khosal, what do you have to tell me?" The King's voice was clear in the nearly empty room. Bopha suddenly wondered if the porch windows were closed so no one there could hear him.

Khosal was facing the King, both sitting cross-legged on cushions, Jayavarman on his higher bench. To Bopha, the minister looked uneasy, and seemed to have trouble meeting the King's eyes. Jayavarman did not seem to notice, maintaining an easy, inviting countenance.

"Well, my Lord. I have heard some rumors that you will not want to hear." Khosal shifted on his cushion. His voice was tight and high, like something was around his throat. The King waited. "They concern Prime Minister Kiri." Bopha nearly fell off her bench, and stifled a gasp. The King waited, frowning slightly. "It seems," Khosal shifted again, "it seems he may have a son that he is hiding from you."

Khosal looked simultaneously sorrowful, concerned and secretly pleased. Bopha was afraid she might have to leave the room and move her bowels. She felt Rithy's eyes on her. After a moment, the urge passed but the young woman did not relax. Her gaze was locked on the two men in front of her.

King Jayavarman's placid expression tightened. "How does this news come to you?"

Khosal shifted again. He looked at the King then down at his hands, then out the window. "I had him followed."

"What caused you to do such a thing?" The King's voice was hard. The minister shifted again.

Khosal had a whiny edge when he replied, "I had heard that he might have had a ... relationship." Khosal looked directly at the King. "Because his wife..."

"Enough!" shouted the King. "You will not speak of my sister." The room still rang when he was quiet again.

Khosal shrugged apologetically, dropping his eyes. Then he said, softly, "He has been keeping the woman in an alley at the market." Suddenly Khosal looked directly at Bopha, triumph vying with   obsequiousness.

CHAPTER 11

1193, Dengue

Bopha wanted to run out of the room, to find Kiri and Kalienne and warn them. Had the King any idea what might be discussed when he told her and Rithy to come? Her thoughts were swirling. She glanced at Rithy, who was closely watching the men's interaction. He felt her gaze and looked quickly at her. Something in her face reflected on his. Bopha suddenly knew that anyone who looked at her would know. She looked at her hands, and gently lifted them into a jeeb of peace. The movement brought some relief and she did a few more, breathing slowly and fully.

When she lifted her eyes, she saw the King had followed Minister Khosal's gaze. His eyes were troubled as he looked at her. She was flooded with longing to protect him from all pain. Her King, this ruler who couldn't eat or drink without fear of poison, who supported her, asking nothing but for her to dance her best and to tell him truth. She met his long gaze, and saw him relax.

Khosal watched them both. Rithy noted the minister quickly hid the envy and hatred that flashed across his face. This man wanted to hurt his sister and his King. When Jayavarman turned back to Khosal, the minister was looking at him with sorrowful calm.

There was a long silence.

"You two may leave now," Jayavarman said, turning again to the young people. When the door had closed behind them, Bopha could hear indistinct voices from inside, the deep rumble of the King and the high whine of his minister.

Boran was waiting for her, but Bopha turned to her brother. "Why did the King call you Nimith Vireak? And when did you get yellow robes?

Rithy looked at her somberly. "It's hard to believe, but I have been here as a novice for seven years. This week, at my full ordination, the abbot gave me the name 'Nimith Vireak.' It means transformation and absence of desire." He paused. "That is a worthy goal," he said wryly, which Bopha understood to mean that he was having a desire he could not express to her. She thought it might be the same one she had. She wanted nothing more than to sit with him under a banyan tree and tell him the whole story. Surely he could advise her what to do.

Instead, the siblings just looked at each other. Then Rithy gave sampeah and turned toward the writing room. Bopha watched him walk away, tall and straight, without a backward glance.

She sighed. The voices inside were still talking indistinctly. Boran looked at her. She shrugged and gave him sampeah. They didn't speak on the walk back to the dancers' dormitory, but at the gate, Bopha turned to the kind guard. "Thank you, Boran, for taking such good care of me. Ever since I was just a little girl." Tears hung in her eyes, invisible in the dark.

Boran bowed slightly, then murmured, "Please take care with yourself, Preah Chan Bopha." She heard worry in his voice.

That night Bopha slept restlessly. Twice she woke suddenly, panting for breath as a huge snake tried to wrap itself around her. The second time, its eyes stared into hers, and she was chilled when she sat up. This woke Nuon, who whispered, "Are you okay?"

"I'm having bad dreams," Bopha whispered back. Then added, "Snakes." The word hissed in the darkness. Bopha pulled a cover over herself when she finally lay down again.

In the morning, Bopha's body felt heavy and her head dull and aching. She tried to follow the dancing but kept stumbling. Finally Kesor pulled her aside.

"What is wrong?"

"My head ached when I got up, and now my whole body feels like it's breaking. And I'm on fire."

Kesor put her hand to Bopha's forehead. "You are burning up. Go to bed. And put on lots of covers." Bopha staggered to the steps and pulled herself up each one. She was feeling worse and worse. Nuon followed her and set out the sleeping mat. She helped Bopha lie down then brought covers. By now Bopha was shivering, which made her muscles and bones hurt even more.

"I'll bring you tea. You need to keep drinking," the younger girl said.

"I feel too sick to drink. I might vomit, but I don't think I can get up."

"Hold on, I'll get a chamber pot," Nuon said, running for the door.

For a week, Bopha lay on the mat. After the first two days, she stopped vomiting but had no appetite. Nuon and Sophea checked on her frequently, bringing tea and small plates of rice, encouraging her. Her head felt like her eyes were going to pop out, so Bopha covered her face whenever the windows were unshuttered.

"You are red all over," Sophea told her one morning, as Bopha lay with a kromah over her eyes. "Your skin is covered with red spots."

Kesor came to look. "I have seen this before. Most people get better after a few weeks," she told the young women. She didn't add that, if they got the rash again a few years later, they often died. Her touch on Bopha's forehead was gentle. "Your fever is better this morning."

But by afternoon, Bopha was so hot she couldn't move except to shiver. She lost track of time. Sometimes it was so bright she had to cover her eyes. The next minute it would be dead of night. People came and went, obscure beings. Once she thought she heard a man's voice. Sometimes she knew it was Nuon or Sophea supporting her head so she could take a sip of bitter liquid. Mostly she couldn't tell who was there, and she didn't care.

Bopha felt the snake squeezing her chest. When she opened her eyes, its narrow, scaly head was right there. The snake flicked its thin tongue in and out. "Now I've got you. What are you going to do about it?" The voice was familiar, high and whiny. But Bopha couldn't remember who sounded like that. She drifted into sleep, too exhausted to run away or to fight the horrid creature.

Vaguely she heard the music of the dance of Garuda killing the Nagas. It came from below. It was dance practice in the courtyard, but to Bopha it was salvation. In her mind, she saw Dara twirling and stamping and clawing. A screeching cry filled her entire being. Then, nothing. When she woke next, Bopha was looking into the stone eye of Garuda. She wasn't shivering. "Do not fear," said the creaky, deep voice. "All will be well." Each feather glinted in angled light from the open windows. Bopha's headache was gone.

She sat up, early morning sun pouring onto her mat. On the floor was a small covered pot. She lifted the lid and inhaled the sweet smell of rice. Suddenly famished, Bopha formed a ball with her fingers and popped it into her mouth. A figure in the door said,

"Hurray, look who's eating!"

Nuon came to sit with her. With awe in her voice, she told Bopha that the King had sent his own doctor to examine her and give medicine. Bopha had a swirly recollection of a bald man with a thin mustache bending over her. Maybe that hadn't been a hallucination. What about the snake? She gasped as a slithery form wriggled out the door. "What's wrong? Are you okay?" Nuon was at her elbow and Bopha returned to the room.

"I thought I saw a snake."

Nuon jumped up and looked around the empty room. Except for Bopha's mat, everything else had been put away for the day. "I don't see it. Are you sure?"

"No, I'm not sure," Bopha said slowly. Her voice sounded funny after two weeks of not being used. "I'm not sure of anything." She turned to Nuon. "You said the King sent me a doctor? And medicine?"

Nuon nodded. "Kesor says he sometimes does that for Apsaras, but it has been a very long time."

The King. Bopha turned the words over in her mind. The King. She could see him on his horse, tall in the saddle, the terrible wound on his back after fighting the Cham. His eyes looking into hers, all the way inside her, after she danced. His face tired. Him laughing until everyone who heard it fell into giggles. The tiny black hairs on his hand, extended in front of her. The smell of sandalwood glistening on his chest. The warmth on her arm where he hadn't touched. His eyes, troubled as he searched hers, then relaxing as her longing to protect him from pain poured out of her, wave upon wave. Bopha stiffened.

Khosal. The snake.

"Do not fear. All will be well." Garuda had come to protect her from the snake. She saw again his stone feathers and deep eye. Her body relaxed.

"I'm better, but I think I need a nap," she told Nuon, who had been watching her friend, concern on her face.

Nuon took the rice bowl. Bopha was asleep before Nuon got to the door.

Next time Bopha woke, it was midday hot. She tried to get up from the sleeping pad. Her bones didn't ache, but she was so weak it took several tries, and then her head was spinning, or the room was spinning, as she stood. Sophea came in just then, and rushed to steady her. Though she was petite, Sophea's arm around her was strong as iron.

"Thanks," said Bopha. "I didn't know I was so weak."

"Well, you've been lying down for two weeks," Sophea told her.

"Two weeks? I guess I lost track of time."

"You did a lot of muttering, and sometimes, when you looked up, you didn't seem to see me. And sometimes you seemed very frightened."

Bopha considered this, as Sophea helped her toward the door. "I think I was very frightened sometimes. I kept seeing snakes. But Garuda came and saved me, and when I woke up the next time, my fever and pain were gone."

"Maybe when you get your strength back, you can give incense prayers to him," Sophea suggested.

"I'd like to go to the stone carvers," said Bopha, nodding, "and thank him in person."

Sophea looked confused and then concerned. "Not that he's a person," said Bopha quickly. She lifted her hand to shelter her eyes. "It sure is bright outside."

With one hand holding tight to the railing and the other on Sophea's shoulder, Bopha got down the steps. It was lunch time and the Apsaras were eating in the shadows. Nuon ran up to help them get to a seat under one of the trees. Bopha sank gratefully onto a banyan knee,

Kesor came up to the three young women. Relief was in her voice. "We are so glad that you are better, Preah Chan Bopha. You have been very sick for several weeks."

Bopha made sampeah. "Thank you for taking care of me, Kesor."

"We can't let anything happen to the King's favorite Apsara," said Kesor, smiling gently. Bopha was surprised by the words, and by something in the older woman's tone. It wasn't envy and it wasn't awe. It was matter-of-fact-ness, and appreciation. "I'll send word about your recovery to the King and to your brother."

"Thank you," Bopha said again. Kesor nodded and left.

"I'll get you lunch," Nuon offered.

"Thank you. You two are such good friends. Where would I be without your help?"

Sophea's smile was genuine and open, and she reached for Bopha's hand. "We were all very worried."

* * *

For several more weeks, Bopha stayed in the dancers' courtyard, slowly regaining her strength. It was a week before she even tried to join the dance practice, and she could only manage an hour. But she sat in the shade and watched, stretching her hands and feet. Her mind returned over and over to the images, so clear when so much else was murky, of the snake and of Garuda. She remembered where her life had been that fateful night at the palace, and she wondered what had happened since.

The King's Man visited the day after Bopha first came downstairs. He was formal and there was no chance to talk privately. "His Majesty is glad that you are better and he wishes you a speedy recovery," was all he said as Bopha sat on a banyan knee among the dancers, before afternoon practice.

Her hands in sampeah, she did dare to answer him, "Please tell His Majesty how much it means to have his good wishes, and thank him for sending his doctor and medicine."

Kiri nodded. He watched some of the practice, then disappeared. Bopha realized she had thought of him as Kiri.

Bopha waited for a chance to talk with Kesor. The woman was very busy since, while Bopha was ill, new Apsaras had graduated into the adepts' courtyard. Sophea and Nuon were both mentoring now, and Bopha's banyan tree welcomed all five of them, plus Thida, who often sat with them. Tevy was round and full of fun, quite a contrast to Sophea's crisp demeanor. Her name meant "angel," and Bopha thought she brought an angel influence to her friend. For her part, Sophea was a kind mentor, not carrying on the tyrannical legacy she had inherited. Theary was tall and slender, towering over Nuon, who would always be on the short side. But she lived up to the meaning "helper." She jumped up to get Bopha whatever she wanted.

"You are all spoiling me. I have to do things for myself or I'll never get strong," Bopha joked.

Late one afternoon, after Bopha managed to complete a full day of dancing, Kesor found her alone under the tree. "How are you feeling after dancing all day?"

"I'm tired, but my strength is returning. Every day is better." Bopha stopped and considered. She was very aware, now, of truth and half-truth. "Well, at least every other day is better. Sometimes if I do too much, I am more tired the next day."

Kesor listened, nodding. "The King's Man will come for you tomorrow." Her eyes gave nothing away, but there was a hint of sadness in them. "In the morning. So you will not come to morning practice." The two women looked at each other as Nuon and Theary came into their shade. "I'm glad you are stronger."

Bopha had been sleeping soundly every night, as if her body soaked up healing while she slept. But this night she woke several times, not from dreams but from roiling thoughts. Was Kalienne still at Bayon? Had the King talked with Kiri? Each time, she heard the grating reassurance, "Do not fear. All will be well," and fell asleep smiling.

After breakfast, the King's Man arrived. He left the horse under a tree and walked in front of Bopha down the road and through the bustling market. It wasn't until they turned into the alley that Bopha asked, "Kiri, did the King talk with you?"

Kiri stopped short at the sound of his real name from the lips of this Apsara who knew his secret. He looked at her sharply. "No. Why do you think he would do so?"

Bopha looked around, but the alley was empty. She told him about Minister Khesol having him followed, and telling the King about Arun Veha and Kalienne. "He did not tell any names, not while I was there," she said.

Kiri's face was stony. "That snake," he said. Bopha recoiled at the word. "What?"

Kiri said grimly, "It's true. He would like nothing better than to have me killed."

Bopha found herself telling the tall man about her vision when she was sick, about being squeezed by the snake. Then she told him about Garuda, and the voice that continued to reassure her.

"Do not fear," Kiri said thoughtfully, appraising Bopha. "Good advice. I certainly hope all will be well."

"I wanted to warn you, but then I got sick," Bopha started.

Two old ladies limped into the alley. Bopha and Kiri stepped back to let them pass.

"Enough for now," said Kiri. "Thank you. I will talk with Jaya. I mean, with the King."

Bopha smiled inside to hear that childhood nickname fall off his tongue. Jaya. She wondered if she would ever know the King well enough to call him that. Suddenly she wanted that more than anything. She could hardly wait to see him again. But when?

It was not up to her. She sighed, and followed Kiri around the turn.

Childish laughter rang against the narrow walls outside Kalienne's room. Arun Veha was throwing stones into a puddle left from last night's rain. His legs were spattered with mud. Kalienne looked up at the sound of Kiri's footsteps. Bopha saw her eyes fill with happiness, then worry as he got closer.

"What's wrong?"

"The King has been warned about us," Kiri told her simply, touching her shoulder gently. "I'm going to talk with him now." Kalienne's beautiful eyes had filled with tears and fear.

Kiri put one finger to her cheek. "I'll be back as soon as I can. With the old horse. We should leave shortly after lunch."

Both young women watched the tall man till he made the turn. Bopha thought his shoulders looked tired. Arun Veha had stopped throwing stones and was trying to follow Kiri, calling "Aupu! Aupu!"

Bopha gathered the little boy up, "Aupouk will be back. Let's go to the baray while we wait."

It was a long wait. They sat watching the water, then showing Arun Veha the little fish in the shallows, then throwing pebbles. Bopha got lunch for them all in the market while Kalienne and her son went to the tiny room. It was cramped and stuffy as they squatted next to the bench to eat. Time crept past. Kalienne had all their things wrapped, then she unpacked the mat and a kromah to give Arun Veha his nap.

Bopha told her about the evening with the King and Minister Khosal, then how sick she had been. "I wanted to come right away, to warn you, but ..."

"I'm glad you are better, Bopha," Kalienne said gently. After a moment's silence she asked, "Tell me again about the voice you heard."

Bopha tried to describe the sound, deep and creaky and grating. The feelings she felt when she heard it were relief, hope, peace.   "Do   not   fear.   All   will   be   well."

CHAPTER 12

Almost

Suddenly Bopha jumped up, whispering to Kalienne, "I have to go. I lost track of time. Kesor released me from morning practice, but now it's long after lunch." Arun Veha turned over on the mat at the sound of her voice, but did not wake. Kalienne nodded.

"I wish I could stay, but..."

"I know. You can't." Kalienne's face was somber in the gloom, but she managed a crooked smile, "Don't worry. All will be well." After a beat she added, "I'll ask Kiri to get you a message before we leave." She stood and the two friends hugged, then Bopha slipped out the door, walking fast down the alley.

Bopha had missed part of practice but not much. Kesor gave her a sharp look but said nothing. Thida looked at her questioningly. She realized that her unexplained absence would give the Apsaras a lot to wonder about, which she regretted. She was starting to understand how dangerous tongues could be, wagging with rumor.

No message came. Bopha sat where she could see the gate as she stretched her feet and half-listened to her friends chatting under the tree around her. She hoped everything was okay with Kalienne. Not knowing was the worst. Sophea had asked her privately why she was so late, but Bopha just shrugged and said, "I lost track of time." That was the truth. Though not the whole truth. Sophea searched her face. Bopha met her gaze, then looked down.

"Okay," was all Sophea said, then, "Take care of yourself, Bopha."

Bopha sighed deeply and nodded. "Thanks for understanding." She squeezed Sophea's hand. "It means a lot."

Sophea caught her eye now, and Bopha realized she had been staring at the gate. She tried to remember what Tevy had just said so she could make some joking comment, but she couldn't think straight. "Maybe I need to take a nap before supper," she said instead. "I'm not completely recovered."

At the top of the steps, she turned to look again at the gate, and saw Sophea watching her. She waved and went into the room. But she couldn't sleep. All her worries wrangled around her as she tossed and turned. Finally Bopha turned to Garuda. "You told me not to worry," she said. "But I can't help it. Please help my friends. Even Kiri, he has become a friend. And he couldn't help falling in love with Kalienne. Please take care of them." No answer came in the late afternoon dimness of the dormitory, but Bopha felt her heart ease. "Thank you. I'll get incense tomorrow morning."

The supper gong sounded just as rain started pounding on the roof. Bopha waited a few minutes till the worst of the downpour passed, then ran to the kitchen porch. It was still raining quite thoroughly. Everyone was crowded back from the drip line. She joined her friends in the line, then they covered their food with their kromahs and rushed to get under the dormitory porch to eat.

"Rainy season!" Tevy's voice was perplexed. "When it's hot season, I can't wait for the rains to start. Now, I can't wait for it to be over. It seems like forever." The young women squatted under shelter and ate.

"Bopha, tomorrow you, Sophea and I are going to the Palace," Thida told her. A messenger came from the King while you were resting."

A messenger! Bopha's heart jumped at the word, but the message sobered her. "Just us three?"

Thida nodded. "I heard the cooks saying that an ambassador from Pagan has come."

"What will we dance?"

"That is up to his Majesty,"Thida reminded her, with a funny look. "Are you sure you're okay?"

Bopha nodded slowly. "Yes. I think so. I'm just feeling distracted. Maybe in the morning we can go to the Garuda atelier in the market. I want to burn some incense because he helped cure my fever. But I don't know if it's okay to do that in the sculpture studio."

117

"They do have a line of finished statues," Theary said. "I saw them just the other day. Maybe you can offer incense to them."

Morning dawned clear and cool. Bopha wrapped her kromah around her shoulders. The six of them walked to the market together before breakfast. Kesor had given permission, and even provided a stick of joss for them to burn when she learned of their plans. Bopha hadn't thought about how she might get incense. Sometimes Kesor would give the dancers a few coins so they could make purchases at the market. But Bopha had used all hers up before she got sick, and hadn't received any more. She was thinking about this — one more way the she could not just do what she might want — when they turned down the street to the stone sculptors.

Four huge Garudas stood in a line next to the road. Bopha had to tip her head back to see their eyes. They were at least half again as tall as she was. Standing next to one, she felt dwarfed by its size and bulk. She looked down at the huge claws, each scale carefully shaped all the way up its leg to where the feathers started.

The artisans were already at work, some in the shadows under the studio roof, some in the day-lit yard. They looked up when the line of dancers stopped, then went back to work. Bopha held the incense out, then realized she had no way to light it. The young women went back to where a middle-aged man was cooking chicken over coals. "Good morning, Bong. May we light our incense from your coals?" Bopha asked him politely.

He was not as polite. He looked them each up and down with a bit of a leer, before saying, "Sure. Help yourself. It's not every day that I get approached by Apsaras." The way he said it made Bopha's skin crawl. She was glad there were six of them and that it was morning.

All she said was, "Arkoun," giving sampeah but not meeting his shifty eyes. He stood in front of the coals now. She stepped to one side and reached the incense into the red embers. Sandalwood wafted up and she stepped back, saying thank you again to the lurking man. She held the incense in front of her, hands folded around it. The young women went back and stopped in front of the Garudas.

Bopha held the incense up, and made little circles, so the smoke swirled. "Arkoun, Garuda," she said, "for healing me and giving me peace." She continued silently, "and please take care of my friend Kalienne, and Arun Veha, and Kiri." Then she said out loud, "And please take care of our King, Jayavarman VII." She repeated this in front of each stone god. To the first three she added, "I'm sorry that we have only one stick of incense."

At the last Garuda, she knelt and pushed the end of the joss stick between several shards of stone on the ground. When she was sure it would not fall over, Bopha stood up and said again, out loud, "Thank you." She felt her friends on each side bow with her. They stood for a moment, looking at the huge statues. The last one had a few feathers on its left leg that were slightly out of place. You had to look closely, and you would need other Garudas whose feathers were different, to notice. Bopha decided she liked this Garuda best, and was glad the incense was in front of it.

Thida, Sophea and Bopha went to the baray to wash after lunch. Theary was almost as good at braiding as Kalienne, and she and Tevy helped them get ready. When Kesor called for them, they went down the steps. Kesor gave Bopha a quick glance and shook her head, just once, quickly. Bopha looked around and realized that the King's Man had not come. Boran stood under a tree near the gate, with several other guards. Her heart sank, but she kept her head up and a slight smile on her lips.

Clouds had massed over the sun, colored from light gray to almost charcoal. To her relief, the promised rain held off until they got to the women's courtyard. So, they would have supper with the women, then go to the King, Bopha thought. She ate lightly, squatting under a porch while thunder burst the clouds.

She was glad to be with other dancers, believing that this would protect her from having the King ask her questions. The rain had stopped by the time they were summoned, and the three Apsaras were ushered into the Great Hall. It was full of courtiers and ladies, dressed in flowing silks of every color, and bejeweled from head to toe. Near the King's bench were several men wearing long skirts, the cloth not pulled up to make trousers. Bopha knew these must be the men from Pagan, far to the west, in their longis. She looked around, but there was no sign of Kiri. She felt the King looking at her.

119

The room fell away as she returned his gaze, losing herself in the dark depths of his eyes. Jaya. The nickname sounded unbidden in her thoughts. Her King. She wanted to thank him for taking care of her when she was sick, for thinking of her with gentle consideration. She wanted so much for all to be well with him, and for him to take care of Kalienne and Kiri. Her eyes poured all these desires into his. Unaware of other sounds, Bopha heard only the creaking reassurance, "Do not worry. All will be well."

She nodded, and heard murmuring. The room returned, and she saw out of the corner of her eyes that the courtiers and ladies were staring at her, as were Thida and Sophea. She made sampeah to the King, and looked at her hands.

"Our Apsaras have arrived," Jayavarman's deep voice filled the room. "Musicians, play the Wishing Dance."

It was unusual for only three dancers to perform this. Thida whispered brief instructions on how to modify the dance, as the musicians tested their instruments and a servant brought each dancer a golden goblet, integral to the dance. When the first notes sounded from the xylophone, the Apsaras were ready. The Wishing Dance. Bopha remembered how much she had wanted to learn it when she was just little. She rarely thought of her village, but now she sent thoughts of wishing well to her family, so long dead. A perfect dance for her tonight, when she had so many wishes. Did the King guess? For a change, instead of dreading the time he would call for her to tell truth, she wished she could stay tonight and tell him everything.

But it was not to be. Rain pounded on the roof when they finished, then the King called for the Blessing Dance. When it was done, the King made his usual speech of praise, and the Apsaras backed out of the room. The rain had stopped, but a light breeze sprinkled them with water from thousands of leaves as they walked home in silence.

* * *

Several more long days passed. Bopha got no message about Kalienne, and there was no sign of Kiri. Was the King's Man in jail? Had he been sent away with Kalienne? If the latter, surely he would have found a way to let Bopha know.

Her practiced steps didn't falter as she danced, but her mind was far away.

"Preah Chan Bopha!" Kesor's voice broke into her reverie. "You have been summoned to the Palace. You will leave immediately."

"May I go first to the baray?"

"No. Boran is here. The King's message was clear. You are to go immediately."

Bopha ran upstairs to put on one of her good sampots and get a kromah. She knew it could be chilly after a rain. It was only a few minutes before she was walking in front of Boran on the familiar road to Bayon. She felt alternately terrified and peaceful, but her training held and there was no outward sign of her turmoil.

King Jayavarman VII, Emperor of Kampuchea, was alone in the room. He waved Boran out, "You may leave us." His deep voice resonated through Bopha's body. "And close the door." She stood in sampeah with her back to the door as it clicked shut. "Come," the voice commanded.

Bopha walked toward the King, still in sampeah, but looking at him. His face was grave.

She stopped a few feet from where he sat in lotus position on his high bench. "Come closer." He gestured to the bench next to him and Bopha stepped up and sat. "Tell me."

Taking a deep breath, Bopha asked, "About the King's Man?" Jayavarman just looked at her. He saw her youth, her beauty, her grace. And her desire to tell him the truth.

"Yes. Tell me all."

So she did. The story poured out, how Kalienne was such a good friend, how sad she had been when Kalienne couldn't stay as a dancer, how she saw her in the market. She told him how angry she was with the King's Man, but how Kiri had won her over with his obvious love for her friend, how he made it possible for Bopha to visit, about the birth of Arun Veha. She told him about how sick she had been and how grateful she was for the medicine he sent, and she told him about Garuda and the snake. "Khosal is a snake.

He came in my hallucinations, but Garuda saved me. He told me not to worry and that all will be well."

Jayavarman watched her closely. There was sorrow but no anger on his face. "They didn't mean to fall in love, Kalienne and Kiri," Bopha said. "They didn't want to hurt your sister, they both love her. But it just happened. It happens, you know. Like it's happening to me now."

Bopha hear her words and realized the truth. She looked into the King's eyes and saw a little surprise, a little amusement. "You ask me for the truth, Your Majesty. I didn't know the truth until just now." She paused. He waited. Bopha dropped her gaze to her hands which had twisted into a jeeb of imprecation. "You can't help falling in love," she whispered, tears filling her eyes.

She saw his hand lift. He wore only two rings today. His fingers were long, but sturdy and strong. One finger touched under her chin. She lifted her head. He was looking into her. "I know you are my King and I am just an Apsara, but I can't help it." She rushed on, "You are so good to me, and when you look at me sometimes I feel you know everything about me. Your eyes touch me to my heart. I want to protect you and hold you and help you. I want to tell you the truth always, even if it means I will be killed. But I don't want to be killed, and I don't want Kiri or Kalienne to be hurt." She stopped suddenly. A few tears dropped onto his finger, which was still on her chin.

He dropped his hand and unfolded his legs. When he stood up, he reached out his hand for hers, holding her eyes. The sandalwood scent was strong from his chest. She was only half a head shorter. When their hands touched, Bopha gasped. A bolt of energy shot from her hand to her head, and down her back. The King lifted his eyebrows. "Your Majesty," she whispered, "I feel," she stopped, then started again. "Energy. Like lightning in my back."

A smile slowly gentled the King's face. "I'm glad, Preah Chan Bopha, that your King's touch might bring you pleasure."

"My Lord," she said softly. "I hope that mine will bring you the same." Their hands were clasped. He brought them to his lips and kissed her fingers, looking at her the whole time. "I don't know," she started.

"I do," he interrupted, his voice so deep it was almost a growl. "I know you don't know. I will teach you." He grinned. "I think you will be a quick study." He slowly drew his fingers out from hers and traced the bones of her face, then down her neck and across her collarbone. Bopha felt the way she had with Kalienne. Her nipples were so hard they almost hurt, and the energy had settled deep in her pelvis. Her breath came in short puffs.

There was a knock on the door. "Not now," said the King.

It was Boran's voice, apologetic but firm. "There is a messenger. It is urgent."

The King gently pushed Bopha back onto the bench and sat again in lotus position.

"Stay, I want to see what you think of this messenger," he told her softly, then louder,

"Enter."

Boran opened the door. A sweaty young man panted his way in, hands in sampeah.

"Your Majesty, I bring a message from the border with Dai Viet." He composed himself, then recited in a chanting manner what he had memorized. Messages were memorized, then the runner would race to the next stop on the highway system that Jayavarman had built across his entire empire. The next messenger would memorize the chant, and so forth, until this young man entered the King's presence. "The Dai Viet are crossing the border, many soldiers like stars in the sky, horses and chariots, bound for war."

Jayavarman's face was stormy. "Message received. Go get something to refresh yourself." The young man staggered to the door, where Boran had been standing. "Boran, go get the King's Man Kiri, and Minister Khosal." Bopha startled. Kiri was here. Boran bowed and left.

"So, Preah Chan Bopha." She looked at him. "I would much rather make love with you than make war with the Dai Viet, but a king is actually not all-powerful." Bopha felt her face redden, but nodded, holding his eyes. "And, yes, Kiri is here. He has been ... under detainment ... while I considered the case."

123

Bopha broke in before she could stop herself, "and Kalienne?"

"Ah, Kalienne. The beautiful seductress. To protect my sister, I have sent the woman away." He looked at his hands. "To punish Kiri would be to invite gossip." Bopha nodded. "We have been friends since the cradle. I trust him more than any other. My heart grieves. But I will not hurt him by punishing the woman or her child. You tell the truth, my dearest Apsara, for which I am grateful. We cannot rule our hearts in matters of love. Thank you for that reminder." He bowed to her, hands in sampeah. Bopha wanted to throw her arms around him. Her smile was radiant. Jayavarman smiled sadly. "And now, to be the King."

They could hear steps approach. "Enter." The door opened. Minister Khosal bowed and waited. "Ah, Minister Khosal. You may enter." The King's voice was neutral.

Khosal looked over at Bopha as he got closer, then back to the King. "Yes, our Apsara is here with me. She will stay." He looked at the door, "Yes, come in." Kiri's tall form looked a bit stooped and his sampot was wrinkled, but he met the King's gaze and nodded.

Khosal's face flashed hatred as Kiri entered, but he hid it quickly. Bopha, so eager to see Kiri, had missed it, but she felt a dark chill emanate from the man. Now she regarded him. He pretended she wasn't there. His thin neck was covered with gold necklaces and chains. Bopha wondered if he slept in them. She wondered where Kiri had been. He wore no jewelry. Without the pomp of accoutrements, he looked like a regular man, but he straightened his back and she saw the King's Man appear.

The King told the message to Khosal and Kiri, who listened gravely. "Kiri, I will lead the army. You are in charge while I am gone." Kiri bowed assent. The King turned and asked sharply, "Khosal, did your intelligence bring you no word that the Dai Viet were on the move?"

Khosal looked shocked. Bopha thought he was pale. She could see sweat start to bead on his forehead. "No, Your Majesty. We have heard nothing." You were too busy spying on Kiri to pay attention to your business for the Kingdom, thought Bopha. "But several of our officers are late in returning from reconnaissance in the northeast. They were expected last week. But the rains ..." he trailed off under the King's glare.

"You are to give the army everything it requires, and arrange for supply trains to start immediately."

"Yes, Your Majesty."

"You may go now." The King was peremptory. Minister Khosal looked at Kiri and Bopha, then backed out the door. "Close it." Khosal did. Bopha thought he looked like he really would rather stay and listen. Maybe the King thought the same, because his next words were spoken very low. "Kiri, Preah Chan Bopha has told me the whole story. She has begged forgiveness for you, and for her friend, the woman Kalienne." Kiri watched the King, emotions chasing themselves across his face, surprise, sorrow, gratitude. "As you know, I believe she tells the truth." Jayavarman looked at her, and she nodded, sending him all her love through her eyes.

"I promised," she whispered.

"You may not see the woman again, but I will not punish you. If I do, people will talk." Kiri nodded sadly. "I will make sure she and the child are taken care of, do not worry,"

The King assured him. "My friend, you and my sister, and this young woman are the only people that I truly trust. Please do not abuse it." He stopped for a moment. Into the silent room, murmuring voices from the courtyard floated through the open windows, many people suddenly very busy. "I am sorry you cannot be with the woman you love, Kiri. I know it will be hard for you." Kiri's eyes were bright with tears, and Jayavarman's with sadness, as they looked at each other.

"You know what to do. You have so many times done this for me. I could not be the King I am, if you were not by my side." Jayavarman reached out and patted his friend on the shoulder. "Go get cleaned up."

"Thank you, my Lord," said Kiri. His voice was husky. At the door he looked at the King questioningly. The King gestured for him to shut it.

When the door closed, the King took a deep breath. "So, my dear Preah Chan Bopha, where were we?" He stood up and drew

125

her into an embrace. His arms were so strong and warm. But the layers of his necklaces poked her chest.

"Be safe, my dear Lord," she murmured into his neck. "Come back to me soon." She looked up at him, and he bent to kiss her. His lips were as soft as his arms were strong, and, if it weren't for the necklaces, Bopha thought she would melt into him and disappear. She wrapped her arms around his lower back and returned his kiss. Her fingers felt a hard ridge running at an angle across his spine. She ran two fingers gently up it, then down to where it disappeared under his wide jeweled belt. She broke off the kiss to whisper, with her arms still around him, "Is this the scar from when you were wounded, fighting the Cham before?" The King's eyes were soft and deep as he nodded. She could feel what Kalienne had told her about Kiri, pressing against her sampot.

"Enough, sweet thing," Jaya warned, pulling away gently. "I don't want to disgrace myself. Not here, not now." He brushed her lips with his hand. "But soon." He paused, thinking, "What was it your Garuda said?"

"Do not worry. All will be well." As she said it, Bopha felt the familiar relief of the great bird's protection. The King nodded, with a sad smile. Bopha kissed him again, then bowed sampeah and walked to the door. He lifted one hand in blessing, then both in sampeah. When would she see him again?

CHAPTER 13
1193 - 1194, Nuon

All of Bayon and Angkor was busy, people walking fast wherever they were going, everyone who passed the gate was loaded down with baskets and bundles. The murmur of conversations and the creak of wagon wheels filled the air. This was the day the King was leading the army to war. When the boom-boom of his drums started, talk and movement stopped. Boom-boom-boom. Tramp-Tramp-Tramp-Tramp.

Bopha was near the road, looking for the first glint of light on Jayavarman's helmet. Because of the rains, there was no dust cloud of warning this time. The road was muddy, with deep tracks. One of the wagons had become mired this morning and had to be completely unloaded to get it free, leaving a wagon-sized mud hole just past the gate.

There! Morning sun was sparkling on so many heads that the army looked like a flood of light. Their tramp was somewhat muted by the mud, but Bopha could feel the vibration, all those feet marching together and shaking the ground. She let the men pass, never moving her gaze from the spot where her King would appear.

It seemed forever, and indeed it was a long time before the foot-soldiers were replaced by horses. The King was dressed in bronze not gold, as befitted a warrior. His shoulders were covered with sheets of hammered bronze that reminded Bopha of feathers. She sent Garuda a prayer, "Please take care of him," as she watched the tall figure on the huge black horse get bigger and closer.

He was looking for her as the horse approached the dancers' gate. Bopha's hands were in sampeah but she couldn't take her eyes off him to bow. When their eyes met, Bopha put her hands to her lips with a little jeeb of pushing the kiss to him. His lips curled just a little and his helmet tipped slightly in her direction. She dropped to the ground, tears dripping into the mud. The horse's hoofs made sucking sounds as it avoided the wagon's mud-hole.

In her mind, Bopha followed the King's straight back, followed the line of the scar that felt so clear to her fingers now.

She heard people getting up, and did so herself as soon as was proper. Now she looked the other way, to the north, watching, watching, seeing only the King, until a crush of cavalry blotted out all but the top of his helmet, still catching the early light. Then, he was gone.

Boran was watching her as she finally turned back into the courtyard. His eyes were full of something she hadn't seen before. Understanding? Pity? She nodded to him and tried to lift her shoulders, pressed down by the weight of loss. He nodded back, unsmiling but not stern. In her mind Bopha saw again the feathers protecting Jayavarman's chest, and felt better.

Weeks dragged by. Gossip was busy with tales of the war. The King's Man came to the courtyard less often, now that he had so much else to do. But he came twice a week to sit with Kesor and watch the dancing, at least for a short time. One afternoon, he waited after practice, leaning against a gnarly knee of the huge banyan. Bopha had been watching him as she danced. To her eyes, he looked older, and tired, with sorrow under his erect posture. She felt badly for him. Her loss was, hopefully, just for a few months. His would be how long?

"Bopha," Kiri said softly as she came to the tree. "It's always refreshing to watch you dance. Thank you."

"Are you watching out for me?"

Kiri smiled sadly, "The King would surely never forgive me if I didn't"

"Have you any news?"

"I can't tell you anything about the war."

"About," Bopha lowered her voice, checking around surreptitiously, "Kalienne and Arun Veha?" She saw the question hit Kiri in the chest. He looked down, and shook his head. "I ask Garuda to take care of them," Bopha assured him.

Kiri nodded. "Me too," he murmured.

* * *

The rains had stopped and the air was clear and dry, at least dry for a jungle. Bopha wore her kromah against the chill at breakfast and dinner. Part of her engaged in music and movement, and chatter with friends. Part of her traveled muddy roads and narrow jungle paths, tracing Jayavarman's old scar with her fingers. Was he fighting now? ... Now?

Although missing her King, Bopha had no sense of dread. Rather, she felt wings of protection wrapping her, as his arms had done. Surely, if something bad happened, she would know immediately.

Of all her friends, Sophea seemed to have an instinct about Bopha, attuned to her moods. She didn't pry but she seemed to listen to what Bopha didn't say. And Bopha wasn't talking about the King. Or Kalienne. Mentoring Tevy had been helpful to the young woman. She had never been withdrawn exactly, but separate. Walled off from really meeting other people. Bopha thought maybe she had been walled off from meeting herself. Now, she seemed more relaxed. She was becoming a wonderful dancer.

One evening the two of them sat in the courtyard. Glimmers flickered from cooking fires all around, from close to deep in the woods. Delicious food aromas wafted on the nearly motionless air. "That smells so good, I could almost eat another dinner," Bopha said.

Sophea chuckled, "Me too. I've never eaten much, but living here I've had the best food in my life. In my homeland we weren't starving. We had enough." Her smile was gone. "But my mother wouldn't let me eat if she was mad at me. My next older sister would try to sneak me something. But if she was caught, she'd be punished too."

Bopha watched Sophea's face in the dim light of the rising half-moon. Her words were fraught, but her face calm and still. "You didn't have it easy as a child," Bopha said.

"No, I didn't. But now, as hard as we work, I have it easy." Sophea looked off into the woods. "So many people here, all around, all through the woods. Some of them have very hard lives. But most of them have a nice smile to give in greeting. They may be poor and hungry, but they try to smile.

129

"I only saw my mother smile once. She was watching the cook fire. I was in the shadows under the house and she didn't know I was there. Usually her face was hard. The lines around her mouth went harshly down on both sides. But that evening, she seemed a different person, just staring into the flames. The rice was boiling and she moved it to where the coals weren't so hot. Then she just squatted there, her face soft. She was far, far away. Then, I saw it. She smiled. It lit up her face. I saw that she could be beautiful. Maybe she had been beautiful at one time, before marriage, before children." Sophea stopped. "I always wondered what she had been thinking, just looking at the flames."

"Maybe her life had been hard," Bopha suggested after a moment.

"She never tired of telling us how easy we had it." She drew her gaze back from the woods and turned to Bopha. "Maybe her life had been hard. I don't want to forgive her, for all those years of abuse. But part of me thinks I should."

The two friends sat in silence, watching flickers through the trees and listening to crickets and the occasional tohkeay. The gibbons had gone to sleep. "How come the monkeys don't fall out of their trees?" Bopha wondered aloud, feeling relaxation sweep through her body. "I just go limp when I sleep. Well, I'm almost limp already. I guess it's time for bed." Then she added, "I'm glad you're my friend, Sophea. And I'm glad you can talk with me. I'm sorry that I can't talk much with you. It's not that I don't want to ..." Bopha trailed off.

Sophea shot her an insightful glance, then murmured, with an impish grin, "It's okay. State secrets!"

Taken by surprise, Bopha grinned and shook her head. "Maybe you can become a fortune teller in your next life." The young women climbed the stairs together. Most of the dancers were already asleep. "Sleep well," Bopha whispered.

"You too. Don't fall out of the tree."

Bopha stifled a giggle. She soon fell asleep, with a smile on her face.

* * *

130

B opha went to the Garuda studio every week and lit incense. The four Garudas had been joined by another two, so she brought six sticks of joss now. She had found a different vendor who let her light them. He was an ancient man, mostly bones, with a few sprigs of almost colorless, fine hair on his head.

"Ah, the Apsara!" he would greet her. "Here to light incense for Garuda. King of birds! Slayer of Snakes!" Grinning toothlessly, he would put his hands in sampeah.

"Arkoun, Taa," Bopha smiled and bowed. Thank you, grandfather. The Garuda with the funny feathers was now in the middle, and Bopha always put the incense at his feet last. She wondered where he would go. Are these statues for Bayon?

Bopha had not seen Rithy for many months, not since the night they met the King with Minister Khosal. While the King was away, the Apsaras danced for a few ceremonies at Angkor Wat, but none went to Bayon for smaller performances. Weeks stretched into months. Gossip said the King had easily vanquished the invaders and was on his way back. Bopha hoped so. There was no gossip about any injuries to her King.

She wondered how Rithy was, what he was learning. She envied him learning to write. She often thought of Kalienne, but had no way to let her know. "Please tell Kalienne that I think of her every day," she told Garuda. "And Rithy. I look forward to the day we see each other again. And thank you for keeping my Jayavarman safe."

Usually Sophea, Thida, Nuon, Tevy and Theary went with her to Garuda. But one day Nuon said she felt ill and went back to bed. When the young women returned, there was no sign of Nuon in the courtyard. Bopha found her on their mat in the darkened dormitory. Nuon was dripping sweat. Bopha touched her arm. Nuon groaned. Her arm was fiery. Bopha ran to get Kesor.

Nuon seemed to have what Bopha had had, but she didn't get better. Instead, her fever got higher and didn't ever drop. She rarely opened her eyes, and when she did, she didn't seem to see anything. Sometimes she muttered, but she didn't answer questions. "Do you think she has been taken by an evil spirit?" Nary whispered.

One day, Nuon got very restless, tossing back and forth on the mat, and Bopha couldn't understand what she was trying to say. One pupil seemed to fill the whole brown of her eye but the other was tiny where light from the window hit it.

The King's Man brought a doctor from the King. He felt Nuon's pulse in several places, and looked at her eyes. Shaking his head, he gave Bopha a powder to put in tea. "If you can get her to take any, it will help."

"Arkoun, Royal Doctor," she said, holding the powder like a gift.

The doctor, kind and sad, looked at her. "It will help keep her calm, so she doesn't have pain. But it won't cure her. I'm afraid nothing can do that."

One of the cooks showed them how to put a strip of fabric in the tea, then in Nuon's mouth. "So she won't choke but she may get the medicine," the woman explained.

Bopha sat for the rest of the day and into the night, wetting the cotton and opening her friend's mouth to push it in. Nuon would clamp her teeth down, and Bopha learned to keep her fingers out of the way. The other young women spelled her, but Bopha rarely left Nuon's side.

In the middle of the night, Nuon's body suddenly went rigid, then her arms and legs flailed and she arched her head back. Bopha, squatting next to her, had dozed off, head on her arms. The movement woke her immediately. "Nuon," she cried, trying to hold her friend still. But every muscle of the small dancer's body was in full action. Her hand hit Bopha hard across the face. Bopha felt her nose crunch, then blood poured into her mouth. She reached for her kromah to staunch the flow. By now, all the dancers were awake and someone had lit a torch.

The seizure lasted and lasted. Kesor joined the young women, in a circle around the mat where Nuon lay thrashing, and grunting like an animal. When it ended, the silence was worse. They watched, helpless to intervene. Nuon's chest heaved, then nothing. Then a big gasp, a little gasp, a puff of breath. Then nothing. Nuon's eyes were open, both pupils now huge. Her chest rose again, once, twice. The flickering light revealed the red of fever fade into the pallor of death. She was gone. Once an

Apsara, so full of energy and kindness. Now, a small body, on a mat in the middle of the night, motionless and empty.

Life returned to the watchers. Kesor knelt and helped Bopha wrap Nuon in the mat. Boran carried her to the end of the porch. By now, the deep predawn blue was chasing night away. Some of the dancers went back to bed, but Sophea, Tevy, Theary and Thida joined Bopha near Nuon's body.

"You'd better have Kesor fix your nose," Sophea said. They had all been so focused on Nuon that they hadn't noticed Bopha's face. "An Apsara wants to be beautiful for her King, not to look like a street fighter."

Bopha grimaced. It seemed wrong to think of her own beauty as something to value, when her friend lay lifeless nearby. But she knew Sophea was right. As usual. So she went down the stairs. Kesor was in the kitchen. One of the cooks had heard the commotion, and was making tea. Kesor looked at Bopha. "Oh my! I guess we'll need some of that hot water to fix our Apsara's nose."

The cook leaned over to get a better look. "That'll want taping," she pronounced. "I've got some gum that will work."

"Anchaly's the one the staff all go to if they have a problem," Kesor told Bopha, then whispered, "sometimes these village healers are just as good if not better than a regular doctor."

Bopha hadn't felt the pain in her nose, after the initial injury, since she was watching Nuon's final agony. But when Anchaly took hold of her nose and pulled — once sharply down, once sharply to her right — Bopha screamed, and reached for Anchaly's hands. Kesor was faster, grabbing them. "Shhh, shhh. That's all," murmured Anchaly. "You don't want your beautiful nose to heal all shoved in and pushed to one side, do you?" Bopha shook her head, very gently. She bit her lip as Anchaly tore several small strips of stiff cotton, put sticky tree gum on them, and wrapped them over and under her nose.

"There you go. Don't take those off for a week. And don't wash your hair. Just wash your face with your kromah. And no dancing. And don't blow your nose." Bopha had been snuffing. "You have blood in there, and it's stopped up so there's no more bleeding. But if you snuff or blow, you can open things up again."

133

Bopha opened her mouth to breath and said stuffily, "Okay. Arkoun, Anchaly."

Streaks of pink and yellow had replaced the deep blue predawn. When Bopha climbed back up to the porch, her friends were impressed by the taping. "It looks worse than it did before," said Sophea, never one to mince words. "But sometimes healing is like that."

"How do you get the sticky gum off?" Tevy chimed in, looking worried.

"You guys! With friends like you, who needs enemies?" Bopha said, with a crooked grin.

* * *

Word traveled fast. Shortly after breakfast, the King's Man arrived, his brown horse parting the gawkers at the gate. He would lead the funeral procession. Three monks were with him, one of them Rithy. When she saw him, Bopha ran up, "My brother, it is such a blessing to see you."

They made sampeah, and Rithy murmured, "It is not usual for a monk such as me, a scribe and so new, to come to the funeral of an Apsara. But the King's Man is kind, and he knew you shared your mat with Nuon. So he made the arrangements." There was no time to talk more.

All the Apsaras were wearing their finest clothes and jewelry. Two burly guards lifted Nuon's body, cradling her between them in her shroud. Truly, she was so petite that one could have lifted her easily, Bopha thought. She took her place right behind the pall bearers. Several guards in front made way through the on-lookers, in front for the musicians, who were beating drums and playing discordant high-toned horns. The King's Man came next, then Nuon, then the Apsaras, followed by all the people who worked in the courtyard carrying banners and flags.

The procession turned away from Bayon and walked for half an hour to where the road split. They took the smaller road, then another even smaller, until they were deep in the jungle. So close to Angkor and Bayon, but the place felt remote. High trees wrapped with vines blocked any sun. Suddenly, the ground fell away into a deep gully. With a final flourish, the music stopped.

The musicians stepped to one side, the King's man to the other. Nuon's carriers swung her body between them at the edge of the ravine, then both let go at the same time. The small bundle flew out, into the air, and disappeared from view, shortly followed by a thud and the crunch of broken bushes. Already vultures were circling high in the white morning sky. Bopha looked up at them. "Eat her fast, to honor her father and mother," she whispered.

After a short prayer by the monks, the line re-formed. This time, the musicians didn't play and the mourners were silent. Back in the courtyard, Anchaly and the cooks had prepared a feast. The King's Man stayed while the monks performed a longer ceremony in front of the dancer's altar, then everyone ate. Bopha sat with Kesor and the King's Man, at Kiri's invitation. They didn't have much to say, not that could be said in public, anyway.

Kesor broke the awkward silence. "With Nuon gone, Theary needs a new mentor. Bopha, you have been chosen. Indeed, had you not been ill at the time, you would already be her mentor." Bopha nodded. Her mind was split in so many directions now. At the war with King Jayavarman, in a village somewhere with Kalienne and Arun Veha, down in a gully with Nuon and the vultures. She had nothing left over for pondering this new role. "I will make the announcement at supper, and meet with the two of you tomorrow morning before dance practice."

Bopha nodded again. Finally she gathered enough thought to say softly, "Thank you for this honor. I hope to show myself worthy." Kesor patted her shoulder.

"Don't worry. We would not have chosen you if we weren't sure. It's been a terrible day. Maybe you can take a nap instead of dancing this afternoon. I know you were up all night."

Suddenly Bopha realized that she didn't have a mat. The one she shared with Nuon was over a cliff in the jungle. Kesor read her face. "We have extra mats. I'll ask Theary to get one for you." As an afterthought, she added, "Would you like to have someone sleep with you?"

Bopha shook her head. "Thank you, Kesor. I think maybe dancing would be good for me. When my body is moving to music, I don't dwell on other thoughts."

"But you have to be careful, Bopha. No dancing for you until your nose heals," Kesor reminded her. Bopha's heart sank, but the small Apsara smile remained on her face as she bowed acknowledgement.

Kiri got up and the monks followed suit. After many sampeahs, they left for Bayon. Bopha went up to the dorm to change into her practice sampot. Even though all the other mats were stored for the day, her spot on the empty floor seemed the emptiest of all.

CHAPTER 14

1194, Sometimes Gold is Good for Nothing

Head up, back straight, her little smile in place, Bopha danced through the days in a fog of sorrow and worry. She missed Nuon, whose small and cheerful presence left a large hole among the Apsaras. After the first night, when she barely slept despite having been up all the previous two days and night, Bopha asked Sophea if she could sleep with her. Sophea's mat was near the corner farthest from the door, a welcome change of location. When Nuon joined the adepts, she had returned to her old place sleeping with Bopha. Sophea had suggested it, assuring them she was happy to sleep alone.

"You don't mind?" Bopha asked.

"I'm happy to sleep alone," Sophea told Bopha, "and I'm happy to share with you. But don't fall out of the tree." They grinned at each other. Bopha slept hard the first night, but only the first. She would lie for hours staring into the dimness of the rafters above, willing herself not to disturb Sophea by tossing and turning.

Dark shadows hung under Bopha's eyes now, reflecting the dark shadows roiling her mind. Was Nuon in a new body already? Surely she'd have a bright future after such a life of goodness. Where was Kalienne? When would Jayavarman return?

* * *

Lines of soldiers marched past, battle-worn but proud. When she saw the King's helmet, Bopha's heart leaped. She knelt but did not prostrate herself, hoping to look into those eyes she had missed so much. But Jayavarman was looking to the other side of the road when he got to where she was. His black horse, its braided tail swishing, carried its rider away as Bopha touched her forehead to the dirt. Tears stung her eyes.

It was another hour before the procession ended and the dancers could cross the road.

137

Back at the courtyard, Kesor was waiting for them. "Where have you been? There is word from the Palace. Preah Chan Bopha, you are to go tonight." The older woman watched closely as Bopha tried to hide her joy. "Boran will take you before sundown."

"Just me?" Bopha blurted out, then wished she hadn't brought more attention to that fact, as other Apsaras clustered around, listening.

Kesor nodded, somewhat curtly. "Come to my room before you leave." She raised her voice. "The excitement is over, ladies. Afternoon practice will start right after lunch."

The afternoon dragged for Bopha. She watched part of the practice then listened to the music, her mind imagining the movements, as Theary braided her hair. Dressed in her best sampot, she knocked on Kesor's door.

"Ah, Bopha. Come in." Kesor's voice was even. "I have something special for you."

She unclasped the latches to the jewelry box and lifted out the necklaces Bopha wore when she danced in a small group. Putting them on a bench, Kesor pulled gently on two ribbons that lay exposed. She had to pull a little harder, then the whole shelf came free from the box. Underneath was a hidden compartment. Bopha and Kesor looked inside.

In the dappled light from the open door and window, Bopha saw a broad necklace, tiers of gold inlaid with gemstones. She gasped involuntarily. Kesor closed the lid, latched it, and handed the box to Bopha. "It is not common for the King to request a single Apsara," she said. "But when he does, he wants her to wear this." Her eyes searched Bopha's, but she didn't say anything else.

Finally Bopha said, "Arkoun, Kesor." Her voice was husky. Both women knew what the request meant. Kesor patted her on the shoulder. Bopha heard Garuda, his deep croak reassuring, "Do not worry. All will be well." She was not worried. Not as such. But her nerves were all thrumming.

Suddenly, it was time. Four guards arrived at the gate, surrounding four men with bulging biceps and strong thighs, who carried a dark wood litter. They placed the litter on the ground. Bopha had seen litters going by in the market, their noble occupants hidden from view. Who was in this one? Boran parted the green silk curtains. No one came out. Bopha stepped closer. The litter was empty. She looked at Kesor, who lifted an eyebrow and tilted her head slightly. "The King has sent it for you, Preah Chan Bopha," said Boran in his kind, gruff voice.

As Bopha ducked inside, she heard faint murmuring from the dancers gathered in the courtyard. In all her years there, she had never seen an Apsara leave in a litter. She was as surprised as the others. Boran pulled the curtains closed. It was almost like being in the jungle, green light filtering through the silk. With a slight lurch, the litter was lifted. Bopha inhaled sharply and reached for a leather strap that hung next to the door. That must be what it was there for, she decided. It was strange to rock along, above the ground, in a green silk cocoon. She peeked through a narrow gap between door frame and curtain. They were just passing the street where the sculpture studio stood. She caught a glimpse of the huge feathered gods, standing in a line. Bopha sat back on the cushioned seat, her heart pounding.

The trip seemed both longer and shorter than when she walked — longer because she wasn't looking around at the sights, shorter because it was effortless. When movement stopped, Bopha thought to hold the strap, which was good. The litter was swung to the ground. Boran opened the curtains. Bopha stepped out into the women's courtyard. It was strangely silent. There were quite a few servants, but they weren't bustling around their business. They stood watching her arrival. Boran and the litter-bearers left. Bopha wasn't sure what to do. She clutched the teak box.

"Preah Chan Bopha?" A young woman stepped forward, smiling softly. She was dressed the way Kalienne had been when she was waiting on Kiri's wife, better than a regular servant but not as fancy as a noble. She was a little older than Bopha, a little shorter, and quite pretty. "I'm Chariya. I'll be helping you." Bopha nodded, stunned.

Chariya led her into a room, empty but for a cushioned bench. The window looked out at the big banyan where Kalienne had met her once. It seemed so long ago.

139

"Would you like some tea?"

"Yes," Bopha managed, "please." Chariya bowed and left. Bopha, still holding the box tightly, walked over to the window. The banyan towered over much of the building. She looked up into its leafy vastness. A breeze rustled the leaves, then blew into the room, lifting the close air and taking it out the door. Bopha's heart lifted with it. She heard Chariya's steps and turned.

"Here," Chariya held out a delicate porcelain cup in her right hand. Her left hand touched her right forearm in the formal gesture of offering.

"Arkoun ... Chariya," said Bopha softly. She put the box on the bench and took the cup with formal acceptance. She sipped gently, expecting bitterness. But the tea was delicate and delicious. She sipped again. "What is this? It's wonderful."

"Jasmine," said Chariya. "It was a gift from the Chinese Ambassador. When the King tasted it, he liked it so much that he has it imported ever since."

Bopha didn't know how to ask the questions that pressed her, or if it was right to ask them of Chariya, or if she would even know the answers. Cooking smells came in on another breeze and Bopha realized how hungry she was.

"The King wants you to dine with him," Chariya said, unbidden. "He will send word when it's time." Two answers. From previous visits, Bopha knew where the mat was.

She asked Chariya, "At that time, will you help me with my necklace?"

"Of course. Is there anything else?"

"Not now. Thank you."

Alone again, Bopha listened to the normal chatter and busyness of the courtyard, which had resumed. She sipped the tea and stroked the lid of the box. Her fingers remembered Jayavarman's scar, and her heart began to thump. Her King. Jaya.

She could feel his arms around her, the scratching of his necklaces on her bare chest, the hardness of his member through

140

his sampot. She longed to see him again, to touch him, to feel him.

Bopha, lost in memory, hadn't noticed how dark the room was. Dusk is brief in Kampuchea, one stroke of color in the sunset, then night. Chariya came with a small torch and placed it in a holder on the wall. "It's time, Lok Srey." The honorific jarred Bopha more than the light.

She unclasped the box and lifted out the necklace. Chariya's eyes got big. "So beautiful." Bopha nodded and showed her how the clasp worked. She handed it to Chariya, who reached around the Apsara's neck. When the heavy treasure settled into place, its lower tiers brushing Bopha's breasts. The touch stiffened her nipples. Maybe that was the point, she thought vaguely.

Almost in a trance, Bopha followed Chariya into the courtyard. Her entrance hushed all conversation. She held her head up and walked to where Boran waited. He led her to the small audience room where she had danced with Thida and Nary, the night she had the hot-cold drink. Soft light flowed out the open door. "Your Majesty," said Boran, bowing, "The Apsara, Preah Chan Bopha." He introduced her as if she were an ambassador, Bopha thought. Past his shoulder, she could see Jayavarman VII sitting on cushions, in front of a low table on which were laid several platters, pots and bowls. She saw him wave for her to enter. Boran stepped back and closed the door behind her.

The King stood up and walked to meet her, eyes soft and welcoming. She made sampeah, and he put his hands around hers. "I didn't see you at the dancer's courtyard today," he said.

"No, Your Majesty. I was at the baray. But you didn't look towards where we stood." Bopha was falling into his eyes. "I wanted so much to see your eyes."

"And I yours." Jayavarman released her hands and touched her cheek gently. "Are you hungry?"

"Yes, my Lord," she said. Her stomach confirmed with a loud grumble. They both laughed.

"Even your stomach tells the truth." They sat next to each other and the King put food in her bowl. "Would you like some of this?" She nodded. "How about pineapple rice?" She laughed.

"Yes, to everything," she said. "But just a taste." That reminded her of the King's taster.

"Shall I taste for you?"

Jayavarman looked at her. "Thank you, but mine has been tasted. And I don't want you to eat anything that hasn't been tasted from now on." His serious tone broke the jesting mood. "I mean that, Preah Chan Bopha, my moon flower. You are now under my special protection, and there may be people who do not like that."

"Like Minister Khosal?" The words were out before she knew it.

The King grimaced. "Yes. For one."

"Why do you keep him then?" Dinner was forgotten for the moment.

"There is a saying, 'Keep your friends close and your enemies closer.' It is good advice for a King." Bopha nodded. "You have much to learn about life at court," Jayavarman continued, "but for now, let's eat, and talk of other things."

The food at the Apsara's courtyard was very good, but what the King ate was beyond excellent. "This is amazing," Bopha told him, after a bite of red curry chicken with lime. "I never really learned to cook anything but rice. I was so young when I came to be a dancer."

"There's more to life than cooking. And more than dancing. Is there anything that you do want to learn?" The King was watching her enjoy the meal, a smile playing on his full lips.

"Oh yes. I want to ride a horse and learn to write." From the surprise on his face, Bopha was afraid she had gone too far. Then he laughed out loud.

"You surprise me every time we meet," he said.

"Well, you asked," she defended herself, mock seriously. "And you know I am sworn to tell you the truth."

"You speak with wisdom." The King reached for a carafe and poured two drinks. He handed her one cup. The liquid was clear, with sprigs of mint floating in it.

"To the truth," he said, lifting his cup, "and the beautiful woman who is not afraid to tell it." He drank his down and watched her sip carefully. She swallowed quickly and went to put her cup down. He stayed her hand, leaning toward her.

"Yes, it is the hot-cold drink you had before. Will you have another sip?" She looked long into his smoldering eyes, then held the gaze while she tipped back the cup. The big gulp was too much and she coughed. Liquid spattered out and the King pulled back, laughing and patting at his chest where droplets shone on the sparse hairs.

"I'm sorry. I'm sorry," said Bopha, when she could catch her breath. Then they were both laughing.

"Your throat and stomach both tell the truth," the King choked out finally, gasping with laughter. "Ah, it is good to laugh." Grinning at her, he said, "You are good for me. I want to be good for you as well."

"Oh, my Lord, just being with you is good for me. Seeing you, watching you." Bopha stopped and dropped her eyes. The room tilted. Jayavarman pulled her to him so she was leaning against his knee. He traced the outline of the necklace on her chest, brushing her nipples once, twice. He bent his head and tickled them with his tongue, then bit one. When she gasped, he lifted his head and looked at her."

"I said that I would teach you," he nearly whispered. "But you must tell me what feels good and what does not. Contrary to myth, I am not a mind-reader." Bopha nodded. He nibbled at her other nipple, looking at her with one eye. She arched her pelvis slightly, feeling a wave of warmth.

"That feels ... good. It hurts a little but in a good way." The warmth was getting stronger and Bopha felt like she might need to urinate. "I'm afraid I should have gone to the mat before I came," she confessed in a tiny voice.

"That may be a good sign," said Jayavarman, nodding. "You don't have to go to the mat." He led her to a concealed door in the back of the room. "You can use this."

He showed her a large ceramic pot with flowers on it. There were even flowers on the lid. "Come out when you are ready."

143

Bopha was so nervous that it took her a while to let go, then she went so much she was glad the pot was big. She put the lid back on, then washed her hands in a matching flowered bowl, pouring water from a matching carafe. On a wooden bar was a clean yellow and brown kromah. She gently dried her hands. She didn't have to pee any more but she still had that feeling of urgency. She opened the door.

"I'm sorry I took so long," she said. The plates had been cleared, but their two cups and the carafe were still on the table. Jayavarman was reclining on one arm on a long wide cushion.

"There is no rush," he reassured her, sitting up and patting the cushion. "Take all the time you need." She sat where he indicated. He put his arm around her. "I did refill our cups." She looked up quickly and he winked. "You don't have to gulp it though, this time." She smiled sheepishly, and reached for the cups.

"To sipping," Bopha said. This time, the sip tasted good. She felt it go down, but it didn't stop at her stomach. Or maybe warmth from below was coming up to meet it in her stomach. Sandalwood flooded her nose from Jayavarman's chest. She leaned over and nuzzled him till she reached his necklace.

"Will you take this off?" he asked her. "Sometimes gold is good for nothing, and wearing nothing is better." Bopha knelt behind him and unclasped the heavy jewelry, letting it go into his waiting hands. The King put the necklace on the table. Bopha watched the scar ripple across his muscles as he moved, then she bent to kiss it, starting from where it came out from under his arm. He groaned slightly as her lips reached his sampot. He lay down and turned toward her. Kissing her stomach from one side to the other, he reached up and rolled her nipple between his fingers. The warmth increased and Bopha shifted. She felt wet, and like she had to use the pot again.

He pulled her down next to him and reached around to take off her necklace. But the clasp was tricky. "You'll need to turn over," he told her. She did and he pulled her hips against him. He kissed the back of her neck and between her shoulder blades, then gently released the lock and dropped the necklace onto the cushion. They reached for it at the same time, arms extended in full contact.

Bopha felt every tiny hair on her arm lift, as if she had a chill. "Are you okay?" His voice was concerned.

"Yes," she whispered. "More than okay. It's just that when I feel your touch ..." she didn't know how to explain.

Jayavarman lifted the necklace gently from her hand, rolled onto his back and laid it next to his own on the table. Bopha rolled so her side met his, then further, so she was lying partly on top of him. Jaya encircled her with his arms. This time, with no necklaces between them, she did melt.

CHAPTER 15

Moving to Bayon

King Jayavarman VII's tender lips touched Bopha's ear, waking her. "Will you stay here with me?" She stirred, then woke. He whispered the question again, his breath tickling her gently.

"Stay here? In the Palace?" They were spooned together on the long cushion. She could smell sandalwood and something musky she didn't recognize. The room was dark but she could see the outline of the window. Since the moon wasn't full, she realized it was dawn. The King's arm was over her and he pulled her closer, grazing his hand from her chin down to the place where her legs met. Warmth followed the touch, swelling until she had to shift her hips. They were both naked. She felt him nod.

"Yes, here in the Palace. I want you near." Jaya's voice almost broke. The softness of his voice contrasted with the hardness she felt against her. His full erection pressed against her buttocks. Bopha tilted back against it until he entered her. She gasped then relaxed, feeling him all the way inside. She started to move involuntarily, but he held her hips. "Wait, my moon flower. Let the energy build until it fills us." He lifted his hand from her hip to her cheek. "You didn't answer."

"Yes, my Lord. I will do whatever you want," Bopha said softly.

"Please, when we are alone together, just call me Jaya," his deep voice rumbled against her cheek. "But do you want to?"

"Yes," she said, then more firmly, "Yes." She paused, then added, "Jaya."

He pulled her even closer, careful not to move inside her. She wanted so much to shift her pelvis. Heat was pulsing through her.

Bopha whispered. "The first time I saw you, I felt your eyes enter me. You seemed to know me. It has been many years now, and you have been so good to me. But that is not what it is. It's a special feeling, a connection. I can't explain." She moved very slightly and they both gasped. "After last night, and now as we lie here like this, as close as two people can ever be, all I want is to be with you."

"I want you to be my wife," the King said gently. Before Bopha could say anything, he thrust into her and she started moving wildly. He guided her motions to a rhythmic, if rapid, rocking, until energy exploded through both of them.

When their breathing had slowed, he traced her arm. The room was starting to get lighter, even with the windows and doors closed. "Will you marry me?"

Bopha pulled away enough to turn onto her back. She kissed him, a long, slow, sweet meeting. "Yes," she whispered. "I'm scared of what it will mean, of what your other wives will think. But yes, I want to be with you, as near as can be."

She watched a smile crease her lover's face. "I've been waiting for you for years," he admitted. "Even as a child, you had something special. When you dance," he trailed off, then tried again. "Watching you dance is like watching the life force move."

Bopha suddenly drew back. "If I marry you, will I stop being an Apsara? Will I stop dancing?"

Jaya's smile faded into sorrow. "Yes. You will stop dancing, except for certain ceremonies. And for me. In private." There was enough light for him to see her face fall. "I'm sorry." He added, "but you will always be an Apsara, and generations to come will sing of your dancing."

Bopha lay back and looked at this man who was changing her life again. He had aged since she first saw him, the lines down his cheeks deeper. Around his eyes the lines showed he had laughed often and frowned less. She realized she didn't know much about him, about his life. There was gossip in the Apsara courtyard. His beloved first wife had died before Bopha came to Bayon. She remembered that one of the first times she danced as an adept was in a ceremony when he married another wife. She thought he had more wives, but didn't know for sure. Where would she live? What would her days be like?

Jaya watched the turmoil of thoughts play across the beautiful face of this young dancer who so moved him. "My dear," he said. "You must have many questions. And I want to answer them all.

147

But it is time to rise. Your lady-in-waiting will take you to your quarters. I look forward to tonight, when we will dine and talk." He cradled her head in both his strong hands. "Trust me, precious Moon Flower. I will take good care of you." Bopha looked deep into his eyes, then nodded. She turned her head to kiss the base of his thumb.

"Now, you can use the chamber first," he said. "But leave some room in the pot for me!" It was a lame joke, but they smiled at each other anyway.

When Bopha came out, the windows were open and there was no sign of the King.

Just outside the door, Chariya was waiting. She bowed in sampeah, and said, "Good morning, Lok Srey. Your rooms are ready." In a stupor, but head high and back straight, Bopha followed the young woman. Lok Srey. Surely that wasn't her.

But it was. Even Boran bowed to her, before leading them to the woman's compound.

Chariya took her to a different building this time. The teak eaves were heavy with ornate carvings of flowers and animals and outlandish creatures, even a few Apsaras.

"Here, Lok Srey," Chariya opened a heavy door and motioned her to go in first. There were six rooms. The largest, the one she entered first, was on the corner, with windows on three sides and another door that led onto a back porch. Doors led from the big room into two smaller rooms, one of which had a hidden closet with a chamber pot. Between these two rooms was a very small room, just large enough for a bamboo sleeping mat and a small bench. The mat was nowhere in sight. "This is where I will stay," Chariya told her.

The last room was almost as big as the first, with windows front and back, and a door onto the back porch as well as one into the room with the chamber pot. Bopha went outside. It felt like being inside a tree. The banyan leaves were close enough to touch. They swayed gently. Were they greeting her? She didn't move her hands, but in her heart she gave sampeah to the ancient tree and asked a silent blessing from its spirit.

The rooms were mostly bare of furniture except for a few, beautifully carved, teak benches and varying sizes of cushions. The bright silk covers of the cushions shone in the morning light. So many colors of silk. "Lok Srey, would you like some breakfast?"

"Arkoun, Chariya. Yes, please."

Bopha stood on the porch, watching the leaves. Below, in the courtyard, servants were busy. When one stopped and looked up at her, she stepped back, out of sight. She sat against the building, under the deep eaves, and started to exercise her hands. The full weight of what was happening hit her. She didn't need to exercise. But it was all she knew. Suddenly Bopha missed the Apsara dormitory, the happy chatter of Nuon, Sophea's dry and trenchant observations on everything, the music filling her days. A tear escaped. Here she was: crying, alone, the King's betrothed. She shook her head and impatiently wiped away the tear.

Chariya cleared her throat. She was in the doorway. "Lok Srey, do you want to eat inside?" The question had more than a little nuance of expectation.

"Chariya, please call me Preah Chan Bopha." Bopha ducked her head, then lifted it and looked at the startled servant. "I'm not used to Lok Srey."

Chariya bowed, smiling a smile that showed she didn't understand and didn't approve and didn't know if she could do that. She said nothing. Bopha sighed and stood.

It was a long day for Bopha. Chariya took her to the women's baray after breakfast. There were several other women there, laughing and chatting. Each of them appraised

Bopha, up and down and up again. Their tight smiles were like a slap in the face. After a moment long enough for Bopha to become uncomfortable, one of them said, "Well, look who's joining us. The Apsara. What is your name, dear?"

Bopha recognized her as the woman who had shamed her years before, when she couldn't eat after the ceremony for her village. She lifted her hands in sampeah, and her chin in recognition of an adversary. Looking the woman in the eyes, she carefully pronounced, "Preah Chan Bopha."

"Preah Chan Bopha. Welcome to Bayon. I am Indradevi." She paused a beat then added, one eyebrow raised slightly, "Your Queen."

Bopha bowed over her hands, glad to break eye contact. She had heard of Indradevi.

She was sister to the King's first wife, who had been very devout Buddhist and influenced the King to adopt Buddhist practices. When his first wife died, Jayavarman VII married her sister.

"Come, it is time to leave," pronounced Indradevi, turning to the other women. Bopha watched them climb the narrow stone steps out of the baray. She noticed that Indradevi seemed to lean hard on a servant's arm. Elegant, cool, powerful — and starting to become decrepit, Bopha thought. No wonder she hates me. Jaya told her he had waited years for Bopha to grow up enough for him to be with her as man and woman. Did Indradevi live with that knowledge? That never spoken, never acknowledged, bitter truth? In the heat of late morning, Bopha shivered.

After the gaggle of court women and their servants left, Bopha and Chariya had the baray to themselves. Chariya told her that the King had built this just for women, the men had another, further away among the high trees that offered welcome shade all over the complex. Bopha relaxed and sank into the warm water. When she practiced floating, as Sophea had taught her so many years ago, the constant sound of hammers on stone disappeared. There was nothing but soft wetness stroking every inch of her skin.

Flushed with the same feeling she had had both last night and again this morning with the King, Bopha gasped involuntarily. She inhaled a mouthful of water as she sank. The baray was not deep, and she got to her feet, coughing. "Are you okay?" Chariya was by her side. She had not called her Lok Srey, but neither had she said her name.

"Yes, fine," Bopha choked out, "I'm fine." There was nothing to do and no one else to talk with, for the first time since Bopha was a young child. She felt at a loss, and asked Chariya, "Have you lived here long, at Bayon?"

Chariya was not shy but she was diplomatic. She answered Bopha's questions about her life in short sentences but did not pry into the Apsara's. The two young women sat on the steps and got to know each other, sometimes sliding back into the water, then climbing out and drying off in the sun. Clouds dappled the surface of the baray.

"It's nearly lunch time," said Chariya, looking up at the sun overhead. "Are you ready to go?"

Bopha nodded. She wrapped her sampot around her full hips and firm buttocks, knotting it below her slim waist. As they strolled back to the women's compound, Bopha tried to think of questions that would not put Chariya on the spot. She wondered how much the King really knew of what went on among his women. She suspected not much. He had an empire to run in the outside world. Indradevi had only a little empire, inside Bayon. How many other wives did he have? How did that work? She would ask Jaya tonight.

"Lok Srey." Chariya's voice was apologetic. Bopha sat up. She had lain on a cushion after lunch and watched the leaves play against the clear blue sky. Now the blue was deeper, with a golden glow. She must have fallen asleep. She rubbed her eyes and looked at Chariya, squatting next to her. "The King will see you soon. Do you want to wear your necklace?" Chariya glanced at Bopha's wrinkled sampot. Bopha followed her gaze, then made useless ironing motions on the wrinkles in her lap. "He has sent you new clothes."

"Arkoun." Bopha decided not to press the issue of Lok Srey versus her name. It wasn't fair to this nice young woman who had a job to do. Chariya helped fasten her hair into a tight bun. Since she wasn't dancing, she didn't need fancy braids. When she was ready, Chariya led her to Boran. The King was in the same room as last night. His face lit up when Boran announced her. When the door closed, Jaya stood up and drew her to him for a warm hug and a long kiss.

"Preah Chan Bopha. How was your day?" He gestured to the cushion next to his place. "I thought of you."

"I thought of you too." Bopha felt shy but decided to tell him about how she felt in the warm water, then how she gasped and sank.

He drank in her face as she talked, then he chuckled. "I knew you would be a fast learner." He touched her nipples, which had hardened. "But don't drown. I want you around a while."

"I want to be around." She touched his lips and he drew her finger gently into his mouth, sucking and nibbling. The warmth started again. He took her hand in his.

"I have something for you." Jaya reached for a small wooden box on the bench where dinner was waiting. He passed it to her. When she opened it, the heavy gold gleamed in the torchlight.

"Oh, my Lord. They are beautiful." Bopha drew out one earring, feeling it weighty in her hand. The emerald flashed in the torchlight.

"Put it on," he suggested. Bopha had worn earrings when she danced, but otherwise not. She tried to slip the large dangler into the hole, but it was too big. She pushed hard, wincing, and finally it slid through. The second earring was just as difficult. "Don't hurt yourself," he cautioned. "We can get your ears pierced larger."

"It's okay," Bopha said, feeling the heavy earring pulling her lobes down. She moved her head gingerly. The jewelry followed, sluggish. "But I don't think I could dance in these." The Buddha's ears were extremely long in all images. Men and women of the court wore heavy earrings from an early age, elongating their lobes. The King's nearly reached his shoulders.

"Do you want my ears to be as long as a female Buddha?" Her tone was teasing, but the King's face stiffened. "I don't mean to be irreverent," she said, hastily. "I'm just ... unsure of myself. This is all so new. And I don't know what you expect. Not really. I met the Queen today, at the baray." She paused. "She doesn't seem to like me."

Jayavarman said, "I'm sorry. I should have introduced you myself. I didn't mean for that to happen. I will arrange a formal meeting for tomorrow. I haven't told her yet of my intention to marry you. I'll do that tomorrow night ... when I stay with her."

Bopha listened, quiet. So that's how it works. She reached for the carafe, poured them each a cup, then handed one to him. "Here's to the future," she said, gently touching her cup to his. She sipped.

152

He sipped. "Preah Chan Bopha, you know a king is not all powerful. So many people depend on me. In the past when I married, I never thought about how it would be for the woman, entering the hierarchy of wives. I never cared that much." He stopped and took her hand. "But this time, I thought I was wiser. And I care very much about you. I know it will be a shock for the Queen. She is a very perceptive woman. I want to be careful not to give her cause to ..."

"I think it's too late for that, my Lord," Bopha interrupted, then apologized. "I'm sorry to interrupt, my Lord."

"Jaya."

"Jaya." Bopha looked up at him. "She hasn't liked me since the first time we met, so many years ago. You had a ceremony here for my family and village, and for my friend Sophea's, after the Cham ..."

He listened carefully, then sighed. "Well, we'll do our best to appease her." He lifted the lid of one of the pots. Robust aromas floated out, cumin, sesame oil. "Shall we eat?"

While they ate, Bopha asked him how he decided which wife to stay with when, and how she would know it was her turn. Would they always meet here or did he sometimes come to the woman's room?

He would tell Kiri, who would arrange it with her lady-in-waiting. His wives always came to the Palace, but usually in his bedchamber. Last night had been impulsive, urgent. Not the norm. "And I'm getting older," he warned her. "Most of the time I just go to the wife and stay the night. We talk, and lie together without," he paused. "You know."

She smiled. "I've never done that," she teased. He looked up sharply, then saw her grin.

"Ah, yes. True." Jaya chuckled. "I make no guarantees to you that all will be chaste between us."

"Do you spend every night with a wife? How many do you have? How do you decide?"

The questions poured out of Bopha, but Jaya didn't seem to mind.

153

"Well, I don't have a schedule, and I often sleep alone. Though now that you are here, that may change. I have three wives. You will be the fourth." Bopha turned his answers over in her mind. Who were the other two? Did Indradevi accept them? Did Jaya know? She didn't ask. The King was watching her. "Tomorrow afternoon, after you meet the Queen, I will have you meet Mach Botum and Sao Nang. This week I will spend a night with each one."

Bopha already missed him. She toyed with her food. "Bopha." She looked quickly up at a man in distress. "This is how it is. Some things I cannot change. But I promise to take care of you. Is there anything you want?"

She asked softly, "Could one of my friends come to visit? Sometime?"

The King touched her cheek gently. "Of course. Kiri can arrange it with Kesor. Maybe this week."

She leaned into his hand. "That would be wonderful." He pulled her into an embrace. She felt the ridge of scar on his back. "Thank you," she whispered into his neck. "Thank you so much." She paused, then added, "Jaya ... My King, my love, soon to be my husband."

As he kissed her, she wondered when the wedding would be. But soon his lips and tongue gave her other things to think about, and she gave herself to them.

CHAPTER 16

Meeting the Queens

Bopha squatted under the eave and watched the banyan-leaf shadows dapple the porch. It was barely noon but the day seemed very long since she returned to her quarters for breakfast. Jaya would send for her in late afternoon, and she would have tea with each of his wives in turn for formal introductions, starting with Indradevi. Queen Indradevi, Bopha corrected her mind.

Finally she heard Chariya looking for her. "I'm on the porch, Chariya," she called softly.

Bopha had decided to sleep in the last room, the big one that looked up into the tree. She could use the closet in the smaller room. It felt strange to use a pot and have someone else empty it, rather than go outside to a mat as she had for her whole life. Bopha was starting to realize how circumscribed her world might become, living in the palace.

Her ears were very sore when she tried to put in the heavy earrings. Chariya drew her to the window and examined the lobes when she saw her mistress wince. "I will get medicine for you," she said. "If you wash them carefully twice a day, and put on the ointment, the holes should heal." Bopha nodded, but the swing of the pendants pulled painfully, and she lifted her hands to stop their movement.

"Thank you," she said, then added, "I don't know what I would do without you, Chariya. This is all so new."

Chariya was pulling the bun tight behind her head, so Bopha couldn't see her face. But she heard sympathy in her murmur. "Yes, Lok Srey. Lots of newness."

Shortly afterwards, Boran led Bopha to the smaller audience chamber. The door was open. This time, there were no long lounging cushions, just a bench on either side of the King's seat, and a small table with tea items and fruit slices on a platter. The Queen sat facing the door. Bopha wondered if Jaya had put her there so she wouldn't have to twist around to see her enter, part of the program to ease her way with the Queen. Indradevi sat straight, face impassive, watching the dancer. Bopha placed her feet carefully, hands in sampeah.

She had seen a flash of delight on the King's face when he saw her, then he settled his features into a peaceful smile. "My Queen," Jayavarman said to Indradevi. His deep voice rumbled through Bopha's chest. "This is the Apsara, Preah Chan Bopha. I gather that you met yesterday, but please allow me to make a formal introduction."

Bopha bowed to him then to the Queen. "Sit," the King told her, gesturing to the bench to his left. He rang a bell. A servant came to pour the tea, then taste it. When the man left, Indradevi handed her husband a cup, then gave one to Bopha. She settled on her bench and lifted her own cup. Her eyes were as hard and dark as ebony. There was a short silence, then she said, "I hope your accommodations are satisfactory?" It wasn't really a question.

Bopha managed to say, "Yes, Your Majesty." Then she stopped, uncertain of protocol. "All is satisfactory."

"If you need something, please do not hesitate to let me know," the Queen continued.

There was no welcome in her voice. Bopha nodded gingerly, not wanting to swing the earrings. "What beautiful earrings," the icy voice continued. Her own earrings were even larger and more elaborate, with large rubies set in a star pattern. The holes were very elongated, and the lobes so long that the jewelry grazed her shoulder. Bopha wondered if it tickled.

Conversation continued, in brief stilted sentences. Finally the King rang the bell and a different servant came to clear the tray. He had told Bopha that would be the sign that the audience was ended. It couldn't come soon enough for her. "Thank you for joining us, Preah Chan Bopha," he said. The Queen inclined her head, hands in a low, loose sampeah. The lines between her eyes frowned even when she was relaxed. Bopha stood, bowed to her then to the King, and backed to the door.

On the porch, she took a deep breath. Boran led her to where Chariya waited. She wasn't in her rooms for long before Boran returned. This time, she met the King's second wife, Mach Botum.

156

She was younger than Queen Indradevi but well into middle-age. Her stomach flowed over her sampot. Jaya had told her that Mach Botum had borne him four children, the second a boy. They were all grown except the youngest daughter. The first daughter was living far to the west, having married a prince of Thailand.

Mach Botum had a jolly demeanor, and conversation was much easier. Bopha recognized her from the baray. She accompanied the Queen but did not make any effort to be too near her, instead sitting among a group of women who chattered and laughed. Her face looked like it had never hosted a scowl.

Sao Nang was a different story. She was the King's third wife. It was at her marriage that Bopha danced as a young child. Sao Nang was clearly pregnant. Not as big as Kalienne had been toward the end, but not too far from delivery. Bopha realized that the King had not told her about this. Her stomach twisted. She wished he wouldn't spend the night with Sao Nang.

This third wife was beautiful, but very crisp in face and bearing. Clearly, she knew how to control her emotions. Her voice was fluid and appealing, a contrast to the sharpness of her features. Her cheekbones were high and her nose almost thin. She had come from Pagan, in a marriage of alliance with a Shan ruler. She was gracious, with none of Indradevi's need to snub the newcomer. But underneath, Bopha felt she was a coiled snake.

"Welcome to Bayon," she purred. "Preah Chan Bopha." She handed the tea around. More tea. Bopha was glad she could go back to her quarters between meetings to empty her bladder.

"Thank you, Queen Sao Nang," Bopha said. This time, the conversation turned to the construction projects, not a usual topic for women. As they talked about the timetable, and when the King expected the main temple to be consecrated, Bopha heard the hammering. It was such a part of life of that she tuned it out most of the time. She wondered if the Garuda with the funny feathers was still standing in the market.

"Do you miss dancing?" The question brought Bopha back to the room. Sao Nang was striking at Bopha's vulnerability.

"Not yet," Bopha said. "But I haven't been here ... long." She didn't want to say much. She felt Sao Nang fishing. She fished right back, "And you? Do you miss Pagan? I hear it is beautiful there."

Sao Nang smiled, almost indulgently, as if Bopha were a child. "It is beautiful. But my King has welcomed me warmly, so this has become home." She let her hand stray to her swollen belly, and rest there as she looked at the King. Jaya smiled back at her. Bopha wanted to run out of the room, out of the palace, and back to the dancers' courtyard. But that wasn't her home any more. She wanted to run to the market and fall at the feathered feet of Garuda. Maybe he would be her new home.

At last the King rang the bell. Back in her rooms, Bopha went into the closet and used the pot. After she washed her hands, she leaned against the bench and sobbed silently. Tears dripped into the water in the bowl, each drop the center of an expanding circle.

Bopha didn't notice. She took a deep breath, splashed water on her red eyes then stood up straight.

Outside her room, the banyan leaves swayed. Bopha lifted her arms into a jeeb and began to sway with the branches, letting remembered music carry her to solace.

That night was the longest in Bopha's life as she tossed and turned. She had never felt trapped before, though she had known there were many things she could not do. She had wanted to come here, to Angkor, to learn to dance for the King. How little she had understood what that might mean. Had Mdeay known? She lay in the dark and tried to conjure her mother's comforting presence. But it was gone.

Dancing was all she knew. Bopha had not realized that to be with the King meant to sacrifice her life. How could she have known? She thought back to the last, long look that Kesor gave her, before she had stepped into the litter chair. Kesor knew, she realized bitterly. But it would have done no good for her to tell the younger woman. The King commanded and that was that. She could not have refused.

She hadn't wanted to refuse. She wanted to go to her King. He had not forced her to do anything. Bopha rolled over again and looked out the window. The setting moon poured in, outlining the leaves in its path. Bopha wondered if her Garuda cast a huge shadow in this moon. When she saw the King, she would ask if

158

she could go to the sculpture studio again. In her mind she could smell the incense as she offered it, and see the funny feathering on the statue's right leg. She looked up at its hooked beak and deep set eyes. The deep creaking voice startled her. "Do not worry. All will be well."

Bopha rolled onto her stomach and stretched her arms out in full prostration. "Thank you, dear Garuda. I forgot your promise. But I don't know what to do," she whispered. She lay listening but heard only the small sounds of a tropical night. Even so, she felt peace seep into her. She slid her hips back over her feet, arms still outstretched in front. "Arkoun, Garuda."

She slept hard after that, and still felt soothed when her eyes opened to early daylight. Kitchen sounds, distant conversational murmuring. An elephant rumbled, then a little one trumpeted. Bopha had seen the elephants at work, dragging huge stones into place, on several occasions at Bayon. The hammering started. She stretched and got up, then stretched some more, twisting and bending all her joints. She started to roll her mat, then realized Chariya would chastise her. It seemed wrong just to leave it there.

Just then, there was a light knock. "Yes," said Bopha. Chariya bowed as she came in, then knelt to roll up the mat. Bopha shook her head. This would all take some getting used to — how long would the strangeness last?

"Are you okay, Lok Srey?" Chariya had stowed the mat and stood looking at her mistress.

"Oh. Yes, thank you. I was just thinking ..." Bopha trailed off, not wanting to burden Chariya. Maybe Chariya would know if they could go to the market. "Chariya, is it possible for you and I to go to the market?"

"Of course, Miss. We can arrange for a litter whenever you want." Bopha's heart leapt. "Do you want to go this morning, or in the afternoon?"

Bopha considered. It would be cooler but more crowded in the morning. If they went in the afternoon, the day would not seem as long. "How about mid-afternoon?"

"I will tell the bearers," Chariya said.

With something to look forward to, the morning sped past. Bopha and Chariya went to the baray right after breakfast. Mach Botum was there but none of the other wives. Was this another blessing from Garuda?

"Preah Chan Bopha," she said, smiling. "Come sit with us." She introduced Bopha to the other women by name and position, 'my daughter,' 'my maidservant,' 'my cousin.' She called Bopha, 'the Apsara.' Everyone was friendly, but no one asked intrusive questions, which Bopha appreciated. She listened to their conversation as it wandered through topics. What would they have for lunch? Who was the new ambassador that had arrived yesterday? Would there be a feast for him? When was Sao Nang's child due? They all had ideas about the best name for a baby, and whether it would be a girl or a boy.

After a few minutes, Bopha excused herself to swim. She had watched Sophea move through the water on her stomach, paddling with her legs and swaying her arms in front of her. She practiced. It felt good to use her body. She decided she would dance every day, even if she only had music in her head. When she climbed up the stones to sit on the edge and dry off, the other women asked her where she had learned to swim like that.

One of the younger maids shyly asked if Bopha could teach her. "Of course. I'm not very good at it, but I'm learning. We can learn together," Bopha assured her. She told them about Sophea, and they asked questions about life in the Apsara courtyard.

The women all walked back to the palace together, then separated to go to their individual quarters. Bopha took the encounter as a good omen. She didn't think she could stomach meeting either Queen Indradevi or Sao Nang. Queen Sao Nang, she reminded herself

When Chariya brought lunch, Bopha asked, "Please. Will you stay and eat with me? I am not used to eating alone." She looked at the bowls and plates set out on the tray.

"There's more than enough for both of us." Chariya didn't answer right away. "I mean, if it's allowed. I'd like it, but I don't want you to get in trouble."

"Oh no, Srey Bopha. I won't get in trouble. Thank you." The two young women squatted together. Bopha rearranged the food so they both had some of each item.

"I'm glad you are here to help me, Chariya. There is so much I don't know about life in the Palace," Bopha said, as she finished a bowl of soup. "Actually, I hardly know anything."

"You'll do fine, Miss. I can see that you want to help people and to be kind." Chariya stopped, looking uncertain how to say the more that she clearly wanted to say.

"But?" prompted Bopha, smiling.

"But it's not always so good to ... " Chariya was uncomfortable.

"To be a push-over? I have to know when to help and when it is better to let things take their natural course?" Bopha suggested. Chariya's face cleared.

"Yes, that's it."

"Thank you for your wisdom and advice. I will need lots of it, so please give it freely. I just spent years learning to dance as an Apsara. Now I need to learn how to ..."

It was Bopha's turn to stop. What did she need to learn how to do? Learn how to stop talking, for one. She had been going to say, "to be a wife of the King." She shook her head. That was not an announcement for her to make. "Well, lots of things." She smiled at Chariya. "Would you like some of this star fruit?"

After Chariya took the lunch tray down to the kitchen, Bopha took a short nap. It wasn't yet hot season, but the day was sunny and plenty warm. When she woke, she went onto the back porch. Sitting in the shadows, she exercised her hands and feet. She had decided tonight to dance the Reamker, the story of the Ramayana. There were parts she wasn't certain of, but she knew most of it and it was long enough to keep her occupied. Who would Jaya be with tonight?

This time the litter had pale blue silk curtains and Chariya pulled them open for her. Bopha moved over on the seat to make room but Chariya shook her head, whispering, "I'll walk behind you." By the time they got to the market, Bopha was sticky with

161

sweat in the closed litter. It was a relief to step out into what passed as fresh air on this afternoon without a breeze.

She suddenly realized that she had not thought to bring incense, nor how to buy it. Her heart dropped and she made a mental note to ask the King. Or Kiri, if she saw him. She hoped Garuda would hear her intentions anyway. As she thought of her feathered protector, she was sure he would.

"Where do you want to go?" Chariya asked.

"Let's smell perfume and then look at toys. One day soon I'll get a present for Sao Nang's baby," Bopha said. She'd suggest the Garuda statues later. The litter bearers accompanied the young women, making sure no one in the crowd jostled them.

After being away from the Apsara courtyard and spending so much time alone, Bopha delighted in the smells and colors of the market. She kept an eye out, but didn't see any dancers in the throng. Usually they came in the morning, she remembered. Maybe next time she'd come then.

After an hour of wandering among the vendors, Bopha led the group to the sculpture street. When they turned the corner, she stopped and stared. The studio was there, but all the statues were gone. Tears sprang to her eyes.

"Miss, are you okay?" Chariya's voice was full of concern.

"There were ... there were six Garudas here just a few days ago. I would bring incense for them," Bopha said slowly.

The sculptors were hammering in the shadows as she walked nearer. She could see that they were making Nagas now. "Good day, Bong," Bopha said to one of the older men. "Where did the Garudas go?"

He shrugged. "The King sent a wagon for them. I guess they're at Bayon."

Bopha made sampeah and turned back to the market, "Well, maybe I can see them there," she said softly to herself. Then, to Chariya, "Do you want to go anywhere else? She did not, so the group made their way back to the litter.

162

Chariya left a torch burning for Bopha after dinner. After she unrolled her sleeping mat and sheets, she asked, "Is there anything else, Lok Srey?"

"No," said Bopha, "thank you. Not tonight." Chariya left, closing the door quietly. The moon was nearly full, peeking in the east window as it cleared the trees. Bopha knelt and rolled up the mat, pushing it against the wall. Then she blew out the torch and stood in the middle of the room in the moonlight.

She danced until the moon lifted above the window, then above the roof. Her body ached, and her left calf had a cramp by the time she was done, but her mind was calm and clear. She may not live in the courtyard any more, but she was still an Apsara.

CHAPTER 17

Perfect Union

Three days dragged along. Bopha went to the baray in the morning and sat, mostly quiet, listening to the women chatter before she swam. When she helped the maidservant Rom Chang float, everyone watched closely. Sweet and friendly, Rom Chang was one of those people who are naturally buoyant and well-coordinated. She made it look easy, like Sophea had.

By the fourth morning, several other women were trying to float. Most of them sank immediately and came up choking, but laughing. "No fair," they told Rom Chang, "you are a water flower so it's easy for you!"

Bopha missed her Apsara friends, but she was starting to recognize some of the palace women and make her place among them. Neither Indradevi nor Sao Nang bathed on those mornings. When Bopha's thoughts strayed to them, she reminded herself of Rithy's saying, "To maintain peacefulness, keep your thoughts on pleasant topics."

To be so near Rithy, but not to see him, was frustrating. Unless the King decided to bring them together, their lives would not normally intersect. "Soon," she thought, "soon, I'll see the King." She did not realize that she was thinking of him again in formal terms, no longer, "Jaya."

Dancing until exhausted in the evenings, Bopha slept well. She danced in the afternoon warmth on the fourth day, thinking she would be summoned that evening. But Chariya brought her supper, with no news from the King. That night Bopha sat in a circle of moonlight in the big dark room, alone. She had not just been hoping to see the King. She had assumed that she would. She watched the circle move across the floor, until she was sitting in shadows. Her body felt sluggish, her abdomen bloated. She would get her moon-bleeding any day.

Bopha curled into a ball on the mat and imagined Garuda standing in front of her, his feathers just a little rumpled. Tomorrow she would try to find where the statues had gone, and how to get incense. Soothed by a plan, she finally slept.

On the morning of the fifth day, the women at the baray were full of news. How did they find out? Bopha wondered. There was to be a big feast for a new emissary who had come all the way from India. Bopha had no idea where India was. Moch Botum gestured vaguely west, "It's beyond the sunset."

Besides a feast, there would be dancing by the Apsaras. Sudden silence followed this announcement by a girl about ten years named Malis, who was Mach Botum's youngest child. Bopha felt sidelong glances as she gasped involuntarily. She dropped her eyes to the steep stone steps that led into the water. Their flat faces were sculpted with flowers and figures. Apsaras gleamed on one stone just under the surface of the baray. She reached down to touch them. Dancers! But not her. She drew slow circles on the stone, and watched their eddies widen. Finally conversation picked up without her. She didn't even know if she was invited to the feast. Bopha straightened her back and lifted her head, on her face the small smile she had learned.

After lunch, Chariya took the tray downstairs, but came back almost immediately. Bopha was sitting on the porch, looking at the banyan and trying not to think. "Lok Srey. The King wishes you to come to him."

Bopha's heart jumped. "Now?"

"Yes." Chariya helped her with the earrings. The ointment had been helping and her ears weren't so sore today. Bopha wore a purple and orange sampot, and all the bangles she had. She was ready quickly.

The King was in the small audience room. When he saw Bopha, he stood up and walked to meet her. "My dear Bopha," he said, clasping her hands. "I wanted to talk with you about tonight." She nodded, silent. "There will be lots of people tonight, so I wanted to see you alone first." He bent his head to kiss her, then wrapped her in his arms. It felt strange at first, then she returned the embrace. When her fingers touched the scar on his back, she suddenly flooded with recognition and affection. She pulled back to look at him, and smiled into his eyes.

"It's nice to see you," she said.

165

"I missed you," he said.

"I missed you too."

"I had hoped to see you yesterday, but I had to entertain the Indian Ambassador for a men's-only evening." He drew her to a bench and they sat next to each other. Jayavarman kept arm around her. "I know it will be hard for you to see the Apsaras and not to be among them." He pulled her closer. "Starting next week, Kesor will let them come visit you here. One or two at a time, every few days." Bopha grinned with relief. "You are very quiet," he told her, moving away enough to watch her.

"Yes, I guess so. I heard about the feast and about the Apsaras, but I didn't know if ..."

She stopped. He waited. "If I was invited," she finished in a tiny voice.

"Oh, Bopha. I'm so sorry. I never thought ..." It was his turn to stop. "I've been very thoughtless. I wanted so much to have you here. My other wives came with their own servants. They sort of brought their own lives. But you came alone, and gave up your life for me." His compassionate tone tugged tears into her eyes. He leaned forward to kiss the corner of each eye. "The many years I was in exile in Champa, I had Kiri and my first wife, and many others in the court. But you ..."

"You're all I have here," she managed.

"I will ask Boran or Kiri to check with you every day, to see if you need anything or have questions. I realize you need some way to reach me. It will be some months still before we can wed." He looked a little abashed. "I have not yet told the Queen of my intention."

"Are you scared of her?" The words were out of Bopha's mouth before she realized. They stared at each other, shocked. Then the King took a deep breath, and smiled wryly.

"I did ask you to tell me the truth," he acknowledged. "And not just the truth I want to hear." He paused. "This is all very new. For both of us. I mean, I have wives and I've had ... concubines ... but it's different with you. We'll have to find our way. Together.

"I've known the Queen since she was born. You know that her older sister was my first wife?"

Bopha nodded. She had heard about the beautiful queen who influenced her husband toward Buddhism and died young, how the King married her much younger sister. "Indradevi is a force of nature, not to be trifled with, not even by a king. Scared is probably too strong a word." He paused. "But not by much. I want to pave the way for our future here, yours and mine, to be smooth. That will take time, and patience."

Bopha considered his words. Then she changed the subject abruptly. "I went to the market the other day, with Chariya. I was going to offer incense to Garuda. But the Garudas are gone. The men said the King had sent a wagon for them. Are they here? Can I see them?" He was listening carefully. She blurted, "And then I realized that I don't have incense or any way to get it at the market. I knew how to do things before, how things worked, but here I'm lost."

Jayavarman shook his head slightly. "So many things I never thought of. I'm glad you tell me. You can get whatever you want at the market. Just tell them it's for the King. The merchants recognize my men who go with you, and they'll keep track. We pay them every week.

"As for Garuda, I don't know. Most of the day-to-day details are handled by my clerks.

I'll ask Kiri to find out for you." Bopha was gleaming with delight. "Don't worry. All will be well," Jaya said softly. "I remember how Garuda took care of you. Of course you can make offerings." He lifted his big hands, one on each side of her face, cradling it.

"He saved your life and I will be forever grateful." Their kiss was long and soft and sweet.

When she returned to her apartment, Bopha felt lighter than she had in days. Jaya had answered all her questions. He was taking care of her. She knew he would send for her tomorrow night, and was eager to sleep in his strong arms. She knew how this evening would progress, where she would sit and with whom. She would be part of the King's entourage, introduced to the Ambassador as his Apsara. Of course she would not dance, but

167

she could barely wait to watch. There would be no time tonight to visit with her friends, but soon.

* * *

True to his word, the King had Boran or Kiri stop by her apartment every morning. It was a few days until Kiri tracked down the Garuda statues. "I can take you today," the tall man with the sorrowful eyes told her.

They were alone on her front porch. "Thank you. That would be wonderful. I can go whenever is convenient for you," Bopha said. Then, more softly, "Kiri, have you heard anything of Kalienne?"

The King's Man shook his head slightly. "Maybe it's better if I don't know. I'm sure the King thinks so. That way I can't get myself in trouble."

"But he said he's taking care of them, and we can trust that," Bopha said quietly. Kiri nodded.

"I'll let Chariya know when we can go find the statues. Oh, and I'll bring incense. Maybe I'll light some myself, and ask for blessings on ..." He stopped as Chariya came up the steps. They all made sampeah and Kiri left. For the first time, Bopha noticed his shoulders were getting a bit stooped.

Late afternoon sun was slanting through the banyan when Chariya came for her. Their shadows were long and thin on the dust ahead as they walked. Kiri led them into a work area behind the temple. Lines of stones, many with parts of figures chipped in bas relief, filled at least an acre. Bopha saw images: tails of fish, an elephant eye and trunk, the arm of an Apsara, men squatting at dice. Workers were maneuvering heavy stones with levers. Others were hammering pictures out of blocks of stone.

Women carried baskets of dirt on their heads, coming from behind the temple and disappearing out of sight. "The King is digging another baray," Kiri told them, gesturing at the women. "And using the dirt to improve the road."

The Garudas were clustered under a tree on the far side of the work area. Beyond them, some workers were squatting over a fire pit. The smell of barbecued chicken hung in the still air. Kiri took

168

the incense over, murmured to the surprised men, and lit it from the fire. He had brought six sticks, and gave each of them two.

Bopha found her rumple-legged favorite farthest from the tree. She looked up into its fierce face. When she reached out her hand to touch a wing feather, the stone was warm. "Be with Kiri," she thought, "And Kalienne and Arun Veha. And of course with Jayavarman. Help me learn my way in this new life, especially with Indradevi and Sao Nang. Thank you for being here." She waved the incense in small circles in front of the huge statue, then in front of the one beside it. She gathered some of the multitude of stone fragments into a small pile and propped up the burning joss in front of her two Garudas.

Bowing a last time to the god, she followed Kiri back through the maze of workmen and stone. She paid close attention to the turns, so she could find her own way another day. It wasn't that far, but there were a lot of people and a lot of work places. The temple of Bayon itself was already higher than the palace, but not as high as the towers at Angkor Wat.

"How high will it be when it's done?" Bopha asked Kiri, as they stopped under a tree and looked back at Bayon.

"Only one more tier to go," Kiri said. "It's a lot shorter than the towers at Angkor, but the temple complex as a whole is larger here."

"Do you know when it will be done?"

Kiri shook his head. "Another few years, at least."

Bopha decided not to ask, "Can I come here with Chariya and light incense?" She couldn't explain the impulse, but she didn't want to have to get permission for every act.

The three walked in silence. Hot season had come, and the sun bore down on them even as it sank. It was a relief to sit at last on her porch, shaded through sunset.

Jayavarman had said that tonight they would be together, so she had danced at dawn, before going to the baray. She pressed her hands back, and then her fingers, extending them as far as they could go, then a little farther, breathing, watching leaf shadows on the porch floor.

169

* * *

She met the King in his bedchamber. It was large room with tightly-fitted teak panels, and windows that had shutters on the inside. When closed, the room was pitch dark. But it was hot season, and all the windows were open. This room was at one end of a high porch, in a building separate from the audience chambers and scribes' workshop. After showing Bopha inside, and closing the door, the guard would stay all night on the porch. Other guards patrolled the grounds around the building.

Thin silk fabric hung from wooden rods set above the windows. Flickering light from oil lamps, burning on several small benches, turned the silk a fiery orange. There was no breeze and the curtains moved not at all. Bopha and Jayavarman sat cross-legged on cushions, eating a dinner laid out a low table in front of them, under the windows where the sun had set.

"How is your visit with the Ambassador from India?" Bopha asked the King as they nibbled on fruit after the meal. "Why does he come?"

"He comes to assure me of his friendship. Kampuchea does not share a border with his land, but I have built roads that run in all directions, across our whole country. They make it easy for messengers — or armies — to travel. Our kingdom stretches from the mountains far to the north, all the way to the western ocean. Ships can cross from the ports on our shores, directly across to India." Bopha remembered what Rithy had said, so long ago, about boats and the ocean.

"Not long before you were born," the King's deep voice continued, "the Cham came all the way to Angkor. They burned everything, stole all the gold and bronze, and defaced the walls and statues." Bopha nodded. She had heard of this when she first arrived at the Apsara courtyard. "I lived with some of the Cham for many years when I was in exile. They have many princes that fight among each other and also fight with us. But other princes are our friends and help us."

He looked at Bopha, adding softly, "Not all the Cham are murderers." Bopha's eyes suddenly filled with tears. Jayavarman gently stroked her cheek, then said, "How about you? What have you been doing?"

170

Bopha told him about the trip to the Garudas, and about the one with the rumpled feathers that she liked best. She didn't tell him about her dancing, not wanting to remind him of her loss. Maybe sometime she could dance just for him.

He poured them each a drink and lifted his cup. "To the most beautiful woman in all of Kampuchea, the one who has stolen the King's heart." She met his eyes. He was smiling softly. Was she supposed to drink to herself? He lifted his chin, indicating that she was. Bopha took a sip. She was getting used to the cold-hot liquid.

She touched his cup with hers, "to my King and my love," she murmured. "May the gods smile upon you forever." They both sipped, looking into each other's eyes.

The King rang a bell on the table. After a moment the door opened and two serving women slipped in, bowing. The center of the room was dominated by a slightly raised platform of very dark wood, polished until it gleamed in the light. The women opened a cupboard where the platform met the wall, and unrolled a thick cushion. Then they spread soft cotton across the cushion and tucked it in on all sides. After plumping several small cushions at the head of the bed, they spread deep purple silk across the whole thing. Bowing again, they gathered the dinner trays and backed to the door.

Jayavarman stood, still graceful despite his age. He extended his hand to Bopha as she rose. They walked to the bed, then undid each other's necklaces. The King took off his sampot and reclined against the pillows, watching Bopha slip off her earrings. As she unknotted her garment, she watched his manhood rising. He pulled her gently on top of him. His hands could be so soft, she thought, as he stroked her back and sides, slowly, rhythmically. She felt her own insides melting. Hard met soft, a perfect union.

* * *

When she woke, early dawn was lighting the curtains. The King was watching her. "You're awake already," Bopha murmured.

"I like to watch you sleep," he said. She rolled onto her side, facing him. With her fingers, she traced his face. Across the broad

171

forehead, around his wide eyes, down weathered cheeks, then down his nose and around his full mouth -- which he opened, capturing her fingers. They both laughed. He pulled her close and she lay her head on his chest, watching the rise and fall of his breath.

"I was thinking about what you told me," Jaya said. Bopha shifted slightly to look at him. "About what you want to learn. The only women here who know how to read and write are the Queen and Sao Nang." Bopha stiffened slightly. "I know," Jaya said. "They aren't an option. But how about Nimith Vireak -- Rithy -- as your teacher?"

Bopha sat up, grinning hugely. "Rithy? That would be wonderful. I haven't seen him in so long."

"Well, he's very accomplished, and has a way of making things clear. Since he's your brother, it would be a good arrangement. There is a small room in this building where you can meet. It gets morning sun."

"Oh, thank you!" Bopha kissed him exuberantly, then again softly, lingering.

Jaya hugged her close, then said, "A King has things he must do, my dear, even if he would prefer to lie abed with you. I will ask Kiri to make the arrangements. Have any of the dancers come to visit yet?" Bopha shook her head. "Well, it would be better if they came in the afternoon, then. Boran can tell Kesor. And you and I can see each other again tonight."

After a few more moments of cuddling and nuzzling, Jayavarman swing to the edge of the bed and stood. He stretched his arms all the way over his head and bent backwards. Bopha could hear his back crick. "Ah, that's better," Jaya said. He did gentle twists right and left, then folded forward till his hands were flat on the floor.

"You could almost be a dancer," she told him. "So flexible."

He slid his legs back until he was lying on his stomach, then lifted his shoulders and head up and back, held for a moment, then flattened. This time he pulled one leg up and arched his back, then switched legs and repeated the posture. Then with legs together behind him, he pushed up on both arms, body and legs aligned at an angle to the floor. Dropping to the floor, he rested a moment, prone, with his arms stretched out above his head. Then, with his elbows beneath his shoulders, he lifted his torso off the floor, bending backwards Lastly, he slid up into a triangle, bottom high, then pulled his hands back to touch his feet, stood and arched back again.

"What is that?" Bopha asked.

"It's an ancient practice from India. The Ambassador showed me yesterday. He calls it Salute to the Sun. I used to do it as a young man but I had forgotten."

"Tomorrow morning, I want to do it with you," she said, wrapping on her sampot.

"I will be honored by your company," laughed the King. He pulled her into a last embrace, then walked her to the door. "Until tonight."

The guard escorted her to the end of the porch, where an older guard took over and walked her to the women's courtyard. It was all so formal, Bopha thought. She walked with her dancer's gait and her head high, but felt naked, realizing that the entire palace was aware of the King's sleeping arrangements.

CHAPTER 18

1194 - 1195, Learning New Ways

Several mornings later, Chariya told Bopha that a guard was waiting, to take her to a monk. They followed a young guard to the building where the King slept. Passing the wide staircase Bopha had climbed to be with him, they went up another set of steps to a porch on the back of the building. Chariya accompanied Bopha to the door, which was open. Rithy heard them coming and met the young women.

"Bopha! It is a blessing to see you again," he said, bowing deeply. Bopha would like to have hugged him, but he was more monk than brother now so she refrained. She introduced Chariya, who would chaperone their meeting, squatting near the door.

Rithy drew his sister toward the east window. Light dappled through trees onto the edge of a table that had a stack of dried and flattened palm leaves. There was a bench in front of the table. "Sit here," Rithy said. He sat next to her. Taking up two palm leaves, he gave one to her, then picked up two slender, polished bamboo reeds. He showed her how to dip the reed in a brass pot. Inside the pot was a black liquid. When he lifted the reed, he made a swirly mark on the palm paper.

Rithy explained that writing was a way to record the sounds of speech. He wrote the alphabet on the paper, having Bopha repeat each letter, along with its name and sound, several times. Time flew past as Bopha tried to make the marks on her paper look like those on Rithy's. She was startled when Chariya cleared her throat softly. The sun was high above the window.

"This is so much fun, Rithy," said Bopha with a big smile. "Can I take my palm leaf with me?"

Rithy smiled back. "Of course. Next time I'll bring you your own ink pot."

"I'm so glad we can meet, brother." Bopha paused. Rithy regarded her solemnly. Did he know about her and the King? He must, she decided. Monks gossip just like everyone else. She knew Chariya was listening discreetly near the door. "It's been a time of changes for me, and I'm glad for your company."

He nodded. They bowed and Bopha carried her palm leaf carefully down the steps. She almost stumbled once, as she was looking at the writing and saying the sounds in her head. The guard looked back to be sure she was okay, and Chariya nearly ran into her from behind as Bopha regained her balance. Bopha nodded to the young guard, "It's okay." She was glad to get back to the privacy of her rooms.

She thought about Jaya. Born a prince, he had always been the object of attention. To him it was natural. For her, it was an unwelcome intrusion. You'd better get used to it, she told herself. This is your life now.

After lunching on fruit and a small portion of rice, Bopha was sitting on the porch when Chariya told her she had a visitor. She jumped up and almost ran to the front door where a small, erect figure stood in shadow. "Sophea!" Bopha hugged her friend. She couldn't stop a few tears from squeezing out, and she clutched Sophea like a drowning person grasps a life line.

Sophea pulled away and looked at Bopha closely. "Are you okay?" Bopha nodded, and inclined her head slightly toward Chariya. "Are you crying?"

"Chariya, will you please bring some refreshment for our guest?" Bopha said. She led Sophea into the front room. "I'm okay," she said softly. "I've just missed you so much.

Tell me all about life in the Apsara courtyard."

"How about you tell me about your new life?" Sophea countered, smiling. "Is this where you live?"

"Yes, these are my quarters. But I'm here alone, except for Chariya." Bopha took Sophea on a tour. "In the evenings that I don't go to the King, I dance in this room."

"By yourself?"

Bopha shrugged, nodding. "I haven't done anything else but dance since I was such a little girl. Well, you know, Sophea." Sophea nodded, sober. "I think dancing has kept me from going crazy here alone. But you're here now. Oh, I'm so glad to see you."

They sat in what Bopha thought of as her dance studio while Chariya served tea, then she left them alone to talk.

Bopha said, "It was wonderful to see you dancing for the Indian Ambassador the other night, Sophea. You make the movements come alive. I wish we could dance together here, but I only hear the music in my mind."

"We've heard the same music for so long, I bet we can hear it together," Sophea suggested. "What do you want to dance?" They decided on the first part of the Wishing Dance, and stood up, positioning arms and legs in the first jeeb. Bopha nodded her head, "1,2,3," and began to move. Sophea followed, keeping the imaginary time as they twirled and bent, weaving in and out as if there were six other dancers with them.

Bopha was almost panting when they stopped. She laughed. "I thought I was staying in shape, but the music is faster with you here." Sophia chuckled.

"I guess I'll have to come more often."

"I surely hope you will. Please, tell me, how are Theary and Thida? Theary didn't come the other night. Is she okay?"

"Just having her moon blood." The young women sat on the back porch where a breeze was ruffling the banyan leaves. They talked and laughed softly until the sun was low. "Kesor says I can come every few days," Sophea said, as she rose to leave.

"You haven't said much about life here, but I can guess some." Bopha nodded. She hadn't said much about the King except that he was kind to her. She said nothing about his wives.

"Oh!" Bopha remembered. "Rithy, you know, my brother, the monk?" Sophea nodded. "He's teaching me to write." Sophea's eyebrows rose in shock. "I need to keep busy, and I can't always be going out, so Ja —". She stopped the word. "The King suggested Rithy could help me." Bopha showed Sophea the palm leaf. She tried to remember the sounds for each letter but only got about a third right. "I'm just starting to learn. Each letter has its own sound! Next time, I'll write you your name."

With that promise, Sophea left. Bopha stood on the porch as her friend followed the young guard down the stairs, her head and back erect as always. She would recognize Sophea's form anywhere, Bopha thought. She wanted to watch until she couldn't see her any more, but she didn't want her vulnerability to be seen by the whole palace. She turned into the sudden gloom of her room. The sun sank.

This evening she would sleep alone. She lay on her soft mat in the darkness, lit by a few torches, until the soft murmuring of voices in the courtyards hushed. A cat shrieked, startling her. It sounded close. Another answered, even closer, then there was the clank of guards chasing the animals away. Bopha tried writing the alphabet in her mind and was soon asleep.

* * *

Bopha's life slowly began to find its new rhythm. She spent the evening and night with Jayavarman several times a week. Most mornings, after going to the baray, she would meet Rithy. She knew the alphabet now and he was teaching her words. A few afternoons, apsaras would visit. When she was alone for the night, she would dance.

Some of the music was fading from her memory and she wished she could hear it more often.

One morning a few weeks after she moved to the Palace, Chariya asked her to come to the main room. At the door was a chubby young man. He bowed. Chariya held out the tray of food to him. He took a spoon and tasted a small mouthful of each item, bowed again, and left.

"Do you want to eat in here?" Chariya asked. Bopha did not, particularly, but she nodded assent. She remembered what Jayavarman said on their first night together, that she should not eat anything that had not been tasted. She shivered, as she sat cross-legged in front of the tray. Apparently he had decided she had been here long enough to pose a threat.

To whom? Queen Indradevi and Khosal leapt to mind. Bopha wondered if those two were allies, or if they each had their individual plots and machinations. The food was suddenly not as delicious. She turned her thoughts consciously to the feathered leg of Garuda, then the Khmer alphabet, for distraction.

At least once a week, Bopha went to the market. The day beforehand, she would ask Chariya to arrange the litter and guards. She liked to go in the mornings when it was busy. She always looked for dancers, and occasionally would be able to chat with a group of them. The apsaras stood out from the crowd by the erectness of their posture, three or four young women together. Bopha always got a few sticks of incense. Now she had big handful stashed on a ledge in the back room, wrapped in a small piece of cloth and tied with a strip of silk.

One afternoon, a day after Sophea and Theary had come for a visit, Bopha decided to try to find the statues. It was another hot day. All the stones gave off heat into the air even more in the workshop acres. Chariya and she were accompanied by the young guard Bopha had almost fallen into while reading. Bopha wondered if he had been assigned to her. His name was Samang and his eyes smiled even when his face was impassive, as befitted a guard.

Bopha thought she could see the tree where the Garudas were, and pointed it out to Samang. But, after their little party wove past groups of workmen, it turned out to be the wrong tree. Sweat poured down their faces and chests and between their shoulder blades. Bopha looked all around. She hadn't realized that the workshop area would change, with completed bas-reliefs moved to other places. She had no idea where they were.

She asked Samang to ask a wiry man whose nearly naked body had been baked almost black by sun. "There are six statues, very tall," Bopha said, reaching her hand up above her head. The man suddenly nodded. Telling his fellows that he would be back, he led the trio. After nearly five hundred meters, Bopha saw the tree (or a tree, she certainly hoped it was the right one). Yes. There were the statues, six in a row. Bopha gave the man sampeah. "Arkoun, bong. We can make our way from here."

In the shadow of the tree it was slightly cooler. As a little gust of wind helped dry her perspiration, Bopha looked around for somewhere to light incense. Since each group of men cooked their own meals, it was easy to find a fire. Samang brought back the six smoking joss sticks and gave them to Chariya. Bopha

178

asked him, "Do you want to make an offering?" From the look on his face and on Chariya's, Bopha could tell she had broken protocol. Samang looked at the ground. "Arkoun, Samang, for getting us the fire," she said.

Bopha stood in front of each huge bird-man and offered the smoke. Chariya followed, doing the same. Then they knelt to leave the incense near the stone claws. Bopha lingered, kneeling, in front of the rumpled feathers. She had much to be thankful for now — the King (when she thought of him, her insides melted and she quickly brought her mind under control), learning to write with Rithy, seeing her apsara friends. She also wanted protection from any danger. And guidance about how to cope with the Queen and Minister Khosal.

After a few minutes, her heart felt ease and warmth. Giving one last sampeah, Bopha rose. The walk back to the Palace compound was much faster, even though they walked into the sun. Bopha realized that she might not be able to find Garuda by herself after all, but she was glad to have gone.

There was no backlash from her excursion, as it turned out, because it was eclipsed by big news. Sao Nang was in labor. Her waters had broken after lunch. This was her first pregnancy, so there was no knowing when the baby might be born.

After so much sweating in the hot sun, Bopha and Chariya went to the baray before dinner. Mach Botum was there with her entourage. The second wife was cheerful and chatty, not just because of her innate good nature but also with the confidence of her position. She had already borne children to her King. Bopha was able to smile warmly at the woman, who always welcomed her, and to offer a few words of support towards Sao Nang. But as soon as seemly, she excused herself.

It was supposed to be Bopha's night with the King. But would this labor change things? All she could do was wait and see.

When Chariya knocked on the door, carrying the box with Bopha's jewels, she knew the answer. Or part of it. Samang and Chariya led her to the small audience chamber, not the King's bedroom. When the door had closed, Jaya stood and opened his arms for her embrace.

179

"You know about Sao Nang?" Bopha nodded into his shoulder. "I wanted to see you. We can have dinner together but …" His words trailed off and she lifted her head to look into his eyes.

"Even though you would not be with her in labor, it is not right for you to be in another woman's arms?"

Jayavarman nodded, squeezing her tight. "I can hardly wait for you to become my wife," he murmured.

They talked softly while eating. Then the King suddenly lifted her up and sat her on his lap. Lovemaking was fast and hard, both of them so eager. Bopha sat on him, her pelvis contracting, until his member softened and slipped out. Their breath had almost returned to normal when the evening air was pierced with a shriek.

Bopha and Jaya quickly straightened themselves. He walked her to the door and opened it himself. She slipped out and found Samang waiting at the bottom of the steps. Before she got to her quarters, several messengers rushed past, heading to the King.

Torches blazed everywhere. Musicians were tuning up at the entrance to the women's courtyard. They started playing. The baby had been born, and it was a boy. A new young prince, Bopha thought. She hadn't asked Jaya how he felt about having this new baby. And they had never talked about having a baby together.

* * *

Slender as Sao Nang was, her labor had been fast and she recovered quickly. In the morning, Chariya helped Bopha dress for her formal visit to the third queen. Her gift had been wrapped for weeks, a small, pure gold Buddha, carefully chosen at the market to be appropriate for prince or princess.

When she entered Sao Nang's chambers, the queen was sitting up on a bed that was a smaller version of the King's. She had dark circles under her eyes but was smiling as she cradled a bundle. Both Indradevi and Mach Botum were leaning over the bed. Bopha knew that in three days, there would be a ceremony to welcome the baby and present him to his father. She approached the bed. Standing next to Mach Botum, she offered her gift. Sao Nang nodded to her to hand it to a waiting servant. Then she

180

pulled back the blanket from the baby's face. His eyes were squinted shut and his full lips made sucking movements as he slept.

"Such a beautiful boy, my Queen. Congratulations." Bopha meant it. She saw Sao Nang recognize that and relax. Indradevi, on the other side of the bed, stiffened slightly. Mach Botum patted Bopha's arm surreptitiously.

The introduction couldn't end fast enough for Bopha. One down, one to go. She practiced writing on her own for the rest of the morning, then after lunch she danced. But it was too hot, so she lay on her mat and watched the banyan leaves until dinner.

On the appointed day, the procession from the women's courtyard to the King's audience chamber was long and loud. Just this once, Sao Nang's litter went first, then Indradevi and Mach Botum, with their retinues. Bopha was surprised to find her litter waiting for her at the bottom of the stairs. She might not be an official wife, but she was being treated as one. Loud music, drums, cymbals, horns accompanied them.

After everyone was arranged in the audience chamber, Jayavarman stood to welcome his son. Sao Nang carried the bundle, now wrapped in gold silk with a peaked, gold and red silk cap, to the King. He lifted it from her arms, looked at the baby's face, and smiled. The baby had been sleeping but now woke up and stared impassively into the King's face until the music started again. Startled then, the baby wailed. Jayavarman laughed and handed the boy back to his mother.

Rithy was among the monks who performed the ceremony. The child received his name: Nimith Sokhem, "transformation and hope." He cried throughout the ceremony, then was given, gasping, to his wet nurse who took him to the back of the room. The sudden silence caused more than a few mouths to smile.

The monks were served first, then men and women ate, separately as was usual. Bopha nibbled and sipped cool ginger tea. She glanced at Sao Nang and thought she looked pale and her smile stiff. She probably wanted the event to end even more than did Bopha.

It was the first time in weeks that Bopha had seen the King's sister, Kiri's wife. Khun Thea looked paler than Sao Nang, and ate

181

almost nothing. She never came to the baray, at least not when Bopha did. Was she all right? Her once full figure had shriveled until the skin was loose and her breasts hung limp.

At last, the gathering recessed. Sao Nang went first, then Khun Thea, then the other queens and Bopha. As she stood at the top of the stairs, waiting for the crowd to get to the bottom, Bopha noticed it was Khun Thea holding things up, as she took each step with great care and gripped her lady-in-waiting's arm tightly.

CHAPTER 19

1195, Sudden Changes

Time slipped by, the rains started. Bopha had been more than six moons at the Palace. Still, the King had not set a date for their wedding. Now Sao Nang brought the baby to bathe in the mornings. More accurately, the baby accompanied her. Being a queen, his mother did little actual care of him. He was cheerful and chubby. Bopha's heart squeezed when she watched him crow and flail his arms. Arun Veha would be how old now? She tried to figure it out. It must be almost a year since he and Kalienne were banished.

There were whispers about Khun Thea. She never appeared in public but Rom Chang had heard from Khun Thea's maid that her mistress hardly ever got out of bed. She was living on ginger tea, and barely kept that down. Bopha remembered Khun Thea's nearly-skeletal fingers clutching the arm of her maid-servant, with enough strength that little wrinkles formed under her grasp.

One morning when Kiri came to see if she needed anything, Bopha asked him. "I've heard that your wife is not well."

Kiri was getting more stooped and lines of sorrow flowed down his face where unshed tears would have trailed. He shook his head, which had much more grey than last year. "She's failing, Bopha. I don't think it will be long before …" His words trailed off and he looked down at the floor.

They were alone. Bopha was sorry for Khun Thea, who was so kind and had so much sadness, and so much physical distress. But she couldn't help wondering what would happen if she died. Would Kalienne be able to return? Not right away, of course, but after a time? She said nothing about these thoughts. "I'm sorry, Kiri. I know she's had a difficult few years. I'll ask Garuda to watch over her." The tall man lifted his eyes to hers and nodded. "And watch over you," Bopha added. The look on his face made her want to cry. Instead, she made sampeah, and sent all the affection she had for him through her eyes.

This man had been such a big part of her life, ever since the day he rode into her village and chose her to become a dancer. She wished he might have happiness again.

A few weeks later, Bopha was awakened in the night by the sound of running feet and lots of murmuring. Then horns began to sound. The courtyard was suddenly blazing with torches and she could see almost as well as if there were a light in her room. She stood up from her mat and went onto the balcony, recognizing the music. Khun Thea! She must have died.

Chariya found her there a few minutes later, bringing her necklaces and earrings. By the time they got to the room where Khun Thea lay, almost everyone who lived in the women's courtyard was crowding the steps, porch and front rooms. Bopha was shocked to see the corpse. There was almost no flesh left for the vultures to eat. Her face was contorted with pain, her mouth hanging open and to one side, though Bopha was sure her maid servants had tried, unsuccessfully, to manipulate the dead skin into a less shocking pose. She thought of Garuda, tried to bring his rumpled stone feathers with her into the room. "May death bring her comfort," she prayed, "and a new life with less pain."

Kiri was standing at the foot of the bed, staring damp-eyed at his wife of many years. He was the only man. Bopha guessed that he had stayed with Khun Thea while she made her passage.

The crowd was moving, backing away, bowing, unable to prostrate themselves in the cramped environs. Bopha turned and saw the King walking purposefully toward the bedroom. Kiri went to meet him, hands in sampeah. Jayavarman nodded, then he embraced his childhood friend. Tears stood in their eyes. Bopha was a few queens away from her lover. He knelt beside his dead sister, and reached for her hands which had been folded over her navel. His big hands completely covered hers. He bent his head for a long moment. There was not a sound in the mass of people.

When Jayavarman finally stood up, he seemed almost in a trance. But he saw Bopha near the back of the room and nodded to her, great sadness filling his face. She gave sampeah, then watched the King and Kiri part the crowd. When she turned back to Khun Thea, Bopha caught the venomous look that Indradevi, next to the bed on the other side, couldn't hide fast enough. She realized that Jaya had only acknowledged Kiri and herself. "If

184

looks could kill," she thought, "I'd be in that bed instead of Khun Thea."

Queen Indradevi spent a few more minutes at the bedside, then left, followed by Mach Botum. Bopha, behind a few large women, hadn't seen the slight figure of Sao Nang until she followed Mach Botum. She felt Chariya touch her shoulder gently, and realized she should be next to leave. She might not be Jaya's wife yet, but her place was set.

Late in the afternoon, under heavy clouds, thousands of people joined the funeral procession. To Bopha's surprise, they went to the same ravine where Nuon had been taken. But it took a long time. Bopha was close to the front, so it wasn't as long for her. She rode in a litter until the last half mile, then she and Chariya walked behind Sao Nang. She could see the tall figures of Kiri and Jayavarman ahead, just behind Khun Thea's bearers. The Queens and the Apsara lined up next to them on the edge of the drop-off, while the musicians played. Then the body was sent into the abyss. Bopha shivered when she heard the thud far below.

The monks chanted the whole Amitabha Sutra, plus the repentance sutra, then the King and Kiri started back down the trail. On both sides of the path, people making their way up bowed. There were so many people. All of Angkor and Bayon must have come, Bopha thought. Before she fell into line, twelve guards in full regalia took their places on the cliff edge. They would watch over the burial site for thirty days. It was not so much to prevent anyone trying to steal the gold and purple silk burial shroud. No one would dare, those colors being reserved for royalty. Not to mention that any so unwise would be dismembered, slowly and in public. This was an honor guard, befitting the sister of Jayavarman VII, King of Kampuchea.

Before they reached Bayon, the clouds opened. It was the most rain Bopha had ever experienced. Deep thunder rumbled and occasionally cracked loudly, then the dimness was lit with flashes. She couldn't see the lightning itself through the silk curtains, which were quickly saturated. Wind whipped the curtains open just as a huge clap rang in her ears. Immediately a line of lightning hit a tree next to the road. Her bearers broke into a jog and she held on, hoping they wouldn't stumble in a rut that couldn't be seen through one of the sudden, deep puddles. The road was shining with rain. People on the sides of the road were turning back, deciding against going to the ravine.

Bopha could barely see the towers of Bayon through sheets of rain. Her curtains hung open and her sampot was soaked. Her bearers took her back to her quarters. The rain continued. The big ceremony for Khun Thea would have to wait for tomorrow.

That night, the King sent for Bopha after dinner. The bed was already made up when she entered quietly. He was sitting on the edge of the platform with his head in his hands, but looked up immediately. "Oh, my dear Bopha, I am so glad you are here." She knelt before him and touched his face gently. He cupped his hands over her fingers, then raised them to his lips. "Hold me," he said softly.

They lay fully clothed, Jaya's head on her breast. She held him close, silently stroking his head, over and over. "I've seen so much death," Jaya murmured. "So much death. And I'm glad my sister is not in pain any more. But Khun Thea was the sister of my heart. Always she stood beside me, and gave advice I could trust." His voice cracked.

He lifted his head and looked at Bopha, then moved to lie facing with her. "Now only Kiri can do that — and you."

She looked into his deep eyes, that were reflecting light from an oil lamp nearby, and she nodded. "No one can take your sister's place, my dearest love. But I will protect and advise you to the best of my ability, as long as I live." Bopha's whispered promise seemed to echo in the quiet room. Her heart melted into him. The only sound was the rain, still pouring down onto the roof.

They did not make love physically, but embraced in their sleep until morning. He was still asleep when she awoke. The lamps had guttered but there were tiny lines of dim light around the window shutters. She looked at the King and thought of Garuda. "Give me the courage to speak truth, and the wisdom to know what that is," she asked her god. Jaya stirred. She had not seen him look old before, but now in the dimness his face held shadows. Even in sleep he was grieving.

Bopha left before most of the palace was awake. She didn't know if that would reduce the gossip, but she hoped so. The look

186

on Indradevi's face at Khun Thea's bedside was etched in her memory.

She did not dance nor practice writing when she got to her quarters. Instead, after breakfast she sat on the balcony and watched the sun try to move clouds out of its way.

Absently, she exercised her limbs. The sun looked to be winning. When it was time to dress for Khun Thea's ceremony, thin streaks of light pierced every cloud.

At the Terrace of the Elephants, banners streamed as the royal procession marched between the crowds on either side. An altar had been set up and a huge golden Buddha, twice life-sized, gleamed under its tent. Long red carpets covered the ground in front of the altar. When the King was seated, lines of saffron-robed monks walked out from either side of the terrace. They bowed to the Buddha, then gave sampeah to the king, then sat cross-legged on the carpets and began to chant. The smell of incense drifted up to Bopha's nose as she watched and listened. She was in the third row, behind the King and Kiri, then the Queens.

It was at least an hour before deep gongs signaled the end of chanting. By now the sun had vanquished its concealer. Canopies over the royal seats protected from direct rays, but it was getting hot. Bopha was glad when the monks filed out again and the King stood.

Under the porches of the palace were now tables, almost groaning they had so much food piled on them. Until she smelled it, Bopha hadn't realized how hungry she was. After the monks had gotten their meals and retreated to banyan trees to eat, servants of the royal retinue gathered at the tables. Her chubby taster appeared at her elbow when Chariya brought their plates. How quickly did poison work? Bopha wondered. Or did it depend on the kind? Could this young man taste it? Would he fall at her feet, seizing like Nuon, or clutch his stomach and scream? She shook her head to clear it, gave the young man sampeah, and accepted the food.

Khun Thea was gone. Bopha looked at the King and Kiri, who were eating with Minister Khosal and some other men, whom Bopha knew to be advisors but whose names she did not know. She sat near the queens, but far enough away that she could only hear murmurs from their conversation. No one was laughing, except Nimith Sokhem. He had just learned how to charm his attendants by doing so. When she heard him, Bopha couldn't help smiling. Jayavarman looked up at the sound, and she could see his amusement. It was nice to see him happy. Kiri did not smile. Was he thinking of Arun Veha?

* * *

Rithy was a good teacher, and Bopha a quick learner. She was starting to read some of the sutras. One evening as she and Jayavarman talked after dinner, he asked how her writing was going. "I love it!" she said. "It's so much fun. I can write your name, and read some sutras." She looked around for paper and reed, but there was none. "Thank you so much for letting Rithy help me."

"I remember your promise, sweet one," Jaya said, "the night after Khun Thea died. It is time for me to honor my promise." He paused. "Preah Chan Bopha, will you marry me?"

Bopha grinned, a very un-Apsara-like grin. She threw her arms around Jaya. "Yes! Oh, yes!" Sandalwood filled her nose as she nuzzled his neck. They kissed long and sweetly.

"I'm thinking the next full moon would be an auspicious time," the King said. "My astrologers have compared our charts." Bopha was surprised. That was almost an announcement in itself. Jaya read her face. "They were sworn to secrecy — or death," he said. He winked, but it wasn't really funny. She knew they might well be put to death, though Jayavarman did not resort to such extremes very often. Still, he was King and that was his prerogative. Mostly she forgot that when they were together. He was Jaya and she Bopha. "What do you think?" His voice brought her back to the moment.

"That would be fine. I mean, it would be wonderful." She was floundering. "What will it mean, really, for us to be married?" She blurted out her concern.

Jayavarman considered. He ran the back of his finger down her cheek. "You will still live in the same quarters," he began, "and our sleeping arrangement will be the same.

188

But I want you to be with me during the day sometimes, when I have meetings with my councilors and with ambassadors. Khun Thea would do that, and we would discuss what she gathered. She was very," he paused, looking for the word. "She had deep intuition and insight. She knew immediately that I was in love with you, for example."

He and Bopha smiled at each other and he kissed her deeply. "Not that it was a very good secret," Jaya continued. "Indradevi also knew right away. She did not like that I used Khun Thea as an advisor instead of her, but she accepted because she was my sister."

"And you her King," Bopha suggested.

"Yes. I'm the King and my decisions are mine to make."

"Do you every change your mind?" Bopha asked suddenly. Jaya looked at her in surprise. "I mean, after you make a decision. Do you ever decide, with more information or a change in circumstances, that there is a better path?"

Silence lay between them. Bopha hadn't been thinking of Kalienne when she asked, but now she wondered. Finally the King said, "Certainly, in war I have made a new decision based on new information." He looked at her sharply. "Were you thinking of anything in particular?"

Bopha looked down. It was a direct question, and she had promised him the truth. She took a deep breath. "Not when I asked," she said. "But ..."

Jaya said nothing. She could feel his eyes boring into her bowed head. She lifted her chin and looked back at him. "But now I'm thinking of Kiri." The King face clouded and his back stiffened. A chill ran down Bopha's. "I promised you the truth," she whispered.

"You should leave," Jayavarman VII said firmly, his face a mask. "Go to your quarters."

189

CHAPTER 20

Leaving

Silence thundered through the room. Preah Chan Bopha stared at Jayavarman VII. He held up his hand, palm facing her, a gesture of finality and dismissal. She stood shakily and backed to the door, hands in sampeah. Her face was also a mask, but hers was shock and horror and sorrow, where his was simple stone.

When she opened the door quietly and crept out, the guard was clearly surprised. He had been sitting with his back against the wall, perhaps dozing. By the time he was standing, spear upright, he had gathered his face into its trained impassive gaze. The small clatter at the bottom of the steps told Bopha that Samang had also been resting. The torch was dim and the porch steps in shadow. Bopha walked down in a stupor. She gestured to Samang in the direction of her quarters.

Chariya was in her own little room when Bopha quietly entered, but she came out quickly and with obvious surprise. "It's okay. I will sleep here tonight," was all Bopha could manage. She had managed to find and put on her small Apsara smile. Chariya quickly set up her mistress's bedding.

"Anything else, Lok Srey? Perhaps a cup of tea?"

"No, arkoun." Bopha shook her head. "I'm just tired." As soon as Chariya had left, Bopha sank onto her knees on the mat, curled over her arms, forehead on the floor. What had happened? She had never seen that look on the King's face. She wished she had never promised him truth, or at least not told it this time. But even as tears poured out her eyes, Bopha knew that wasn't true. It was her life-duty to be honest with this man whom she loved so dearly. Bopha tried not to sob, but her chest heaved. Great gulps of air were the only sound as she wept.

The sky was starting to light when Bopha finally cried herself out and fell into a restless sleep. After breakfast, which she couldn't eat, Boran came to the door. His gentle eyes looked at the apsara, whose eyes were puffy and red. "Bopha," he started, then cleared his throat. "Preah Chan Bopha, you will be leaving the palace with me tonight after dark. Chariya and Samang will come with us." He stopped, sadness pulling down the corners of his mouth. After a moment, he made sampeah and left.

Bopha knew he had wanted to say, "I'm sorry," but it was not his place. Still, it made her feel a little better. Until she realized.

What he said meant she had been banished.

* * *

There was no meeting with Rithy, no visits from Apsaras that day. Chariya was very subdued and barely met Bopha's eyes when she had to ask a question. Suddenly Bopha wondered whether Chariya had a life outside of their quarters. Friends? Family? She was pretty sure Chariya didn't have a husband or suitor. Regret at upending this sweet young woman's life added to the weight pressing down on Bopha. How about Samang? She did not know who had told them they would be leaving, nor what they knew. She was pretty sure they had been threatened into silence. Was leaving after dark was a bit of courtesy from the King? Or was he protecting himself, she thought bitterly.

She ate almost nothing all day. "Lok Srey, you need to eat something and drink a little," Chariya wheedled. "You'll need strength for the journey."

Wouldn't she. Finally Bopha nibbled some rice and squash and drank a cup of tea. She would need more strength than Chariya could imagine. As she sat in the gathering gloom on the balcony, she saw feathers, rumpled above a stone claw. "Garuda. I never thought of you today. Thank you for reminding me." In her mind rumbled the words, 'do not worry, all will be well.' She took a deep breath. She heard Chariya at the door, holding two bundles. Bopha stood up, then gathered the reed pen, ink pot, and packet of incense.

"Is there room for these?"

Chariya nodded, then knelt and untied the cloth. Inside were the few items Bopha was taking. She saw two kromahs and her old sampots from when she was a dancer. Who had decided what she would have? Bopha realized it didn't matter. It was what it

191

was. She was wearing the first sampot that the King had given her. Chariya retied the bundle.

Taking a deep breath, Bopha wrapped a purple and violet kromah around her shoulders against the evening chill. She looked around at the big room. Then, straightening her shoulders, lifting her head, and putting on a small smile, she led the way to the porch and down the steps.

Samang was waiting. He also had a small bundle in one hand, his spear in the other. He led them along a path through the royal gardens to a seldom-used gate. There was no moonlight and Samang did not carry a torch, but the way was smooth underfoot and murky border shrubs were visible enough to guide them.

A guard came out of his small shelter, where he had a small lamp, and creaked open the wooden gate. Boran detached himself from shadows outside and made sampeah. Bopha and her companions returned it. "Let me help you up," Boran said quietly, his deep voice loud enough to silence for a moment the insects chirping in the trees. Bopha had not seen Boran for weeks and was glad for his company. The King was sending her with one of his most trusted aides. She made out a wooden wagon under the trees. It was large enough for all of them. The small driver had an enormous head, but when he turned to watch them, she saw he had wrapped a kromah to make a turban. The horse turned its head as well, and blew out a wet breath through its nostrils.

Boran sat next to the driver on a bench behind the horse. Bopha sat cross legged in the back. Chariya and Samang prepared to walk behind but Boran said, "You ride also." Bopha moved over so she and Chariya were next to each other, facing the back. They could lean against the driver's bench. Samang sat toward the back, on one side. The driver made a chiching sound, and the cart began to roll. Before they turned onto the main road, Bopha saw the roofs of Jayavarman's palace. She was glad of the dark, which hid her sudden tears.

No one was on the road, the market empty. The horse clop-clipped along, the wagon creaked and rocked. After a while, Bopha drifted in and out of sleep, jarring awake when the wheels went over ruts and stones. But the road was surprisingly smooth. She remembered Jayavarman telling her of building good roads in all directions. He had also built hospitals along the routes, which doubled as hostels for travelers.

At daybreak, they stopped next to a large stone house. "We'll stop here," Boran said. After hours of silence, his voice was rusty. The passengers in back stood, then climbed out somewhat creakily, after so long sitting.

A middle-aged man came out of the house. As soon as he looked at Boran, he bowed his sampeah. "Your rooms are ready," he said. Then, "Bong," he greeted the driver, "the stable is around in back." Inside, a woman who looked like she had recently been awakened was bringing pots of food to a low table. It smelled good. Bopha realized she had barely eaten since … Her stomach turned as she remembered.

But she was a trained Apsara, and knew when she needed to take care of her body even if she didn't want to do so. So she sat and ate — some — then Chariya and she followed the woman to the mat out back before going to bed. How long had it been since Bopha used a mat? It seemed a lifetime. Morning light from the small window in their cramped room showed two sleeping pads, with barely space to step between them. Nonetheless, Bopha fell asleep almost immediately.

* * *

When she woke, she wasn't sure where she was. She could tell from the light that it was late afternoon. She was alone in a yellow stone room. When she came more fully to her senses, Bopha thought, "I really don't know where I am. And I don't know where I'm going." A slight breeze came through the window, as if moved by huge, slowly-beating wings. Thinking of Garuda brought a real smile to Bopha's lips, and ease to her aching heart.

They left the hostel after another meal. The sun was nearing the horizon as the wagon trundled onto the road and headed south. Bopha watched the landscape disappear behind her. They passed through a small village every hour or so. People stacking rice straw would put down their rakes and gaze at the wagon. It was not a fancy wagon. There was no royal insignia. Boran and Samang were not holding their spears at the ready. Maybe the

193

villagers were used to seeing wagons piled only with goods, not bearing people.

For two days they bumped south, stopping earlier each evening, so by the third day it was mid-morning when the wagon turned west. Short and heavy rain poured down in the afternoons and they would shelter as best they could under big trees until the sky was merely dripping. The wet road was harder going for the horse. Bopha felt sorry for the animal.

Bopha had not been out of the Angkor-Bayon complex since her arrival so many years before. But when she saw rice paddies, with their impossibly green sprouts, she was flooded with memories of her village. Her father and her brothers cared for their fields meticulously. Sometimes she would help with weeding. She remembered how her hands would sting after pulling plants all morning in the hot sun. It was such a relief when afternoon clouds sent them home, leaving the rain to bless their rice. She could not picture her parents' faces, nor hear her mother's voice.

How had Rithy found out she was gone from Bayon? He was all she had of family, and now he too was taken from her. Bopha shook her head slightly, to clear the sudden sadness before it came to tears. This landscape was not so different from her childhood. A variety of greens, from the almost iridescent rice to a deep green of big trees, paler small shrubs, pastures with skinny white cows and rounder, black water buffalo nibbling grass. She admired the two thick half-moons of the buffalos' horns as the animals got smaller and smaller behind them.

Samang was leaning against the side of the wagon and he could look both forward and back. Suddenly, he got to his knees, pointing west. Bopha and Chariya turned to follow his finger. There was a gleam on the road far ahead.

"Tonle Sap," was all Boran said. It had been a very silent journey, each traveler keeping their own thoughts. Three were heading into the unknown. Bopha remembered Boran telling stories in the Apsara courtyard. What had he said then about Tonle Sap?

"When King Jayavarman VII took back Angkor from the Cham, we chased them all the way to Tonle Sap. So much blood flowed from our enemies, and from our Kampuchean heroes, that the lake turned red." She could hear his words, and see him pantomime cleaving the Cham with his sword, as Dara Davuth listened with his mouth open. Dara who danced as Garuda, leaping and stomping on the snake people, entranced by tales of war. In truth, they had all, boys and girls, been entranced. Bopha wished she were back there, in that golden time when dancing was her life, before she knew too much of the world.

The young people knelt on the wooden floor until their knees hurt too much, watching the shimmering light grow larger. Then the wagon went down a slight incline and the lake was lost to view. The women sat opposite Samang then, as the driver pulled the brake lever so the poor horse wasn't pushed down the hill by the cart. Everyone except the horse looked ahead. The horse just looked at the road ahead of its feet. The road ended at a wide, muddy river.

A small wagon with a canopy on it floated on the brown water. It was tied to a post on the bank with thick rope. As the passengers got out of the wagon and stretched, a thin young man loped up and gave Boran sampeah. Behind him followed a string of naked children, who stopped and stared from a safe distance. One little one was clothed in rags, and carried two bundles. She handed these to the young man then retreated quickly to safety. He knelt in the mud and reached for the wagon, pulling it close to the bank. He put the bundles under the canopy.

Suddenly Bopha knew what she was seeing. This wagon on the water must be a boat! Was she going to ride in a boat? Clearly so, since there was only a narrow footpath along the bank on both sides of the river. Too narrow for the horse and wagon.

Seeing the young man's bundles reminded Samang and Chariya of their bundles, which they retrieved and handed to the boatman. There were a few spindly houses on very high stilts nearby. Gesturing to them, the man said, "My wife has made us food. Please, come." He looked too young to be married, Bopha thought.

A very young woman met them under the porch, gave sampeah and gestured them to sit. There was only a bowl of rice and one pot, but its fish amok was very fragrant and Bopha was suddenly starving. The wife-child handed each of them a banana leaf and served the meal. She didn't say a word, nor meet the eyes of her guests. The naked children watched from behind the porch uprights.

The food was as delicious as it smelled. With many thanks and sampeahs, the travelers returned to the boat. "Lok Srey," the boatman addressed Boran, "if you will please sit here, the boat will balance better in the water." Boran nodded and took his place. The boat rocked as he did so. When Bopha followed the directions to her seat, she nearly fell overboard. The boat responded to every movement of her body. She decided to be very still until she knew more about this boat-dance.

Another young man came down the track and boarded. "My brother," said the boatman. "He is very strong." The new arrival was as stringy as his sibling. The youths picked up paddles and sat on a bench in the middle of the boat. They faced Boran, who sat in back, where the boat was wider. Samang was in front, in the narrowest part. The young women sat facing forward, in front of the rowers. One of the children untied the rope and threw it toward the boat. It fell in the water with a splash. Samang leaned to pick up the rope, and the boat tipped. Bopha reached for the side of the boat, instinctively leaning the other way. The boat righted itself and the brothers began pulling their oars. They were indeed strong, slicing the water cleanly, the boat leaping forward with each stroke.

Little boys, as brown as the water, waded up to their shoulders in the river, lifting nets. Sometimes a silver gleam flashed, trapped. Old men sat on the banks and mended fish nets. In front of some houses, poles stuck up out of the water, with woven bamboo walls that disappeared under the surface. Floating vegetation filled the space between poles.

"Fish farms," said the skipper, who looked over his shoulder to steal a glance at his beautiful passenger, then followed her gaze into the water. Bopha nodded. There were other boats on the river, many just big enough for one person, or two. The men and boys on these craft were dragging nets.

A woman carrying a pot climbed down the steep bank to a flat space above the water. She squatted next to a hole in the dirt and put the pot in the hole. When she lifted it up, the pot was dripping. "When you fill a hole with water from the river, the dirt settles in the bottom. Then the rest of the water is clean." Boran cleared his throat and the young captain returned to rowing and kept silent. Bopha had appreciated his explanations but she said nothing.

* * *

The river was busy with boats, fishermen, scattered villages. Children played on the banks or swam in the brown water. After an hour or two, Bopha's boat passed some boats that had houses on them. Did people live there, like Rithy had told her? She couldn't imagine living on something so small. The day was getting hot and sun reflected on the water, making the air under the canopy even hotter. So far, the sky was clear. Now houses were fewer and farther between and each had a small shrine, visible on a high post set back from the river's edge.

After a long time, their boat turned toward shore where a houseboat sat unmoving. Bopha watched a woman come out onto its porch, and heard her voice but not its words. Several children came to stare as they approached. The boatman put his oar down and grabbed onto the the woman's porch, which was just slightly above the water.

His brother walked, crab-like, forward to get the rope from near Samang's feet. The boat barely rocked, his tread was so sure. He handed the rope to one of the children on the porch. Then he stood with legs apart and offered his hand to Chariya. She took it as lightly as possible, but then had to hold on harder when the boat tipped at her step. Once she was on the porch, she gave sampeah.

Bopha held the proffered hand and paid great attention to how she placed her feet. She felt the boatman shift his weight to keep the vessel steady as she got to the side. Chariya reached to help her the rest of the way. Boran did not take a hand, but grunted as he got one knee on the porch and pushed himself up.

Samang tried to jump from the boat to the houseboat, but he misjudged both the dance and the distance. The boat tipped so far that each boatmen sank into a crouch and grabbed the side. Samang's splash got everybody wet. The children screamed with laughter, and even Boran chuckled.

This houseboat was a riverside restaurant. On the shore side, a narrow plank was the land access. After using the mat there,

197

Bopha and Chariya balanced their way back across the plank into the dimness of the house. The woman had prepared tea and rice snacks.

The travelers stayed in the restaurant long enough to let a sudden rain squall pass. When they got back in their boat, the western sky was full of red and orange and pink. The river was getting wider and the sky bigger. Bopha had to shield her eyes as the last rays shone right into the canopy. She looked to the side, and couldn't see the river bank. Nor on the other bank. They had reached the lake. Tonle Sap.

The blue of evening filled the world, sky reflected on water. The oarsmen rested and turned to look. The boat drifted a few minutes. In the distance, another boat was getting bigger. The rowers returned to their task. Bopha watched. The other boat was in fact bigger. A houseboat, it had a large canopy toward the front and another toward the back. There was a pole sticking up between them. On the pole was a huge yellowish sheet, dangling limply. Then the sheet bellied full and a breeze ruffled Bopha's hair. The houseboat came closer and closer.

When it was quite near, she could see a large man walking on the houseboat deck. He pulled something and the sheet fell down at his feet. Another man, thinner and shorter, and a big woman, joined him, looking across the water as the two boats neared. The rowers eased their stroke and let their vessel drift within reach of the houseboat. The man threw a rope. This time Samang caught it neatly and pulled until the boats touched.

Chariya, Bopha, Boran and Samang clambered onto the houseboat. The brothers stayed behind. "Arkoun, Bong," Boran said, nodding to each young man. Everyone made sampeah, then the boatmen picked up their paddles and turned toward home. Bopha watched them get smaller for a moment, then turned toward the people waiting to greet her.

CHAPTER 21

Exile

Bopha awoke to pitch blackness. The room was rocking. That was what had wakened her. They were sleeping on the houseboat. She heard a snapping sound. Her eyes adjusted and she could barely make out the canopy above her, snapping in the wind. The boat rocked more, then thunder crashed overhead and lightning tore a jagged line through the sky. Moments later, rain poured down, drumming on their shelter. The canopy shed most of the rain, but wind whipped some under the sides of the shelter. Bopha could feel Chariya sitting up next to her. They huddled together in the middle of the boat and waited out the storm.

Boran and Samang had settled on the back of the boat, and the boat people slept inside the central wooden shelter. This houseboat was larger than most of those on the lake. After supper, Chariya and Bopha had watched several families float past in much smaller craft, with just a fabric shelter stretched over bent poles. One of the men on their boat was very big, with huge thick eyebrows and a gravelly voice. He was garrulous and ignored (or didn't understand) Boran's occasional throat-clearing cues to be quiet. He told them all about life in this watery world.

People lived their whole lives on the lake, fishing. They took their catch to the mouth of the river and sold it to waiting river-boatmen, who would then sell the fish in the biggest town on the river. He and his thin son were not fishermen. They just caught what they needed to eat. His was the boat that the King summoned to ferry passengers across Tonle Sap. He had met the King during the battle on the lake years ago, and won favor. His other children had their own boats and were fishermen, except one daughter whose husband kept a small store on the far bank of the lake. "You'll meet her. When we get to that side of the lake, we dock right in front."

Thunder boomed, rain pelted the young women. The world was wet and black around them. After a while, Bopha's stomach became queasy with the constant jerky motion. Suddenly she scrambled to the side of the boat and returned her dinner to the water.

This happened many times, until she just lay on her pad, soaking wet and hoping for death.

Finally the thunder grumbled away and the wind gentled. It still poured rain but the vessel stopped pitching. For a long time it remained very dark. Bopha lay and shivered, mostly with her eyes closed. There was nothing to see anyway. Finally a thin line of paler grey began to grow, until it separated clouds from lake. The big man had said they would spend two nights on the lake, "If the winds bless us. Otherwise it could be three nights." She prayed for wind.

She heard the big man cough and spit, then he started to talk. She couldn't understand any words. Occasionally his wife would murmur something. When she lit a candle in their shelter, Bopha could see she was rolling up their sleeping mats. The rain eased as the sky became brighter. There was no sunrise, but it was clearly dawn. By the time the woman brought her tea, Bopha was shivering so hard she couldn't hold the cup steady.

"You are soaking wet. I told my husband the storm was coming and you should sleep inside. But he never listens to anyone but himself." The woman looked at her sick young passenger. "I'll be right back." Bopha lay and waited until she returned. "Here. Take off that wet thing and put on this." She handed Bopha a blanket.

Bopha was unsteady even on her knees, so Chariya helped her undress, and wrapped her mistress in the rough cloth. Then she sat Bopha down and brought the cup to her lips so she could sip tea. At first Bopha gagged when the liquid hit her stomach, but Chariya was patient and persistent. The boat woman watched a few moments, then harrumphed back into the shelter, where she clattered pots.

After a while, the violent spasms slowed, then stopped. Bopha's body was sore from such shaking, but she began to feel warm. The surface of the lake was flat, as if there were no such thing as a wave in the whole world. Her stomach settled and she ate a little rice for breakfast. By the time the sun poked through the clouds, she was ready to give the blanket back to her hostess.

"Arkoun. I've never been on a boat before yesterday. I never even saw one."

"Sometimes I wish I'd never seen one," the woman muttered, nodding in her husband's direction. He was sitting at the back door of the shelter talking with — or to — Boran and Samang. "But we can't choose our fate." She looked at Bopha. "You look like you feel better."

Bopha nodded. "Yes. Thank you for taking care of me." She turned toward Chariya.

"And you as well. Arkoun, Chariya." Chariya's face looked a little grim, but softened at Bopha's words. The boat woman took their cups and went into the shelter.

"Chariya," Bopha said softly, "I'm sorry that you had to leave Bayon because of me. But I am so grateful that you are here." Chariya looked down at her hands. "I don't know much about your life, but I want you to know I'm sorry." The serving woman nodded, then met her mistress's eyes.

"We can't choose our fate." Her soft echo of the other woman's words hit Bopha hard.

Was that true, she thought. Are we all just doing what fate decreed long before our birth? Are the gods up there laughing, as they watch us try so hard to do this or that? Surely not Garuda. And not the Buddha. They're not laughing. Bopha shook her head.

"You might be right," was all she said.

Mid-morning, a breeze picked up the sail. Water shushed along the sides of the boat as it glided along, but the vessel didn't rock. Bopha was grateful. She looked out at endless water and sky, with occasionally the dot of a distant boat, until her eyes hurt. It had been a long and unpleasant night, and she didn't feel all that good. She lay on her side under the canopy and drifted to sleep. She was being embraced and kissed so gently and lovingly by Jaya, then she saw his hand raised, not to hit but to stop her. She ran out of the room, tripping over the guard and falling down the stairs. Bruised and bewildered, she lay in a heap. Now what?

Waking from the dream did not answer the question. During the days until they got to this boat, there was distraction to keep

201

her mind from brooding. Now, she couldn't stop wondering. Her heart twisted, taking her stomach with it. She forced herself to eat a bit of lunch, then lay down again. She didn't want to sleep but she couldn't stand to see another drop of water. With her whole being, she prayed to Garuda. "Please keep me safe from danger, both outside and in. Let me see your deep stone eyes and feathered arms, instead of dwelling on this terrible loss. Keep me strong whatever comes. And please remind me, again and again, 'Do not worry, all be well.'" After a moment, she added, "And please protect the King. Now he has no one but Kiri to advise him."

In late afternoon, there was more rain, but not the terrifying waves. The boatman announced that he would keep the sail up all night if there was wind enough, and stars enough to steer by. By dark the sky had cleared but there was no moon, just more stars than anyone could count in many lifetimes. Bopha could see bulk of the boatman, sitting in the opening of the shelter. She felt his eyes on her and curled up small, hoping the night impaired his vision. For the first time, she wished she were not so beautiful. She was glad Jaya had sent Samang to accompany her.

Jaya. Suddenly her heart was full of love for him. She knew he had not wanted to send her away, but didn't see any choice. Her question stood between them. Now he had two decisions he might regret. Maybe he would change his mind. Someday. A sense of peace surrounded her, and she fell asleep smiling softly.

The boat made good time. By early afternoon the next day, the horizon was slightly green and lumpy, then trees became visible. There were more and more boats. The boatman loudly hailed many who came near. He seemed to know everyone. Bopha thought he would certainly gossip about his beautiful passenger. Boran's face was stormy and she figured he felt the same way about the boatman.

Finally they got close enough to see a platform sticking out from the land, with buildings on stilts all along the lakeshore. "That's my daughter's store," said the wife, pointing. She had come to sit with Bopha and Chariya under the canopy. Bopha moved until the woman's bulk hid her a bit from the boatman. But he was busy with the sail until they got near enough that he and his son could row them in to the dock.

The boat's arrival attracted notice, and several men stood on the dock, ready to catch and secure ropes. Many children flocked onto the dock, but were shooed back by one of the men. A heavy board was pushed from the dock onto the back of the boat. Boran walked up it, then turned to help the women if they needed. Samang stood on the deck and offered his hand to Bopha. "Thank you, Samang, I'm fine," she said.

Going up the plank was no problem. But trying to walk on the dock was a different story. She felt like the deck wobbled, and she staggered.

The boatman had been watching her, and now laughed. He called out, his voice carrying to the whole village, "You got your sea legs, but now you need to get your land legs back!"

Chariya had the same trouble. She held one bundle in each hand, arms away from her body for balance. "Don't worry," said Boran. His deep voice was a blessing. He had barely spoken on this entire journey so far. "You'll soon adjust to being on land again."

He gave sampeah to the boatman and his wife and son, then led the way to the bank, where a wagon waited, this one with a patient ox in harness.

* * *

That night they stayed in another of the King's hostels. The vegetation and topography on this side of the lake were the same, except in the distance were high, blue shadows. Boran called them the the Cardamom mountains. They had traveled west from the lake, and now were going south. In late afternoon, the wagon stopped in front of a small house, down a path from a large village. Within moments, they were surrounded by children. Bopha could see their mothers watching from the edge of the crowd.

"Bopha?" Bopha couldn't believe her ears. Who here knew her name? She looked around, then behind her.

"Kalienne?"

The two young women fell into each other's arms. Over Kalienne's shoulder, Bopha could see Boran's face. He was almost smiling.

"Who are you?" The high-pitched question came from a wiry little boy with a mop of dark hair, who stood next to Kalienne, his legs apart in a sturdy stance. He stared at Bopha.

"Arun Veha?" Bopha asked, squatting to be eye level.

He regarded her solemnly. "How do you know my name?"

"I'm a friend of your mother's," Bopha told him. "In fact, I was in the room when you were born. You certainly have grown since I saw you last."

"Why haven't you seen me?"

"I have been living far away." The boy nodded but kept watching as Bopha and Kalienne linked arms and turned to face Boran.

"Boran, I don't know what to say. Thank you so much," said Bopha. "I had no idea where we were going."

"Thank the King," Boran said. "And the King's Man." He paused, looking like he was going to say more but changed his mind. Then he added, "I was sworn to secrecy."

"I understand," said Bopha. "But thank you." She saw Chariya and Samang standing to one side, bundles in hand.

"Kalienne, this is Chariya, and this Samang," Bopha introduced them. They gave as much sampeah as the bundles allowed. "And this is Kalienne. She was a dancer with me for years when I first came to Bayon."

"Let's go inside," Kalienne invited the new arrivals. "I'll make dinner. Arun Veha, please go tell Auntie Leap that we need more groceries — fruit and fish, and some greens — for guests." The little boy ran off, disappearing into the crowd of people, who watched the visitors go into the house before dispersing.

Kalienne's' house was clean and spare, three rooms. "You can sleep with me," she told Bopha.

"She will have her own house next door," said Boran quietly.

204

"Next door? The big house? Where the widow lives?" Boran nodded.

"Come, I'll show you." Boran led the way back to the road, then down a path under huge banyans and another kind of tree that Bopha had never seen before. This house was more than twice the size of Kalienne's. It had actual steps not just a ladder going up to the porch. At the bottom of the steps, a tiny old woman was giving sampeah. She must be the widow, Bopha thought.

Tiny and old, she might be, but the woman climbed the stairs briskly, without touching the handrail. Her name was Sikha. Bopha went first, then Kalienne, then Chariya and Samang with their bundles. Boran brought up the rear.

There were three large and two small rooms in the house. The main room went through from front to back, where another porch looked over a well-tended garden. Beyond that, a woven wood fence, then a small field in which grazed two fat cows and a water buffalo. "You will sleep here," the old woman said, pointing Bopha into the large room that overlooked the garden. The woman opened the door to her own large room, then showed Chariya and Samang to the smaller rooms.

"Mdeay!" Arun Veha's piercing voice carried from Kalienne's house. "Mdeay!"

She went onto the porch and called back, "We're over here, next door." The boy quickly came running, along a narrow path between the two houses.

"What are you doing here?" Arun Veha barely stopped for breath, "Hi, Yeay."

"Bopha and her friends will be living here with me," said the old woman, who had joined Kalienne on the porch. Bopha watched through the door.

"Can I come live with you, Yeay?

"But your Mdeay would be miss you and be sad."

"She can come too," suggested the boy.

Life with Arun Veha was nothing if not entertaining. Even Boran was enchanted when he was adopted as "Chitea." Kalienne went back to her house to bring groceries, and her son continued his questions.

Samang was stumped when Arun Veha asked who he was. Bopha realized that the young man probably didn't know any more. He had been a royal palace guard, in charge of protecting the King's Apsara. Maybe he still was, she thought. Just not in the palace. "He's my friend and protector. He makes sure no harm comes to me or Chariya."

"Will you be my friend and protector?"

Samang nodded, smiling. "Of course." Satisfied, the boy went to pester his mother and Sikha who were cooking in the kitchen area under the house. His piping voice came through the floor.

After supper, Chariya helped Sikha clean the kitchen. Samang and Boran sat quietly on the porch, listening to night noises but not talking. Kalienne and Bopha went over to put Arun Veha to bed, then lingered on that porch.

"Oh, Bopha, it's so good to see you. But why are you here?" Kalienne's beautiful eyes shone in the starlight.

Bopha told her the whole story. They sat with their arms around each other. "But to see you again makes this whole thing bearable. How did you possibly endure, Kalienne?"

"Well, I had Arun Veha. He helped keep my mind off ... troubles. Bopha nodded. "And Sikha has been a great help. Over time, I've made some friends in the village. But I can't talk about my life at Bayon, and everyone knows there are secrets." She turned to look at Bopha. "It will be the same for you, I'm sure."

The two friends leaned into each other. Arun Veha asked a question in his sleep and they chuckled. "Even in sleep?" Bopha asked. "Really?"

"That's my boy," grinned Kalienne.

CHAPTER 22

1195, Sikha

The quiet woke Bopha before the sun actually rose. She went out onto the porch and watched the world brighten. The cows and water buffalo grazed placidly. Distant sounds of a town waking interrupted the insects who were chiching and skreeking. A monkey screamed. Bayon with its hustle and hammering was a lifetime away.

"It's beautiful here." Sikha appeared so quietly that Bopha hadn't heard her.

"Have you lived here your whole life?"

"Nearly. I was born in a village just over that hill." Sikha gestured beyond the pasture. "My father made pots. The hill is all clay. My family and my whole village have made pots forever, all kinds and shapes."

"Did the bowls we ate from last night come from your village?" Bopha had noticed their lovely shape and the brightly-painted, intricate patterns, different on each bowl.

"Yes. I've heard that the King even gives our bowls and pots as gifts to foreign emissaries."

The King.

Sikha noticed Bopha stiffen. "I met him," she said quietly. "When he was injured during the war against the Cham. Boran brought him to me because I am known as a healer." Bopha turned to look at Sikha. "He stayed in the room that you are in." Bopha caught her breath. "That's why he sent Kalienne to me. I know when to speak and when to keep my peace." Sikha paused. "He is a good man, Jayavarman VII."

Tears filled Bopha's eyes. Sikha patted her arm and went back inside the house. Bopha wept silently. When she heard Chariya and Sikha talking in the kitchen, she wiped her eyes on her sampot and went down to help.

"Oh no, Lok Srey, we are okay," Chariya was horrified but tried to hide it when Bopha offered assistance.

"Chariya, my dear," said Sikha. "While you are here Bopha will help — and you cannot call her Lok Srey." Chariya was stricken. "You could call her Srey Bopha. That is not quite so formal, you know." Chariya nodded. Sikha continued, "There will be a lot of things that are different here. But I know you'll get used to it quickly."

Something about the old woman was immensely comforting. Bopha took a deep breath. "Arkoun, Sikha." She heard Chariya take a deep, somewhat shaky, breath also.

"We will need your teaching," Bopha said.

"That's why I'm here. Or rather, why you are here with me." Sikha smiled softly. "Now, Bopha why don't you make the tea? Chariya and I will prepare food. Boran is leaving after breakfast." She seemed to know everything.

It had been so long since Bopha had done such simple tasks. Her life had been to dance. All other details were taken care of by others. In the dimness under the porch, Bopha felt herself getting smaller, becoming the little girl who helped Mdeay. Her first job had been to make tea. When she was older, her mother showed her how to make the fire from small sticks, how to keep the fire just so, to cook rice without burning.

Boran and Samang returned from wherever they had been. Bopha hadn't heard Samang leave. The young guard was athletic, strong but agile, and his steps were light on the boards of the floor. He could move silently when he wanted. Some men stomped heavily with every step, like the big man on the houseboat. Why would the King use such a bombastic blowhard for delicate missions? Bopha wondered idly as she brought tea to the men.

Arun Veha raced down the path from his house, followed by a slower Kalienne. He burst into Sikha's yard. "Yeay! I'm here!"

"So you are," Sikha laughed. "Maybe Samang can teach you how to walk quietly one of these days. You know, sometimes it's important to be very quiet."

"But not now," suggested the boy, plopping down next to Samang, who was sitting cross legged on the raked dirt floor.

"Have you had breakfast?" Bopha asked the child.

"Yes, but I can have another one." The answer was immediate and slightly wheedling.

"Oh, you can? Does that mean you want more to eat?"

Arun Veha studied Bopha a moment, then said, "Yes, please, Auntie Bopha."

"That's better," said Sikha. "It's important to learn good manners, young man." She handed a bowl of rice and fruit to Arun Veha.

"Arkoun, Yeay," he said, before taking a huge mouthful.

* * *

An ox cart rattled down the drive toward the house. Boran stood up, saying, "Thank you, Srey Sikha. For everything. The King thanks you."

Sikha patted his arm. "You tell him from me that I'll take good care of his Apsara." Bopha was only a little surprised that Sikha knew who she was, but she was very surprised that she had touched Boran.

And more so that the old warrior had accepted her touch as a matter of course. He bent in sampeah to the old woman. "I will give your message to the King." His smile held sorrow as well as reassurance.

They stood in a line along the road, giving sampeah as Boran climbed into the wagon.

A few townspeople stopped to gawk, but the driver shook the reins. The ox leaned into his harness and the people scattered.

How much planning had gone into this, Bopha thought, and all done so fast. It must not have been the first time. Well, certainly it wasn't, she realized. Kalienne was here. But there must have been runners that long day after she left the King, or men on horseback galloping down the road to the river. Other men rowing small craft, hard and fast down the river and across the lake, to get everything ready. It was the first time Bopha directly experienced the long reach of the King. Would she see him again? She sent a fervent prayer to Garuda, as she walked slowly down the path back to Sikha's. Kalienne slipped her arm through Bopha's. She knows better than anyone, Bopha thought, how I feel.

* * *

Days turned into weeks, a moon passed. Arun Veha appeared early each morning and stuck to Samang like a burr. The guard took the boy with him on errands, and whittled him a small sword. They practiced sword fighting in the yard. After Samang showed the child some Chinese fighting moves, Arun Veha spent hours kicking his legs up and out to the side, grunting and shouting, "Ha!" Kalienne told Bopha she was glad that her son finally had a good male to teach him.

Chariya barely spoke. Bopha worried that the woman was too homesick. "Chariya, please, talk to me. We are not at the palace now. The rules are all different. Here we are more equal. It's okay to talk. You need to talk." But her handmaid, who was no longer exactly that, just nodded dully. "Please. Please talk. I know it's hard for you, harder than for any of us. I have Kalienne, a friend I knew for years. Samang has Arun Veha. You don't have anyone here. I want to be your friend." Chariya looked at her hands. Bopha sighed. "Okay, I won't pester you. But I'm here whenever you want to talk."

Bopha was very tired. All she wanted to do was sleep. Often, she couldn't eat dinner and the smell of food turned her stomach. Chariya didn't seem to notice but Sikha did, and Kalienne. One evening, after Bopha had run to the mat and vomited, Sikha asked,

"Bopha, when was your last moon-bleeding?"

"I don't know," Bopha said slowly. Right after the emissary from India came, right after Sao Nang's baby was born. That was at least two moons ago. Could she be pregnant?

She looked into Sikha's sharp eyes. "Maybe two moons ago?"

Sikha made her some tea to help with nausea, and told her to eat small amounts throughout the day. "You should feel better in a few weeks," Sikha told her.

Mornings were better. Bopha sat on the porch, looking at the cows and practicing writing. She had collected palm leaves, which were now dry enough to use as paper. Arun Veha liked to watch her, and she showed him how to form the letters and repeat their names. Kalienne sometimes came with him.

"That is so amazing," she said to Bopha one day, "that you know how to read and write."

"Do you want to learn?" Bopha asked her friend.

"Oh, I don't think I could."

"You could try."

"Well, I guess so."

They gathered more palm leaves to dry. Bopha didn't have much ink, so she began to write in the soft dirt. The three squatted in the shade of the fragrant agarwood tree and drew with sharp sticks. Samang watched from a banyan knee.

"Samang, do you want to try?" Bopha asked one day, handing him a stick. He shook his head and didn't reach for the wood. "It won't bite," Bopha chuckled. "And I don't think it can hurt you to read and write." Reluctantly, Samang joined them. Bopha was a patient teacher, and found she loved seeing her students learn.

"You are a natural teacher," Sikha told her one day, having watched the class from the shadows under the house. She had dipped a kromah in water and was cooling Bopha's forehead and the back of her neck. The young woman lay on her side, trying not to vomit in the afternoon heat. Bopha nodded, then got up quickly and went to the mat.

Weeks passed and so did the rains. It was starting to get hot. Bopha had to tie her sampot in a different place. Her hip bones were prominent now. Except for breakfast, she was unable to keep anything down. One day as she lay trying not to think, she felt something poke her. But it was from inside. Then her stomach did a little swirling jump, not nausea. Something else. Was it the baby?

When Kalienne came to sit with her, Bopha asked. Kalienne grinned with delight. "Yes, my dear Bopha. That's the baby." The two of them watched Bopha's belly, but there was no more jumping.

Sikha tried different teas and potions. Nothing worked. More time passed. Bopha couldn't even eat breakfast now, let alone sit in the yard with her students. She lay on her pad, getting thinner and weaker. She had a basin by her side, unable to get down the stairs to the mat in time. Even standing up was an effort. The old woman's face was solemn as she squatted next to Bopha. The baby was all there was in Bopha's abdomen, and its every movement showed. "At least it was still moving, poor thing," thought Sikha. Unless Bopha could start eating, both she and the baby would die.

One night Bopha was wakened by a strange shooshing sound. She felt a sweet, cooling breeze across her face. It was very dark in the room. But she could see the stars out the window, between the leaves of a huge tree. She rolled onto her back.

A very large shape was nearby, its sides moving rhythmically. The shooshing and the light breeze were coming from the shape. Bopha had no feeling of fear. Whatever it was radiated love and peace. With each puff of air, a strange scent, not unpleasant, wafted with it. The baby swam to a new corner of her belly. "Hello, little one," Bopha said. She didn't know if she spoke out loud or not. "Hello, big one," she said to the shape.

She heard Garuda's deep croak in reply, "Do not worry, all will be well." Bopha took a deep breath, then sank into darkness, lulled by gentle puffs of air and the undefinable, reassuring odor.

Bopha woke hungry, to full daylight. She sat up and the baby jumped. "You don't like when I move? Well, you'll need to get used to it." She got to her knees, then stood. She was a little shaky, but her stomach was still eager for food.

"Well, well. Look who came for breakfast," said Sikha, when Bopha made it to the bottom of the steps.

"Yes. Here I am at last." She lay in a hammock and watched Chariya and Sikha. Chariya brought her tea. "Arkoun, my friend." Chariya gave a small smile and nod.

"It's nice to see you, Srey Bopha."

After eating, Bopha went back upstairs, but sat on the back porch instead of lying down. She rested her back against the wall and her hand across her stomach. The baby kicked at the hand. Sikha joined her. Bopha told the old healer about the shape in the night, and the breeze and the smell, and how she felt no fear. Sikha's eyes were hooded but sharp. She nodded as she listened.

"Your guardian has come." She spoke with certainty. Bopha remembered when she was so sick in the Apsara courtyard.

"Garuda," she murmured. "It must have been Garuda. He came to me before. I used to give incense to him." She stopped, thinking of the huge statues at Bayon. "Is there a Garuda in the town here?"

"Yes," Sikha said thoughtfully. "In fact, the King had one made for the Wat here, after he was healed. He is Buddhist but has a special feeling for Garuda. He told me that Garuda came to him one night, in that very room. His wound was badly infected and we didn't know if he would survive. But after that vision — or visit — The King began to get better." She added, "He founded Wat Bakan then, and supports the monks ever since."

"I would like to go. To give thanks," said Bopha. "Not today, but when I am a little stronger. I even brought incense from Bayon."

By the end of a week, Bopha was able to walk to Wat Bakan. Samang walked in front with Arun Veha, who walked, ran, retraced his steps, jumped from one side of the road to the other. Kalienne and Bopha watched him. "He sure has energy," Bopha said. "Do you think he'll give me some?"

Sikha and Chariya were last, walking together. Bopha could hear Sikha murmuring to Chariya. She decided to pray for healing for her helper.

The pagoda spire gleamed in the morning sun. "He's on the east side," said Sikha, leading the way through the gate and among the squat buildings to the pagoda's other side. This Garuda was not as tall as the ones at Bayon, only a little taller than Samang. His wings were extended. His eyes were fierce but he had one leg up, as if he were dancing.

"Is he fighting?" Arun Veha kicked as he asked, and shouted, "Ha!"

Maybe Garuda was fighting, Bopha thought. She hoped he fought with the King to change his mind. She untied the silk on her packet and gave a stick of incense to each of them. A young

213

monk, not many years older than Arun Veha, had attached himself to their group as they passed one of the small buildings. "Come with me," he said, "we have fire inside."

He led them up the steep, narrow steps into the pagoda, where candles were burning on an ornate altar. In the dim light, Bopha could see that all the walls and even the ceiling were painted with scenes from the life of the Buddha, depicted in gold and red and blue and green. They gave sampeah to the huge golden Buddha sitting in regal bliss on his throne above the candles. Then they lit their joss, backed out the door, and turned to walk down the steps.

At the foot of the feathered god was a stone tray filled with sand, from which protruded the burnt ends of incense sticks. Bopha prayed intensely, while the baby kicked fiercely.

Was he dancing or fighting, this little new life? She thanked Garuda for healing her, and asked him to take care of her baby, and his father, and especially to help Chariya. She thanked him for Sikha, for being brought to this place, for being reunited with Kalienne and Arun Veha.

By the time they got back to Sikha's, the day was hot. Bopha was glad to rest in the shade. When Chariya brought her tea, Bopha asked her to sit. "How are you doing, my helper? I've been too sick to talk, but I've been praying that you would find your way here."

Chariya was looking at Bopha, not at her own hands. A good sign, Bopha thought. "I'm okay," she said softly. "Sikha has been helping me adjust. You were right, what you said. It is all new here. I didn't get to see my family often when I lived at the palace, but I knew that they were nearby. Now..." she stopped and did look at her hands. Bopha waited. After a moment, Chariya took a breath. "I don't know if I'll ever see my family again." Tears filled her eyes. Bopha nodded, and reached for Chariya's hands. She didn't say anything. She too had tears.

They sat in the shade, holding hands for a long moment. "You know, I didn't realize before," Bopha said finally. "But once you become part of the palace, whether as a dancer or a handmaiden or," she paused. Everyone knew, why not say it? "A concubine," her voice cracked and she stopped again. "After that, you don't

214

really have a say in what happens to you." She took a very deep breath. "I guess all we can do now is the best we can, where we are."

Arun Veha ran up — Bopha didn't think she'd ever seen him walk. "Auntie Bopha, are you all better? Can we do writing?"

"I think we can," she told the eager child.

"I'll get sticks," he said, on the run again.

"Chariya, would you join us in writing?" Now Chariya didn't look at her, just shook her head. "Will you at least sit with us?" Chariya nodded shyly. Arun Veha returned and handed her a stick, which the young woman accepted hesitantly. But refusing it would have brought her to Arun Veha's attention, with his endless questions.

Sometimes in the early mornings, Bopha and Kalienne would dance on the hard-packed dirt behind Sikha's house. Arun Veha loved when they did. Bopha told him about Garuda killing the snake people, and about the boy Dara Davuth who was such a good dancer. "I want to be a dancer," he said. Then he went off to fight with Samang.

Dancing with Kalienne was different from being with Sophea. It had been too many years since Kalienne left the courtyard. She couldn't remember the music or the moves. But it was still refreshing to practice the jeebs, and to twirl and bend and sway. They stayed behind the house, far from prying eyes. The villagers had great respect for Sikha, so the arrival of Bopha, Chariya and Samang was accepted without actual questions. Of course, Bopha knew, they would ask questions among themselves. If they saw her dancing, it would feed more questions.

Often in the afternoon, people would come for healing help. Sikha treated them in the shade under the porch, giving packets of herbs, making poultices for wounds, singing prayers, occasionally massaging head, foot, hand, back. Bopha began to recognize some of the people, but had yet to meet them formally.

Samang had immediately become part of the community, from the first morning when he met Boran at a tea house. His easy smile and banter welcomed people. Bopha could hardly remember the trained impassivity that his face wore in the palace.

Sometimes in the evenings, he ate elsewhere, but he was always back before bedtime. One night, when the baby sat on her bladder and she had to get up to use the mat, Bopha found Samang sitting on the front porch, holding his spear lightly. When she returned, she sat on a step near him.

"Are you on guard, Samang?"

"Yes, Srey Bopha. Always." His teeth gleamed in the pale light of a gibbous moon.

"And you are well? I mean, you are doing well here? I have never told you how much I regret that you had to leave your life at the palace. You have been banished along with me."

"Ah. No, Srey Bopha. I am not banished. I am at work. This is where I belong, with you. Boran explained it to me. Do you know that he is my grandfather?"

Bopha was very surprised, then realized it made sense. "Is that why I was given into your care? Because the King trusts your grandfather so much?"

"Yes. I am blessed to have this honor." He paused. "And it is more fun here than at the palace. I have more free time, and can even go into the village."

"I never thought of that," said Bopha, "how much you had to just wait around while I was inside somewhere. Anyway, I'm glad that you are here with me. Thank you."

Samang gave sampeah, and she returned it. "Good night, Samang."

"Good night, Srey Bopha. And Lok Baby, or Lok Srey baby," Samang chuckled.

The baby leapt in answer and Bopha put a hand on her belly, now so large. "He or she says arkoun and good night."

CHAPTER 23

1196, Big Miracle and Golden Surprise

The final weeks dragged, as Bopha's abdomen bulged huge over her sampot. Her ankles began to swell, and Sikha made her lie down in the afternoons. Sometimes she thought the baby wanted to fight or dance its way out thought her stomach. One day Bopha was resting in the shadows of her room. The baby had been very busy, then suddenly stopped. At first she was glad for the respite, and fell asleep briefly. But as the afternoon grew dark with clouds, and her huge belly remained quiescent, she became concerned.

She went down to find Sikha, who was starting supper with Chariya's help. "Sikha, the baby suddenly stopped moving. He was dancing all over the place ..." she trailed off.

Sikha handed her spoon to Chariya as she said, "Let's go upstairs." Bopha caught Chariya's worried look as they turned to leave.

The old woman squatted next to her as she lay on the mat. Her hands were crooked but strong. She pushed and prodded, first feeling the sides, then from top to bottom of Bopha's pregnant belly. "I'll be right back," she said. Bopha could hear a wooden lid creak open, and the sound of rummaging." Sikha returned with a silver bell whose base was a big as her hand. It had no clapper. Instead of a handle, it had a narrow silver tube on top, which attached to a small shallow cup. The silver gleamed in the semi-dark of the room

Bopha lay on her back and Sikha pressed the bell into her abdomen then put her ear into the cup on top. She listened a moment, then moved the bell into a different spot. Her face was inscrutable. Sikha returned several times to a particular area, then sat back and put the silver bell to one side.

"I'm not sure if I'm hearing anything or not," she admitted.

"What is that?"

217

"The King sent it to me. It is a tool to hear a baby's heartbeat. It came from China."

"And you can't hear the heartbeat?" Bopha's own heart was racing and squeezing.

Sikha shook her head. "Rest on your side for a while. Chariya will bring dinner up to you. I'll check again in a few hours. It may be the baby is resting because it knows you are going to go into labor soon."

"I am?"

Sikha nodded. Bopha could see her soft smile in the gloom. "Soon."

Bopha lay listening to the sounds coming through the floor from the kitchen. One of the cows bawled and a gibbon replied. Then she heard distant thunder, and rain tapped on the roof. Within moments it was pounding. When a thunder clap resounded right overhead, Bopha jumped and gasped. So close. She settled back on her mat, waiting for another booming crash. It came within seconds, and she heard a crack next to the house. Then a crash as wood splintered over her head and rain poured in the hole.

Bopha jumped up and raced down the stairs as the ceiling caved in, bringing the wall with it. She nearly ran into Samang, who grabbed her arm and shielded her with his body, pushing her away from the house. With an enormous crunching sound, the house fell to the ground behind them. They ran down the path toward Kalienne's house. Sikha and Chariya stood panting and dripping under her porch. Arun Veha for once was silent, staring at the refugees with big scared eyes.

"We heard the crash," Kalienne said. Her soft voice was barely audible over the din of the rain and thunder. They moved deeper under the porch and watched sheets of water pour from the roof. When the storm finally eased, Kalienne lit a torch.

Samang was sitting on the dirt, leaning against a post and trying to look behind him.

"Are you hurt?" Kalienne asked.

"I think so."

"Let's have a look," said Sikha, gesturing for Kalienne to bring the torch close. The flickering light showed a huge splinter of wood protruding from his flank, and blood had already stained his sampot. "Chariya, will you boil water?" Just then Bopha felt a deep pain in her belly and groaned. Sikha gave her a sharp look, then said, "Lots of water, please, Chariya."

"We'll have to leave that piece of wood in the wound for now," she told Samang, who nodded, wincing. "Arun Veha, go the village and tell Sokhem — the old Sokhem, you know who that is?" The boy nodded. She dictated, "Tell him 'Sikha's house is destroyed and we need a sharp knife, needle and thread, and bandages'." She had Arun Veha repeat the sentence twice, then sent him running.

"Samang, you go into the front room and Bopha, you into Kalienne's room." Sikha climbed the ladder quickly. Bopha followed, stopping for another pain half way up.

Chariya steadied Samang as he stood, then climbed the ladder slowly. A burble of blood came out on each rung.

Kalienne started the water to boil, dipped a pot of cool water from the cistern then carried both it and the torch up the ladder. Chariya was waiting on the porch. "I'll bring the water as soon as it heats," she told Kalienne.

Sikha already had Samang lying on a mat in the big room. Kalienne lit two more torches. "You go sit with Bopha while I tend to Samang." Kalienne nodded, leaving two lights with Sikha and taking the third into her own bedroom.

"How are you doing?" Kalienne's soft voice was filled with love and concern.

"Okay, I guess," Bopha said. "Until the pain comes."

"I remember!" There was laughter in Kalienne's voice. "You were with me then. I'm so glad I can be with you now." She squatted next to Bopha and held her hand. "Try to breathe when the pain starts, and think of something you love."

Jayavarman, Bopha immediately thought. But that thought brought its own pain to add to the contraction. She confessed to Kalienne, "I thought of Jaya but that doesn't help."

Kalienne shook her head. "What else?"

"Garuda! I can think of him. I like the way he is dancing at Wat Bakan, or fighting, and you can't tell which." Another pain. She gripped Kalienne's hand tightly.

"Breathe …. Breathe … Breathe with me."

Bopha tried to focus on the sound of her friend's voice, and on one feathered leg, lifted. Maybe he is dancing the dance about Killing the Snake People. Both dancing and fighting at the same time. Fight for my baby, please.

Breathe. Focus. Rest.

"I'm going to check you now." Sikha had come in silently, her voice at Bopha's ear.

"Turn onto your back and bend your legs up." Sikha touched the back of her hand to the inside of Bopha's upper thigh. Another contraction, this one so long and hard Bopha lost both breath and focus. "Okay, now we'll see what's up with this baby." Her fingers were gentle but Bopha was tense and tender, and she grunted. "Please, bring the light near." The fingers probed. "I can feel hair! Almost there. Good job, Bopha."

There was no time, just pressure, intensity, pain. Respite for a breath or two only, when leaned back against Kalienne's stomach. Sikha repeated the instructions Bopha vaguely remembered from Arun Veha's midwife. "Push unless I say to stop. Then stop and pant."

She pushed. Kalienne counted, "1, 2, 3, 4, 5, 6…" until the contraction eased. The pressure between her legs was more than anything Bopha had ever experienced. She pushed again.

"No. Stop." How could such a tiny woman have such a commanding voice? "Now pant." Bopha panted. Kalienne panted with her. Sikha's fingers moved. "Okay, now push. One big push. Push, push, push!"

Suddenly, the pressure was gone. Bopha had her eyes squeezed shut but they popped open. She and Kalienne looked to where the old healer was holding something. "You have a boy," Sikha told Bopha. There was no wailing. Sikha turned the baby upside down, then rubbed its back vigorously with the waiting blanket. Silence. She did it again, then lay the little body on the blanket and flicked its feet with her fingers. Nothing.

Sikha bent over the baby, covering its mouth and nose with her mouth. She puffed gently. Puff … puff … puff … puff.

Bopha wasn't breathing. Everything in her willed her baby, her son — Jaya's son — to breathe. Please, Garuda. Please, Buddha. Please, little baby.

Sikha breathed for the baby a long time, then sat back on her heels. She wrapped the limp body and picked it up tenderly.

"Please, let me hold him," said Bopha, tears pouring from her eyes. As she lifted him to her chest, another contraction convulsed her. Kalienne quickly took the baby and patted Bopha's shoulder.

"Just one contraction now, then you are done," Sikha assured her.

But she wasn't done. There were more, and more, wave after wave of pain.

"I think you have another baby coming," said Sikha.

Kalienne lay the motionless baby gently nearby, and resumed her coaching. This time, the baby came fast. Sikha slipped the cord from around its neck as it slid out into her other hand. Again, silence. The three women prayed as Sikha dried the little body and patted its back. Finally, a squeak, a cough, a tiny cry.

"Quickly, give him to me!" Bopha couldn't wait for the baby to be wrapped. She nestled it on her stomach, listening joyfully as it started to wail. Sikha draped the blanket over her arms. The baby pushed itself against her now-soft belly like it was climbing a steep mountain.

"I think he's trying to get to your breast," chuckled Sikha. He. Bopha heard with one ear but both eyes were glued to the tiny being working its way to a first meal. Two sons. Twins. The baby climbed, rested, opened his mouth, cried a little, climbed. His eyes were open and he seemed to see his mother. Finally, he reached his goal and clamped on to her nipple, sucking vigorously.

"Ouch!" Bopha wanted to pull away from the little beast, but knew better.

"It gets easier," said Sikha. "I'll be back." She left to check her other patient.

Kalienne sat near Bopha, watching the baby nurse. "He's beautiful," she said. "And he sure knows what he wants."

Bopha nodded, smiling. Then she remembered her other son. "Please, can I hold my other baby?" Kalienne lifted the tiny bundle next to her. She reached across the nursing infant to place its twin in Bopha's arm. "Will you unwrap his head?" Kalienne stood and walked around the mat. She pulled back the blanket.

"His eyes are open," Kalienne said. "Do you want me to close them?"

"No. I want to see him." Bopha looked from one tiny baby to the other. The second twin had fallen asleep, but one hand was reaching toward his brother. She stared at the first twin. She thought she had seen his full lips move. "Kalienne, I think he's alive! Sikha!"

It was true. With a sudden gasp, the baby opened its eyes wider. Then the sound of its full-bodied wail filled the room with joy. Kalienne took the sleeping twin and wrapped it tightly, while Sikha took the crying baby. The three women were all grinning widely.

"Let me hold him without the blanket," said Bopha. "Please." When he felt her skin, the baby stopped crying and started sucking movements. He didn't try to climb to her nipple, so Bopha lifted him to it. Her nipple looked impossibly huge next to his tiny lips. Sikha tickled him gently on his cheek and he turned toward the touch, opening his mouth. His suck was tentative. He stopped and stared into his mother's eyes. "It's okay, little one. Eat. You'll like it. I promise." As if he understood, the baby sucked a little more.

"He's had a hard start," said Sikha. "But he'll get the idea."

"How is Samang?" Bopha suddenly remembered about her protector. If he hadn't shielded her, that wound would have been in her body. "He saved my life. Not just mine. Mine and the babies."

"He's young and strong. He'll heal. I gave him some tea to help him sleep and ease the pain. Arun Veha and Chariya are watching over him."

"I'm so glad. What would we do without you, Sikha?"

Sikha patted her arm. "How about putting those little cucumbers down, and getting some sleep yourself?"

Bopha shook her head. Her body thrummed with energy, a kind she hadn't felt since she had been a dancer. "I'm way too excited to sleep." She looked down at her sons, both sleeping now. Their fingers almost touched. "But my arms are going to sleep, so I guess I'll put them down. And I'm hungry!"

Chariya brought her dinner, which tasted delicious. "Congratulations, Srey Bopha. What a surprise!"

"Indeed," smiled Bopha. "It wasn't one baby that was too busy after all. But two will keep us all busy, I think." They laughed. "Thank you for the delicious meal, Chariya. You are a very good cook."

Chariya looked shyly pleased. "May I see the babies?" She cooed over the sleeping bundles, which Kalienne had nestled next to each other in a basket that usually held onions. "They look so much alike!" Bopha nodded, but she thought the first twin had bigger ears. He was also a little bigger. His hat was pulled down below his ears now, so you couldn't tell.

"It will be nice to see them in daylight tomorrow," she said. Suddenly a huge yawn overpowered her and she was bone-tired.

Chariya insisted Bopha use a pot. "Tomorrow will be plenty of time to go down the ladder to the mat." Then she took the used linens and made the mat up fresh.

"Thank you," said Bopha, sinking gratefully onto the pad. "This feels wonderful."

She fell immediately into a deep and dreamless sleep.

* * *

With two babies, she did not have much sleep after that. She nursed them both. The four women shared other baby chores. One day Bopha realized, as the boys were simultaneously sucking, that if she were married to Jayavarman and living in the palace, she would not be nursing them. They would have a wet nurse. Or two wet nurses. She loved holding their small bodies, giving them life from her own body and watching as they sucked until they fell off the nipple into a deep milk-sleep.

Sikha and Chariya would often feed the boys milk from the cows, mixed with sugar syrup. They reminded Bopha nursing wasn't enough. Bopha wasn't sure she believed that, but she was grateful for their help and the twins were already noticeably bigger. Mr. Big-Ears was bigger than his brother, but not by much.

She was going to take them to the Wat to be named by the oldest monk, since their father was not available. She wondered if Jaya would have a favorite between them. Then her eyes filled with tears. Would he ever meet these sons of his?

Arun Veha was not impressed by the babies. "All they do is cry and sleep," he complained. "I thought we could play."

"Babies start really small, and it takes them quite a while before they can walk," Bopha told him. "It's hard to wait, I know."

Arun Veha shrugged. "Why did you cry?"

"When did I cry?"

"Well, it was more like yelling," said the boy. "Last night."

"Ah. I guess I didn't notice. It's a lot of work to get a baby to come out, even though it's so small."

"The yelling woke up Samang. He listened, then told me it was okay. Then he fell asleep again. I just sat next to him, wishing he would stay awake."

"That was a long night for you," said Bopha.

Arun Veha nodded. The sound of men talking came in through the window. "Who's that noise?"

"I don't know," said Bopha. The big-eared twin had finished nursing and she put him next to his sleeping brother. "It sounds like it's coming from Sikha's." Arun Veha was already out the door. She heard him clattering down the ladder.

He was back soon. There were lots of men looking at Sikha's broken house, trying to figure out how to move the tree.

"What we need is an elephant," said Old Sokhem. "This is too big for an ox or a water buffalo." He and his middle-aged son, young Sokhem, were directing the workers. But there were no elephants in the neighborhood. It took them three days of sawing and chipping and burning at the huge tree before they could even move its bulk. Then they started carefully to dismantle what remained of the house, saving what could be used to rebuild.

Men came from all the surrounding areas to help. Over the years, there wasn't a family who hadn't been blessed by Sikha's gift of healing. Their wives and children came also. They cooked meals over small fires. It was almost like a festival. Even the monks came to watch, and the women gave them food.

Arun Veha ran down the path to Sikha's first thing in the morning. He ran back to Kalienne's to report as they ate breakfast, then ran back to the worksite. He played with the children there and kept an eye on what was happening with the tree and the salvage operation.

Samang had been regaining his strength but he still grunted when he got up, and walked favoring his right side. He wanted to help the village men, but Sikha said he needed to be careful not to open the wound by lifting too much too soon.

Naming day was set for ten days after the birth, a date determined to be auspicious by the old monk. Kalienne had to go to the construction site to collect a reluctant Arun Veha for the ceremony. As he dragged his feet slowly behind his mother, word spread among the children and thus to the women, then the men. By the time Bopha and Kalienne reached the road, each carrying a baby, there was a line of people waiting to follow them to the temple.

Bopha had forgotten to bring incense for Garuda. Between the busyness of new motherhood and lack of sleep, her mind was garbled. As she passed the bird-man-god's statue, she lifted the baby she carried, the first twin, in sampeah with her. "He wouldn't be here except for you," she thought. "Arkoun. I can never thank you enough."

The statue stood guard, silent and still. "I'll come back with incense later," Bopha promised.

A row of saffron-robed monks stood in front of the altar, each with a stick of burning incense. When the people had crowded inside the Wat, one monk struck a large bronze gong with a wooden mallet. The sound reverberated from all the surfaces and thrummed Bopha's heart. She held the first twin more closely to her chest. Then twenty voiced chanted together, a droning Sanskrit sutra. She didn't understand the sacred verses but the sound was soothing. After the gong rang again, the oldest monk turned to her and Kalienne.

"Which is the first twin," he asked, "the one that was born dead?"

Bopha held out her sleeping big-eared son, warmly wrapped and wearing both hat and mittens. The monk pronounced his name: Big Miracle (Apphoutheto Thom). The gong sounded and the monk chanted a short prayer. Kalienne offered the second twin. The monk named him Golden Surprise (Phnheaphaael Vanna), then blessed him. After another long droning chant and a final gong, Bopha and Kalienne went down the line of monks making sampeah to each. Sikha, Chariya, Arun Veha and Samang followed, doing the same.

Ordinarily many gifts would have been given to the Wat, but everyone knew that all Sikha owned was still under the wreckage of her house. However, an abundance of food had been prepared by Sikha, Chariya, Kalienne and Bopha. In addition, the workers' women had brought food. Everyone sat cross-legged under a huge pavilion, feasting, with lots of chatter, banter and laughter. Before leaving, each person made sampeah to Bopha and Kalienne who held the twins.

As they walked back through the village, people called out greetings. Bopha thought that Jayavarman had been very thoughtful when he sent her here. It was a safe and welcoming place. She wondered what these people thought, really, about her sudden arrival. Besides Kalienne, had there been others sent by the King? She would ask Sikha, she decided. Then she realized that Sikha would never tell. Vanna started to cry in Kalienne's arms and they picked up their pace. He was hungry, her golden surprise. Vanna's wails woke up Thom, and the two women chuckled as he joined his brother in voicing need.

226

"Soon, soon, little Big one. You'll have to learn some patience one of these days," Bopha told him. "We're almost home." Home. She was feeling at home. Life in the Palace was fading, as had life in the Apsara courtyard. She would never forget her wonderful nights with the King, but this was home now.

CHAPTER 24

1197, Return

Time ran fast and slow at the same time, each day lasting forever but suddenly the twins were more than a moon old. Now, another breath and they were starting to push themselves across the wide floorboards on their stomachs. At least Vanna was.

Sikha's new house had been built fast. It looked much like the original one. Bopha liked how the walls in her room had both old weathered boards and freshly cut ones. She squatted, watching Vanna struggle to reach her. "Come on, little golden cucumber, you can do it." Vanna pushed himself into a tripod position, then flopped back onto his belly. Thom was content to lift his head and watch, then lay it down again.

Sikha reassured her that babies grow at different rates. Thom was not only older but bigger, and sometimes big babies were slower. Thom lifted his head and looked at his mother, who lay down so her head was on the same level. "Hi there, older one." Thom gave her a big wet grin and gurgled. "Are you getting a tooth? You are certainly making enough drool." Bopha reached for the nearby kromah — always there needed to be a kromah near a baby — and patted at Thom's chin. He smiled again.

His lips were very full and his ears still bigger than Vanna's. Buddha had enormous ears in all the statues. It was a sign of grace. Suddenly, Bopha could see Jayavarman's ears, then his full lips curve into a smile as he pulled her close. Tears came with the memory. How she missed him. She had not expected to hear from him, but still, every night she wished she could lie in his arms and tell him what the babies had done.

Arun Veha continued to keep his distance from the twins. Samang was completely healed, and he and the boy spent all day together. "He's growing so fast," Kalienne lamented. She sat with Bopha on the porch and watched her son practice marching with Samang. They marched down the lane to the road and disappeared. "I'm glad he's healthy and strong, and I'm glad

Samang is here for him. But I miss the days when he would cuddle in my lap and listen to stories from the Reamker."

The twins were both sleeping. Bopha linked her arm through Kalienne's. "I remember. He is so tall now." She paused. "Like Kiri." She felt her friend stiffen. "Do you think of him? Of Kiri?" Then she admitted, softly, "I think so much of Jayavarman, especially in the night."

Kalienne took a deep breath, then said softly. "Of course. I always think of Kiri."

They sat in silence in the late afternoon shade. Bopha watched the sun behind the house cast long shadows eastward from the trees along the path, toward the road. Rains were long gone but the heat hadn't yet started to press down on the land. A horse passed on the road. Was it really a horse? There were not many horses in this part of the country, and that one had looked big.

Bopha listened and was sure she heard the muffled clop-clop of hooves in the dirt. "Do you hear that horse?" She turned to ask Kalienne, but her friend's face had gone ashen and she was staring down the lane.

Kalienne sprang up and rushed down the steps and into the trees. Bopha watched.

The horse was coming down their path, a tall figure sitting straight on its back. "Kiri!"

Kalienne's voice was strangled with tears. The man jumped off and ran toward her.

In the shadows, Bopha could see them fall into each other's arms, pull back to look at each other, and embrace again.

Kiri. Bopha's mind was swirling with questions. She stood, ready to go find some answers, when both twins started crying at the same time. She dimly saw Kiri's head turn toward the sound. She gave brief sampeah from the porch, and went in to get her sons.

Kalienne and Kiri took the small path to her house, so she could show him where she and his child had been living. Arun Veha came back from the village with Samang, and immediately wanted to know why there was a horse in Sikha's yard. Bopha sent him to ask his mother, not wanting to tell him the wrong thing.

Chariya had seen the reunion from the hearth under the porch. She recognized Kiri, of course, from the Palace. Samang recognized the horse itself, who was lathered from a hard ride, and took him to the stable to groom and feed him.

Early that morning, Sikha had been called to a birth on the far side of the village. She finally returned, walking a little stiffly but her back was still straight. Kalienne and Kiri had come back with Arun Veha. Everyone was sitting under the porch, except for Chariya who was cooking. Bopha had fed both twins and was absentmindedly swinging them in a hammock, watching Kiri. No one was talking, not even Arun Veha.

"Srey Sikha," Kiri stood to greet her, with deep sampeah. Bopha had never seen him bow like that.

"Lok Kiri," said the old woman, looking even tinier as she craned to meet the eyes of the King's Man. "Welcome. It is good to see you again."

"It has been too long," said Kiri. He looked a little older than when Bopha had last seen him, but the stoop was gone. His face was lined with smiles. "Thank you so much. It is clear that my family has been in good hands here."

Arun Veha sat between Kiri and Samang, but closer to Samang. He looked at the tall man, supposedly his father, with a mix of awe and suspicion. Kalienne had never told him anything about who his father was, or why he was not with them. "When you are older," she always said, in answer to his queries. All he knew now was that this man had come. And on a big horse.

His clothes were travel-worn and unremarkable, but there was something about the way he walked and held his head. The child did not know the words "confidence" and "leader," but he recognized the attributes in the King's Man. He had not seen it before, except in the tiny old lady he called grandmother. In Sikha it was not so obvious. But when she spoke in a certain way, everyone listened and obeyed. Even Old Sokhem.

That evening Kiri did not say anything about why he had come. He and Sikha talked about old times, after the Tonle Sap battle, and about her new house. No word about life in the Palace, no admission that he was even from Bayon. Bopha tossed all night and got up with dark shadows under her eyes. She did not begrudge her friend this blessing, but to see her so happy with Kiri was like a sharp blade in her heart. She couldn't sleep, so went downstairs to make tea and start breakfast. The sky was thinking about getting light, but it was dark under the house

"Bopha." He had come up so softly she didn't hear a rustle or step. She twirled and faced him. "The King has sent me." She waited, her eyes fierce with tears. "He wants you to return with me." He paused, then said, "You and the twins. And Kalienne and Arun Veha." He stopped. Tears dripped down her face but her eyes were still angry. Kiri dropped his voice lower. "I think he wants to apologize."

"Apologize!" Bopha spat the word. It echoed against the floorboards above their heads. She heard Samang stir. She lowered her voice to match his. "Now he wants me, after all this time. He wants me, so I'm supposed to come and be grateful." Her body trembled with rage. All her months of sorrow crystallized into an overpowering hatred.

Kiri had stepped back at her first word. Now he sank to a stump, and held his head in his hands. "I'm sorry," he said, finally. "I was so happy to see Kalienne that I didn't..."

"You didn't think what it would be like for me?" Bopha's voice was flat. Kiri shook his head.

The water boiled and Bopha turned to pour it into a teapot. She moved the rice closer to the center of the fire. They heard Chariya get up, then her quiet step on the stairs. "Well. I'll think about it." Bopha said. One of the babies started to cry. "Later." Bopha left the tall man sitting on the stump.

* * *

What could she do? Really, what could she do? Thom was staring into her eyes as he nursed. "What can I do, little big one?" She stroked the soft, dark hair that sprouted wildly all over his head. The King was the King. It was he who made this nice life of hers possible, he who sent money.

231

He who could decide not to. Then what would she do? Thom burped, bringing up a fat bubble of milk. Bopha wiped both her breast and the baby's mouth, then raised him to her shoulder and patted his back. She felt the next burp dribble down her back. The smell of sour milk filled the room. Vanna turned over but did not wake. Bopha leaned against the wall, setting Thom in her lap. "What do you think?" Thom smiled his big goofy smile and Bopha grinned back in spite of herself. "You are a silly boy," she told him lovingly, "and I bless you."

Thom said, "Taa." Or something similar.

"Did you just say, Taa'?" Bopha regarded her older son. He had not said anything remotely similar before. Maybe Ba or Ma. He didn't babble as much as Vanna, who came up with new sounds almost every day.

"Ta," Thom said.

"Well, you don't have any grandfathers," his mother informed him. "And it will be a while until you can say 'aupouk.'" Thom smiled again. "Do you want to go meet your aupouk?"

"Pou," said the baby.

Bopha started to cry soundlessly, tears pouring down her face. Thom looked at her and smiled, then looked concerned. Her breaths were great gasps. Thom started to wail. That woke Vanna, who joined the chorus. Bopha just sat, her back to the wall, weeping with her sons, until Sikha knocked gently on the door.

The old woman knelt to pick up Vanna and pat him. Then she sat next to Bopha with her knees up, and put Vanna on her lap. She took Thom from Bopha and put him next to his brother. She cooed to the boys and made clicking sounds with her tongue until they stopped crying. Then she patted Bopha's knee.

"I knew this day would come," she told the young dancer. "When the King gives his heart, he is loyal and true." Bopha cried harder. Sikha cooed and clicked to the twins, her bony body pressed against Bopha's side. Bopha could feel heat and calm radiating out from Sikha. Her heart began to ease, and with it, her tears. She wiped her face with a last shuddering breath.

"Srey Sikha, you are a miracle. Being here with you has made this time of my life so much more bearable. I feel like this is my home." She paused, then said, "Bayon was never my home."

Sikha shook her head, slowly. "Not Bayon, no. But Jayavarman. He is your home."

To hear his name spoken by the old woman shocked Bopha. No one used the King's name except Kiri and his wives. And Bopha. But Sikha had a long history with the ruler of Kampuchea. Long, and apparently more intimate than Bopha had realized.

She leaned her head back against the wall. The women sat quietly a few minutes, then Vanna got restless for his meal. Sikha patted Bopha's knee again, handed her Vanna, and took Thom downstairs.

After feeding Vanna, Bopha took the steps one at a time, slowly. Her head was spinning. Vanna bounced in her arms. Kalienne appeared on the path from her house just then. She walked fast to meet Bopha. "Are you okay?" Bopha shook her head. "Here, give me Vanna." She put her arm around Bopha's waist and walked her to a seat under the house. "I'll get you some tea."

Bopha sipped listlessly at the warm liquid. When Kiri came down the path, she said to Kalienne, "I think I'm going to take a nap. Will you watch the boys?" Now her head both spun and throbbed. The swirl of thoughts was making her sick, she decided.

Upstairs, she fell on the mat, and slept hard. When she woke, the spinning had stopped. She looked up at the rafters, listening to the murmur of conversation below. She didn't want to hear it, didn't want to make any plans, didn't want to leave this comfortable house. Didn't want to see the King.

She turned over and closed her eyes. But no sleep gave respite. Finally Bopha got up and rolled the pad, storing it under a bench. Everyone gave sampeah when she joined them. "We were just talking about tomorrow," said Sikha. "Old Sokhem has heard that Kiri is here, and is giving a feast. Then, the next morning, you will all go back to Bayon."

Word of the King's Man had travelled only a day slower through the villages than he had on his horse. Bopha suddenly

233

remembered the first time she had heard of him. It had been years since she had been able to see her mother's face, but now it was clear.

She was a little girl in a dusty yard, Mdeay putting down the water pot and telling her that the King was looking for girls to teach how to dance at court. Beautiful girls. She remembered that she hadn't been excited at first.

Then she remembered tucking the pebble in her sampot, and the way her back felt as she started to dance. It was the first time she had been taken up by a dance, the first time that energy had thrummed her spine. Tears came to her eyes but she willed them not to fall. She missed dancing. She missed so much of her past life.

"Look, Vanna's going to crawl!" Chariya's excited voice cut into Bopha's trance. Her younger son was on hands and knees, rocking. Then he moved one knee forward, and looked around. Kalienne and Chariya clapped. Thom was sitting on Sikha's lap and started to bounce. The old woman put him down on his belly. Thom squirmed toward his brother.

"Thom is not to be outdone by his baby brother," chuckled Sikha. Arun Veha watched the adults but failed to understand the excitement.

"Can we go practice throwing spears?" He sat next to Samang Kiri was on the other side of Kalienne. Samang gave Kiri a questioning look. Kiri nodded.

"Sure, let's go, little man," said Samang. Bopha saw Kiri watch the boy leave. His face had a shadow of loss. He missed all those years of his son's life, she thought. All because of the King. This re-ignited her anger and cleared the cobwebs from her mind.

The King. The all-powerful ruler who can cut people's lives off at will. Anger gave Bopha strength and clarity. She could not refuse to return to Bayon, nor to see the King, but she could wall her heart from further hurt.

* * *

On the appointed morning, villagers clustered on the road at the end of Sikha's lane. The King's Man led the small procession. Samang walked at the rear, wearing his impassive Bayon-guard face, his spear upright in his hand.

Sikha walked between Bopha and Kalienne as far as the road. Then, to Bopha's surprise, she continued on with them. Her eyes sparkled as she nodded to Bopha. "Yes, I will come with you. It is time to see the King."

The presence of the tiny, wise woman lifted Bopha's spirits, and with that, her head. She put on the small smile of the Apsara, straightened her back, adjusted Thom in his kromah-sling across her chest, and stepped purposefully forward.

They walked until mid-afternoon, except for a lunch stop. Arun Veha hung back near Samang, sometimes pacing with him and pretending to carry a spear. Sometimes he walked with the women, and occasionally near the horse. At the top of a small rise, they stopped again. "What's that?" Arun Veha was next to Kiri now, but keeping well away from the horse's hooves, as he had been warned.

"That's Tonle Sap," his father told him. "That's where we're going."

"Why is it sparkling?"

"You'll see. We only have a little further to go." Kiri clucked his horse to a walk before his son could ask another question. When they made the final turn into the village at the lake's edge, they paused. Sparkling water, tinged pink and orange from the setting sun behind them, spread as far as they could see.

"It's the sun hitting the water that makes it sparkle," Kiri told Arun Veha. "We are going to cross that water."

"But I can't swim," protested the boy.

"Ah. You don't have to swim. See that boat there?" Kiri pointed. Arun Veha shook his head. "We are going to get on the boat and the boat will take us to the other side." His son was unconvinced.

Bopha listened to the conversation, remembering Rithy telling her about boats. "A boat is like a wagon that floats on water," Bopha told the boy. This one was huge, with two cabins on the top platform and many round holes in the sides on the deck below. It also had a mast, but the sail was shrouded.

"What about your horse?" Arun Veha asked.

"He'll get on the boat," Kiri said, smiling.

By now, villagers had come to watch. They accompanied the newcomers to the dock, murmuring and giving sampeah. Arun Veha walked next to Kiri. When Kiri swing off the horse, he handed the reins to the boy. "Here, you hold these." The horse looked at the child with one yellow eye, then nodded his head, pulling Arun Veha's arms up. But the boy held tight, and the horse settled down. Kiri watched until he was sure about his son. Samang came up to the other side of the horse.

Kiri turned to greet a short, sturdy soldier who wore a huge, shining helmet. "Everything is ready, your honor," said the soldier.

This boat had two sturdy planks running from dock to deck. The women went first, carrying Thom and Vanna. Another soldier, taller and leaner, and wearing a smaller helmet, met them on board. He showed them a set of narrow stairs to the upper deck. They climbed up, then looked over the railing as Samang led the horse across the planks and tied him to the railing of the lower deck. Kiri and Arun Veha boarded together, and joined the women at the upper railing.

When the planks were stowed away, village men untied the ropes and threw them expertly toward waiting soldiers. Creaking, the boat turned. Bopha could see long sticks with big flat ends that poked out of holes on the deck below.

"What are those?" Arun Veha spoke her question. Kiri explained about rowers, then took his son to see where they sat.

"He seems to enjoy beng with his father," Bopha whispered to Kalienne.

"I'm so glad," her friend whispered back. "I was getting worried."

"Do not worry, all will be well." It was the clear, soft sound of Sikha's voice. She had come up next to them.

But Garuda's deep screeching croak repeated them in Bopha's heart. "Thank you," she told the feathered god, "thank you, and please be with us all."

CHAPTER 25

Welcome

Crossing Tonle Sap in the royal barge was smooth, fast and comfortable. In the early afternoon of the second day, Bopha stood at the rail on the upper deck under the bright red and green canopy, watching for land. She rested her hand next to an intricate bronze decoration depicting Garuda's head. His beak was slightly open, showing pointed teeth, and his human hands held lotus flowers above the feathers of his head. These busts were spaced every few meters along the railing. She was grateful for the protection, but had not offered incense. When she returned to Bayon, that would be one of the first things to do, she decided.

Her stomach was in knots and she had to use the pot in her large cabin several times that morning, anxiety squirting out almost uncontrollably. Now she was beyond anxiety, into a state of flat denial. She wished it were the peace of the Buddha, but that was beyond her now. There were still two days of travel, she knew, to reach the palace.

Vanna and Thom were good distractions. Arun Veha spent his time with Samang and his father, leaving Kalienne to sit with Bopha and Sikha. The women did not talk of the future together, but encouraged the twins to wriggle and squirm between them. Vanna was starting to crawl. Thom, noticeable larger than his brother, was getting the hang of movement at last, but was less voluble. Vanna babbled almost continuously unless he was asleep.

"Did Arun Veha talk so much when he was this age?" Bopha asked Kalienne.

"No. Not that I remember. But he made up for it when he started using words." His high, inquiring voice drifted up from the lower deck, where Samang was showing the child how to groom a horse. The women chuckled. Now the twins were both sleeping, a somewhat rare occurrence, and Bopha was alone with her thoughts.

She tried not to think. She watched the water sparkle, very blue under a cloudless sky. The light was almost blinding. Then, she saw it. Land. The rowers increased their speed. Within an hour, the barge was heading up the river, scattering smaller vessels ahead of it. Fishermen and villagers stared at the big boat as it passed. Most made sampeah. The royal pennant hung limply from the top of the mast in the heavy afternoon air.

By the time they reached the dock, clouds were filling the southern sky. They would not give rain, Bopha knew, just trap the increasing heat and reflect it back to earth. Her back was damp and perspiration beaded under her heavy breasts. Nursing two babies had enlarged them noticeably. Even though they were eating lots of other foods now, they still liked milk before and after any sleep. Would they have to be weaned when they got to Bayon?

As if reading her thoughts, both boys awoke. Milk dripped from both nipples as Bopha went into the cabin. They were trying to sit up in their hammock, which Chariya had been gently swinging. The boat touched land with a slight bump and the twins fell back into the hammock. "Hello, little ones. We just got to the other side of the lake," their mother told them. She picked up Vanna, who stared at her a little cross-eyed before smiling hugely. He moved to start nursing, but she put him over her shoulder where he babbled crossly. "We have to get off the boat. Then you can have some milk."

There were no trees near the river, just long heavy grass and a wide dirt path, not quite a road, that led up to the top of the bank. Kiri and the horse disembarked first, then the women and children, then Samang. A small crowd of villagers gave them sampeah from a respectful distance. A large, well-built wagon with a canopy waited where the path met the road, harnessed to a big horse. The driver was a soldier with a small bright helmet. As soon as the passengers were settled on cushions, he took off at a rapid trot, following Kiri.

The twins stared as the world sped past. The women helped them to stand and grasp the side of the wagon. Arun Veha told them what they were seeing. "Look at that huge tree!" "See that little shrine?" "That's my father on his horse!" The almost-toddlers turned to stare at him when he talked. Chariya produced small rice cakes and pieces of mango. By the time everyone had eaten, they were all sticky and covered with grains of rice. Sikha poured water onto a kromah and washed faces and hands. Bopha and Kalienne brushed the boys off and then their own sampots.

This time the trip seemed fast. Before Bopha knew it, the wagons were stopped at a hostel for the night. Early the next morning, as the sky was just getting light, they continued the journey. By early afternoon, villages were close together. More wagons and people were on the road. When they saw the King's wagon coming, people moved to the side to let it pass. Before sunset, the wagon reached Angkor. The serrated towers stood high and clear against a pink sky. Bopha's heart began to pound.

The driver stopped to give the horses a chance to drink. Their coats were dark with sweat. When the clatter of hoof and wagon ceased, the sound of thousands of people, and distant hammering on stone, filled the air. After so long in Sikha's quiet village, this clamor startled Bopha. She had forgotten what it was really like to live in the city. Kiri told the group that they should freshen up before they got to the palace, so they washed as best they could in the baray in front of Angkor.

* * *

When the wagon started to move, Bopha recognized everything. Each turn, each building, as they made their way more slowly through the crowds, was filled with memories. Passing the market, she looked for the sculpture studio but her view was blocked by a wagon piled impossibly high with woven baskets. Too soon, they jolted to a halt under the enormous trees of Bayon palace. It was nearly dark but torches flickered all around them. There were soldiers in two lines, holding their spears at attention.

Samang jumped down and helped Sikha out of the wagon. The tiny elderly woman took a moment to straighten up, then she stood as tall as she could. Her white hair shone in the torchlight. Kiri came to give a hand to Bopha and Kalienne. Arun Veha scrambled out and stood next to his mother. His eyes were huge, and he was silent as he looked at the soldiers with their gleaming spears. Everyone was stiff from travel.

Chariya handed the twins to Kalienne and Bopha before she got out herself, with help from Samang. They stood in a ragged cluster. Kiri nodded to them to turn. He was facing the line of soldiers, his head high, a smile on his face. To Bopha's amazement, King Jayavarman VII was standing at the head of the soldiers, hands in sampeah. Behind him were his wives and the rest of the court, dressed as if for a feast. Jewels flashed, golden necklaces sparkled.

They processed toward the King in a line: Kiri, Sikha, Bopha with Thom, Kalienne with Vanna, Arun Veha, Samang. Hands at hearts, walking slowly. Chariya hung back, melting into the shadow of the wagon. Bopha could not take her eyes off the King. He looked much older, but his smile was full and welcoming. Jaya. She had intended to hold her heart away from him, locked safely from further hurt. But instead she was flooded with love and relief.

He looked directly into her eyes as she approached. Tears suddenly formed, but she kept her head up and smiled softly. He nodded, once, then shifted his gaze to Kiri.

"Arkoun, my friend," he said. Kiri smiled back, and bowed sampeah.

The petite old woman was almost grinning at the King as she approached, hands at her heart. When he wrapped his hands around Sikha's, the crowd rustled but made no other sound. This was so unusual. The whole event was extraordinary. Bopha could hear the King rumble something to his old friend and healer, and her higher-pitched murmur in reply. They smiled at each other, then Sikha moved to the side.

Bopha turned Thom to face his father as she stepped forward, offering him with both hands. Jaya looked at her, then put his hands around hers and the child. "Thom," she whispered, "Apphoutheto Thom." Jayavarman's smile broadened as he dropped his hands. "He's the first twin."

Jaya nodded, then looked past her to Kalienne. Bopha turned slightly, tucking Thom against her right hip, still facing forward. Kalienne did not try to meet the eyes of the King, but handed Vanna to his mother, and bowed a deep sampeah, then backed away. She didn't get far. Kiri had moved behind her. He did not touch his beloved, but indicated she and Arun Veha should stand next to him.

Turning back to Jayavarman, Bopha shifted Vanna to her left hip. He stared at the King, whose broad chest necklace was catching light. "Ba, ba, pa," he babbled, drooling. Jaya chuckled. "Vanna," said Bopha, introducing him. "Phnheaphaael Vanna. The surprise twin."

"Welcome home, my dear Bopha. You will never know how much I missed you and how glad I am that you are safe." The king's voice was so soft that only she heard the words. She nodded. Tears were not staying in her eyes but dripping down her cheeks. With both hands full, she could not wipe them. Jaya touched his own cheek, then kissed his finger. This was not the place for him to dry her face, she knew. Bopha felt the gentle touch he did not actually give her. "Later I will have more time to meet these wonderful boys," he assured her.

She stood next to Sikha, who reached to hold Vanna. They watched as Kiri moved forward to introduce his family. The flickering lights revealed Kalienne's beauty more than daylight, thought Bopha, as her friend bowed to the King, still not meeting his eyes.

Jayavarman lifted his hands, palms outward. "We welcome back to court these faithful friends." He paused and the crowd murmured. "We honor that they have been loyal and true through hardship and loneliness. Their devotion is a lesson from which we can all learn." Putting his hands together at his heart, he bowed his head slightly. Behind him, the crowd realized what he was doing and followed his example. Bopha could see the tension and resistance in Queen Indradevi's face, but she managed a tiny nod.

"Now for the feast!" With this announcement, the King turned and led the way to the great banquet hall. The crowd of queens and courtiers followed.

"Preah Chan Bopha, would you like to change your clothes?" Kiri's voice was soft. "Your quarters are ready."

"Thank you," said Bopha. She heard him make the same offer to Sikha and Kalienne. Chariya met the women at the wagon. They went to the women's courtyard where other maid servants waited. On the porch outside Bopha's old rooms was a chubby young woman.

"Chou will take the twins," said Chariya.

"Take them?" Bopha asked.

"Take care of them," Chariya assured her. "They can stay in the smaller bedroom. I will move to the other small bedroom, and Chou will be in my old room."

"Oh, okay." Bopha was suddenly so tired all she wanted was to lie down and sleep for a whole moon. But she gathered her Apsara training, washed, and dressed for the feast. Chariya fixed her hair. She could hear Chou talking to the twins in the next room, and them babbling in response.

"The King sent this," Chariya offered Bopha a polished teak box. Inside was a wide golden necklace inlaid with sapphires and emeralds in intricate patterns. Bopha lifted it, watching the gems catch light from the small wall sconces. When Chariya had clasped the necklace around her long, sculpted neck, Bopha put her hands in sampeah, then went to the door. Samang, in a spotless sampot, his hair still damp from bathing, stood at attention. Wordlessly, they walked toward the sounds of feasting.

All the doors and windows were open and light flooded into the trees. Bopha could see a few heads, as people walked around, but most of the celebrants were already seated.

She lifted her chin and stepped gracefully up the wide stairs. From the door, she could see Jayavarman on his dais, and recognized the narrow face of Minister Khosal next to him. That face tightened when he saw Bopha. The King followed his look, then he rose from his seat and met Bopha, hands in sampeah. The room was suddenly silent as all faces turned toward the King and the Apsara.

"Your Majesty," she said, bowing.

"Preah Chan Bopha. Welcome home." Jayavarman's eyes glistened, and he blinked a few times before leading her to the long low table where the queens were sitting. "My bride to be," he announced to the quiet room, "Preah Chan Bopha."

Mach Botum recovered first and stood up to greet Bopha. Indradevi inclined her head in a cold welcome. Sao Nang slowly followed Mach Botum's example, her sharp nose and high cheekbones exaggerated in the wavering light from torches along the walls.

Bopha held her hands in sampeah, bowing slightly to each of the King's wives.

Conversation in the room started again slowly after she sat down. To her relief, no one but Mach Botum asked her any questions. "Bride to be," she beamed. "How nice."

Bopha nodded, stunned by the announcement and the welcome. "Do you know when?"

Bopha shook her head. "I guess when the astronomers say it is auspicious," she managed. "How have you been? Is Malis here?" Bopha asked questions to avoid her own answers. She did not expect to have any appetite, but it had been a long day and she was young and healthy. As the platters and bowls were served, her nose and stomach agreed that she should eat. "I forgot how delicious the food is in the Palace," she told Malis, who had come to sit next to her.

Queen Indradevi glanced at her occasionally. Bopha smiled at her, as she lifted a spoonful of fragrant fish amok to her full lips. How long had it been since the Queen humiliated her for not eating? Tonight, Bopha was ascendant, she knew. Indradevi and everyone else knew it also. Bopha's smile widened as she reached   for   another   mouthful.

CHAPTER 26

Meeting the Twins

When the meal was done, people milled about again. Many courtier approached Bopha, bowing sampeah and introducing themselves. She remembered no names but some of the faces were familiar. Jayavarman caught her eye a couple of times, smiling gently. Once he gestured to her to come meet Muni, his Minister of Construction. Muni was of medium build, wiry and full of intensity. His eyes flashed and his back was straight.

"I hope to talk with you more one day, about your construction projects," Bopha said.

"Between water systems, roads, hospitals, temples — you must be very busy."

"Yes, it is wonderful what our King is doing. No other ruler anywhere has ever done so much in such a short time," Muni said with enthusiasm and appreciation. "I am honored to be helping."

Bopha found Kalienne in the crowd. She was sitting with Mach Botum, who asked about Arun Veha.

"He sounds like my second child," laughed the plump queen. "Always asking questions."

"Is your son at the palace now?" Bopha asked.

"No." A shadow passed across the sweet face. "He was killed in the battle for Angkor."

"I'm so sorry," Bopha said. "We can all thank him for his heroism."

"He was only 13," Mach Botum said softly. "Too young, really, to be there. But he was the King's favorite child, and wanted so much to be part of the action. You know how young boys are. The King kept him behind the lines, but a stray arrow struck him as he watched from across the baray." Her voice faltered. Then she regained some of her usual cheer. "Tell me about the twins. We heard that the older one was not alive when he was born."

245

Bopha told the story, adding, "I think it was Sikha, breathing into him, that gave him life."

"I have never met her before now, but there are many stories about her healing people," said Mach Botum. They looked around, and saw the tiny figure sitting next to the King, talking with Boran. Bopha realized suddenly that Boran might actually be the head of the King's armies. She would ask. Yet Jaya had sent Boran with her to Sikha's village. He wanted to keep her safe, she understood. Kiri was the king's most trusted friend, second in command of the whole kingdom. Boran the most trusted guard. Was that why he had been at the Apsara courtyard? Keeping an eye on her? Or on all the Apsaras, so dear to the King's heart?

A sudden yawn overpowered Bopha. She tried to stifle it but could not. The King saw it. When he stood, those in the crowd who were not already standing scrambled to their feet. He announced, "It has been a long journey for our friends, so we will not keep them up too late. Good night and thank you all for coming." He walked to the door, followed by Sikha, Boran, Kiri, Khosal. The queens followed, Bopha in line behind Sao Nang.

At the foot of the stairs, Samang met her. Instead of heading for the women's courtyard, he took her to the King's bedroom. It had been hours since Bopha had nursed. As she walked up the stairs, she thought of the twins, sleeping in an unfamiliar room with an unfamiliar woman. Would they be okay? Milk seeped from her breasts, fragrant and slightly syrupy. Of course, Chariya was there. They would be fine, Bopha assured herself.

Jayavarman came to her, hands in sampeah, as soon as his guard closed the door. Her hands were at her heart and her forearms stuck slightly to her milky breasts when she dropped them to her sides. She was no longer the girl she had been the last time she was in this room.

They stood looking at each other. Bopha stood straight, suddenly flooded with anger at this man who so carelessly upended her life. He put out a tentative finger to her cheek. The gentle touch sent a shiver down her spine. Anger dissolved into that feeling of connection and oneness she remembered so well. Jaya. He moved only that one finger, tracing her cheekbone.

246

"I'm sorry, Bopha. I was wrong. And stupid. And pig-headed. I should never have sent you away." The king's words were soft with remorse, as were his eyes. "You were right. You told me the truth and I rewarded your loyalty with …"

Tears were in his eyes then. "With …" Drops fell. One hit her hand which had reached toward the big man. She lifted it to touch his wet cheek, then kissed her fingers, never breaking eye contact.

"With banishment," she said. Her quiet word hit Jaya, who suddenly inhaled. "Yes," she continued. "With banishment. I am grateful for your apology. Do you still want me to tell you truth?"

Jaya nodded mutely. Then he whispered, "Yes… Please." His voice was almost pleading. "I do not want to live without you near me. You know how much I loved my first wife. When she died, so did a part of my heart. I never thought I would feel that way again. But now." His voice cracked. "Sometimes it is so hard to be King. So many demands, so many details, so many people wanting things from me. But you, all you ever wanted was my heart." Bopha nodded. Now tears fell from her eyes also.

The King finished so quietly she could barely hear him. "And you have it. All of it. My heart is yours, Preah Chan Bopha."

She took a step toward him, her breasts grazing his chest. On tiptoe she lifted her lips to his, still looking into his eyes. "I'm here," she said softly, and kissed him.

Sometime in the night, Bopha awoke. She was damp from sweat and breast milk. The King lay on his back, one arm over his eyes, his breathing not quite a snore. The other hand was entwined with hers. Gently she disentangled and went to use the pot. On her return, eyes adjusted to the dark, she could see his eyes were open and following her.

She lay back down and snuggled into his arms, wrapping her upper arm around his back. Her hand traced the scar there, a line so full of memories. He put both hands around her head gently, and kissed her, his lips so soft that she melted into them. "I missed you so much," Jaya said.

"And I you."

"This morning there is a council meeting." Jaya told her after a moment, tone more business-like. "I want you to come," he said.

247

Bopha pulled back to look at him. "Afterwards, we can talk," he continued. "And then, I want to meet my new sons." His teeth glinted in the near-dark as he grinned. "Twins! Imagine."

"You won't have to imagine any longer," Bopha teased him.

"No one else teases me," Jaya said, pulling her close. "Khun Thea would. But not Kiri."

"Well, you can count on me to tell you the truth — and to tease you."

Jayavarman took a deep breath. She could feel him nodding his head. "But if you ever do something like this again," Bopha warned the King of Kampuchea. "I will not return." She shook her head. "I would rather die." Her tone was dead serious.

"I won't," he promised. "Never. I would rather die than have you leave." He put his palm flat across his heart.

Bopha resisted the urge to say she hoped he wouldn't change his mind about that.

Talk about changing his mind had started the whole thing. She put her hand over his, then kissed his chest.

When he traced her nipples, milk eased out, surprising him. "It's been too long since I nursed," Bopha explained. "My breasts want my babies."

"You nursed both boys?"

"Of course." She didn't point out that she was in no financial position to hire a wet nurse even if she had wanted. "It's the most wonderful thing."

"Not something a man can know," Jaya said, somewhat ruefully."

"No, I guess not."

"I'll arrange for a wet nurse today."

"No, please don't." Bopha's certainty surprised both of them. "I mean, thank you for your offer. But I like nursing the boys. It won't be for much longer. They are starting to drink from a cup. And they eat," she laughed, "they eat and wear lots of different foods."

"Wear?"

"Have you ever watched a toddler learn to eat?"

"No," Jaya admitted.

"Everyone nearby needs a bath afterwards," she chuckled.

In the silence after Bopha's remark, her words sat. "I have not had much to do with my children," admitted Jayavarman. "Any of them. Until they were older, and even then ..."

"It is the way of Kings," suggested Bopha, then added, "And Queens. But I was born in a village, a different way of life. So nursing and taking care of my babies seems normal."

By now the room was starting to get light. "Time to go," said Bopha. "The world calls." She paused, then asked, "How is Rithy?"

"Your brother is very well. Such a smart young man. He is now assistant to my chief scribe." After a beat, Jaya continued, "Would you like to continue your lessons?"

"Oh, yes. Very much," said Bopha. "We practiced every day at Sikha's, until the twins were born. Then, only a few times a week."

"We?"

"Arun Veha, Kalienne, Samang, Chariya."

"Chariya?"

"My maid servant," said Bopha. "She didn't want to learn, didn't think it was right for her, in her station, but Arun Veha gave her a stick. He was very keen that everyone have a stick. We drew letters in the dirt of the yard."

"Ah," said the King, nodding slightly. "Your maid servant. You are an unusual woman, my dear Preah Chan Bopha. Full of surprises."

* * *

The twins were playing in the front room with Chariya and Chou when Bopha returned.

When they saw their mother, they put out their arms for her to pick them up. By now her breasts were so full that it was a little difficult for them to latch, but they were big and eager. Bopha decided to talk with Sikha about how to wean them. Kalienne would also know, she realized. But where was Kalienne?

They made a procession to the baray. Chariya and Chou insisted on carrying the boys and Bopha didn't argue. As they got close, they could see a lot of women there, Kalienne's tall figure among them. No sign Indradevi, to Bopha's relief. Malis squealed when she saw the twins, and came to sit with them, showing them how to slap the water and to make waves. Except for the stop at Angkor yesterday, the boys had never seen a baray. They were used to bathing in a bucket, but it was clear that this was much more fun. They crowed and splashed, getting everyone near wet. Arun Veha joined the game vigorously.

Sao Nang arrived with Nimith Sokhem, now a rowdy almost two-year old. As soon as he was in the water, he started splashing the twins and demanded, "Who are you?"

"This is Vanna and this is Thom," said Bopha, pointing. She added, not really for Nimith Sokhem's benefit, "Your half-brothers." She surprised herself. All the adults knew that already. But Bopha did not intend to be cowed this time around. She was an Apsara, and had survived banishment and given twin sons to the King. She was his betrothed and his beloved. She was invited to a council meeting. She was determined to hold her own in these exalted environs.

"Can you come over this afternoon?" Bopha asked Kalienne, adding very softly. "I want to hear about everything."

Kalienne smiled broadly and nodded. She was radiant. Bopha hadn't seen her look so beautiful and happy in many years, since before she left the Apsara courtyard to be Khun Thea's lady in waiting.

There were many sampots and boxes of jewelry in Bopha's quarters when she returned.

She dressed for the council meeting in a blue sampot shot with gold thread. The earrings Jaya had given her — how long ago it seemed — were in a small box. She had not worn earrings since she left the palace, and had to push hard to get them through her

250

ears. She chose a simple gold necklace, its tiers held together by slender gold chains.

Samang arrived and led the way to the King's small audience chamber. The King stood when she arrived, so all the other men did as well. All men, Bopha noted: Kiri, Khosal, Muni, and four others she did not know. After introductions, they sat again.

There were formal speeches from each man, full of flowery praise for the King, and kernels of information. The most pressing matter was water. Muni explained the problem, then invited the water master to give more details. Jayavarman VII was greatly expanding the system of waterworks, barays and canals that supported agriculture and brought water to Angkor and Bayon. Last rainy season had not been as abundant, the cities were growing, and so was their need for water. Jaya approved the plan for diversion of another river to support Angkor and Bayon.

The second item was also in Muni's jurisdiction. A bridge was needed in Kampong Kdei. Architects had designed one with twenty-five arches, spanning the river. Drawings of the bridge were passed around and admired. It would be the longest bridge in the world. "A fitting tribute, to last a thousand years, for our great King," declared Muni.

Several scribes were scribbling at a low table on the side of the room. They filled pages, blotted them, then piled them under small bronze statues. Bopha recognized Garuda, the elephant god Ganesh, and an Apsara. When the wind picked up, the papers fluttered but did not blow off the table.

Later Rithy told her that there was a whole room under the scribes' studio, full of papers filed by date and subject. He took Bopha to meet the wizened monk who monitored the library.

"Oh yes, I know where every document is, Lok Srey," the bald and wrinkled man assured her. "If there is an inscription to be chiseled in stone, they come to me. I give them a copy to take away, but always I keep one here."

Kalienne came after lunch, and the two old friends sat on the back porch talking quietly.

The King had given Kiri permission to marry Kalienne. Arun Veha was to be taught by royal tutors, just like any child of the king. "It's hard to believe," said Kalienne, tears in her eyes. "After all these years, Kiri and I can be together. He's so wonderful."

Bopha nodded. She knew how it was. "But, Bopha, Kiri has aged. Our years apart were so hard for him. You know, he and the King have been friends since they were children, they were together in exile in Champa, they fought together to restore Kampuchea to the Cambodians. Many years." She looked at her friend. "And the King himself is," she paused, looking for the right words. "Not a young man." There was a moment of silence, then Kalienne shook herself, "But they are both strong and vital, very healthy." She sounded almost like she was trying to convince herself. Already, both Kiri and the King had outlived many men.

Bopha hadn't thought much about how old Jaya was. She knew he was older than herself by many years. But how much older? She had no idea. Time was not a clear concept for her, other than days and moons and seasons. She had no idea how old she was herself. She changed the subject. "Will you have a big wedding?"

Kalienne shook her head. "Not so big. A blessing by the priests. A feast."

"Where will the blessing be held?"

Kalienne shrugged. "Bopha, this is all so new. There is so much I don't know. Life was one way, a quiet life in a quiet village, a quiet sorrow but love from Sikha, and always entertainment from Arun Veha. Now, suddenly, in less than a week, here we are at the Palace. You were an Apsara. But I was just a lady-in-waiting, a step above a maid." She paused, then sighed. "You always seem so calm and confident. How do you do it?"

Bopha put an arm around her friend and hugged her. "I am a village girl who became an Apsara. First a … lover? … concubine? … to the King. Then banished. Now here I am, as you, suddenly with a new life. I'm far from calm." She looked at Kalienne. "Do I really look calm?"

"Yes, really. Calm and beautiful. Regal, actually."

Bopha chuckled. "Regal. Hunh. Maybe being an Apsara taught me how to carry myself, despite what I felt on the inside. And confident? I never thought of myself that way." She paused, then continued soberly, "But last night, at the feast, something shifted. Now I believe I can be a true partner to the King." Her tone changed. She spoke firmly, "And a worthy opponent to any who wish me harm."

Kalienne stared at her. "Do you think anyone wishes you harm?" Bopha shrugged. She would not burden her friend further. Kalienne was a dear, wonderful friend, but an innocent. This was not a conversation she needed to have. Bopha had no proof, just suspicions. She had not shared them with the King. Not yet.

Chariya came to the porch. "Lok Srey, Samang has come. The King is ready to meet his sons."

The royal sons were dingy from rolling on the floor together. They were kind of like puppies, Bopha thought. It did not take long to give them a quick wash and dress them, clean cloths wrapped around their waists then tucked up to make a diaper, finally tiny sampots in an identical orange pattern. Most people would not be able to tell them apart. But Bopha could. She took Vanna from Chou and Chariya picked up Thom.

Jayavarman was waiting in his bedroom. "Hello, hello, come in." Bopha entered but Chariya hesitated at the door. "Come, come," he told her. She walked in, cringing like someone might hit her.

"It's okay, Chariya," Bopha reassured her.

"Ah, Chariya. I hear you have been learning to write." At the king's deep rumbled words, the young woman looked like she wished to die right there. Recovering herself, she made sampeah awkwardly, clutching Thom to her shoulder and gazing at the floor.

Then she nodded.

"Do not worry," Jayavarman reassured her. "You may continue to learn. Here, let me get a look at this boy. Which one is which?"

Bopha spared Chariya from speaking. "That's Thom. His ears are bigger, and he's a little bigger."

Jaya reached for the child and placed him on one knee. Thom looked into his eyes then gave his goofy grin. "Oh, teeth. I see teeth," said his father. Thom babbled and drooled. The king jostled him up and down on his knee, saying, "Do you want to ride a horse?" The knee went faster and faster. Thom's grin faded, then he threw up onto his father's leg. "Whoa!" Jaya held him at arm's length.

Bopha handed Vanna to Chariya, grabbed the spare kromah on her shoulder, and patted at the vomit. Jaya handed her the baby. Thom turned his head to keep looking at the big man with the deep voice.

"I'm almost afraid to say hello to you, young man," Jaya told Vanna, who was also twisted around, keeping an eye on this new man. But the king held out his hands and Chariya gave him the boy. Vanna regarded his father with a serious expression. As Jayvarman settled Vanna on his lap, there was a loud squirting fart. Jaya quickly held the baby away from him.

"Not to be outdone by his older brother," laughed Bopha. Chariya was trying not to laugh so made a choking gurgle. The sound was so unusual that the King's lips curved up, then he started laughing as well, still holding Vanna at a safe distance.

When he collected himself, he said, "I'm glad I decided for us to meet here. It's so much easier to change so I don't have to walk through the courtyards with a lap full of ..." Laughter overtook him. "Well, you know. Here, take this little bundle of," he giggled, "joy and poop."

Bopha, a big grin on her face, said, "Say 'nice to meet you Aupouk'.'" She also held Vanna away from her body. Chariya had already backed to the door. Bopha took one of Vanna's small chubby hands and waved it at Jaya, then held both his hands between hers, giving sampeah. "Now we know why you don't spend much time with your young children."

They could hear Jaya chuckling as they closed the door. Samang, waiting on the porch, looked non-plussed. "It was a most ... unusual meeting," Bopha told him. "The twins gave the King all they had." Samang still looked confused, but led them down the stairs. Vanna continued to flap his hand.

CHAPTER 27

1197, Weddings

On a hot and cloudless afternoon, Kalienne and Kiri were wed. Despite Kalienne's wish to have a simple ceremony, the King took charge. He and Bopha talked about it. He wanted to honor his best friend, and cement his position as the second most powerful man in Kampuchea. Bopha explained the dynamics to her friend, who could do nothing but accept.

The sun beat down on the Terrace of the Elephants. The canopy over Queens and courtiers was stifling. Young boys pulled rhythmically at long ropes attached to huge, woven-bamboo fans that hung from the wood struts holding up the roof. Small gusts of hot air did nothing to reduce the temperature inside.

Bopha sat next to Sao Nang, just behind Minister Muni, while Indradevi sat behind the King. Kiri sat at the King's right and Kalienne at his left. After long prayers and the offering of many sticks of incense at the central altar, the crowd of saffron-robed monks sat on the ground in front of the platform where the court sat.

It was time for the traditional Bongvil Popil part of the wedding ceremony. So long ago no one knew when, a man asked God for a blessing tool to use when human beings married. God took diamond sand from the universe to make a golden banyan leaf, representing the woman's vagina. Then he took a diamond rock from the Himalaya Mountains to make a candle, the man's penis. The candle was wrapped in the banyan leaf, and the two blessings were carried three times around the bride and groom, to bring harmony and joyfulness to the union.

Kiri and Kalienne stood, then walked to the center of the terrace in front of the altar. Kiri put out his hands and she placed hers, palm to palm, on his. The most senior monk of Angkor circled them three times. He held a candle wrapped in a banyan leaf in one hand, which he waved in small circles as he walked slowly around the couple. In the other hand, he held a stick of incense which he waved in the same manner. Bopha could see tears coursing down Kalienne's cheeks. She had a big smile, and her large, beautiful eyes never left Kiri's face. Kiri was not crying, but his eyes glistened as he gazed back at her.

Bopha's eyes dampened as she watched. There were many other elements to the wedding, all based on ancient legend. Finally, the priest nodded and a deep gong sounded three times. Kiri and Kalienne took their seats, next to each other, at the King's feet. It was time for the Apsaras to dance.

Despite the sapping heat, Bopha was eager to see this. She had herself only performed the Wedding Dance once, at the marriage of Jayavarman and Sao Nang. She remembered how much she had wanted to learn this dance when she was just a small girl, in her long-ago village. "And look at you now," she heard Mdeay murmur. "The King calls you the greatest Apsara, and will marry you by the next moon." The sound of Mdeay's voice shocked Bopha. If she had tried, she would not have been able to remember that voice, and her mother's face had also faded over the years. She quickly turned her head to catch a glimpse of Mdeay, but saw only Sao Nang's chiseled cheeks.

Just then, the music started. From the hidden stairs at the side of the Terrace, the Apsaras walked gracefully to the center of the parade ground. There were three lines of ten females and one line of men. The dancers circled until Sophea's petite upright form was in the center, facing Dara. Bopha's heart flip flopped. She recognized Thida, Theary, Nary, Tevy. How she longed to dance with her friends.

Before she could feel sorrow, the dance began. The music and movement carried Bopha. She could hardly keep her arms and feet from forming the familiar jeebs. Somehow, she suddenly knew in her marrow, she needed to keep dancing. But not this minute. With the discipline of an Apsara, she sat still on her bench until the last tones stopped. The crowd aahhhed and patted their benches loudly. The King himself stood in sampeah, which caused everyone else to do so, in great haste.

The dancers filed out, a line of embodied music. Bopha's eyes followed them. She knew the twists in those stairs, all the different bas reliefs that rose on both sides, higher than two men standing on top of each other. Most bas reliefs at Angkor were huge, many carved stones piecing together a big picture. But this staircase was different, no more than two to four carvings per image, and the stones were smaller. On some, a single image filed the stone. A fish, its mouth hugely open. A monkey reaching for a banana. The dancers would not attend the feast, but trudge back to their courtyard in the heavy, still, heat of late afternoon.

Bopha felt Sao Nang step away from her, and realized that the King had started back to the Palace, where many white tents were set up, under which tables covered with white cloths were piled with foods for the huge feast. Kiri and Kalienne, hand in hand, were right behind the King. They would sit with him for the meal, then more prayers, then hours of exaggerated, polite speeches to wish them well. Bopha was glad for her friend to be honored in this way, though she knew both she and Kalienne would be relieved when the three days of celebration were finished. She wasn't really looking forward to her own marriage, soon to come, with five days of ceremony and feasting.

Children were invited to the feast but not the ceremony. Chou and Chariya brought the twins, who were starting to cruise, pulling themselves up on any available object. Bopha could see the two women, in the next tent over, with other ladies-in-waiting. Sometimes one of them picked up a crying twin. Once consoled, the child squirmed until he was put back on the ground again, out of Bopha's line of sight. Arun Veha was running between the tents with a group of boys. Nimith Sokhem was trying to keep up with them, his chubby legs churning. He was a fast runner, but still a few years younger than the others. Bopha didn't recognize the leader of the pack, who had spindly legs and long arms. Something in his face was vaguely familiar.

"Who is that child?" She asked Mach Botum, who was sitting between her and Kalienne. "The one leading the boys." She pointed with her chin, it being impolite to use a finger. Mach Botum's eyes followed the gesture.

"Oh, that's Visothirith. He's Minister Khosal's son." She lowered her voice, "But far from heavenly or pure. If there's any mischief to be found, that boy will be first in line."

"And who is his mother?"

"At the end of the table, wearing a green sampot with orange flowers."

Bopha looked. Khosal's wife, despite her bright clothing, looked mousy and scared.

She was listening to a long story her neighbor was droning, nodding and trying to smile.

The woman seemed to feel Bopha looking at her, and suddenly turned her way. When their eyes met, Bopha made sampeah. Flustered, the woman returned it. This caught her neighbor's attention, and they both looked at Bopha. Out of the corner of her eye, she saw Minister Khosal, on Kiri's right, notice the interaction. He looked down the table at his wife, frowning, then back at Bopha. His wife cowered and looked down.

Bopha, her face impassive except for an apsara smile, inclined her head slightly to the minister, then turned to Mach Botum. "The wife of Minister Khosal?"

"Yes." Mach Botum paused and added, almost inaudibly, "poor thing."

"Indeed," agreed Bopha. A servant reached between them, offering a platter of sesame cookies. "Thank you," she said to the servant, who looked startled before shifting her gaze and backing away.

"You have a kind heart," Mach Botum said, diplomatically.

"I may never learn how to behave at court," admitted Bopha. "To be served ..." She decided that her village roots were not necessarily bad and that treating servants with courtesy was a virtue. No matter what people like Indradevi — Queen Indradevi, her mind interjected — and Khosal might think. She would be courteous, but not too friendly. It was a fine balance in such a hierarchical society. She took a deep breath, then a bite of the cookie. When she stole a glance at Khosal's wife, the woman had gone.

* * *

It seemed no time passed before Bopha was the bride, looking into Jaya's eyes as the candle, this one wrapped in heavy gold fashioned in the shape of a banyan leaf, circled them. He lifted her hands to his lips, a break from tradition. She heard a slight, collective intake of breath. Then the King opened his palms, and bride and groom turned to the priest, giving sampeah.

Their wedding was a five-day affair, starting with a huge parade that went all the way from the Palace at Bayon to Angkor. Soldiers in full regalia led the procession, followed by colorfully-clad men who carried flags and banners, interspersed with musicians marching as they played flutes, drums, fiddles, gongs. Several hundred palace women carried candles, flames lit even though it was morning. Their necklaces, sampots and hair were decorated with flowers of all colors and shades. Following them, more palace women marched, these ones carrying lances and shields.

All the King's Apsaras followed, both young and adept, their arms in various jeebs. Four thousand gestures were in the classical repertoire, and the dancers would change positions as they walked. Every so often, their musicians would play, long enough for the dancers to twirl three times, their legs lifting and feet twisting into a new movement on each rotation. The crowds along the way aaahhhed the loudest for the Apsaras. Until Bopha and the King arrived, that is.

The King's private guards came next, swords held upright, helmets gleaming. Carts drawn by horses and goats, both cart and animal covered with gold ornamentation, carried the lower members of the court. Mounted on elephants, high ranking Ministers and royal cousins, splendidly attired and sparkling with gold and jewels, lurched along. Their red umbrellas could be seen from afar.

If Jayavarman had had concubines, these would have come next. But he had sent them all away years before, as he waited for Bopha to come of age. He had been loathe to lose Bopha as an Apsara, so much did he admire the way she brought heaven to earth with her grace, and he waited longer than he would otherwise.

Behind the ministers, Kiri rode his magnificent sorrel horse, man and animal bedecked with silver and silk. He held a very long, very sharp spear. The intricately worked silver of the shaft glinted in the sun.

Kalienne, ranking now just below Bopha and the queens, led the procession of royal women. She rode in a carriage festooned with silk banners. A huge black ox pulled the wagon, with colorfully dressed men holding the slim gold reins on each side. In its nose was a large metal ring. In front of the ox marched a man holding upright a polished teak pole with a sturdy metal hook in the end, in case the animal took a notion to get away from the crowds. Kalienne sat, tall and graceful, blue silk sampot clinging to her shapely form. Her wide eyes watched from under a wide circlet of gold. Her thick braids pouffed up above the band, and stood out from her head on all sides below it.

Sikha had told the King that she wanted to see this marriage before she left Bayon for home. "This Apsara will bring you great good fortune, my Lord. So please, treat her well." Only Sikha could have admonished the ruler. But he took it meekly.

"Don't worry, old friend. I have learned my lesson. Thank you again for taking such good care of her."

As befitted her relation with the king, Sikha now surveyed the parade from a litter. She was so tiny she hardly needed the four sturdy men who hefted the poles. She had asked to have the front curtains pulled apart, as well as having the sides open. She wanted to see everything. Her sampot was deep purple. The only concession she made to the King's imprecation, that she be clothed as he might want to see his mother, was to wear a solid gold bangle on each arm, formed of two serpents twining up each withered bicep. "I appreciate your wish to honor me," she told Jayavarman. "And that you have adopted me as mother. But I am a simple village healer and cannot betray those roots." So great was his regard for Sikha, that he honored her wishes.

Sao Nang rode a magnificent black horse. Its mane was braided with gold and red silk, matching her sampot. The bridle was gold and Sao Nang's arms shone with wide arm bangles from bicep to wrist. She sat upright, calmly and firmly guiding the big steed.

Also bedecked with gold, Mach Botum followed in a carriage pulled by two white horses.

Her blue sampot had intricate patterns woven in gold thread, of great ibis bringing blessings.

Indradevi was in a palanquin of solid gold. The green silk curtains were pulled back, allowing the crowds along the way a rare sight of the King's first wife. She wore a crown that sparkled with emeralds, and an enormous breastplate of gold. Although first wife, today she rode ahead of the bride-to-be.

Bopha had never ridden on an elephant until that week. When Jaya had explained how the parade would progress, she said she preferred to try a horse. But he told her the elephant was more of an honor, and he wished everyone to know her rank. So she had spent a few hours with one of the royal mahouts. Despite the lurching gait of the huge animal, Bopha now sat gracefully in the solid gold howdah. Its roof was supported by four chains of turtles, their backs encrusted with all manner of gemstones. Her sampot was pure gold thread.

Early that morning, Kesor had sent Thida to fix her hair in the traditional Apsara braids. While Thida was doing this, Chariya had come in, followed by Samang carrying a large mahogany box that had two doors inlaid with ivory. When they opened the doors, the red velvet lining showcased a golden headdress. Despite its delicate construction, the crown was heavy. Waves of gold rope framed her forehead and wrapped securely around the back of her head. Progressively thicker flames of beaten gold, twenty one of them, rose to a peak almost two hand-spans high. Rows of rubies were embedded in the flames.

Paroxysms of aaahhhs followed Bopha through the streets.

Finally King Jayavarman VII, ruler of Kampuchea appeared. He stood on the back of an elephant whose tusks were encased in gold. In his hand, he brandished the sacred sword. People were torn between staring, shouting, and prostrating themselves. Most did all three, haphazardly.

Behind the King, Boran led a contingent of the most highly-placed soldiers, on smaller and less decorated elephants. When the last elephants had crossed onto the bridge at the South Gate of Angkor, soldiers formed a blockade. The first ceremony of the wedding would be private. As private as a parade of thousands could be.

* * *

261

Bopha was grateful when the elephant lumbered to its knees. She had practiced this part many times, at first nearly falling out of the wooden howdah. The mahout warned her that the uprights on the gold palanquin used for the parade would not be sturdy enough for her to hold on to, so there would be straps hidden in each side of the roof.

A wooden ladder with wide steps was rolled up to the kneeling elephant, and Bopha stepped down, glad for her youth and physical agility. She knew now why Queen Indradevi had not been on an elephant.

It was a relief to enter the cool stone building in the Angkor complex, monks' quarters that had been prepared for the royal party. To cover the not-quite-four kilometers from Bayon Palace to Angkor Wat had taken the parade more than two hours. By now, the sun was near its zenith. Bopha's neck ached from holding up the crown, and the gold threads of her sampot itched. Chariya helped her remove the headgear once she was inside her assigned small room.

"Would you like tea? And some fruit?" Chariya offered.

"Yes, please. And maybe a bit of rice and dried fish?" Bopha was suddenly famished.

Because preparations were so extensive, she had eaten at dawn.

The twins and Arun Veha had watched the procession prepare, in the open spaces behind the Terrace of the Elephants. Vanna and Thom ogled and pointed at the light sparkling off the gold decorations, while Arun Veha was more interested in the soldiers and the animals.

"I want to ride an elephant," he told Bopha. From a safe distance the day before, he had watched, along with the other young boys, as she practiced getting on and off the huge beast.

"Maybe someday," Bopha told him. "Talk with your father." The boy had quickly bonded with the tall older man, and followed him whenever he was allowed. He mostly avoided the twins, nowhere near as much fun as the gang of palace boys with whom he ran. They all took writing and lessons from a young monk.

"All we do is repeat what he says, on and on, over and over," Arun Veha complained. "I liked it better learning from you." Bopha laughed.

"Thank you, young man. But I want to hear that you give proper attention to your lessons with the monk!" Arun Veha shook his head. "Unh-unh," said Bopha. "You need to honor your teacher."

"Okay." The boy sighed. Bopha was sure he had grown just in the few months since they returned to Bayon. "But can I come sometimes and practice with you?"

"Yes. That would be nice. But not till after the wedding." Rithy and she were meeting every few days now. To see again her big brother, whose narrow shoulders were filling out as he matured, had been a joy. She told him the whole story of her time away, including the boats and being sick crossing Tonle Sap.

Rithy listened carefully, regarding her with an expression between compassion and impassivity. Nothing seemed to ruffle him, Bopha thought. Truly, he was following the Buddha's path. "I too am glad to see you again," he told her. "I missed you. But the Buddha teaches not to worry, and I try to obey."

"Next week," he continued, "I will be joining the scribes during Council meetings." He paused. When Bopha said nothing, he admitted, "I heard that you have been there."

"Yes, my Lord wishes me to attend. You know I am bound to tell truth to him." Rithy nodded. She sighed. "Even though it led to my exile, I do not regret my role. He has promised ...". She trailed off. Rithy waited. "He has promised never to punish me for that again. I told him I would never return if he did." She looked at her brother defiantly. "I will die first."

Rithy raised his eyebrows but said nothing. She blurted out, "Since we will both be at Council, and you are teaching me to read and write, maybe we can talk about the meetings together? So many years ago, we both agreed to tell truth to power," she reminded him.

"When you are Queen," Rithy began.

But Bopha interrupted. "When I am Queen, you will still be my brother. I will need you more than ever."

263

Rithy bowed his head slightly. "I will always be your brother," he said softly, then met her gaze. "Always."

CHAPTER 28

Queen

Five days of parade, ceremonies, feasting for every inhabitant of Bayon and Angkor, so many changes of clothes. By the evening of the last feast, Bopha was exhausted. She looked down the long table from her place at Jayavarman's left hand. Queen Indradevi was to his right, then Kiri and Minister Khosal. To her left were the other queens and Kalienne. Despite the gaudy costumes, everyone looked a bit worse for the wear, she thought. She noticed that Indradevi had deep circles under her eyes.

At the foot of the table she glimpsed Khosal's wife. The torches were flickering, but Bopha thought she saw bruising on the cowed woman's cheek, and the eye on that side definitely seemed smaller. She heard Khosal's smooth voice talking with Kiri. The sound made her feel like she had been covered with oil and she wanted to go to the baray and wash. She listened more closely, without giving away her intentions.

"But my dear Minister," Khosal said to Kiri, "the King's Man is bound to support his Lord no matter what." Kiri's face hardened. What were they talking about? Bopha wondered.

She felt the King's arm tense, where it touched hers. He must have heard as well. No doubt that was Khosal's intention. She would have to wait to find out what he knew about the conversation. Mach Botum was asking about the twins.

"They are growing so fast," Bopha said. "Vanna is about to start walking. And Thom is not far behind."

Finally the King stood. The entire crowd did as well. His deep voice rumbled, "These past five days have been to honor my beautiful bride, the Apsara Preah Chan Bopha." He gestured for her to stand with him. As she did, she heard murmurs on all sides, from all tents. Bopha felt a chill. Why was he putting her in this position, opening her to threats from the Queens and the Council?

He reached for her hand, then lifted their joined hands, turning his palm up, so everyone could see. The gesture pulled their hips together, side to side. Warmth from his hand ran up her arm and down her back. Suddenly, her spine felt like it was bursting with energy, as it had sometimes in the past when she danced. Power coursed down, then up from tailbone to the top of her head, where the heavy gold crown pressed down on her neck. She could barely remain standing, nor keep breathing, as the jolts hit.

Jaya must have felt her body's tension. He did not turn his head to look at her, but lowered their hands, and put his in sampeah. She managed to do so as well, amid a general hubbub of sampeahs. He took her hand again and led her out of the tent. She leaned heavily on his hand. Boran and Samang materialized to escort them. People scurried out of the way bowing.

By the time they got to the staircase up to the King's bedchamber, Bopha could barely walk. Jaya put his arm around her and half-carried her. He murmured, "What is wrong? Are you ill?" She shook her head.

"It's my back." She couldn't say more.

Once the door had closed, the King carried her to the bed, which had been made up earlier. She shivered and jolted when he lay her down. His face grave and worried, Jaya lifted off her crown and removed the heavy necklace. He stroked her hair. "I'll call the doctor."

"No, please. Don't." It seemed an eternity, but was really only moments before the jolting stopped. Her back felt like empty space. "I'm getting better." Jaya moved around the bed to lie facing her. Her vision was clear, but she saw golden and blue light surrounding him, pulsing gently. The colors shifted through the rainbow as she tried to explain what had happened.

"This has happened before," Bopha started. "Never so intense. But the first time I danced for Kiri, when I was just a little girl in my village, my back was filled with energy when the music started. I didn't even know I was dancing. Afterwards, my body felt like a dream. And sometimes, when I danced for you, it would come over me again, both the vibrations and the dream."

Jaya said nothing, just listened with his entire focus on her face, head resting on one hand. She reached to touch his other hand, which lay between them. "When it is over, I am so tired. But full of peace." She stroked his hand, and he grasped hers tightly. His fingers were warm. "I've never told anyone," she whispered.

"Your hand is so cold," he said, concerned. Shades of green and red radiated in a wide arc around him.

She smiled. "And yours so warm." After a moment, her hand also warmed.

"I was afraid," Bopha admitted in a voice so soft Jaya moved his head closer to hear. "When you had me stand in front of everyone. It seemed so ... unusual. Have you done that at your other weddings?"

The King shook his head. Bopha continued, "I was afraid of what Queen Indradevi and Sao Nang and Minister Khosal might do, if you honor me so much."

Jaya sighed. "The Kingdom needs to know where you stand with me. Of course, I do not ever want to endanger you. There will be trusted guards around your quarters at all times. Also for the twins. But I want you next to me. You are not only young and beautiful, but also wise beyond your years. You are able to see into people. I can do that myself, to some degree. But you..."

Violet and orange light shimmered. "Your insights I can trust." He stopped a moment, staring at her. Then he said softly, almost in awe, "Sikha told me so. But last night, Garuda came to me in a dream. I was standing on top of a mountain at the full moon. Suddenly there was the most ..."

The King searched for words. "The whole world was filled with the loudest sound. A shrieking cry. It was so loud it nearly pushed me to my knees. I saw a huge shape flying toward me, black against the moon. There was no threat, no feeling of danger. Just this enormous creature. When it came closer, I realized it was Garuda. He was carrying you on his back. He landed gently at my feet. You slid down to the ground, to stand in front of me. Garuda opened his wings around you. The moon outlined each feather. His wings were open for your eternal protection."

Bopha was speechless. Indigo and golden light pulsed around the King. "Garuda," she finally whispered. Jaya nodded. Then he pulled her to him, holding her as if she might slip away somehow.

After a few minutes of tight embrace, he drew back and looked at her. "I knew I could trust you before, but now I know I do not need to fear for you. You have a protector much more powerful than I am." Bopha and Jayavarman each took a deep breath at the same time, and smiled at the synchronicity between them.

Bopha touched his cheek, then traced his face from brow to chin on each side. There was nothing she could say. He turned his face into her hand and rested there.

* * *

They drifted off to sleep in that position. It was full daylight before either stirred. Bopha opened her eyes and saw the King, smiling slightly, his eyelids quivering. Was he dreaming? She remembered Garuda, coming to him in a dream, bringing her to him. There was surely some mysterious power that had pulled them together.

Jayavarman stirred, and saw her watching him. "Ah, my sweet new Queen. How are you this morning?" His deep voice was even deeper as he roused from sleep. They heard a discreet throat clearing come from the closed door. He kissed her gently then rolled on to his back. "The Kingdom calls," he observed ruefully.

Bopha had never slept late in her whole life. She didn't want to now, but felt a little strange to have to leave the King's bed even if she wasn't quite ready. They did not have the luxury of lovemaking this morning, which was fine. But something in the sleeping arrangements made her feel vulnerable today. This was the King's bedchamber, not their room together.

Jaya came out of the small room where the chamber pot was, and the washing bowl. His face was still a little damp when it touched her cheek as he gave her a hug. She watched him put on a fresh sampot. "What do you say to going on a trip with me? I'd like to see the bridge being built at Kampong Kdei and then I'll show you Preah Khan Kampong Srey. That's where I stayed to make preparations for retaking Angkor from the Cham."

"That sounds wonderful," said Bopha without hesitation.

"And you might even be able to ride a horse," Jaya teased her. He remembered everything, Bopha thought.

"Just say when," she told him.

The King opened the door. Bopha caught a glimpse of Boran and Kiri as the three men walked down the porch. She waited a few minutes, then followed. Her golden-threaded wedding sampot was the only one she had, and it sparkled in the morning sun. She wished she had one that did not draw attention to the fact that she was wearing yesterday's outfit. But she lifted her head, met Samang at the foot of the steps, and walked to her quarters without meeting anyone's eye. She did hear the occasional murmur as she passed knots of people. She would talk with Jaya about her wardrobe options for his bedroom.

The twins were delighted to see her. Vanna got on his unsteady feet and managed a few steps in her direction before plopping onto his bottom. Thom stood up, looking for something to hold on to, but there was nothing near enough. He too sat down suddenly.

"You two!" Bopha laughed. They both got up again immediately, and she squatted near them and gathered both in a hug.

Babbling a long story, Vanna looked at his mother. "I see," she said. "Then what happened?" He continued, as if in answer. Chou and Chariya were laughing quietly.

Thom watched his brother seriously, then broke in with an emphatic "Bababa, mama, pa!" Then he pointed to Bopha's sampot.

"Yes, you're right. I wore this yesterday. I really need to go to the baray. Do you want to come?" Both boys answered effusively. "Okay, just let me change." She went into her room. The twins tried to follow but she could hear Chou and Chariya distracting them. When her door shut, the sudden stillness hit Bopha hard. When was the last time she had just sat quietly and watched leaf shadows? How long had it been since Sophea came to dance with her? Her life was suddenly so full of outside activity that she felt almost dizzy.

She would ask Chariya or Samang where the Garudas were. This afternoon would be a good time to go visit and give thanks. Her incense was sitting on a small shelf. The banyan leaf wrapper had disintegrated. Suddenly she wondered if there were small statues of Garuda in the market, or if she could ask one of the sculptors to carve one. She would like to have a little altar in the corner of her room, with both the Buddha and Garuda.

* * *

Bopha and her entourage had just settled on the stones at the women's baray when Queen Indradevi arrived. "Preah Chan Bopha," said the Queen, once she was seated.

"Are you recovered from the celebrations?" Her eyes were hooded and she looked like a fierce bird of prey.

Reminded of Garuda, Bopha was emboldened to answer. "Not quite, my Queen. Five days is a few days too long."

Indradevi's featured stiffened. "Yes. Too long." Just then Thom, who had been holding on to the stone steps, lost his balance and splashed into the water. A few drops hit the queen, who grimaced, but Bopha didn't see. She leapt in after her son, and dragged him to the surface.

Thom coughed, then laughed. "So, you liked that, you naughty boy?" He gave her a big grin and tried to wiggle out of her grasp. "I guess we'll have to teach you to swim very soon." Thom settled for hitting the water hard, then laughed as the water droplets flew into the air, each one catching a sunbeam before falling. "I'm sorry, Queen Indradevi," Bopha said, watching the King's first wife draw back. "We'll move over to the other side and leave you in peace." Holding Thom on her chest with one hand, she lay down on her back and carried him away with gentle kicks. He was delighted. Vanna was bereft.

Chou carried the golden surprise by land, then stepped down the steep stones and put him in the baray as his mother and brother paddled up. "Your turn," said Bopha. "Here you go, Chou." They traded boys, and Bopha swirled Vanna around in the water. He crowed.

Malis had learned to float, and she practiced, making her way to where the twins and Bopha were. They made a merry group. When Sao Nang arrived, Nimith Sokhem ran immediately to where the action was. Then Arun Veha came with Kalienne. Suddenly, Bopha realized that Queen Indradevi was alone, with just her ladies in waiting and Mach Botum. There was nothing Bopha could do to make amends. Trying to get the raucous group of children back to the other side would draw more attention to the situation.

Bopha rolled onto her stomach, pushed her arms out in front of her, then swept them to her sides. This propelled her body through the water. Doing a high jeeb with both legs, then pushing them together, added momentum. Before she knew it, she had reached Mach Botum, who was sitting half in the water next to Indradevi.

"What is that you are doing?" Mach Botum asked, with real interest.

"I don't know," Bopha admitted. "Just moving my arms and legs. Doing jeebs. It's fun." She paused, then chuckled, "and fast. Faster than floating."

Queen Indradevi said nothing. But if she were a frog and Bopha a nymph fly, the frog would have eaten her in a heartbeat. Bopha stood and waded to the steps. Without staring, she could see that the Queen still had the dark circles under her eyes. The Queen lifted her chin in a quick gesture to her servant, who came to steady her as she stood. "We will see you another time," Indradevi said, a chill in her voice.

Bopha gave sampeah and tried to smile. She managed an Apsara smile. "Yes, my lady," she said. She watched the tall, thin queen walk down the path. Her head was high, but her shoulders stooped a little, and her gait did not flow smoothly. Her right arm did not swing freely. Realizing that she was staring this time, Bopha turned and looked across the baray to where the children were splashing and screeching.

She sat down in companionable silence with Mach Botum. The day would be warm, but clouds were gathering. One day soon, rains would come. The tall trees around the water offered plenty of shade, while their reflections swirled on the surface as waves from the other side traveled across.

"How did you meet the King?" Bopha asked after a while. She felt comfortable asking such a question of the plump and cheerful woman.

"My father was leader of one of the clans, before Jayavarman VII came to power. He and his brothers had alliances with many other kinship groups. From an early age, I knew my marriage

271

would be a political union." Mach Botum paused, and lifted a big leaf from the water. It was larger than her hand. She spun it slowly, then let it drop, where it kept spinning gently. "I was lucky that such a kind and handsome man as Jaya wanted to marry me."

Bopha recoiled slightly, to hear that name, Jaya, from this other ... wife. Mach Botum was watching the leaf, which still turned languidly in the pool. "But he was not King when you wed?"

Mach Botum lifted her eyes, pensive and sweet. She shook her head. "No. But anyone who met him could see that he would be. The way he held himself. He has such assurance. But still he listens when people talk. Always wanting to learn." The two women looked at each other. "He has treated me well. I have no regrets," Mach Botum finished.

"I had no idea how things worked when I came. I didn't even know how many wives the King had." Bopha had a sudden urge to confide. But to say what? Mach Botum was watching her, relaxed. "I knew life as an Apsara," Bopha continued. "But not as a Queen. If you have any suggestions about how." She stopped. "How best to fulfill my new duties without ... stepping on toes ..." Her words faltered.

"Some toes are in the way you must walk," Mach Botum smiled. "I'm sure you'll find your way." Was she talking about Queen Indradevi? That there was no way to avoid treading on her sense of power? Mach Botum looked up at the sky. "Time to go. Nice to see you." Then she added, "Queen Preah Chan Bopha."

The title slapped Bopha, but she was sure Mach Botum meant nothing bad. She jumped into the water and swam quickly to where her little family and her dearest friend were playing.

CHAPTER 29

1198, Kampong Kdei Bridge

The trip to see the bridge at Kampong Kdei was delayed for many months. The rains started early and roads turned into deep mud. No one traveled who did not have urgent need.

The King finally told his newest queen that they would not be alone on their journey. "Sao Nang has been very interested in all my construction projects," he admitted. "She has a sharp mind for such things and has made many good suggestions. I cannot really go to the bridge at Kampong Kdei without bringing her along."

He watched Bopha carefully. She didn't see. She had dropped her eyes at Sao Nang's name and was looking at their joined hands. They lay facing each other after a long, sweet love-making. "Please, Bopha, try to understand."

She sighed deeply and dragged her glistening eyes up to his face. After a moment, she said, "I will try." They looked at each other. She continued, "I know it is important to you, to the Kingdom. Maybe to my relationship with Sao Nang. I won't lie and say it's fine. But I guess I do understand. I had hoped we could spend time together, just us, without all the Palace demands and intrigue."

It was Jaya's turn to sigh. He rolled onto his back, wrapping one arm around her and pulling her next to him. She rested her head on his chest, listening to the thump-thump-thump of his heart. "I would like that as well." He paused. "How about we make two trips? One to the bridge, with Sao Nang, then in a few weeks you and I can go together to visit..." He stopped and Bopha looked up at him.

"What?"

"Mach Botum comes from Kampong Svay." The king's voice was soft and full of regret.

"Hcchhh." Bopha made a scraping noise in her throat. Her body sagged and she looked down, at her husband's navel. His abdomen was muscular, but the skin was loosening some with

273

age. "So she would have to go along, to see her family. Or we cannot go." She felt him nod.

"I'm sorry." They lay quietly in the dim room. Distant night sounds came through the open windows to the back porch. The moon was close to full, and had crossed over the top of the building so its light shone through the openings. Round shadows from the bead-strings, which hung close together from the top of each window to repel insects, lay across the polished floor. It was still several hours until dawn.

Bopha reached across Jaya's chest to hug him. He lifted her on top of him. She kissed him, so gently, their lips soft and melting together. "I remember you told me that a king is not really all-powerful," she said, mouth next to his. "I guess this is one of those times. Powerful in war, but maybe not as much in marriage." Her lips curved into a smile. She felt him start to tense, then he felt her smile.

"Are you teasing me, Queen Preah Chan Bopha?"

"Indeed, my Lord, King Jayavarman VII, ruler of Kampuchea. Who else will?"

The ruler of Kampuchea chuckled as he kissed her again. She felt his manhood stir. He is far from a young man, Bopha thought, but still so full of vitality. She moved slightly down his body, opening her legs to meet him.

* * *

When a King goes on a journey, it is not a simple matter of mounting his horse and taking a small bag of food. A full week of preparations was required. Messengers were sent to the hostels along the road. Both Bopha and Sao Nang would take a lady in waiting, as well as their personal guards. Minister Muni, in charge of public works, would come, as would several scribes and small contingent of Royal Guards. There were grooms and drivers and cooks, food for people and animals, ox cart wagons.

Kiri would stay at Bayon, designated to act on the King's behalf. And, Bopha thought, to keep an eye on Khosal. She had never found out what the slimy minister had meant at the feast. Maybe he was just sowing dissension, trying to cast doubt in the

274

King's mind about his childhood friend. Khosal was not called the finance minister as such, but his job was to safeguard the Royal Treasury and be sure manpower and monies were available for all projects in the kingdom.

Three mornings a week Bopha took riding lessons from one of the royal grooms.

She was glad for her Apsara athletic training, but still her inner thighs ached and her bottom was sore after only a few hours on a horse. Her teacher told her she needed to be boss of the animal. She had never learned to be boss of anything or anyone, except herself.

On the second day, when she approached the horse, it flattened its ears and reared, almost lifting the groom who held its reins. "My Lady," the groom suggested, when he had the animal under close rein, "perhaps you would like to ride a different horse?"

Bopha was almost ready to say she didn't want to ride any horse, but she nodded. He led the animal, who was now kicking, back to the stables. Bopha squatted in the shade of one of the barns, where Samang had been watching her ride inside the woven bamboo fence which surrounded the dirt practice yard. "I'll get you a treat for your new horse," he said. In a few minutes he came back with a big carrot.

The groom appeared with a smaller, light brown mare. Bopha stood up and entered the arena.

"Here you go. Toch should be better mannered." The mare's ears swiveled at the sound of her name.

"Young one," said Bopha, approaching with her palm up, offering Samang's carrot. "Aren't you pretty?" The soft, whiskered nose sniffed her hand, then picked up the treat. Bopha stroked her neck as the mare chewed. Her shoulders came up to Bopha's nose. She turned her head, big dark eyes watching as Bopha stepped into the groom's hands and swing onto the blanket spread over the horse's back. "Okay, let's go," Bopha told the animal, shaking the reins gently and squeezing her legs around the horse's big rib cage. Toch stepped forward. Her gait was much smoother than the big stallion's, and Bopha found herself enjoying the ride.

When Bopha arrived at the arena on the third morning, her groom had two horses tied to the fence. "Let's go for a short ride outside the palace grounds," he suggested.

Bopha had brought sugar cane for Toch, which the mare eagerly mouthed. She was still chewing as Bopha mounted. The groom jumped up on his horse and led the way. They took a well-worn path from the back of the palace grounds, and circled around until they were in front of Bayon. The top tier was rising now, and some towers had faces on them. From the drawings Muni showed to the Council, Bopha knew that there would be many towers, each with four faces. The stylized features could be Buddha or Jayavarman, she thought. Her heart jumped a bit to see that beloved face looking down on her.

Samang walked behind them, spear upright, until the horses began to trot toward the southern gate. Then, he jogged. For Bopha, the time went fast. She talked to Toch from time to time, watching the large ears turn to listen. Back at the arena, she gave sampeah to the guard, stroked Toch's soft nose and whispered, "Arkoun." Toch nickered softly. The sound made Bopha happy. Today, her legs were not sore as she walked back to her quarters. "Toch," she thought, "small one, you are the perfect horse for me."

The road to the Kampong Kdei bridge was wide enough for two horses abreast, so Bopha and Sao Nang rode next to each other, behind the King. Sao Nang was on the big black horse she had ridden during the wedding parade. "Where did you learn to ride?" Bopha asked, after an hour of silence.

"My father loves horses," Sao Nang said, turning her chiseled features toward Bopha briefly, then back to watch the road. "He had all of us learn to ride, boys and girls, from when we could barely walk."

"Is this horse one of your father's?"

"Yes. His name is Ny. He came with me when I married. My father gave him to me for my thirteenth birthday." Sao Nang paused, then added so softly Bopha could barely hear. "He has been a good companion."

"He's like a piece of home," Bopha blurted, "in a new land."

Sao Nang looked at her sharply, then seemed to realize Bopha was not making a criticism but an observation. "Yes. He is a piece of home." She stretched forward to pat the long black neck. Ny nodded his head and swiveled his ears. "He is very smart."

Bopha hadn't had such a long and natural conversation ever with this queen. "My family was killed, except for my brother Rithy, when I was a little girl. And my village burned." Sao Nang said nothing. "The Apsara courtyard was home for a long time. I'm still getting used to Bayon," Bopha continued, her mind cautioning her to be quiet.

Sao Nang nodded, without looking at her. "Yes, it can take time to settle in at Bayon."

Bopha wondered if Queen Indradevi had been mean when Sao Nang came. Probably.

Rithy had taught Bopha to count, along with reading and writing. She was fuzzy on the past but figured it had probably been about ten years from the time when she danced at Sao Nang's wedding to the King and when she herself had moved to Bayon. Now another three years or more had passed. The twins would soon be three years old, born in rainy season. She stole a glance at Sao Nang's profile.

This queen must have been quite young when she was given in marriage. But it was so many years later that she had Nimith Sokhem. Had she had trouble conceiving? Had she lost a baby? Was she so young that the King had waited to lie with her?

Bopha shook her head. She had no one who could tell her these answers. As if reading her mind, Toch shook her head, bringing a smile to the apsara's lips. She patted the horse. Maybe it was a good thing after all for her and Sao Nang to travel together. Jaya had warned her that he would sleep alone during the entire trip. She suddenly missed his warm lips and strong arms and … Her pelvis moved involuntarily against Toch's blanket.

Toch took this to signal "go faster," and broke into a trot, bringing Bopha back to the present. "Sorry," she whispered to the horse, as she pulled gently on the reins. "That's not what I meant." She heard Sao Nang chuckle as she rode up next to Bopha.

"Talking to your horse again?"

Bopha laughed out loud. Jaya heard the sound and looked back. "Yes, I guess so, Srey Sao Nang. It's nice to be with someone who understands." The two young women smiled at each other.

Traveling with the King was a new experience. In every village, people would pour out of houses and fields to catch a glimpse of the royal caravan. Dogs and naked children followed after them. The villages along this wide road were larger than the ones going to Tonle Sap, with more prosperous houses. The horses did not go faster than the ox wagons, so the trip would take two nights and more than two days.

Sikha was riding in a colorful wagon, with a canopy and flags. She had insisted that Chariya and Sao Nang's lady in waiting ride with her. Jayavarman, as always, acquiesced to the tiny woman. "Yes, mother," he teased. "Your wish is my command. But are you sure you want to return to your village? We would so much like to have you stay here in Bayon."

"I am sure. To see you marry Preah Chan Bopha was a wonderful blessing. But city life is not for me, as you know. I leave you in good hands with your new queen."

On the return trip, the King would take her to Tonle Sap. Bopha would miss the wise old woman. She and Kalienne were the only women with whom she could speak freely.

"You will be fine," Sikha prophesied, patting her hand. They sat on Sikha's porch, a few buildings from Bopha's own quarters. The twins were walking up and down, Vanna almost running, Thom holding on to the railing. "My work here is done."

On the first night, the locals prepared a feast. Jaya told Bopha he had sent food ahead, so as not to burden his people. "When the armies move, it is different, we must be self-sufficient, and there is not time for celebrations. But when I travel for other purposes, the people need to have ceremony."

The two Queens and Sikha retired after a long banquet and performances by local dancers, actors and musicians. As she lay on her silk sheets, Bopha could hear laughter and singing from the courtyard. The room was small, as were all the rooms in the hostel, but she was sleeping alone, Chariya in the room next to her. How long ago she and Chariya had taken the exile road, and

278

lain next to each other on rough mats in a similar room. Bopha turned on to her side, listening to the deep rumble of Jayavarman's voice as he toasted the village leaders. Her Jaya. She would recognize his voice anywhere.

* * *

The next morning, Bopha didn't feel well. Although she had slept soundly, she woke tired. Breakfast had not settled. By the time they stopped for lunch, she needed a nap.

Sikha told her to give the horse to the groom, or tie it to her wagon. She could lie down until they got to the next hostel. Bopha didn't want to, but she didn't want to throw up while riding Toch. She slept restlessly under the canopy, rousing from time to time when the procession slowed to pass through a crowded village.

"Will you give my excuses to the King," she asked Sikha when they were settled in their rooms. "I don't think I can eat tonight." The old woman looked at the beautiful dancer, noticing the circles under her eyes. She got a packet from her box, and gave it to Chariya with instructions for preparation. Chariya returned with a cup of the tea, and a small bowl of rice and a banana. The tea smelled of mint and something Bopha could not identify. It was slightly bitter, but she felt better as she sipped. Sikha and Chariya watched her.

"What will I do without you, dearest Sikha?" Bopha asked as she lay down on her mat.

"You always know what to do." She drifted off, not sure whose voice was reassuring her not to worry.

Sometime in the night, she felt a presence in her room and smelled the familiar sandalwood of Jayavarman. She rolled on her back. His outline was dim in the waning moon. "Are you all right, my love?" Jaya's voice was soft with worry. "Sikha told me you needed sleep. But I wanted to see you with my own eyes. No emissary, no matter how wise, can take the place of being with you."

Bopha sat up, but the room swirled, so she lay down again and reached for his hand. He settled on his side next to her, gently cradling her head in one hand and stroking her hair. She slept again.

Morning was cooler than it had been for days. Bopha awoke alone, with both appetite and energy. Had the King come or was it just a dream? She did a few jeebs from the wishing dance, then joined the company in the courtyard. The King was talking with the Sangat leader and Muni, but nodded and smiled when he saw her. She gave sampeah, and smiled back at him.

Before the sun reached zenith, they arrived at the construction site. The road had narrowed so Bopha rode behind Sao Nang. She was grateful for the tall trees on both sides. Sweat dripped between her breasts and her sampot stuck to Toch's blanket as she tried to slide off the horse. It was not a graceful dismount, but Samang's strong arm kept her from embarrassment.

Ahead, the trees had been cut far back from the road. There were crowds of men in loin cloths shoveling dirt into buckets. Women lifted the buckets to their heads and carried them up the steep bank. In the distance on one side, water shimmered against a high wall of dirt. "That's where they have made a dam," Sao Nang pointed. "So the foundations can be built."

Small stone towers rose from the dirt of the dry river bed. On the far bank, the towers were high, and they arched until they met each other. Bopha could see workmen carrying large stones and fitting them together. "See, three of the pillars are finished. There will be twenty-five arches. It will be the longest bridge in the world." Sao Nang's voice was filled with pride. "It will be called the Dragon Bridge. Already, the King has sculptors making huge naga heads for each end, and the body of the snake will curve along the top to make a railing."

Bopha was very impressed, both at the how the bridge was being built and at how much Sao Nang knew. "You could be an engineer," she said. Sao Nang's face hardened. "I mean, you know so much, you could probably design bridges yourself. I don't mean to disrespect you. I think you are amazing."

But the damage was done. Sao Nang turned away, toward where the King stood. Minister Muni was next to him, gesturing and talking. Bopha's heart sank. Just when she almost thought she and Sao Nang might be friends. She joined the group at the edge of the riverbank, but on the side away from Sao Nang.

Watching the laborers toil, Bopha wondered who they were. Were they farmers who couldn't work in their fields until the rains came? Or people who could not pay their debts and were thus forced to work as slaves. Or Cham slaves, prisoners of war? She was suddenly overwhelmed with how difficult their lives were, compared with her own. Her gorge rose and she ran, a hand to her mouth, into the trees.

There were encampments on the side of the river by the dam, on both banks, where the laborers lived in small thatched huts. Bopha lay in Sikha's wagon while the rest of the company, except Chariya and Samang, went to visit the nearest encampment and have lunch. The thought of food almost made her throw up again, so she watched leaf shadows play across the canopy until her stomach settled.

As she leaned back against the cushions, her mind drifting, she suddenly knew. She was not sick. She was pregnant.

Why does Sikha have to leave now? Bopha remembered the long night of the twins' birth. Thom would have been given to the raptors if not for Sikha. "Please," she prayed, picturing the feathered legs and hooked beak of her protector, "please be with us." Her heart ached. There was no reassuring voice. And she never thought to be excited by this new life growing within her.

CHAPTER 30

1199, Welcoming Life

Bopha remained ill for months, able to eat only small amounts. She was gaunt, except for the small mound in her womb. The King finally sent word to Sikha, asking if she would return to Bayon until the baby was born. None of his physicians could treat Bopha's nausea. She told him how she had been sick with the twins but Sikha had brewed teas that helped.

She was lying on her mat, watching the twins on the porch. Soon after they returned to Bayon, another nursemaid came to help Chou. Bopha guessed that Chariya had not wished to be demoted to babysitter, when she pressed her case to be simply lady-in-waiting. The two caregivers squatted in the shade not far from Bopha's door. They had gathered seeds from a plant that grew wild and were showing Thom and Vanna how the seed would pop when placed in a cup of water.

The twins stared into the water then shrieked with fear and glee when the seed suddenly popped its casing. They ran to the far end of the porch, then ran back shouting, "Again! Again!" Bopha remembered showing Reasmey those surprising seeds. Very unpredictable. One may pop immediately, the next may take a breath or two. Or five. And just when you put your face close, POP!

"Soursdey, Queen Bopha." The strong voice startled her, then filled her with joy. Sikha! Bopha turned over slowly to greet the tiny old woman. Even so, the movement stirred her nausea, and she panted a bit before speaking.

"Oh, Sikha. Thank you so much for coming. I know you prefer your village to the palace. But I've been so sick." She stopped to pant, then reached for the basin, retching. Nothing came up but drips of thin, bitter, green liquid. Chariya heard the sound and came with a clean basin. Sikha dipped a cloth in the bowl of water set nearby, and wiped Bopha's forehead then the back of her neck.

"So I see. Chariya, will you please bring boiling water in a pot?" Sikha reached into her kromah-bag and pulled out a packet wrapped in dried banana leaf. "We will hope that this helps. Now, close your eyes. It is time to talk with your baby."

As if in answer, Bopha's abdomen rolled visibly, while Bopha gasped at the words. "Yes, little one. We want to talk with you," Sikha said, with a small chuckle. "Put your attention on the toes of your left foot, Bopha. Relax all the little bones and muscles. Breathe in and out gently. There is nothing you need to do but relax your toes."

They had relaxed up to the dancer's belly when Chariya came softly in with a pot of boiling water. Sikha opened the packet, poured its contents into the water and swirled the pot a few times. She replaced the lid of the pot and handed it to Chariya with a nod.

"Please, put this in the corner under the altar." To Bopha she said, "Place your attention on your stomach. Relax your stomach. Imagine a bluish-green light moving gently around your abdomen, up the right side, across the top just under your chest, down your left side. Allow this light to fill your belly. Breathe in and out. As you breathe in, imagine the light rising softly up and across. As you breathe out, let the light flow down your left side, carrying away any tension."

The twins had gone to the baray. Bopha lay with her eyes closed in the sudden silence. Sikha sat cross-legged next to her. After a moment, Sikha guided the dancer-queen through the rest of the meditation, relaxing her chest, neck, face, head. "Now draw in golden healing light through the top of your head," the ancient woman said softly. "Let it flow down through your entire body, cleansing and relaxing you. Let the light fill you with vibrant energy and push out all tension through the bottom of your feet. Let the tension flow into the earth, and leave you free." There was no sound but Bopha's breathing, as she focused on Sikha's instructions.

Then Sikha said, "Greetings, little one, whoever you are. Do you like the new light your mother is bringing to you? Will you please tell her what it is that you want from her?"

Bopha took another deep breath and lay very still, listening inside herself.

Finally, Sikha said, "You can open your eyes now." Bopha did. The room seemed somehow different, lighter. A ray of sun

283

touched the corner altar where Buddha and Garuda stood on a gold and blue silk cloth.

Bopha stretched. Sikha poured her a cup of tea from the pot. Bopha sat up enough to hold the cup. Chariya pushed pillows under her back. The tea was very bitter and Bopha made a wry face. After a few sips, she put the cup down and cleared her throat.

"I did not want another child," she admitted, almost inaudibly. "Not now at least. I have not welcomed this pregnancy. But I don't want to lose the baby. I realize I never told her that." She paused. "Her or him. But I think her." Tears formed in Bopha's eyes as she lay back on the cushions and cupped both hands around the swelling of her abdomen. "She wanted to know if she had to die to make me happy. No, no. I do not want you to die. Let us both live, and be happy together." The tears were pouring down her face. "Please, believe me. I will protect you and love you as much as I possibly can."

Chariya, squatting nearby, was weeping. Sikha nodded, eyes full of peace. She gave sampeah to Bopha's belly. "Well done, little one. We look forward to meeting you one day soon."

With Sikha nearby, offering healing herbs and meditation, Bopha slowly gained appetite and strength. It was a slow process, and she still vomited nearly every day. But she was able to hold down enough to maintain her weight at least. She couldn't believe how weak she was. On the day she finally went to the baray, she had to stop and rest twice, and to hold Chariya's hand on the steep, narrow stone steps. She sat with the other queens, including Indradevi. The children were screaming with laughter and splashing on the other side.

"So you are well enough to join us at last," Indradevi said. It was a simple statement made in an almost flat voice, offered with a low, brief sampeah. Bopha returned her snub with a polite sampeah and an Apsara smile.

"Yes, my queen. Thanks to Sikha." Bopha added, "And Garuda."

Indradevi's eyebrow went up at her last word. "Indeed."

"Yes, Garuda." She was going to say, "He is my protector," but heard the challenge in the tone she would have used, and refrained. Instead she said, "It's so nice to get outside at last, into the fresh air." Clouds were piling up on a small breeze. "I think I'll swim before the rain."

Bopha slid into the water and turned on her back, moving to the center of the baray with small strokes of her arms. Her abdomen was so much smaller than it had been with the twins, but the baby was active. She sent up a small prayer of gratitude. Now out of earshot, Bopha whispered, "Do you like swimming? I'm so glad. When you come out, I'll teach you." Her belly jumped. "You like that idea?" She rolled over and moved arms and legs until she reached the children's area.

"Mdeay! Mdeay!" The twins squirmed out of restraining arms and threw themselves into the water. Bopha caught Thom first, then lifted Vanna. He was coughing.

"You can't swim yet, Vanna," Bopha scolded him. "So you can't jump in or you'll choke. Like you are doing now." Vanna coughed a few more times, then hit the water with both hands and laughed. "What are we going to do with you, you little trouble-maker."

She and Malis had been teaching the older children to swim before she became ill, and Malis continued the lessons without her. Nimith Sokhem jumped in now and paddled up to the twins. "See, this is how you do it!" The little boys watched a moment then tried to get into the water again. "Malis, will you help Thom and I'll hold Vanna?" Supported by hands under their bellies, the twins kicked, splashed and screamed with laughter.

It wasn't long before Bopha had had enough. "Okay, I'm going back to the other side. You are wearing me out. But I'm getting stronger, so watch out!" She handed Vanna to Chou, then tickle-poked him in his tummy. "Watch out, I'm going to get you!" Bopha laughed, waggling all her fingers toward him, slowly then faster and faster, until she tickled him all the way up to his chin. "You too, Thom," she said, repeating her antics, to her son's delight.

She floated a few minutes in the middle of the baray before getting out, imagining light filling her, as Sikha had instructed. The water had done her good, Bopha thought. She needed to stop only once on the way to her rooms. She was even hungry for lunch. Rainy season was almost over, but a few strong storms came to remind her of the twins' birth.

"You still have a few weeks," Sikha said one day. "This baby will be small, but seems strong."

While she was sick, Bopha had stayed in her quarters, but now she again slept with the King several nights a week. She told him of Sikha's meditation, and her realizations about the baby. He listened, softly tracing around the small lump of her belly, up the right, across, down the left. He even talked softly to the bump, and when he touched his lips to kiss it, a fist or foot poked him in the mouth.

He laughed, "No one gets away with poking the King in the mouth! No one but you!"

He held Bopha close and stroked her back. She traced his scar. "I'm glad you are better," he murmured. "Losing a baby is one thing, but to lose you…" his voice trailed off and he pulled her closer, kissing her hair.

Bopha's days were full. Besides playing with the twins, she was studying with Rithy several times a week, and visiting with Sophea, Nary and Theary. When Sophea came alone, they would still dance. Bopha was losing her muscle-memory skills, and her connection with the music, but she did not have time to brood or grieve.

She was back at her place in the Council. Minister Khosal was full of worries about money and manpower. Jayavarman had so many projects going at the same time, spread over such a large kingdom. Where were the resources? Bopha still disliked the man intensely, but he had some points worthy of consideration. At least the provinces were secure, for now. Several of the King's oldest sons and daughters had married royalty, and those former kingdoms recognized Jayavarman as liege lord.

* * *

One night, Bopha woke to find her mat wet. She was glad she was not in the King's bed. Soon after, pains started. She woke Chariya, who went to get Sikha. The night was cool and breezy, so the women closed all the windows and doors.

A mother and a newborn baby needed to be kept warm. Jayavarman had insisted he be told as soon as Bopha started labor, so a message was sent.

Compared to the twins, this birth was fast and relatively easy. Kalienne had come to be with Bopha, holding her hand, supporting her back, breathing with her. After a final push, and then sudden relief, Bopha heard the infant suck in a deep breath, then wail. "Do you have a name for a girl?" Sikha asked, grinning. She held up the naked squalling baby. Bopha put out her arms, and cuddled the damp little form, who immediately started swimming toward the breast.

As her daughter's dark eyes stared into hers, and the tiny mouth sucked with surprising strength on her nipple, Bopha said, "Welcome. We meet at last." Kalienne put blankets over the two them and Sikha managed to get a hat on the baby's head as she nursed.

Bopha leaned back against the cushions as the afterbirth was delivered.

"No second baby this time," Sikha joked.

"That's fine with me! I'm glad for this one. She seems so much smaller than the boys."

"She is smaller," said Sikha. "But strong. Full of life force."

Jaya and Bopha had discussed names. He and the priests would decide, but Bopha would urge that this tiny girl be named Kravann, for the tiny golden-brown flower that decorated bas reliefs throughout the empire. She would accept as her second name either Chenda, for "thought/intelligence," or Chivy, "life." Khmer had no acceptable name for a female that meant "strong."

"Which you are, for sure," she assured the baby, whose eyes were starting to droop.

Bopha was too excited to rest after Kravann fell asleep. She handed her to Kalienne and got up to use the chamber pot. Morning light was peeking through the cracks around the windows. She could hear the twins waking up in their room, Vanna talking as soon as his eyes were open. She opened the door to the porch and stepped out, wrapped in several warm layers. After giving sampeah to the big banyan tree, she went back inside, careful to

287

close the door again. This building was so big that no fire underneath would heat her room.

Lighting incense, she knelt in front of her altar, giving thanks yet again for being healed from the months of vomiting, as well for such a fast and safe delivery, and for the gift of this tiny, healthy Kravann. After eating breakfast, she lay down and slept until it was time to feed the baby again. Her orders were clear. "Wake me when the baby wakes. I will nurse her."

Bopha was surprised to find how firm she could be. Usually she was easy-going and mild. But when it came to her children's welfare, she would fight, even taking a challenge head-on if necessary. Maybe, she thought, her years of training as an Apsara had changed her. She had learned to push her body beyond where it wanted to go, keeping her mind and will in charge, persevering to reach a goal. She could barely remember the little girl who had walked to Angkor years ago, so full of homesickness and trepidation. Now she was even getting used to being addressed as Queen Preah Chan Bopha.

The monks, after consulting the stars, chose the name Kravann Chivy for the King's newest child. They knew the small girl had clung to life during her mother's illness. During the naming ceremony, she looked impossibly tiny in her father's large hands, but she looked steadily at Jayavarman's golden crown, trying to lift her head. Indeed, she watched everything, though only a week old, until it was time to eat.

Bopha had just sat down with her plate, between Mach Botum and Kalienne, when Kravann's loud cries momentarily stilled conversation. Bopha got up and took the girl from Chou, looking for a quiet corner in the crowd. Indradevi and Sao Nang, faces identical in polite disapprobation, watched her turn away from the room to nurse. Khosal's wife, Mony, was further down the table, her face a study in envy and pain. She was eating with her left hand since her right arm was in a sling. Polished flat sticks peeked out from under a tightly wrapped bandage. She had tripped, she said. So stupid. So clumsy. Tripped over her own feet and fell against a table.

* * *

288

That wasn't what Sikha had heard. Her bedroom was just behind the house where Minister Khosal lived. She had been wakened by his shouts, and listened to his wife whimpering. Dull thuds were followed by loud crying, a big crash, and screams. Dressing quickly, the old healer picked up the basket she kept near the door, and crossed the yard. At the bottom of the stairs, her own guard was watching the Khosal's house. She indicated her intention, and he walked her across.

Khosal's guard was pacing on the porch at the top of the steps. His worried face relaxed somewhat when he saw Sikha. He knocked on the door. Khosal yelled to leave them alone. His wife's sobbing was subdued but with each breath she said, "Ow, ow, ow." Sikha stood in front of the door and said in a clear but low voice, "Minister Khosal. This is Sikha. Please open the door and let me take care of your wife."

Both guards moved in front of the tiny woman as the door was yanked open. Khosal's face was red and puffy and his breath foul with alcohol. His necklace was askew and his sampot stained. The guards held their spears at an angle, prepared for trouble. Even in his impaired state, Khosal recognized that he was outnumbered. He backed into the room and sank onto cushions on the far side from the door.

Mony was bent over in a corner, holding one arm with the other. She looked up when Sikha squatted next to her. The guards stood between Khosal and the women, watching the man closely. Sikha murmured, then reached to support the woman's forearm, which bent crazily. "Please, bring her to my house. I will give her some medicine for pain, then we can fix this arm." She turned to Khosal, "Your wife's arm is badly broken. Do not touch her again."

Khosal spluttered and made a move to stand. The guards lowered their spears toward him, but it was unnecessary. The Minister's legs gave out and he fell, landing on the cushions.

He was snoring before the guards had made a seat of their arms to carry Mony down the stairs. Khosal's guard stayed at Sikha's long enough to help set the bones, then returned to his place at Khosal's steps. Other servants had heard the commotion and there was a small crowd in the dark, but no one lit a torch. The guard said nothing, and people returned to their beds.

Sikha kept Mony at her house for nearly a week. In addition to the broken arm, the minister's wife had bruising across her abdomen and one eye was black and blue.

Mony refused to tell Sikha what had happened, though Sikha told her she had heard the fight.

Bopha, in the bliss of new motherhood and at a distance from Khosal's house, had heard nothing of this. Since Mony begged Sikha not to tell, the King also did not learn of the abuse.

By the naming ceremony, Mony was back at home. Khosal had cried and told her how sorry he was, begging her to forgive him, telling her how much she meant to him. It was not the first time. Not by a long shot. He had fixated on Mony when she was still a girl, one of the youngsters who served Queen Indradevi. He waited impatiently till her moon blood started, and wed immediately.

They had only one child and both parents doted on Visothirith. Mony had had many miscarriages, which she privately blamed on her husband beating her, almost always below the sampot so no sign was visible. He was convinced she was looking at other men. But she barely looked at anybody ever, so afraid was she of making a wrong move and provoking Khosal yet again.

Sometimes Mony wished she could just die. Surely she wasn't as bad a person as her husband said. But even if she were, maybe it would be better to return as a jackal or a frog than to continue in this life of terror and hurt. She dreamed of jumping from a bridge or running in front of an elephant. She held on for the sake of her son.

CHAPTER 31

1200, Visothirith

Months passed, hot season came and went. Sikha returned to her village before the rains started. Kravann put on weight but was still tiny compared with other babies her age. Her features were stunningly beautiful, and she was already saying a few words.

The twins were big and sturdy. They now followed Arun Veha everywhere, running with the palace boys. Visothirith found endless ways to get them all in trouble. One day the boys opened a gate and let out the unruly black stallion. By the time he was caught, he had kicked a groom in the head and enraged the elephants. The palace grounds were in an uproar. Elephants trumpeted, the horse brayed, people screamed as they scrambled out of the way. This time, finally, the parents heard of the mischief, and disciplined severely. Before this, their nannies had protected the boys, meting out punishment on their own, lest they themselves be punished for not giving proper supervision.

The King himself spanked Thom and Vanna when he learned of the escapade. "You need to learn respect," he growled, as the twins cried and held their bottoms. "Respect for others, respect for property, and respect for yourselves. You are the sons of the King of Kampuchea, not some street ruffians. I don't ever want to hear that you have misbehaved again."

He looked at each of them severely. "Do you understand?" They looked at the floor, crying still. "Look at me, Thom." Unwillingly, the little boy lifted his eyes and met his father's gaze. "Do not follow the lead of someone who is doing mischief." Thom nodded, tears falling off his chin onto the floor.

"Vanna?"

"Yes, Aupouk." Vanna had watched his brother's reprimand and now met Jaya's eye.

"You will be leaders. You are not followers. You have to be good examples for your people."

291

"Yes, Aupouk," the twins said together.

"Go now," the King said. Much subdued, they gave him sampeah and followed Bopha out the door of the small audience chamber.

For Visothirith, the consequences were worse. As the oldest, he should have known better. His father took a bamboo rod and beat him until Mony gathered her courage to intervene. Her child had fallen at Khosal's feet, whimpering.

"Please, Khosal. He is just a boy. You might hurt him."

"He will remember this day," Khosal declared, and brought the rod down again.

"I will remember, I will," pleaded Visothirith. "I won't be bad again."

Khosal struck the floor next to him so hard the rod broke. The boy and Mony both jumped. Khosal threw the pieces of wood down and strode out the door. They heard him stomp down the stairs.

Kneeling, Mony gathered her son in her arms. At nine years old, he was almost as tall as his mother. He had not cried during the beating, but now he sobbed. She rocked him until he was cried out. "Shhh, shhh, shhh. It's okay. It's over now." Visothirith had never been hit before but now she was afraid for him. Her husband had always taken out his anger on her. Khosal had crossed a line and she was terrified for the boy.

"Please, my son, my dearest, do not provoke your father. Please. Please think before you do anything that might be bad."

After a few minutes, the boy pulled away from his mother and wiped his hand across his face. He did not meet her gaze.

"Visothirith?" Mony asked. He did not reply, just poked at the pieces of bamboo on the floor. She asked again, "Visothirith? Please look at me." His dark eyes smoldered when he finally looked up. She saw he was not repentant but enraged. "Will you promise to think before you act?" He shrugged and dropped his eyes again.

"I know you are a smart boy, but you don't always act like one. Now is the time for that to change." Mony was more forceful than

292

she had been in her whole life, but she was desperate for her son to understand. She didn't want to speak ill of Khosal, but the boy must be warned.

"He's a monster," Visothirith muttered. "I know what he does to you. I wish he were dead."

Mony gasped. She had never allowed herself to think of what her son heard in the next room, as his father beat her. But she couldn't speak the words he needed to hear now.

After a moment, Visothirith jumped to his feet. "You are a coward and he is a monster!" He ran out of the room and down the steps. Mony crumpled into a ball on the floor and wept bitter tears in silence.

* * *

All the boys were worked hard after this escapade. They spent longer hours studying with the monks, then learned techniques of fighting. Each boy was assigned a young soldier, under Boran's tutelage, who was a mentor. Not exactly a babysitter, but the children's free time was much limited, and much more strictly monitored. They had grown beyond the supervision of women.

"This is the first time I've ever had to intervene with children," Jaya told Bopha. "Maybe because the twins are so much younger than the other boys, they were led into more trouble."

"Or maybe it's Minister Khosal's son," said Bopha in a soft voice.

"What do you mean?"

"Maybe he's a bad influence. He seems wild in a way most children are not." She lay with her head on Jaya's shoulder, in the evening after the twins were disciplined. "I've watched him at the baray. He always pushes the limits. Much more than Nimith Sokhem." She felt the king stiffen. "I don't mean to tell tales, or interfere with your other children, my dear."

Jaya took a deep breath. "I disciplined Nimith Sokhem as well."

"Yes," she agreed. "Let's hope that all the boys learn from this." She paused. "You know, I tried to ride that horse, before we went to the Kampong Kdei bridge. The one who went on a rampage today. He is not a nice animal."

"Then he doesn't belong here," Jaya said vehemently. "I don't want that seed among my herd. There's a difference between being strong and being mean."

"Yes. But not all animals — or all people — know that," she said. She leaned back to look at her husband. "You are a good man, Jayavarman. A good man, a good king, a good father."

He gazed at her, then said softly, "I hope a good husband as well."

She smiled widely, "Oh yes. And a good husband." She leaned in for a deep, soft kiss.

"A very good husband."

* * *

Rainy season was longer and more intense than in recent memory. A dam broke in the waterworks system far upstream from Bayon, flooding a village, killing many people. Although everyone had been praying for relief from the years of drought, this was not what they had wanted.

As the weeks of damp heat went on and on, there were whispers in the palace grounds. Small dead animals were found. Not just dead, but tortured. Decapitated. Limbs and tails not just cut off, but torn. Lizards, birds, cats, even a puppy.

One day between thunderstorms, Bopha went to the baray with Kalienne. They formed quite a group, with four children, three nannies, ladies-in-waiting. The boys ran ahead, then stopped instead of splashing into the water. They stared, then all started talking at once. Thom was crying loudly. Samang and Kalienne's guard usually waited a discreet distance away while the women bathed, but they came forward at the commotion. A gibbon, its head nearly torn off, floated near the steps. Kalienne's guard waded in and lifted the poor animal on his lance. Face grim, he carried it away.

"No swimming today," Samang said. "I'm sorry. We'll have to wait for rain, then ask the monks to say prayers."

"That was no accident?" Bopha said, her voice ending in a question.

Samang shook his head. "No. No accident, my Queen."

"What happened to that gibbon? Why was he in the baray?" The children were full of questions as they walked home. Bopha didn't know what to say, except that it was very sad and a terrible accident.

"But you said it wasn't an accident," objected Arun Veha. He was growing into a very observant youth.

Bopha shook her head. "Yes," she said softly, "I did say that. But maybe I'm wrong."

It was Arun Veha's turn to shake his head. "I don't think you are wrong, Auntie Bopha. I've heard the servants talking. Many bodies have been found. All kinds of animals. All tortured and killed."

Bopha stopped and stared at him. "You've heard that? This is not the first time?"

"No. Ask the grooms at the stable. They've found many."

"Many what?" Vanna asked. The twins had run ahead but turned back when their mother stopped.

"We'll talk later," she said, looking sharply at Arun Veha. There was a huge roll of thunder. "Let's get home quickly before it rains." The thunder distracted her sons, and they raced each other through the compound. Arun Veha, quiet for once, walked between Bopha and Kalienne.

The dead gibbon caused a furor. It turned out that many palace servants had found or heard of some animal. It seemed that at first they were small. Mice, bats, geckos. Then birds and cats. The gibbon was big. It had been pierced with something sharp through its abdomen. Its neck was cut part way, then torn. Who would do such a thing? Had anyone seen suspicious activity?

People blamed a ghost, or a wicked tree spirit. They looked at each other, wondering, watching every move. Nothing like this had ever happened at Bayon. The astrologers consulted their stars. It was all very inauspicious.

A few mornings later, most of the people in the Palace followed the monks to the women's baray. The ceremony was long, and the priests walked three times around the whole baray, chanting. Before they were done with the third circuit, the heavens opened, pouring rain into the contaminated water. It was too wet to burn incense. When lightning started, the crowd streamed back to shelter. Had the blessing worked? Or had it ended before the cleansing was complete?

* * *

For whatever reason, no more bodies were found. Gradually, life at Bayon returned to normal. Rains ended, hot season returned. The Kingdom of Kampuchea was at peace. Jayavarman VII welcomed ambassadors from many lands, Bopha at his side. She had a gift for languages, it turned out, and would listen carefully when visitors came. A petite woman in the entourage of the Chinese Ambassador was teaching her to speak that language. By now she and Rithy were proficient in reading and writing Sanskrit and Khmer.

Visitors brought gifts of gold and jewels and slaves. The Kampong Kdei Bridge was completed. Most of the palace went on the journey to celebrate its opening. Jayavarman VII, mounted on his biggest elephant, led the parade across the new span. The towers of Bayon were almost ready to be consecrated, though no date had been set.

Then dead animals began to appear again. Now they were set out like offerings, arranged into bizarre and convoluted positions. Children were kept close to nannies. Guards tightened around each royal counselor and family. That last seemed to help. It was many weeks between corpses. But emotions were fragile and fear close to the surface.

This was an enemy that the King could not simply fight and conquer. Jayavarman was frustrated. "I thought it was over," he complained to Bopha, after the body of a cormorant was found, with a tohkeay in its mouth.

Bopha was thoughtful. "After you had more guards around each member of the royal family and the council, it was months between killings," she observed.

"What do you mean?"

"I'm not sure. Just that more guards seemed to help." She suddenly looked at Jaya, horror in her face. "Do you think the killer could be someone who was being guarded? Someone who couldn't act as freely under those circumstances?"

"You mean someone in the palace household or in that of one of my counselors?"

Bopha nodded sadly. "I don't think the murderer is a ghost or tree spirit," she said. "I think it's a cruel and deranged person."

Jaya sighed deeply. "I agree. But ... someone we know so well?"

Bopha shrugged. "I would hope not. But ..."

Tensions were set to explode. One night a huge thunderstorm pounded the palace. The storm was so loud, it took a while for people to recognize human screams in the noise. By the time they did, the cries had stopped. In the meantime Khosal's guard had run down the stairs to get help. Sleep-rumpled people gathered under porches, watching through the downpour as several soldiers battered down the door. Light poured out, showing that the men had stopped in the doorway. One at a time, they walked gingerly inside. When they came out again, after only a moment or two, a small figure was between them.

Down the steps, through the rain, the soldiers marched, disappearing in the direction of their barracks. One stayed behind to guard the steps. They had not closed the door to Khosal's house.

As the rain eased, people lit torches and murmured, crossing between houses to carry news. A dozen soldiers came back, accompanying the King's physician up the stairs. Again, there was a long pause before the group entered the house.

Palace houses were built at angles, so it was not easy to see into one house from another's porch. But word spread. Minister Khosal and his wife were dead. A bloodbath in the room. Their son, Visothirith, was locked in the barracks.   Mony had been beaten to death, her head bashed until her brains spilled out. Minister Khosal, arm still upraised and holding a heavy stick, lay on his face with a lance through his back. He had killed his wife. Then his young son had killed him with his own ceremonial weapon.

Now people admitted to hearing fights from that house. They didn't want to interfere.   A man was in charge of his own household, after all. No one had given a thought to the boy who lay   rigid,   listening,   year   after   year.

CHAPTER 32

1200 to 1204, Indradevi, Bayon, Kiri

Visothirith squatted in the corner of a small cell for two days, refusing food, speaking not a word. He did not attend the funeral of his parents, which was a very subdued though crowded procession, long on chanting and short on music.

On the third morning, he obeyed when told to stand up, and walked under guard to the courtroom. The judge was short and fat, with many rings on all his fingers. His eyes were watery and red as he stared from his bench down at the boy. His eyes were always watery and red. Rumor held that he would soon lose his vision.

"Did you kill your father?" The fat man's voice was harsh. Boran stood to one side, watching the proceedings. He would report to the King. He, the judge, the boy, and the six guards were alone in the big room. The murmuring of many voices just outside the closed door betrayed a throng outside. Word spread fast, and people lusted after gory details

Visothirith was silent, staring at the floor.

"Look at me!" The judge shouted. The boy did not respond. "I know you are not deaf," the fat man said, loudly but not shouting. "Look at me, or you will be sorry."

Visothirith did not. His clenched jaw and fists alone signaled that he heard. The judge stared at him. "Take him away," he said finally, gesturing to the guards. "He can rot in prison."

It took all six guards, lances forward, to make progress through the crowd outside.

"That was so fast." "What did the judge say?" "What did the boy say?" "Where is he going now?" "Was he sentenced to death?" Loud questions surrounded them as they walked back to the barracks.

299

"Now what?" Jayavarman VII fumed at the news Boran brought. He and Bopha were in the small audience room. "That stupid judge has tied my hands. The boy is sentenced to prison, as if he were an adult, just because he didn't speak. Isn't Khosal the real criminal here?" Boran shifted his weight, where he stood in front of the throne. He knew the King was not really asking him a question. "Thank you, Boran, for your report." He took a deep breath. "We will consider things. Meanwhile, keep the child at the barracks. And keep him safe."

Boran nodded, then said, "My Lord, may I speak?" Jayavarman gave him a sharp look, then nodded. He had known Boran for many years, and knew him to be both honorable and wise. "My youngest son was the mentor for Visothirith. He thinks the boy was the one who killed those animals."

Bopha gasped. Then she put the pieces together. Of course.

The King nodded slowly, then asked, "Does your son think the boy is doomed to be forever twisted?" Jayavarman searched Boran's face.

Boran shook his head sadly. "No. Not necessarily. But his home life has left a mark. He will need a strong but kind hand, from someone he can trust."

"Thank you, Boran. You are a wise counselor," Jaya smiled at his old friend.

Boran gave sampeah and left.

"I can't just release him," Jaya said to Bopha. "But there is not really any good place to send him. He can't stay at Bayon. Khosal is … was … a cousin of Indradevi. His wife came from a village that was destroyed by the Cham when they were on the way to sack Angkor, so she has no relatives." He paused. "It would be wrong to kill him, since his actions were in defense of his mother."

After a few moments of silence Bopha suggested, "Could we ask Garuda what to do?"

She was now sitting next to him. Jaya put his arm around her and kissed the top of her head. "We could," he murmured.

People wanted the King to do something, to say something, to render a royal judgement. He couldn't wait long. The next

300

morning, at the council meeting, he announced his decision, which would be carried by criers throughout Bayon and Angkor.

"The boy, Visothirith, will be banished from Bayon, but he will be kept under watch for seven years. He will not be free but he will not be in prison. If his actions are honorable in those years, he will have earned liberty. If not, he will receive just punishment."

No one sat in the spot where Khosal had sat as Minister for so many years. The King glanced at the empty space, then asked for suggestions about who might succeed him. Finally, Kiri cleared his throat, and offered a name. Muni, Boran and other ministers also had ideas, which they offered diffidently. It was a short and subdued meeting.

"Next time, we will hear from Minister Muni about when the long and arduous work to build our most majestic Bayon Temple will be complete." The King ended the meeting.

Bopha woke in the night. Some different sound, but she could not identify it. Then she heard it again. A soft nicker. She glided to her porch and looked down its length. The moon came out from behind a cloud. At the far end of the gardens, two shapes neared the old gate. One was tall, the other very short. When the gate swung open, they disappeared. Visothirith and Samang's brother were on their way to Sikha's village. Bopha sent along a prayer for the boy's recovery. And another for long life to the ancient healer who had saved her life and those of all her children.

* * *

When the rains ceased, heat pressed upon the land. Despite storms that had been more tumultuous than anyone could remember, the rainfall had not been enough. Some barays dried up completely. Irrigation ditches ran sluggishly. Would the rice harvest survive this drought?

Minister Muni told the King that more workers were needed to divert rivers far from Bayon, lest the royal palaces themselves lose their water supply. It turned out that Khosal had kept poor records. Meas, the new Finance Minister, was still trying to sort out what resources were actually in the royal treasury. Luckily, Bayon Temple was almost completed. Council meetings were long and indecisive.

301

"Just do it!" Jayavarman said finally. "We need that water."

"Yes, my Lord," said Meas, bowing. Then he said hesitantly, "If I may speak, my Lord."

The King nodded curtly. "My name means gold, but I cannot make it out of nothing. I implore you for patience." He turned to Muni, "Please, sir, give me the numbers, and we will do our best to supply your needs."

But water ran out before the new irrigation projects could be completed. Crowds begging for rice gathered in front of the Terrace of the Elephants. It was not rebellion but desperation. Jayavarman ordered food to be released from royal granaries, preventing mass starvation. Luckily, the next rains brought succor. But the King was still concerned. In each province, he built storehouses and appointed ministers for food.

Water was on his mind.

Queen Indradevi was slower and slower when she came to the baray. Her voice was still as sharp as her eyes. "Queen Preah Chan Bopha," she said, inclining her head minutely. "Are you well?"

"Yes, my Queen." In the years since her return, Bopha had never learned how to talk with this woman. Maybe there was no way to do so. Should she return the question? Anyone could see she was failing. "And you?"

The Queen gave a little snort of derision. "Do I not look well?"

This question could not be answered, so Bopha just smiled a little. "Yes, my Queen."

That answer could be interpreted in so many ways that Bopha was proud of herself.

A few days later, word came that the Queen had been struck dumb in the night, and could not move one side of her body. The King went to her chambers for a visit.

"How is she?" Bopha asked when she saw him a few nights later.

"She is leaving her body," Jayavarman said bluntly. Bopha hugged him close.

"You know that my relation with Queen Indradevi has never been warm," she whispered, "but she has been with you since way before you became King. I'm sorry. It must be very hard for you."

Jaya nodded sadly. "Yes. She has never been easy to get along with, but she never failed in her support of me."

The Queen lingered, a strong spirit loath to let go of anything. For many weeks, the King visited her bedside daily. "It's okay, my dear Queen," he finally murmured in her ear. "You have been a good and faithful wife. Thank you." He was holding the hand that she could still move.

She turned her head to look at him, gripped his hand hard, and nodded once. A single tear sprang to her eye. The other eye, on the dead side, was closed. A few minutes later she took a gasping breath. Then another. Then, she was gone.

Her funeral was a celebration of gold, jewels, and all the panoply the Kingdom of Kampuchea could display. Hundreds of monks led the King and his remaining queens to the burial site. Troupes of musicians were interspersed with courtiers. Everyone wore their most glittering outfit. The procession took an hour to go through the Gate of the Dead, past thousands of inhabitants bowing in sampeah.

* * *

Months later, Ambassadors from both the Srivijayan Empire and the Mon states arrived within days of each other. The King of Kampuchea gave them his most lavish welcome. It was the first time since Queen Indradevi's death that the palace grounds had rung with such music and feasting.

Bopha sat next to Mach Botum to watch the Apsaras dance. Sophea was even more exquisite than in the past, each jeeb bringing heaven to earth. For the first time, though, Bopha could not anticipate all the moves, and it was no struggle to keep her limbs from dancing. The realization was bittersweet.

"I'm no longer an Apsara," she told Jaya as they lay entwined.

"How so?"

"I don't remember every jeeb. And my body doesn't crave the movement," she said ruefully.

"You will always be the most renowned Apsara," Jaya told her. "The one who bewitched the King and brought him love when he thought it impossible."

Bopha laughed softly. "A worthy trade," she said.

"Queen Preah Chan Bopha," he murmured. "Apsara."

* * *

The next rainy season was normal, but water levels remained low in all the barays except in Angkor and the royal palace near Bayon. Muni made sure that the King would be last to be affected by the lack of water.

"It's because so many people live here," explained Minister Muni to the council. "We just can't keep up with the water needs. Every time we finish another diversion, the population grows."

"Why don't we move people back out to the provinces, to their villages?" Jayavarman asked. The council members looked at the floor. No one spoke. He persisted, "Well? If there are too many people, the solution looks easy."

Finally Boran broke the silence. "Your Highness, that is a solution. But it is not easy. Most of these people are not slaves." He didn't finish the thought, leaving it up to the King, who sighed.

"Yes, we can move slaves. But it would cause much ill will to try to make free persons go where they do not want to go. What else can be done?"

There was no easy solution, despite many long meetings. Kampucheans wanted to be near their King. Even when Bayon was done, and those resources freed for irrigation projects, the people would remain.

* * *

The consecration of Bayon was the biggest and most lavish celebration anyone could remember, which was saying something in an empire renowned for its displays of power and wealth. It lasted a full week long. The parade was configured similarly to the one for Bopha and Jaya's wedding, but it started at Angkor Wat and ended at Bayon. When Jayavarman VII held up

304

the sacred sword, atop the biggest elephant ever seen, the crowds cheered wildly.

After the last dinner, and more dancing by select Apsaras, Jayavarman VII stood up from his throne.

"My countrymen," he said, "We have accomplished the biggest building projects in the history of Kampuchea. Roads, bridges, hospitals, waterworks, Banteay Chhmer, and many other wats. And now, the Temple of Bayon, which will last a thousand years. Your lives have been commemorated in its bas-reliefs. Untold generations will gaze on its splendor and remember this day. We give thanks to Buddha and to all the gods, who have granted us grace to bring to completion this project dearest to our hearts."

Far beyond their usual wah-wah's, the courtiers cheered lustily. Outside the tent, other palace workers added their praise. Finally the King gave sampeah, and the noise subsided.

"Go in peace. Treat each other with consideration and respect. Work hard. Ask heaven for wisdom." He paused, and looked around at many faces. "Good night."

He led his queens out of the tent into the hot, still night. So many torches blazed that Bopha could not see a star. Samang was waiting for her. She would stay with the King tonight.

"You did it!" Her voice was soft but filled with pride as she wrapped her arms around him. "Congratulations, my Lord and my love. Bayon is the most beautiful temple in the world."

It had been a long time since they made love. Despite the rigorous pace of the past few days, particularly holding up a sword while standing atop an elephant, Jaya was invigorated. She could feel his eager manhood now, and kissed him deeply as she sat upon it. "I'm ready," she said. And she was. Orgasm was fast and powerful for both of them.

"Let's go there," Jaya said, when he caught his breath.

"Go there?" Bopha was still sitting on his lap.

"To Bayon. Let's go. Now."

They organized their sampots, and went to the door. When it opened, his guard and Samang stood up immediately. By now, the courtyards were dark and empty except for a few dim torches.

The tents were still up, but the tables stood bare and attendants had all gone to bed.

The King's guard led the way. The four walked quietly through the grounds and into the north gate of the new temple. Stars filled the sky above the silent stone faces, covered with gold leaf. Garuda stood fierce on each side of the stone path. The gold on his beak and feathers gleamed slightly in the moonless night, but the ruby eyes had no light to reflect.

"Stay here," said the King quietly to the guards when they reached the steps. He led Bopha into the temple. They climbed up, and up, turning with the narrow stairway until they reached the highest terrace.

When they came out the doorway at the top, they stopped. Jaya reached for her hand. Neither spoke. For long moments, they just looked, turning their heads. The intricate carvings could not be seen, apsaras and rishis shrouded by night. But the faces were everywhere. Two hundred and sixteen identical, peaceful faces, watching over the fifty-four provinces in the Empire of King Jayavarman VII. Fifty-four pairs of all seeing eyes looked in each direction.

Jayavarman stepped onto the terrace, then sat down with his back against the tower. Bopha followed. They sat together in silence, shoulders touching, backs against the stone wall. She lost track of time. They sat in the gaze of Avelokiteshvara until the sky turned grey.

Finally Jaya spoke, his voice gravelly. "Bless us. And bless this my kingdom." He lifted his hands in sampeah, then stood and bowed to the four directions, hands at his heart.

It was not quite dawn when they headed back, but the first cooks were in their kitchens. They, and the boys starting the cook fires, stared. Was that really the King? Walking at such an hour with his Apsara queen?

In the morning Bopha watched Jayavarman sleeping. His cheeks were slack and the skin of his arm sagged where it wasn't touching her shoulder. Her beloved was getting old. When he was awake, his personality radiated power. But in the vulnerability of sleep, his age was showing. He stirred, pulling her close. She nestled into him. "Please, Garuda, take good care of this man. Kampuchea needs him so much," she whispered to herself.

* * *

Arun Veha was in his fourth year in the monastery at Angkor. He did not want to be a monk, but rather emulated his father. However, Kiri and Kalienne decided he needed the solid foundation that monastic training would supply, especially after the events of 1200. Their son had been close to Visothirith, almost from the moment he arrived at Bayon. He looked up to the older boy and was happy to be his accomplice in adventure and mischief. Nimith Sokhem had never welcomed him, but Visothirith defended Arun Veha from the young prince's scorn.

Thom and Vanna missed Arun Veha, but they were busy with school and martial arts. Next year, his parents needed to decide about sending them to the monastery.

Bopha and Kalienne sat on the porch in the shade.

"When will Arun Veha come back to Bayon?" Bopha asked. "I know how much you miss him."

"Yes, I do," said Kalienne softly. She and Kiri had never had another child. "I know it's wrong to be so attached, but I can't help it. He and Kiri mean the world to me." She paused. "He'll never really come back, you know. He will live in the barracks here, and start his intensive military training."

Bopha nodded. She was glad the twins were still living with her. Even when they left, for monastery or barracks, Kravann Chivy would still be home for many years.

"Bopha, I'm worried about Kiri. He's been having pains in his chest."

"Oh no," said her friend. "Has he seen the doctor? Does Jayavarman know?"

Kalienne shook her head. "He says he's fine, that it's nothing. But I know that's not true."

She was right. A few days later at a heated council meeting again discussing water, population and resources, Kiri collapsed. "An elephant is on my chest," he groaned. But before the doctor

307

could be summoned, he turned blue. Then his neck and face turned a deep purple-red. He was dead.

For the funeral, Bopha walked with Kalienne and Arun Veha. It was a break with tradition, but the King had given permission. They led the mourners, right behind the pallet with Kiri's body. All three were weeping silently. The King of Kampuchea took his place behind them. Those closest could see tears coursing down the ruler's cheeks.

"I never got to see him again," whispered Arun Veha, as his father's body crashed down into the ravine. "Can I come home now?"

* * *

Jayavarman stood in as patriarch for his childhood friend, and Arun Veha was allowed to return to Bayon. For a few weeks, he lived with his mother. Then he moved into the barracks. He had the King's permission to have dinner with Kalienne several times a week. Bopha made a point of visiting her friend every few days.

The King would care for Kiri's widow and son as if they were his blood, so she did not need to worry on that count. But Kalienne was heartbroken. "I knew he was much older than me," she told Bopha. "It felt like we lived on time we took from death ever since he came to Sikha's village." She couldn't hold back tears. "I knew, but it doesn't help."

Bopha put her arm around her friend, then held her while she sobbed. Kiri and Jaya are the same age, she thought, unwillingly. How much longer do we have?

CHAPTER 33

1207, Vengeance is Mine

Jayavarman awoke from his nap with a loud knock. "What now?" His voice was almost querulous. Bopha had lain down beside him, snuggling close despite the afternoon heat. But she was not tired and got up when he began to snore.

She drew her palm leaf, ink, and brush from their box in a corner and began to practice Chinese calligraphy. Since she did this almost every afternoon, she was improving. It was true that she should use the brush, as Xiuying so often said. The bamboo pen did not have the same flow. Bopha now had two brushes, one in her rooms and one in the King's bed chamber.

Xiuying had been given special dispensation to stay and teach Chinese to her and Rithy. Though the official ambassador and other members of the delegation came and went, Xiuying and several others were on permanent assignment. Jayavarman had even built a special building for the Chinese emissaries.

Rithy had a better grasp of the characters, but Bopha had an ear for the music in the spoken language. She could understand most of what the Chinese dignitaries said in meetings. Their interpreters quickly learned of her ability, and were more careful afterwards in how specifically to translate what King Jayavarman actually said and the emissaries' replies.

Muffled words from the door gave no information about what now, so Bopha rose and opened it a crack, as the King sat up slowly.

The big guard apologized then said, "There is a messenger from Tonle Sap."

"I will see him in the small audience chamber." The King's deep voice was not as deep as it had been when Bopha first heard it. In fact it was either a growl or almost a quaver and he had to clear his throat often. This order was a growl. The guard bowed and Bopha closed the door. Jayavarman stood up, waited for a moment, then went to the little room to use the chamber pot. It was nearly five minutes before the door opened again.

309

"Dribble, dribble," the King complained, this time quavering. "What I would give for a good stream, and only twice a day, not ten times." Bopha had gotten a fresh sampot ready. She murmured soothingly, not really saying anything. Jaya grunted as he bent over to pull up the garment. He had gained weight. His skin didn't sag, but his belly did. She handed him the royal necklaces, then did the clasps as he held them up around his neck.

"Let's go," he said. "I never like a message from Tonle Sap."

He didn't like this one. A scrawny young man bowed and scraped his way toward the throne, then stood up straight and recited, "The boy Visothirith and his guard Poeu Meaker will arrive at Angkor tomorrow." The King gave sampeah and waved the youth away.

"Seven years already," he mused. "All reports have been positive. Even after Sikha's death, the boy behaved well and studied hard." Bopha nodded. She had followed Visothirith's progress. He must be nearly sixteen now, she calculated. News of their dear friend's death had come a few years ago. Afterwards, the boy had moved into the village monastery, still with Boran's youngest son as mentor and monitor. Bopha hoped the troubled boy had been with the old healer long enough for her to untangle his heart. But she was filled with foreboding.

She, Jaya and Boran discussed how to handle the boy's return. Obviously, there would be no celebration. It was best if he came unnoticed. The rumor mill would start, but a child, in seven years, grew into a youth no one could recognize. He and Poeu Meaker would stay in the monastery at Angkor for a few weeks. If the monks there confirmed Visothirith was no threat, he could return to Bayon. He was good with numbers, the reports said, very good. He wanted to train to be a clerk in the King's treasury.

"As the father, so the son?" Bopha asked.

"I hope not," Jaya replied. Bopha grimaced.

They had not said anything of Visothirith's return to the twins, now studying at the Angkor monastery and longing for the day they would move to the barracks like Arun Veha and Nimith Sokhem. At least Vanna was longing.

310

* * *

A few weeks later, the King summoned his three sons. They stood in the doorway like stepping stones, the tallest wearing a soldier's loin cloth, the twins' orange robes bright in the afternoon sun.

"Come, come," Jayavarman growled. Hands in sampeah, the boys approached his bench. "Sit." They sat cross legged in front of him. Jayavarman wore necklaces of royal pearls that covered his chest. "How are your studies?"

He looked first at Nimith Sokhem. "Do you still want to be a soldier, now that you have had some years of practice?"

"Yes, my Lord." Nimith Sokhem's voice cracked on 'Lord,' dropping an octave.

"And what kind of soldier do you want to be?"

"I want to lead an army to war!" The son of Sao Nang was emphatic.

Jayavarman raised his eyebrows. "And if there is no war?"

His older son was nonplussed, then stammered, "No war?"

"No war. There is not always war, you know." The King's growl began to quaver.

"What kind of soldier do you want to be if there is peace?"

Nimith Sokhem had obviously never considered this possibility. His shoulders drooped.

"Think about it and tell me next time," his father said. The boy nodded glumly, but straightened his back and shoulders.

"And you, Apphoutheto Thom. What do you have to say for yourself?"

Thom was noticeably taller and heavier than his twin. His face was cheerful. It took a moment for him to gather words. He spoke slowly. "Father, I want to stay in the monastery, with the monks. I am not good at reading or writing. Not good at all. And numbers make no sense. But the chanting fills me up. That's what I want to do."

"You want to chant prayers?" Jayavarman was surprised.

311

"Yes, Aupouk," Thom beamed.

His father sighed, studying the chubby boy. "There are worse things a prince could do," he said at last.

"Thank you," Thom's lifted his hands in sampeah, and the King returned the gesture. Something about the sweet smile on the boy's face made him feel less old.

He turned his gaze to the smallest son, whose build reminded him of a coiled leather whip, lean and strong, ready to snap into action. "Phnheaphaael Vanna, how about you? Do you want to chant prayers? Or be a soldier?"

Vanna looked Jayavarman in the eye. "No, my King. Not either. I want to be like you."

Nimith Sokhem sucked in a sharp breath. The old man tilted his head. "Like me?"

"Yes, the best ruler in the whole world, who brings peace to a huge empire and knows how to act with honor." He paused, then added, "And when to wreak vengeance."

Jayavarman pursed his lips. "That is the balance a ruler needs to know, you are right."

He nodded, giving the boy a small smile. He shifted on his chair. His knees no longer bent into lotus position willingly.

"I am glad to hear of your aspirations, my sons. But I have news, and I want you to hear it from me." The three boys leaned toward him slightly, expectant. "I hope it will be good news. We will see. It has been seven years since Minister Khosal's son was sent away. All reports are that he has behaved well and studied hard. Therefore, Visothirith is returning to Bayon."

Amazement bloomed on the boys' faces.

"He's coming back?" Nimith Sokhem interrupted, his voice echoing off the teak walls. Then he realized what he had done. "I'm sorry, my Lord. I'm just so surprised..." He trailed off under the King's withering glance. "I'm sorry," he repeated softly. "He was my friend."

Jayavarman's face softened. "Yes, I remember," he said. "That's why I want to tell you myself. He has fulfilled all the requirements to return. But," he looked from one upturned face to the other. "But, if he misbehaves in any way, he will have to face the consequences." He did not say, "He will be killed." Did his sons know? Did Visothirith? He needed to speak with the boy. He would tell him in person. How had Vanna phrased it? "Peace, honor, vengeance." He continued, his growl strong now.

"Nimith Sokhem, you will be seeing him, because he will be living in the barracks." The tall boy, nodded, looking at the floor. "Look at me." The dark eyes were murky when they met Jayavarman's. Conflicting emotions raged. "You are the same age, but he will not be training with you. He has been in a monastery while you practiced weaponry. However, you will eat together and …" It was the King's turn to trail off.

There was a moment of silence, then the King said, "I am proud of you, my sons. You are each so different and each so strong. Study hard." He looked at Nimith Sokhem then Vanna and added, "Go in peace. Avoid all fights you do not have to fight. Sometimes the strongest man is the one with forbearance, the one who can control his emotions." He lifted his hands in sampeah, ending the audience. The boys scrambled to their feet and returned the blessing.

When the door closed behind them, Jayavarman uncrossed his legs with difficulty. Pain radiated up to his knees when he put his feet on the floor. When it subsided enough, he stood and limped to the hidden room to use the chamber pot.

* * *

Bopha and the King were eating dinner. "How did it go?" He was reclining on the cushions with his long legs stretched out. His ankles were slightly swollen.

"They are three different boys," Jaya said after recounting the meeting. "But I'm glad I told them. I can only hope that Nimith Sokhem accepts Visothirith. He is very angry." He sighed. "Maybe it's the challenge he needs for his next lesson." He reached for a slice of mango and slid it between his full lips. Many of his teeth had fallen out and he appreciated the soothing

313

softness of the fruit on his gums. "I want to talk with Visothirith in person."

Bopha was sipping tea and nearly choked. Jaya continued, "I need to be sure he knows the consequences of any misbehavior."

"You will have him killed?"

The King nodded somberly. "I would have no choice. Murdering your father under such circumstances is one thing. It is understandable. But the torture of those animals." He shook his head. "Someone who does that may not ever be healed. Sikha died after only a few years with the boy."

Bopha reached for his hand, lifted it to her mouth and kissed it gently. "May it not get to that," she said softly.

* * *

No one noticed when a big burly soldier and a tall slender youth walked through the palace grounds. It was late in the day. The smells of curry, and chicken skewers cooking over open flame, filled the air. Poeu Meaker was the youngest of Boran's children, but he had been so big at birth that he got two names, "youngest," and "greatest." His arms were huge, shoulders broad, and the muscles of his chest rippled as he walked, spear held loosely at his side.

Visothirith was a few finger-widths taller, but only about half Meaker's weight. His head was long and narrow on a thin neck. His gait was graceful, almost feline. Meaker had been with the boy for so many years he had hardly noticed what he looked like, just that he was tall and thin. He didn't see Khosal in his build and face.

But when they got to the barracks, Boran nearly gasped. His training held and that surprise did not translate to his face. The Minister of the Army was waiting for his son and Visothirith, wearing his bronze helmet, leather cross-chest straps, and sword belt. Official wear but not ceremonial. He kept under lock and key the silk ribbon with its huge, golden seal of office, only donning it for major events. His hair was thin under the helmet, and full of gray, and he was almost twice the man he had been when Bopha first met him. Every few years, the leather workers had to make him new chest straps. For all his weight, he was lithe and vigorous still.

"Welcome to Bayon, Visothirith," rumbled Boran. He lifted his hands in sampeah, as did Visothirith, who glanced at the old soldier's face then back at the ground. "Welcome back, my son Poeu." Meaker put his hands in sampeah, bowing to his father, face wreathed in un-soldierly smiles. "Dinner is almost ready. Let's get you settled." A young soldier appeared and took Visothirith into the barracks.

Boran put his hand on his son's arm. "Let's talk a bit," he murmured. "I want to hear your thoughts. I have read all the reports, but … None of them prepared me to see Khosal in this boy."

"Khosal?" Meaker was startled, then slowly nodded. "You mean, he looks like his father?"

"Very much so. You were not at court, and you were young when you went away. But the courtiers will immediately know who he is. I need to tell the King. Please, keep him away from the main palace grounds for a few days. Also, the King wants to meet with him in person, to be sure he understands his circumstances."

"Yes, father, of course." Meaker shook his head in wonder, then frowned. "Khosal! I had no idea. Do you think the boy knows?"

"He would if he ever looked into a still pool," Boran said. "That can't be easy." He sighed. Meaker's stomach growled. "Don't tell me you are still growing," his father joked, poking at a bulging bicep.

"Maybe," the strapping young man replied. "I'm always ready for a meal."

* * *

Some weeks later, Meaker and Boran accompanied Visothirith to the small audience chamber. King Jayavarman VII sat on his golden chair adorned in royal pearls. His feet were on the floor instead of crossed on the throne. His sampot covered his swollen ankles. He radiated power. Bopha stood behind him. Visothirith stood between Boran and Meaker, in front

315

of the King. All three were dressed as soldiers, with short swords on their belts, and bronze helmets that rose to a point.

After a few pleasantries about the trip across the lake and life in the barracks, the King cleared his throat.

"Visothirith, son of Khosal, all reports are that you have done well while you were gone from the palace. Your behavior is irreproachable. I think you know that. But I want to be sure you understand the consequences if you misbehave in future." He paused, looking straight at the tall youth. His resemblance to his father was in truth uncanny, Jayavarman thought, grateful for Boran's warning.

Visothirith stood at attention and met the King's eyes. His expression was unreadable. "Yes, your majesty." Bopha felt a fluttering of wings behind her and turned her head.

Nothing. But a cold chill ran up her arms, raising the little hairs, as she turned back.

"If you do anything that could constitute danger, or less than honorable behavior, I will have no choice but to have you beheaded." The King paused. Something hard crossed Visothirith's face, and he shifted his stance slightly, left leg in front. "Do you understand?"

"Yes, your majesty." The words were cold. "I've been waiting for seven years." Suddenly, he cried, "And now you die!" Visothirith drew his sword in a flash and rushed toward the old man on the throne. It was only two steps and the boy was fast. Bopha screamed.

Jayavarman still had the instincts of an old warrior. His body knew which way the blow would come, and leaned him to his right as the sword sliced into the throne where the King's head had been. Boran and Meaker each grabbed one of Visothirith's arms, as the boy tried to pull the sword out from the wood that held it. He was shouting curses at the King and Bopha when they wrestled him to the ground.

"It's all your fault. You and your beauty seduced the useless King and turned him away from my father. Yes, my father was a monster, but you two pushed him to it. He always said that, when he was beating my mother. 'One for Jayavarman, one for his bitch!'"

Boran broke the youth's jaw with one punch, cutting off his diatribe. Jayavarman regained his balance and sat upright. "Take him away. He will die for all to see."

Bopha's scream and Visothirith's shouts had rung through the courtyards. Soldiers rattled up the steps with swords drawn and lances at the ready. It was chaos. A crowd of cooks and courtiers and workmen gathered as six soldiers carried the writhing prisoner toward the barracks. A trail of blood from his broken face dripped into the packed dirt.

The blade had nicked the King's shoulder. Bopha was staunching the blood with her kromah as Jayavarman grumbled, "It's nothing." He looked at Boran and his son, whose faces were white. "We will talk later." They gave sampeah and left reluctantly. It was their fault that the untried boy had worn a sword. The doctors arrived and bandaged the wound. It was not nothing, but neither was it deep. It should heal quickly they told the King.

"Go. Leave us," he commanded. The room cleared. "I need to go to the small chamber," he muttered to Bopha. She stood by to steady him as he stood a moment before walking. "I'm okay. Stop hovering."

She took a step back. "Yes, my love. I'm just so glad you are okay."

He relented, "Yes, yes, I know. But I have to go right now." He tottered a bit but Bopha let him go alone. She knew he hated getting old. So many indignities for this man who was used to being in charge of an empire. He ruled the biggest kingdom in Southeast Asia, but could no longer rule his own body.

As she waited for her husband to be done in the small room, Bopha remembered the wings, fluttering just before the attack. Had Garuda saved the King? She brought out cushions, and set them on low benches near the wall, not directly facing the throne. The gouge from Visothirith's blow was ragged and black in the throne's gold back. She shivered. So close. She went to the door and asked the guards, who now numbered five and stood lances forward, for tea.

317

Jayavarman and Bopha sat on the cushions, sipping tea. They talked about the assassination attempt, how Jaya had felt his body moving him to safety without him consciously doing it. She told him about the wings. They embraced. Tonight, she would bring her small Garuda to his chambers. Later, they would offer incense to the Garudas on the causeway at Bayon.

"The Council has to meet," Jaya said. "And everyone must see that I have not been harmed. I have to tell Boran to be sure no one kills the boy before he is beheaded. Many people are enraged at him."

Bopha nodded. In all her years at the palace, she had never seen an execution, but she knew this was one she must attend. It was rare for Jayavarman to order such punishment in any case. Sometimes his judges would do so, but most crimes were distant from the King and not his business to be involved.

"What about Boran?" Bopha ventured the question. That the attack should have been possible at all was a grave misjudgment.

Jaya sighed. "Yes. He made a big mistake. Visothirith should never have been given a sword. But Boran has been loyal to me for forty years. He saved my life at the battle on Tonle Sap, and was gravely injured thereby. I sent him to the Apsara courtyard for several years until he recovered fully. He is a great general, closer to me than any man except Kiri." He sighed.

"There is no one I trust as much. But how I wish Kiri were here." He paused, then continued, "There will be advisors who tell me to have Boran put to death, or sent from Bayon at the very least." He looked at Bopha.

"You know, if Visothirith had sliced my head instead of the throne, his next thrust would have killed you as well. Boran and his son saved not only my life today, but yours as well." The King's voice was a deep growl. Then he admitted, in a low voice that quavered, "I don't want to lose him." He took a deep breath. "So, through my magnanimity, Boran will retain his seal as Minister for the Army. But he and I will have a long, private talk."

* * *

318

On the appointed day, the court gathered on the Terrace of the Elephants. In the center of the parade ground, a platform had been erected, with steps on one side. On the side facing the terrace, two hinged boards were set, each carved out to accommodate a neck. When closed together, the neck would be secure.

Concentric circles of soldiers in full battle regalia stood in the hot sun, with masses of townspeople behind them. Never in the history of the Kingdom of Kampuchea had the King's life been threatened in such a manner. Aside from war, and the occasional poison attempt that was settled quietly, nothing had come so close to harming him.

After the courtiers were settled, the three queens were carried in on their gold palanquins. The King had been persuaded by Bopha not to try horseback, let alone his favorite mount, the elephant. His dismount would viewed by thousands. So he also came in an open-topped palanquin, which was bejeweled and fluttering with silk banners of royal gold and blue. Eight burly men carried it. Sweat poured down their faces and chests under the King's weight.

Jayavarman VII stepped out and stood in front of the throne, which gleamed in the afternoon sun. He had so much gold on his chest that the sparkles almost hid his face.

When the cheers and wahs had settled, the King lifted his hands in sampeah. In a strong voice, as deep and steady as when Bopha first heard it, he said, "My dear Kampucheans. It is with a heavy heart that I come today, to watch with you as a life is ended. Among the duties of a King are to maintain peace and to mete out justice. Sometimes, as today, it is a sad duty.

"Many of you knew Minister Khosal. Seven years ago, he was killed by his son, Visothirith. At that time, the boy was barely nine years old and trying to protect his mother. Alas, she had already been beaten to death by his father. We offered clemency to the child, and sent him away. For seven years, he studied hard and behaved well, fulfilling all the requirements to return to Bayon.

"But instead of being grateful for his life, he spent those years hiding a fire of revenge against me. As you have no doubt heard, when he was granted an audience with me, he attempted to kill me. For this, he is sentenced to be beheaded. My life was saved by the head of the Armed Forces, Boran, and his son Poeu Meaker." He gestured to Boran, standing next to the platform. "Bring the prisoner. And proceed."

The King sat. All the people craned their necks instead of sitting. Arun Veha and Nimith Sokhem were in the last circle of soldiers on the parade ground, farthest from the scaffold. Bopha hoped they would not be able to see past the tall men. Four rows of monks sat in front of the king, facing the golden altar and its gold Buddha. Bopha was glad to see the twins closest to the throne, their view of the parade ground also blocked by taller men.

Visothirith was dragged toward the platform by four soldiers. A cloth gag was in his mouth. People closest could hear muffled words and grunts. His wrists were bound together, as were his legs, but he resisted as best he could. Bopha saw the wisdom in having a device to hold a prisoner's neck steady. The boy put up quite a fight, but the soldiers were strong and lifted him up the stairs. They pulled his legs out behind him, not roughly, and lowered his shoulders until his neck touched the curved board. The executioner closed the second board. Visothirith's body writhed until the soldiers knelt and held him down.

A gong sounded, deep and heavy, vibrating across the terrace and parade grounds. Again, and once again. Three times. The monks began to chant the Heart Sutra. Bopha saw Khosal and Mony's son stop fighting and lie still. The droning filled the sultry air, penetrating. Gibbons and birds were silenced. The gong sounded again, three times.

Tears sprang to Bopha's eyes. The boy had never had a chance at life. She hoped his next life would have more happiness. The executioner raised his sword high. The steel gleamed as it fell. A dull, wet sound, severing life. Visothirith's head fell onto the parade ground. A soldier picked it up and lifted it toward the king. Bopha hoped her sons could not see the dead staring eyes. Another soldier had moved a basin to catch the blood that poured forth. In moments, only a few drops hit the dark red pool.

Another gong. The King stood, hands in sampeah to his monks, soldiers, countrymen.

Visothirith's body was carried down the steps to where a white cloth lay. The soldiers lay the body on the cloth, brought the head to join it, and wrapped them tightly. They lifted the pall, lowered it briefly toward the king, as if in a final bow, and waited. At the final gong, the King turned away and got back in his palanquin. Visothirith would have a soldier escort to the ravine, but no mourners, no music, no monks.

CHAPTER 34

1214, Kravann

Bopha and Jayavarman lay facing each other as early morning light crept through the slats in the shutters. "My love and my Lord, please. I want our daughter to be as happy as you and I have been." Already it was hot. Bopha wanted to get up and slide open the wooden blinds on the side of the room that had a private porch with no stairs, hence no listeners. But they were continuing a discussion from last night and she did not want to disturb.

His face softened as his voice quavered, "We have been happy, have we not?"

Bopha leaned and kissed his lips, still full but somewhat shrunken. "Yes, my dear. Truly, our love is a blessing."

Jaya sighed. "You are right. So many of my children have made good alliances. Nimith Sokhem last year. He writes of how the customs are different in the Mon states. I suspect he still longs for a war to fight, but he is being a warrior for peace there, with his young wife." He took a deep breath. "And Sambath is, after all, a grandson of Boran. He may not be of royal blood, but his family has proven brave and loyal for so many years. You really think Kravann Chivy is in love? She is so young. How could she know?"

"I was only a few years older when I knew," Bopha reminded him. "Even as a young girl I searched for your eyes when you passed the Apsara gate."

The King chuckled. "Yes, I remember."

"Kravann says she saw Sambath at the New Year's festival parade last year, and felt like hot tea filled her whole body. She could not look away when his eye reached for hers." Bopha felt the King stiffen. "My dear, he looked at her, yes. But he is a soldier, not a monk, and high-born though not royal."

Jaya relaxed and rolled onto his back, wrapping his arm around her, still strong. They lay in silence for a moment. She listened to his heart beat with one ear, while the other heard early morning sounds in the compound.

Finally Jaya said. "All right. Love wins. Kravann Chivy can marry Sambath."

Bopha hugged him hard. "She will be filled with joy to hear this. In the past few months she has lost so much weight. She says she cannot bear to eat when she thinks she might be forced to marry someone else."

"That you did not tell me, wife," growled Jayavarman.

"No," Bopha agreed. "I did not. But I feared for her. As a man, and a King, you may not have thought about how a woman might feel. So many women live nearly like slaves, unable to speak of their wishes, submitting to their husband's needs..." She trailed off as Jaya lifted himself, grunting, to a sitting position against the pillows.

"Are you suggesting that my own daughters might be so unhappy?"

"I am not. I hope that they have found their husbands to be kind and gentle and understanding, like their father." Bopha did not add, "in addition to their being powerful allies."

The King scowled. She knew he was pondering this new idea. She continued, "Most of your children had married and moved away before I came to Bayon. But I know that Malis is happy," she said. "She was so glad when you chose Meas as her husband, even though he is much older. She did not know him but Mach Botum had told her how wise and gentle he is. And when she did meet him, she saw how handsome he is despite his age. Of course, she is also glad she is able to stay near her mother and all her friends here." Meas was doing a wonderful job, Bopha thought, balancing in his difficult role as Minister of the Treasury, the new title for Khosal's old position.

Malis's wedding was in the year Bayon was consecrated. Bopha thought back over all the years since she moved to the Palace. So much had happened. She remembered how virile Jaya had been, how strong and agile. In those days, he would work all day and make love all night. It had been many seasons now since his manhood rose to her. She had learned to count long ago, so Bopha knew Jaya was nearing ninety. All of his friends had died. Boran, though much younger, had been struck down with fever and died in three days, shortly after the execution of Visothirith. Bopha was glad that he had lived long enough to know that the King, to whom he had given service for so long, still appreciated him.

She gave the King another kiss. "Thank you, dear Jayavarman, for your wise and kind decision about our daughter's future. Do you want to tell her yourself or shall I?"

"I will. Bring her to me after the Council meeting today."

Bopha got out of bed, and stood discreetly nearby as the King worked to swing his legs out of bed. He noticed, and admonished her, "You hover!"

"Yes, my love." She took a step away and busied herself with her sampot, watching out of the corner of his eye as he finally stood and balanced. His body had shrunken some over the past ten years, but he was still a formidable presence. And his mind was very sharp.

He shuffled his first steps toward the small chamber, then he walked with more confidence. Bopha let the guards know they were ready for breakfast, then organized his clothes and jewelry, her thoughts on the upcoming Council meeting. Despite more and more resources being available for irrigation projects, water remained a problem. Rainy seasons had been too short for almost ten years, while Bayon grew and grew.

Now, when she rode out of the city, villages that had been separated by miles of rice paddies were one long mass of buildings. It took nearly two hours to reach fields, longer to get to where big trees hung over the road. All those people, cutting wood for fires and houses, while they built homes in the paddies and expected to eat. And wanted water.

She shook her head, face solemn. Maybe this year the rains would be longer and heavier. She sent a prayer to Garuda. Who else could help?

When Jayavarman returned, she gathered a smile onto her face. It was not hard to smile when she saw him, this man she loved so well and for so long. He was watching his feet but felt her smile and looked up, "What are you smiling about?"

"Nothing. I just love you," she murmured.

He grinned and nodded. She handed him his clothes. She would have time between breakfast and the Council meeting to talk with Kravann Chivy.

* * *

The young woman's face was uncertain as she gave her mother sampeah. Then she saw Bopha's smile and knew. "He said yes?" Bopha nodded. "He wants to tell you himself, after the Council Meeting this morning. But you have guessed."

Kravann Chivy squealed with delight and rushed to hug her mother, who was almost a head taller. The two were equally beautiful. Kravann's face was slightly broader, like Jayavarman's, and perfectly formed. She could have been an Apsara, were she not royal. She walked with exquisite grace and had spent hours practicing jeebs with Bopha as a youngster.

She had also inherited Bopha's gift for languages. Starting at age four, she begged to stay for Bopha's lessons with Xiuying. Chinese characters gave her some trouble, but she had learned the tones of both Chinese and Cham, and her uncle Rithy welcomed her for writing lessons. Now she was learning Sanskrit. Jayavarman approved of her scholarship. Both his first wife and Indradevi had been women of learning, so to him it felt natural for Bopha and Kravann to engage in studies.

Kravann chattered on about her father's decision, interrupting herself. "Who will tell Sambath? He and I have talked — of course with my maid present. He is so handsome, just looking at him makes me feel like I'm swimming in warm water. When will the wedding be?"

Bopha laughed. "Such exuberance! My dear daughter, your delight brings joy to my heart. I recommend that you suggest Sambath ask for an audience with the King, to get his blessing. And, of course, the astrologers will determine the date, you know that."

Kravann's face fell, "Of course. I forgot about them. Do I seem too eager?"

"Not too eager when you talk with me, but too eager for anyone outside this chamber to hear," Bopha warned gently. Kravann nodded. "Our family has been blessed, these many years. Health, beauty, the favor of the King. There is much that might be envied."

She looked at her daughter and sighed. "I'm not suggesting you practice any deception. Just discretion. You understand the difference?"

"Yes, Mdeay. Not to flaunt my blessings. But it's hard. I'm so happy I just want to dance and sing and tell the world." She threw out her arms, then lifted them into the first jeeb of the Wishing Dance. Bopha relented, smiling, and joined her. The two women danced to imagined music, following the jeebs, twirling together. Kravann was in the blush of youth, barely fifteen years into life, her mother in the fullness of mature beauty, not yet forty.

Their dance was interrupted by a discreet knock. "Yes? Come in," Bopha said, as she hugged her daughter with a decidedly un-Apsara-like grin. Chariya opened the door, then gave sampeah. "Lok Srey, you have a visitor."

Sophea still lived at the Apsara courtyard and now was the chief dancer. Bopha often enjoyed watching her perform for small gatherings at the Palace. When they could, the two old friends would share tea or a meal. Now, Bopha could tell Sophea had something on her mind.

"Come in, come in. Kravann and I were just doing a little of the Wishing Dance."

Sophea smiled, "It's good to know that you have not lost your inner music."

"Kravann, will you please let Rithy know I won't be able to come for lessons today?" Bopha said. Her skin was glistening with perspiration and she reached for a kromah to pat her neck and chest.

"Am I interrupting?" Sophea asked.

"Not at all. The unexpected chance to speak with an old friend is most welcome."

Kravann gave sampeah and left, her step light, followed by Chariya who went to get the women tea and fruit.

"She looks happy," Sophea observed.

"Indeed." Bopha resisted the urge to tell her friend why. "She is a good girl, and full of life. But I think you may be here to talk about something else." She led the way to the private back porch. Between a gentle breeze and the banyan's shade, Bopha began to feel cooler. "I don't know how you can dance so long and so often. I have barely breath after part of one dance."

Sophie looked somberly at the floor. "That's why I'm here, actually." She paused, then met Bopha's eyes. "I can still do it, but it is not easy," she admitted. "I think it's time for me to retire."

"Really? What will you do?"

"That's what I want to talk about. The logical thing would be to become lead instructor for the Apsaras."

"But?"

Sophea shrugged. "But ... I am not drawn to that. I want to do something different. My whole life so far has been dance. I am grateful, of course, that I was blessed with ability and opportunity." She paused.

"But you wonder what else is out there, in the rest of the world?"

"Yes, that's it. I've lived in the courtyard since I was six years old. Kalienne left when she was fourteen, you when you were nineteen. Tevy and Theary are still dancing, but Thida retired a few years ago."

Bopha considered. "And she married almost immediately." Sophea's face clouded. "Which is not something you want to do, at least not now."

"Right. Maybe someday. But only for love. In truth, I have never been attracted to any man." She caught Bopha's glance. "No, nor any woman. I don't seem to have that ... whatever it is. That kind of interest." Sophea paused, then finished in a burst of words, "But I do want to travel. I cannot read or write. I don't speak any other languages. But when I hear about tigers and giraffes and lands with snow, I want to go see them."

"I can hear that," Bopha said. "In all these years I've never heard such passion in your voice. Usually you are so careful, so considered,"

"Wrapped tightly like a butterfly in a cocoon," suggested Sophea. "That's what I want. To let go of this need to control every step and word and thought. To leave my cocoon and fly.

"An Apsara trains for years to control every step and thought," said Bopha thoughtfully. "And you have been one of the best dancers in all of history. But now you want something different."

"Yes. Exactly."

Chariya knocked lightly and brought refreshments, then left.

Bopha served the tea, then put a cookie and some mango and rambutan on a small porcelain plate. The women sipped in companionable silence. Finally Sophea asked,

"Do you have any ideas, Bopha?"

"Not right away, but I will consider. Maybe Garuda will give me an inspiration." She enjoyed the rambutan, spitting seeds into her palm and placing them on the plate. At royal banquets, rambutan was pitted carefully, but she had instructed Chariya that she would prefer them whole when she ate at home.

"I wonder how the King would feel about sending a small group of Apsaras on a good-will tour, at least to Pagan? Last time I saw their Ambassador, he couldn't stop talking about our Khmer dancing."

"Do you think he might?" Sophea was elated. "After all, a few years ago we hosted some Indian dancers."

A few nights later, Bopha suggested the plan to Jayavarman. After slow consideration, the King approved. "In all this time, I have sent only men abroad, and kept the Apsaras at home for show. But maybe it's time for them to be ambassadors." He looked sharply at Bopha, "And do you have someone in mind?"

"You know me, so well, my lord," she admitted, and told him of her visit from Sophea, and the idea that came to her right after she asked Garuda for inspiration. "But it is true that Sophea would be perfect for the role."

"You are right, my dear. She is an exceptional woman and an exquisite dancer."

* * *

Bopha spent more time with the King than any other person, attending council meetings and spending the night with him several times a week. She cherished their time together. He had plans to build more temples, in every part of his kingdom. These would honor the Buddha, and give his subjects places to worship and learn. Bopha never tired of discussing these projects.

"I want my people to know the teachings of the Buddha," Jaya told her. They were enjoying a quiet dinner alone. "But one his teachings is tolerance. So there are Hindu gods at Bayon. And I leave the bas reliefs of Hindu mythology that decorate Angkor Wat. As long as I am alive, we will not fight about religion."

"I'm so glad, my dear. I offer incense to the Buddha, and I know the four Noble Truths and the Noble Eightfold Path. But," she paused and looked up into Jaya's dark eyes. "What would I do without Garuda?"

He lifted his hand and stroked her cheek with one wrinkled, gentle finger. "And so, we welcome Garuda into Kampuchea." Bopha kissed his finger, then leaned her cheek into his offered palm.

Jayavarman VII had already outlived two wives, almost every soldier who fought to secure his realm, and every childhood friend. His oldest son had died and his second son, by Queen Indradevi, had been living in Champa for longer than Bopha had been at Bayon. "Speaking of welcoming to Kampuchea," the King continued, "I have written my son Indravarman. He will be arriving sometime this month."

Bopha's heart clenched. The succession. She had not wanted to ask. But here it was.

329

She supposed it was better for the Kingdom that Jayavarman VII designate his successor, but the thought of him being gone filled her with dread.

* * *

He carried himself like a king, thought Bopha, as she stood with the King and court when Indravarman rode into Bayon. Regal on a huge white horse festooned with gold and jewels, the man radiated health and power, younger than his fifty years. He knelt in sampeah in front of Jayavarman, who raised him up and embraced.

"It has been so many years, my son. My eyes bless the sight of you." The King's voice quavered and he cleared his throat.

"Aupouk, you bless my eyes likewise." Indravarman's voice was so smooth it was almost oily. As the King introduced him to the Queens and court, Indravarman offered sampeah to each, murmuring appreciations.

"Queen Preah Chan Bopha," said Jayavarman.

"Ah, the Apsara Queen," said Indravarman, looking her over, almost impolitely. "I have heard much about you." Bopha wondered if Queen Indradevi was one of his informants.

"It is a blessing for us to meet at last," she said. But a shiver went up her spine and she was glad when he moved on to Minister Meas.

Indravarman, of course, began to attend Council meetings. At first he listened politely, but over time he asked more questions, then offered suggestions. Jayavarman seemed delighted by his engagement. Several times a week, he would dine with his son.

When his wife, Jorani, came to the baray, she had little to say except to Sao Nang. She was coldly polite to Mach Botum and Bopha. "She is too old to be a reincarnation of Indradevi," thought Bopha. "But she might as well be."

* * *

Kravann's wedding displayed all the pomp and wealth of Kampuchea, over four days of feasting and ceremony. Everyone agreed that no bride had ever looked so beautiful.

330

On the day she and Sambath were to be encircled by the banyan wrapped candle, her dress had so many pearls she complained to Bopha. "I can barely walk. I hope my sampot doesn't fall off from the weight."

"I'm sure you'll survive," her mother said, tightening the knot just to be sure. Kravann's chest was almost completely covered with tiers of pearl necklaces. "Sambath is a lucky young man."

Dignitaries came from all parts of the Kingdom for the celebration, parades, elephants, gold and jewels, banquets. On the final evening, the Chinese Ambassador's gift turned out to be a spectacular display of fireworks. Crowds of thousands packed the parade ground and cheered. The finale spread Chinese characters for health, wealth, love and happiness across the sky above the parade ground.

Bopha spooned into Jaya that night. "What beautiful fireworks," she said. She had to speak fairly loudly, so she lay with her mouth near his good ear. "Congratulations, Jayavarman VII, on the wedding of your daughter."

"Our daughter," the King said. "Our most beautiful daughter. Goodnight, my dear queen. Sleep well. This has been a wonderful but exhausting week." He was asleep almost immediately.

Bopha lay in the darkness, replaying the panoply of events. She was grateful that Kravann would remain at Bayon. Thom, of course, would. He was as cheerful as always, engrossed in life as a priest. In another four years, he would take his solemn vows. His smile glowed as he had chanted for his beloved little sister.

Vanna now towered over most other soldiers and took his role seriously, so he had no smile during the celebrations. But he had come to wish Kravann well the night before.

"If Sambath doesn't treat you well, dear sister, just tell me and I will take care of him," Vanna swore. This was not a threat which Sambath's almost-wife wanted to hear.

"Vanna, if you so much as touch a hair of his head, you will have to answer to me," Kravann cautioned.

"Children, children," Bopha chuckled. "I'm glad you are both so protective, and have so much love for each other. But this is a time for present celebration, not worries about the future." In truth, she was not worried about Sambath. If he was anything like Boran or Samang, his grandfather and uncle, he was a man of honor, wisdom, kindness and strength.

Suddenly Bopha remembered being a small girl in a remote village, slipping in the mud as she tried to carry two heavy water buckets up from the river. She felt the slick mud under her bare toes, then on her knees, then her chest. She bent her head back slightly so her chin didn't get smacked on the bank. That was the day the King's Man came to the village and her life changed forever.

Gently separating from Jaya, Bopha got up and knelt at the altar, giving thanks for all the blessings of her life. She lit no incense, but in her mind's eye, she saw again the rumpled feathers on Garuda's leg, and felt protective wings around her.

* * *

Kalienne and Bopha met almost every day at the baray. They usually sat with Mach Botum, who continued placid and pleasant. Bopha had not, in all these years, heard a mean remark pass her lips. Rarely, Sao Nang would come at the same time, and always she was distant. Sao Nang had never had another child, and Bopha felt her enmity. Although the King continued to spend at least one night a week with his other queens, most of the time Bopha was his sleeping mate. He hadn't said so, but she believed he was not mating with anyone else. Of course, he was of an age now when no one would expect him to have that ability. But Sao Nang exuded controlled hostility, a banked fire ready to explode under the right conditions.

Before the Apsaras left for India, there was a ceremony with several hundred priests chanting for hours, then Jayavarman feted the dancers with a huge banquet. Sophea was in the seat of honor, between the King and Indravarman. The other six dancers sat interspersed with members of the Council.

Bopha remembered her own difficulty talking under such circumstances, when she first came to Bayon. She wondered if these young women felt the same. Sophea and she had discussed who should go. The women would not just be dancers but also Ambassadors for Kampuchea, and should be able to hold their own in distant courts.   Bopha watched and saw no hesitations, no blushes. These Apsaras would be fine emissaries.

CHAPTER 35

1218, Garuda

She stood on the parapet before the sun rose, a lithe figure with hair pulled tight in two buns, one on each side of her head. Her left hand rested on the cool stone balustrade. She could hear, distantly, the sounds of many people already hard at work. They were preparing for her husband's funeral, soon to take place on the Terrace of the Elephants. Unable to sleep, she took refuge here, high above the waiting world. She turned her head left, then slowly circled until her back leaned against the supporting stone. Everywhere she looked his face beamed back at her with that beloved, enigmatic smile. Some said the faces were Avelokiteshvara. To her, they were both

Barely twenty-four hours ago, Jaya's body curled against the length of hers in post-coital sleep. They had not made love for many years, and it had been a surprise to both of them. "Well, well, look who's awake," Jaya said. He stood, with some difficulty, from the floor and reached for Bopha's hand. She saw his sampot standing at attention. He undid the knot in her gown, as she undid his. Despite being ninety years old, his arms were strong as they encircled her.

Their love-making was long and slow and sweet. Bopha came many times before Jaya finally reached climax. "I love you so much," she whispered.

She could feel his lips against her shoulder, curving into a smile. "And I you, my dearest Moon Flower."

It was the cold that woke her. Cold was not a sensation normal for this time of year, in a country of gibbons and mangos. Jaya's arm felt stiff over hers, pinning her down. She came fully awake. The torches were snuffed and the chamber very dark at the new moon. The room was silent, the palace compound still. She shivered. That chill seeping into her back was death.

Bopha pushed wildly at Jayavarman's arm, then twisted out from under it as his full weight fought her. She cried out into the

334

darkness, "Help, bring a light!"   She grabbed for the sheet, wrapping it over her nakedness.

There was sudden commotion from the corridor outside, Samang clattering to his feet. He had been dozing, at guard in full armor. When the door swung open, and his torch lit up the room, he saw her and bowed. With his head still down he asked, "Yes, my lady?"

"Samang, my lord is dead!" Bopha's voice, normally soft and fluid, shrilled. It carried throughout the compound. "Please!" She was desperate. Jaya's body was jumbled, his bare bottom and genitals higher than his head, the white scar that ran from armpit to thigh gleaming in the light from Samang's torch. "Cover him!"

She had backed into a corner by the window, pulling the sheet tighter. Her silk gown was in a pile with his, on the floor by the low table where they had sat on pillows and talked for hours. He was so full of plans, her Jaya.

Samang understood and looked around.   The purple and yellow silk quilt had fallen off the foot of the bed. He grabbed it. Sleepy voices were coming closer, mumbling concern. Samang was very strong. He lifted Jayavarman's body, turning it over and straightening the legs. Then he gently covered his chief with the quilt. Bopha sighed in relief. With the sigh came tears. She sank to her knees, sobbing, as the door, then the room, filled with people.

Chariya, was one of the first to arrive. She knelt now, next to her mistress, murmuring, "Come, my lady.   Come with me." Chariya half-lifted her until Bopha came to her senses enough to rise. She was tall for a woman, taller by half a head than Chariya, as tall as Samang. She kept her eyes down but her back straight as she walked to the door, Chariya in front of her, to protect her undressed body from stares. The crowd parted ahead of them.

She had cried herself out, alone in her room. Chariya brought food but she had eaten nothing, and asked to be given privacy. The maidservant had still come in every hour or so, quietly opening the teak door and slipping inside. Bopha ignored the intrusion, sitting at the window and staring blankly as the sky got light, then bright, then dim, then dark.

Finally, she stood up, stretched, and slipped out the door. Samang stood on the porch. "I need to go to the temple," she whispered. She hadn't spoken in so many hours that her voice was a croak. "Alone."

Samang nodded. He walked silently before her through the dark and empty palace grounds, down the wide road to the temple. She climbed the steep steps, the same steps she and Jaya had climbed years ago, before the consecration of Bayon. At the top, Bopha paused, then walked onto the high balcony. She leaned back against the balustrade. Her eyes had adjusted to the dark, and she could vaguely see the faces all around.

Her body felt hollow, unreal. The only reality was the hardness of the stones against her back. What now? As the favorite wife of Jayavarman VII, she had been safe from court intrigue, especially safe from Sao Nang, who hated her, and Indravarman and his wife, Jorani. But now?

Sweet, slow Thom had become a dedicated monk and would pose no threat to Indravarman when he ascended the throne. She was grateful that Vanna was safely in China. Jayavarman had assigned him to escort Sophea and the Apsaras on this longest of trips. Reports were universally favorable. The experiment with these female emissaries was a complete success.

But what would become of her? All these years she had been provided for, owning nothing, having no other home than the palace and the man she loved. Now she had nothing.

The eastern sky was turning red as Preah Chan Bopha faced it. She put her hands together palm to palm, raising her arms. Lifting her right knee up and to the side, she began to dance. Her back pulsed with energy, rising from the base of her spine and flowing out the top of her head. She welcomed the flow and gave herself to the music, so clear in her head that she could hardly believe there were no real musicians playing.

* * *

Suddenly, the sky was rent with a sound that filled the world. A screech, deeper and louder than anything Bopha had ever heard. She knew instantly.

Garuda. She had prayed to him almost her entire life, but had no idea really who he was. Her feathered god was real, and he was coming. A shadow appeared in the eastern sky, flying toward Bayon. Huge wings beat above the stone towers, their swoosh echoing as the bird-god lowered in front of her. His talons were each longer than her entire hand, and his eyes gleamed gold, with black pupils the size of coconuts.

Bopha bent her head back to stare into the eye that was watching her as the enormous beast alighted on the stones. Her arms were still lifted from the dance, in a jeeb of welcome and praise. She was so absorbed that she made no sampeah.

"It is time." The voice filled her body, vibrating throughout, as if her whole being were a drum. Slowly she brought her arms down, palms together at her forehead, then her heart. Garuda towered over her, his sharp curved beak as big as her head. He closed his wings behind his back. Bopha saw that his arms were covered with gold bangles. The sun had yet to rise, but early rays sparkled on the gold. He returned sampeah.

"Come." He knelt and made a cup of his hands. Bopha didn't understand. Garuda waited. She took a step forward. He smelled of incense. His feathers lay smooth across his broad chest. Then she knew. His hands were cupped like the groom's when she went riding. She lifted one foot and placed it gingerly on the palm, which was much larger than her feet. In one smooth motion, Garuda lifted her onto his back. His jeweled necklace was a thick rope of gold where it nestled in the feathers behind his head. Preah Chan Bopha grasped it as Garuda stood, then opened his wings.

The sun rose, blinding her as her body lifted into the air.

337

AFTERWORD

This book had a long incubation after 2013, but then was written in less than two years. In a way, it wrote itself, I just had to sit down and listen. My thanks go out to many people who have supported me to write.

Easy Writers has patiently listened to drafts, and focused me to provide a timeline and more historical context. My daughter made it possible for me to revisit Bayon when it was empty during the Covid pandemic. DeEtta Vincent, Kate Lipper Thompson and Carl Vigeland read the final draft and made helpful suggestions.

The people of Cambodia have welcomed me sweetly. Much appreciation goes to Naga Cambo, who was my guide at Siem Reap. He also suggested I go Tonle Sap and took me Banteay Chhmar (where I was only the second visitor that day, so different from the hordes at Angkor Wat). He is on Facebook, and I heartily recommend his services.

Unfortunately, I was unable to find a Khmer reader to check me for cultural sensitivity, a phrase I dislike but a concept I support. It is easy to offend without realizing. If I have done so, I sincerely apologize.

I also do not wish to offend anyone with Hyperemesis Gravidarum (Bopha's condition in her last pregnancy). The causes of this are not understood, and people I have known who suffered it were desperate to keep their babies. Bopha's cure was a miracle of sorts. That said, Sikha's meditation might be a beneficial adjunct to treatment of any number of troubles.

So far, I self-publish, though this time around Simon Gerber has been a blessing. To navigate the format-jungle takes specific skills.

I hope this story inspires people to go to Cambodia and wander among its ancient temples, pondering the amazing feats of construction and the lives lived so long ago.

Pearl Whitfield

HISTORICAL NOTES

All that remains of the enormous city that was Jayavarman's capital (as big as all five boroughs of New York City) are the stones. Wood was reclaimed by jungle in the thousand years since the disintegration of the empire he created. There are stone monuments with inscriptions throughout Cambodia, mostly in Sanskrit, that testify to heroic acts and generous donations, but nothing remains if made from recyclable material.

Because the written record from medieval Cambodia is gone, historians rely on an emissary who came from China to the Khmer Empire for a year, from 1295-1296. Zhou Daguan wrote extensive reports home on all aspects of life in Kampuchea, and the Chinese preserved these. Also, one long gallery at Bayon is dedicated to depictions of everyday life.

Ancient Cambodian building projects continue to be explored and resurrected from the jungle. Some of these are in modern Thailand. Jayavarman built hundreds of miles of canals and dikes to divert water to Bayon, providing both irrigation for rice paddies and water for the city. Tree ring samples recently confirmed that there were severe droughts in the early thirteenth century, which likely contributed to the fall of Kampuchea.

Most historians agree that the Cham sacked Angkor in 1178, and Jayavarman chased them out in 1181. Many other dates are not so clear. For example, Jayavarman might have been born in 1120, 1122, 1123 or 1125. I have chosen what worked for this story. All agree that he lived an extremely long life, likely dying at ninety. I have used names that are current today for historical people and places, hence more recognizable, rather than the names by which they were known when they were alive. Also, many words and names have variant spellings since transliteration is a tricky task. I chose what I liked best.

I beg forgiveness from Queen Indradevi. After she appeared in my story as a rather unpleasant individual and the younger sister, I learned that in fact she was the older sister of King Jayavarman's first wife. Also, she was a supporter of what we might call women's rights, founding and supporting many schools for girls.

If it seems to rain a lot in this book, that is because Cambodia has only two seasons, wet and dry. Steps in ancient temples and barays are extremely narrow, so one has to step up sideways, and each riser is steep. Most of these risers have been carved with images. When the images of Naga and Garuda appear together, they symbolize peace. The energy in Bopha's back is kundalini (see Yoga Journal in References).

One of the pleasures of a trip to Siem Reap is to see the acres of stones that have not yet found a home in the temples. These excavations create a giant jigsaw puzzle of bas reliefs to challenge and   confound   archeologists.

REFERENCES

Books

Burgess, John. A Woman of Angkor (a novel),

Chhuor, Cham Riya. Jayavarman VII, Le Roi d'Angkor et son Espouse Indradevi (ebook paru en mai 2015).

Coe, Michael D. Angkor and the Khmer Civilization, Thames & Hudson, 2003.

Singer, Guy. Gathering of Dragons (a novel), The Dragon Series — Book 1. 2015.

Shors, John. Temple of a Thousand Faces (a novel). New American Library, 2013.

Zhou, Daguan.   A Record of Cambodia: the Land and its People, Translated, with an introduction and notes by Pieter Harris, Silkworm Books 2007.

Internet

"Ancient Secrets Decoded: Bayon, Angkor, Cambodia." Phalikan.com

Davis, Kent. "Ancient Queens Who Shaped an Asian Empire: Indradevi and Jayarajadevi." 5 September 2010. Devata.org.

Davis, Kent. "Are Ancient Goddesses Actually 12th Century Khmer Queens?" 1 April 2010. Devata.org.

"Cambodia — Culture, Etiquette and Business Practices." (Undated). Commisceo Global.

"Fundamental teachings." The Buddhist Society. (https://www.thebuddhistsociety.org).

Cambodia Museum: https://www.Cambodia museum.info/encollection/stoneobject/Jayavarman.html

Encyclopedia.com. "Jayavarman VII."

Ethnomed.org, on naming a child in Cambodia.

Garuda: https://shellybryant.com/2013/01/26/garuda-and-naga/

Hendrickson, Mitch. "Historic routes to Angkor: development of the Khmer road system (ninth to thirteenth centuries AD) in mainland Southeast Asia." faculty.Washington.edu. Undated.

MacLoughlin, Shaun. "The Flying Palaces of Angkor. The Greatest of Kings: Jayavarman VII. Drama. Englishwordplay.com.

Marissa. "A Guide to Cambodia's Traditional Apsara Dance." Theculturetrip.com. 9 January 2018.

Nieptupski, Paul. "Medieval Khmer Society: The Life and Times of Jayavarman VII (ca. 1120-1218)." Asia Network Exchange. (Has excellent map of empire).

Nureyev, Rudolph, excerpts from letter he wrote to dance community while dying of aids (posted by Mavs Favs on Facebook, 25 July 2021, not fact-checked at the time and unable to verify at time "of publication).

Orientalarchitecture.com. "Angkor Thom South Gate, Angkor Cambodia."

Pagan: https://www.newworldencyclopedia.org/entry/Pagan_Kingdom

POV. "The Flute Player: Conduct a Cambodian Ensemble." archive.POV.org ("19 years ago")

Reynolds, Frank E. "Jayavarman VII, King of Khmer Empire." Britannica.com.

"Roles, Relationships and Key Concepts of Khmer Kings." Khmer Knowledge Keepers. Weebly.com.

Shapiro-Phim, Toni. "Reamker. The Cambodian Version of the Ramayana." Center for Global Education, Asia Society.

"Something fishy? All about Cambodia's prahok." Travelfish.org

"The Khmer Empire —Fall of the God-kings." YouTube. HTTPS://www.YouTube.com/watch?v=ghmjlBD2Fd4&feature= youtu.be

"Why Prahok is so important for Khmer food." Jul 23, 2019. Dinewiththelocals.com

Wikipedia for: "Champa," "Culture of Cambodia," "Jayavarman VI," "Indravarman II," "Jayavarman VII," "Indravarman III," "Spean Praptos", "Kampong Kdei Bridge," "Khmer traditional clothing."

World History Encyclopedia: Khmer Empire map.

Yoga Journal on Kundalini: https://www.yogajournal.com/yoga-101/energy-rising/

Periodicals

Conn, David and Politzer, Malia. "Offshore loot: how notorious dealer used trusts to hoard Khmer treasure." The Guardian, 4 October 2021.

Ellen, Rosa. "The Living Sound of Angkor," The Phnom Penh Post, 7Days, May 10-16, 2013.

Mashberg, Tom. "With a Gift of Art, a Daughtor Honors, if Not Absolves, Her Father (Re Douglas Latchford). New York Times, Jan 29, 2021.

McPherson, Poppy. 'The Quantas steward who fought the Khmer Rouge," The Phnom Penh Post, 7Days, May 17-23, 2013.

Normenn-Smith, Ingrid Olivia. "Meditation, Medication, Molecularization? Examining the Remediation of Cambodia's 'Mental Health Crisis.'" 2019. Pulitzercenter.org.

Stone, Richard. "Divining Angkor", National Geographic, July 2009, pages 26-55.

Whorskey, Peter and Poliltzer, Malia. "Denver Art Museum announces return of four artifacts to Cambodia after Pandora Papers coverage of indicted art dealer." Washington Post, 16 October 2021.

"You and Me: 'During Pol Pot I didn't want to write in public," The Phnom Penh Post, 7Days, May 10-16, 2013.

Other Sources

Chanthara, "Life During the Golden-age of Angkor!" 26 October 2020. Nerd Night Phnom Penh.

Interpretive signage at the Killing Fields outside of Phnom Penh Cambodia, 2013.

Royal Cambodian Dance Troupe performance of traditional dance, Phnom Penh, 2020.

Traditional Cambodian Dance performance in Siem Reap, 2013.

Visits made by the author to Tonle Sap, Angkor Wat, Angkor Thom (including Bayon), Banteay Chhmar, and other temple sites in 2013 and 2021.

The map of Jayavarman's empire I concocted from many sources, but drew myself.

DISCUSSION QUESTIONS FOR APSARA

1. What are some power dynamics explored in the book? Is love among them?

2. How does Bopha change from simple village girl to Apsara, then to Queen?

3. Is Jayavarman a sympathetic character?

4. Are there similarities between life for women in 12th century Cambodia and in your country today? How about for men?

5. What do you think happened at the end of the book?

ABOUT THE AUTHOR

Pearl Whitfield

Pearl Whitfield was a nurse for some forty years. In retirement, she began to write. This is her second book.

Her first novel, *The Storekeeper, A Tale of Small Town Life*, was published in 2020.

Her books are available through your local independent bookstore (via Ingram), or on Amazon (where they are also available as eBooks on Kindle). If your book group misses Whitfield's book tour, you may be able to arrange a zoom meeting with her.

She lives in eastern Oregon, where time among ponderosa and sage brings peace and inspiration.

Made in the USA
Middletown, DE
30 December 2021